SONG OF THE EARTH

Looking back, it might not have happened had Dewi been home and the shifts stayed normal. But with the heavier stall of the two, Dada linked with me, and left the inside one for Ifor, Billie Softo and Jed Donkey.

It was a mistake, for there wasn't two ounces of brains between the three of them.

Alehouse Jones, who was in the next stall, said it was a bellstone. Manuel Cotari, the Italian, said it was a face-slip that trapped them first, then took the roof. To this day Owain and Phylip Benyon reckoned that Billie was clearing the gas with a cover board and candle, like I used to do, and the stone dropped as Ifor came in with Jed Donkey.

Whatever it was, it laid sixteen tons on them, and when they roped Ifor's feet for the haul-out he would not come, said Albert Crocker, for his arms were wrapped around Billie Softo.

'She liked that,' said my father. 'Miss Carey liked that. . . .'

**Also by the same author,
and available in Coronet Books:**

Song of the Earth

Alexander Cordell

CORONET BOOKS
Hodder and Stoughton

First published in Great Britain 1969 by
Victor Gollancz Limited

Coronet edition 1976
Second impression 1980

Printed and bound in Great Britain for
Hodder and Stoughton Paperbacks, a
division of Hodder and Stoughton Ltd.,
Mill Road, Dunton Green, Sevenoaks,
Kent (Editorial Office: 47 Bedford
Square, London, WC1 3DP) by
Richard Clay (The Chaucer Press) Ltd.,
Bungay, Suffolk

ISBN 0 340 20516 4

For
Clayton Thatcher

The coming hope, the future day
When Wrong to Right shall bow.
And hearts that have the courage, man,
To make that future now.

ERNEST JONES, Chartist poet

I

I REMEMBER red light that beamed and flashed on the black clouds above Dowlais. Distantly, on the wind, came the bellow of the iron as the furnacemen built up the heat. The iron ran liquid in the moulds, and I could hear it sighing and moaning as they tore it from the rock by fire. The mountains trembled. The old workings by Pont Storehouse echoed thunder to the beat of the drop-hammers. The new rail consignment for Spain belled and clanged in the stackyards. Flinging aside the Dowlais blanket I got out of bed and ran to the window, shivering in the night-shirt my mam had cut down from my brother Ifor last Monday, before she had been taken ill. Toes crinkling to the nip of the boards, I stared into a world of frost, a land made beautiful in hoops of gold and crimson as they tapped the furnace bungs from Pontyclun to Merthyr, and the little rivers of sparkling iron hissed and leaped into shape to last a million years.

Bitter old winter, that one in 1845. Indignant to the frost the skeleton trees crouched in moody scarecrows down Bridge Street, Merthyr, and the mountains beyond were all over white like Church of England wedding-cake, and above the freezing hills of Brecon the moon was sitting on the peaks all bare and beautiful: down the red-black, flickering street the glazed China dogs of Solly Jew raised their poodle sniffs at a world of ice and fire. Daft old world, come to think of it, with the iron up there being boiled to a frizzle and us down here freezing to death.

'What you doing out there, boy?' asked Gwen, from the bed.

A minute back she was out to the wide, her red button nose snuffling over the Dowlais blanket, this being so called since my wicked old Granfer Ben Evan lifted it off a gentry bed twenty years back, and what he was doing around gentry beds

9

is anyone's guess, said Dewi, my brother, he being an expert in this particular line himself.

'What you doing, Bryn?' asked Gwen, now beside me, all podges and bright curls, aged seven, three years younger than me: amazing how the dead will up and walk when bent on other people's business.

'Just looking,' I answered.

'Aye? Well, Dada said no looking for us, just bed.'

'I want to see our mam go,' I said.

'Gran will come in and hell will set alight.'

Setting alight now, it seemed. Dowlais again, burning and flaring on the snow, reflecting off the slate roof of Bethania, the little square cottages with their backs to the Taff withering and shrinking into strange shapes: faintly, above the thunder of the iron, I heard the beating of the accident gong. Gwen stiffened against me, finger up, eyes switching. 'Listen!'

I thought I heard the scream and scurries and for God's sake this and for Christ's sake that: legs one moment, mounds of rags and blood the next. They were always catching it up in Dowlais especially, said my father; as good as the Shambles slaughter-house any day of the week; one chopping block for men, another for animals.

'Any sign of Mam yet?' asked Gwen, and she put her arm around my neck and her hair against my cheek and I was warm and soft inside me for this sister, though you would never have thought us related. For Gwen was all wrist bangles and double chins, and I was inches taller, a herring in boots, said Ifor.

My big brothers Dewi and Ifor were sixteen, and identical twins when it came to womanising, but alike in no other respect. Six feet in socks, Ifor was a tap-room brawler, with a dent in his nose and raging black hair: Dewi, topping him by an inch, was dark, handsome and slim, with a fierce Silurian face: very hot for a revolution, was Dewi, and down with the Queen.

Gwen now, hugging herself, her breath steaming on the window.

'Cold to hell, I am, boy,' said she. 'Back into bed with us, is it, and leave Mam till morning?'

'By morning she will be gone,' I answered.

'Eh, dafto! Hobo Churchyard do come in daylight.'

'Coming at midnight, just to cheat us children,' I said.

'O, aye? Hobo is too frit to bury in the dark—too much on his conscience, says Sharon.'

'Listen!' I whispered. 'Is that Sharon crying down the street?'

Sleeping next door but eight was my sister Sharon, we being a bit short of room in by here.

'Not Sharon,' replied Gwen, getting in under the blanket. 'It is Mrs. Willie Shenkins.'

'Crying for our mam?'

'Crying for her Willie,' said Gwen.

Night and day, frost or shine, Mrs. Shenkins sits out the back of her Number Sixteen Bridge Street, Merthyr, hoping for a chill that will send her to her Willie. Big for his age was he and down in the low levels of the Cyfarthfa collieries since the age of six, but they brought him up last winter because his eyes were getting bad, like the ponies. And the agent sent him over to the puddlers, and the glare took him when they were tapping the bungs into the six-ton cauldron, and a puddler pulled him clear. Later, he fell again, head first, so they cooled the cauldron with Willie inside, and gave it a decent burial; Chapel and Church of England, Roman Catholic and Jew, and God be with Willie Shenkins, they sang, as Willie went six feet down, what was left of him, in the Company cauldron.

There was no sound in the room but Mrs. Shenkins sobbing.

'Do not mind her,' said Gwen. 'Not quite a full pound she isn't.'

Often I had seen the women cry in Merthyr, with their sack aprons to their faces, for a death or a drunk, but nobody ever cried in my life like Mrs. Shenkins cried for Willie.

I said, 'Gwen, you there?'

'Aye, man,' said she, her nose over the blanket.

'When Hobo Churchyard comes he will bring two black horses with feathers.'

'Aye, and the preacher and the Inspector of Nuisances.'

'Like when old Jack Curly died, remember?'

'A beautiful death had old Jack Curly,' Gwen said warmly.

11

'They cried and sang all the way to the chapel.'

I said, 'But first they burned the bedding and sprinkled carbolic on the floor of the house. Will the Inspector do that here?' I got into the bed beside her and she was hot and plump like a Christmas chicken, wings and elbows going, crying:

'Eh, hop it! Cold as ice, you are, and chattering to freeze.'

'Black horses do frit me, especially at funerals.'

'White horses for weddings are best,' said Gwen.

I did not speak to her.

'*Whisht*, you, Bryn. Do not cry,' she said.

Footsteps on the landing, open came the door. My father stood with the lantern held high, his shadow on the wall like an ape dancing, and my grandmother said:

'Do not heed them, Mostyn. Look, dead asleep for a grave, they are.'

Hand in hand we lay, Gwen and me, breathing for embalmed corpses.

'Take her, Mostyn,' she repeated.

But I was at the window when Hobo Churchyard came with a cart and a droopy black horse. Ifor and Dewi carried Mam out, and they stood in the snow with their lanterns painting circles of yellow about their feet. Later, the Inspector of Nuisances came and burned the bedding. Nose pressed to the window I watched the black cinders spread where the fire had been: up the stairs came the smell of the carbolic. Gwen said from the bed, 'It do not seem right to put carbolic where our mam has been.'

I was watching the road and the undertaker's cart moving black and squat along the road to Vaynor. Gwen said, 'Has Mam gone, then?'

'Aye.' There were black wheel-ruts in the snow, I remember.

'Come on in, boy.' She held the blanket wide.

Hobo Churchyard had gone. And behind the Castle Dowlais went on fire again, lighting the room with furnace glow.

I bowed my head to the flashing light of the window.

'It will be a good death tomorrow, mind,' said Gwen, 'with singing and crying and plenty to eat.'

2

NEXT morning, after my mam had gone, it was as if she had never existed, save that Gran laid her place at table. Otherwise everything was much as usual, with Ifor and Dewi side by side at the bosh, shaving, braces dangling, holding up nose-tips and making faces at the razor. Most mornings I would stand on the chair without a back and look into the mirror they looked into, this being about seven foot up, but no sign of whiskers rooting yet, black, fair or ginger, said Dada. This morning, however, my father said little, being in a chapel-quiet and with pew-dust in his heart, said Gran.

Gorgeous was my gran, but more of her later.

'There is a beautiful day, Mostyn, isn't it?'

Silent he sits, fist on knee.

'Chilly, mind, but beautiful.'

There is no sound but the scur of the razors and the scrape of hobnails on the flags of the kitchen.

'A decent meal when we get back, son, and your slippers by the fire, eh?'

'Dada,' I said, coming down from the bedroom.

'Leave him, Bryn,' whispered Gran.

'You heard Mrs. Ten Benyon has another one developing?' asked Dewi.

'Please do not be indelicate,' said Gran from the hob.

Bacon on the go now, sizzling sweet and brown, the pig playing a large part in our existence, said Dada, servant and master, and no wild flower do smell as beautiful.

'What is indelicate in having a baby?' asked Ifor.

'Indelicate when applied to Mrs. Ten Benyon,' said Gran, 'and the children are listening. Up to table sharp now, for it is a busy day coming.' For head of the house was our gran. They can say what they like about Welshmen, fighting at the drop of a hat and solid in the jaw, but their women run the households. My beautiful sister Sharon came into the kitchen then, she having slept with Mr. and Mrs. Isan Chapel next door but eight, they having a spare room because of a relative now deceased, there being no room in our house for fourteen-year-old sisters with ten-year-old brothers peeping over bed-clothes; and she winked at me as she pulled her chair to the table. Wicked in the eye was she, and Welsh dark, with long black hair in waves on her shoulders to drive the boys mooney in town, like Mrs. Ten Benyon must have looked about half a century back, said Dewi, when the Irish unloaded themselves at Fishguard. Three of them came to Merthyr, one after the other, and they all collected Mrs. Ten Benyon, and in her good time she saw the boots off and the shrouds on all three of them, but they got their own back by landing her with ten boys. 'Eh, dear me,' Mrs. Ten used to say, 'thirteen men I have known in all lengths from six inches to six-feet-six—men, all men, I am, pestered in the breast and loins.'

'There is a slut for you, mind, talking like that,' said Gran, forking the bacon, 'and us decent Chapel people. Fourteenth on the way, is it?'

Prim as a poke-bonnet one moment, scandal very sweet the next, for Gran.

'The new agent Man Arfon been seen in the vicinity, they say,' said Sharon.

My father stirred at the grate. 'Do you think we could have a little more hospitality towards Mrs. Ten Benyon and a little less of the scandal, considering it is a rather special day?' and this put us all quiet since my father was gentle when it came to women labouring in mine or childbirth, never passing one in town without knocking up his hat. I scrambled up to table then but Gran pulled me out of it.

'You been out the back?'

'Not yet.'

'Then out and see to it and back here with hands washed.'

It is astonishing to me how people arrange such matters, me being the best to know the call or not, and, anyway, Gwen was out there all dopey from the bed, and once I opened the door in haste and she came out head first, curled up on my boots and slipped off again without a sigh.

'Hurry up,' and I took my fist to the panel.

'Hop it,' said Gwen.

The dawn mist was curling smokey fingers round the back; the old tin bath on the nail crying at being out all night, and drips from the water-spouts freezing teeth in sockets as I broke off an icicle and sucked, waiting for Gwen. All down the wall the colliers and furnace-workers were getting up in shouts and groans, and I saw in the eye of my mind six hundred bare elbows sawing on bread boards and cheese being hunkered for doorsteps and small-beer and ale being poured into flagons for the scourers, rodders and rollers of Cyfartha. Dogs were fighting for breakfast scraps, cats belting each other down alleys, babies shrieking. Hairless and wrinkled, the aged teetered from the beds out of habit or to let a shift-worker in: like Mr. Isan Chapel next door but eight, aged eighty. Blinded by a furnace blow-back, was Mr. Isan Chapel, poor soul, and every morning trying to find his way down the garden path to the little seat that hung over the river, and no help from his bull-dog missus either, she being upper class since collecting third prize for a sampler from Lady Charlotte Guest, and she thought nothing of hammering poor old Isan if he didn't behave. Only five feet high was he, and never got used to the blindness, but wandering, arms out, with no sense of direction, said Dada, and he could even remember Bacon the Pig of Merthyr selling cannon to America in the War of Independence, whatever that might be. Seeing him, I vaulted the garden wall and went to guide him, for I would never forgive myself if he fell in the Taff as he did last autumn, and half the neighbourhood floundering around with ropes and clothes-poles, trying to fish him out until my dada arrived and waded into the river and carried him to the bank.

'Eh dear, you poor little soul,' said my father.

I will always remember him kneeling there with Mr. Isan Chapel held against him. And the circle of faces above them was the dregs of the community, not one of them Welsh; stamping, guffawing, until my father rose, facing them.

'Because you live like animals do you have to act like them?'

Half-drowned was Mr. Isan Chapel.

I said now, steadying him, 'You all right, sir?'

'As right as I will ever be, child, if it wasn't for the

15

indignity,' said he in Welsh, for he came from King Arthur stock up in the beautiful Prescelleys.

I got him on the seat. 'Shut the door, is it, Mr. Chapel?'

Often he left the door open facing the river, which was daft, for the Pont Storehouse urchins would arrive and heave clods at him, trying to hit him off the seat. And there was no point in me showing him respect if he was going to sit there heading off clods.

'Bryn,' called Gran from the back.

'Ay ay!'

'What you up to, then?'

'Helping Mr. Chapel.'

'Good lad. Come now, the bacon is leathering,' she cried, and I was away sharp for the bacon, for if there is anything I cannot stand it is old age and its indignity, and I only helped to make a good impression on Dada: clods it would be from me also, given half a chance.

Cut my throat before I end up as helpless as that.

'A good boy you are, Bryn,' said he, 'helping Mr. Isan Chapel.'

After breakfast, my father said, 'No work today, no school. We are going up to Vaynor, to be with Mam.'

Strange, come to think of it, that our mam should be Church of England, she having the blood of the Cornish tin-miners in a place called Bodmin, while on my father's side the family have been Methodist since Job was a comforter. Up in the room with Gwen I got into Dewi's best home-spun trews cut down, boots to shave in, a shirt front with no arms and tail and a starched collar under my ears. With my hair smoothed down and watered like the mountain fighters I stood rigid because of the creases, waiting for Gran.

'Am I pretty?' asked Gwen, turning in her funeral dress, and I did not spare her a glance, for you can dress a County Cork porker in a crinoline and never make him presentable. I would prefer her seventeen, for girls of seven I do hate, all wriggles and giggles and baby fat, with her black-buttoned boots to her knees and red bows in her long, plaited hair. 'A throw-back, this one,' said my father, 'we are dark and she is

16

fair, her blood coursing from the old Brythonic plains. But she is a Celt, remember—same as you.'

'Bows out,' said Gran, coming up the stairs. 'It is your mam's funeral you are attending, not Michaelmas Fair.' She hooked me closer for inspection. 'Face soaped up, washed behind the ears. Eh, my!' And a great softness sprang into her eyes. 'There is a sight for a dead mam, and your Granfer Ben proud in the stomach to see you so respectable.'

Stuffed and cooked we had this Granfer Ben, for breakfast, dinner and tea.

'Yes, Gran.'

'Be a good boy now, leave the crying to the women.'

'Yes, Gran.'

'And Bryn . . .'

I turned back to her and she did a queer little sniff and pulled me hard against her. 'Away,' she snapped, heaving me off. 'Are we standing around all day?'

Worth a mention, this gran.

A big-fleshed woman, she was, vigorous in the breast and glorious in the brow, looking seven foot high with her hair piled up on a comb, the same as Queen Victoria, and the best layer-out this side of Brecon. Five sons she bore my wicked old Granfer Ben, every one but my father being taken by the Top Town cholera. On my mother's side, apparently, things came respectable. The worst thing that happened in her branch was when my Uncle Waldo went a semi-tone flat exalting every valley in the public hall in Dowlais in 1835, and within a week he was emigrated to North America on the end of a boot, the Welsh being a trifle sensitive when it comes to disrupting Handel. Aye, practically gentry on my mother's side, said Gran, the men collecting shiners through turning the other cheek to the bruisers, which is a bloody stupid thing to do in Dowlais at the best of times, said Ifor. Three times to church every Sunday, the men in top hats and frock coats, the women in bonnets and crinolines with bowed good mornings left and right and alcohol and fisticuffs a long way down their list, and fornication something that was practised in London only, mainly Whitechapel.

'But,' said Gran that talkative day, 'your people on my side

17

of the family do not stand deep examination.' And she told of Granfer Ben who was large in the copper-works band down the Vale of Neath and singing the *Messiah*, sounding the trumpet double bass while shaving with the cut-throat, being glorious in the lower registers. Handsome devil, apparently, handy with the mountain fighters and spare-time on the females.

'But best of all with the Penny Gaffs on Fair Day?' cried Sharon.

'Played in the company of Siddons, give him credit,' said Dada, 'and under Macready of the Swansea theatre!' and he cried, taking off Granfer Ben, ' "For beauty, starv'd with her severity, cuts beauty off from all posterity. She is too fair, too wise, wisely too fair to merit bliss by making me despair." '

'Romeo and Juliet!' shrieked Sharon, who was strong for the Penny Gaffs and people like Taliesen the Poet who had long hair, and I wouldn't trust him with a maiden aunt as far as I could throw him, let alone the likes of Sharon.

Most artistic, my family—Dada and Sharon mainly, while Dewi, Ifor and me were more bent on thick ears and ale and saw-dust. Gran said:

'Eh, grief, he was a born actor—this Shakespeare chap was clay in his hands, and very keen on the opposite sex—did my best, but no woman on earth could suffice him. And when Brigham Young's people came to the Top Towns on speculation, he was off to Salt Lake City and the Latter Day Saints. No sight nor sound of him since—must have died of women, I reckon.'

'There are worse ways of dying,' said Dewi, and I saw my father give him a queer old look and a sigh.

'Oh, he must have been exciting, exciting!' cried Sharon, and she picked a piece of herring out of Gran's pan and sucked it reflectively, her actress eyes, large in her high-boned face, going dreamy in the lamplight.

Excellent with the herrings was my gran, doing acres of them in the big, black pan on the shining, black-leaded grate; all sizzling and sending up a silver perfume, glad to be out of that murky old Baglan Bay and into the bellies of Mostyn Evan and fighters. Ach, I do love the nights of the herrings, with Sharon at the ironing and Gwen on the samplers and Gran kneeling by the hob with the big wooden spoon out of the wash-tub.

'Damned old reprobate he do sound to me,' observed Ifor, who, on times, could be solid marble between the ears.

'Who, now?' asked Gran, looking up from the herrings.

'Granfer Ben,' said Ifor, all unsuspecting, and I saw my father open the *Cambrian* and get well down behind it, always a sign of trouble afoot.

'As God is my judge, I'll not be responsible,' said Gran, putting her spoon under Ifor's nose. 'You sit there passing lewd remarks . . .'

'But, Gran . . . !'

'Don't you gran me, you useless big oaf, scandalising your own grandfather,' which sounded Irish, and was, for Gran always went Limerick when under deep provocation.

'Sorry, Gran,' cried Ifor, backing off.

'And you big louts also—you hear me?'

'Oh, yes, Gran!' Dewi and I shouted in chorus.

'No finer man than your Granfer Ben walked in twin boots, and there's no apology for a man here fit to clean them!'

'Yes, Gran,' we all said, including Sharon and Gwen, and my dada stirred at the fire, took out his pipe, and grumbled:

'Smitten with the tongues of angels, we are. Why the hell we have to have Granfer Ben every time we have herrings do beat me,' and he rose. 'We will wash all tears from eyes. My father, Ben Evan, was the finest Falstaff in the Swansea theatre, and my mother, Ceinwen Evan, is the best cook in Christendom. All wounds healed. Up to the table sharp, sharp, sharp!'

And now we were off to the funeral.

'Bryn, Gwen, Gran!' called my father from the bottom of the stairs. 'It is half past ten and we are off directly.'

'Coming, Mostyn,' Gran called back, and took our hands in hers, saying, 'No tears, remember. Your dada is dying inside and is covering it with smiles. I will not have him brought down, you hear me?' She swallowed hard and cried deep in her throat. 'You hear me, children?'

'Yes, Gran,' we said, hand in hand now.

And she led the way down to the pony and trap.

She could have been going to a wedding for all the pomp and size of her, and when she stepped on the back step of the trap the pony up in the shafts, but we did not giggle, we did not even speak.

This is living on the tip of tears, on the breath between grief and laughter.

But often, I believe, Gran cried for Granfer Ben.

Some mornings, when she came down, her face was pale and proud and riven with unshed tears, and her lips were as red as cherries as if she had been kissed in sleep.

Aye, well, let me gabble on about grans and granfers and funeral suits and herrings and Latter Day Saints, for while I am doing this I am not thinking about my mother.

And forget the day in November when we put her six feet down in Vaynor.

3

COME spring, I was still at school on Tramroadside, for although most children were down the mines before the age of ten, my father reckoned that I was a bit of a scholar and ought to be given a chance. So it was one and sixpence a week with me and down to the private school run by Miss Bronwen Rees of Abergavenny and become a professor in an American university.

I do love the spring and her bright colours, and the lambs doing cart-wheels down in Fair Meadow, which is what they called it until the ironmasters got hold of it and plundered and spoiled it.

But up above Vaynor the country was sweet and green, and there I would go most Sundays after Chapel and lie on my ear on the earth and listen to its music. For the earth speaks, says my teacher: the stones talk to the clay, the loam and pebbles give their opinion. For what is earth, says she, except the tongues of men gone to dust?

In love, me.

In love with Miss Bronwen Rees.

'Hurry!' cried Gwen, 'we are late!' And away down Bridge Street she went, fair hair flying, very keen, though she was not too special between the ears and twice two are seven.

'Good morning, Bryn!'

''Morning, Mr. Waldo Phillips.'

'Another scholar for Miss Bronwen Rees, is it?' This from Mrs. Ten Benyon hanging out of her top window, very flourishing, as ladies are when they are making babies.

'Ay ay, Mrs. Ten!' Very fond of me was Mrs. Ten since I had been giving private lessons after school to her Owain and Cynfor; taking in Granfer Ben's books and reading aloud to the family about how point five is half of one and the Union Jack is the colour of blood and if you put down a shilling the change out of three pints is ninepence at the New Inn but watch it at the Vaughan in Neath. And I reckon my granfer was the only drover in Wales who knew about places like Pola and Treviso and Roman generals like Ostorius Scapula.

'Here are more of his books,' my father used to say. 'Learn, Bryn, learn. A scholar is worth ten labourers—anyone like me can lead a barge-horse.'

Spelling and making up poetry I am good at, but arithmetic, said my brother Ifor, who couldn't count up to fifty, is mainly learned to help the masters make a fatter profit. Dewi, also, was dead against anybody making a profit, and he spent all his spare time reading papers by a chap called Engels and back copies of *The Trumpet of Wales* and pamphlets by William Lovett and Feargus O'Connor. And my gran used to get her fists up and shout about the flames of Hell and disbelief in God; though why this Engels boy and God should disagree on anything beat me, for both are bent on feeding the hungry, which was more than the masters were about this time on The Top.

Down Bridge Street after Gwen now, weaving through the gangs of colliers coming from the levels on the old canal, lovely with their noise and banter, many being Irish from the famine ships of Fishguard, and in rags: women were out on their doorsteps, scrubbing their little half-circles of purity into the world; others brooming away the night-soil tippling down the gutters, for there was no place in Bridge Street for it save fling it out of the window, and the whiff of it curled your nose first thing in the morning. In ranks five abreast went the colliers on shift, cold tea under their arms, picks and shovels on their shoulders, and the language they were raising must have stripped the paint off the door of Bethania half a mile south. Into their ranks I slipped, stretching my thighs to keep up with them.

'*Bore da*' *chwi*, Evan, lad!'

''Morning, Mr. Shonko!'

'Off to school, is it?'

'Ay, man!'

'Make the most of it before old Crawshay gets hold of you.'

'Yes, thank you, Mr. Shonko.'

'That lovely sister of yours still activating?'

'Sad for your mam I am, my son,' said Mr. Noah Morgan.

There was Afron Shavings, the carpenter, Bili Jones and Wil Shout, the old pack-horser, all down Crawshay's canal levels, and Dai Central Eating with one tooth in his head: very partial to my mother, was Dai, in the Sunday School she took each week in the old Bethania, and I loved them all with their backslaps and insults.

I ran like a hare for the next half mile, through Pontmorlais, up to the school door: turn the handle; stand there gasping.

See her standing there in beauty, Miss Bronwen Rees of Abergavenny.

'Good morning, Miss Rees.'

'Good morning, Bryn Evan.'

Although she was Welsh speaking, she never spoke Welsh. Her grandfather, it seemed, though Welsh in name, was born fifty yards over the Hereford border, and she had an uncle living in London who was a quarter English, on his mother's side. Besides, in fifty years Welsh will be a foreign language, said she, so anbody talking it in by here I will hit to Cyfarthfa and back return journey.

But Welsh or English, one day I will set up house with Miss

Bronwen Rees. I will build this house four square to the wind; boarded floors I will give it, two rooms up, two down. And I will make a track from the mail-coach road through the Beacons, with flowers either side and more around the door. Nine boys and one girl I will fetch from Miss Bronwen Rees, God willing.

'Take your seat, please, Bryn Evan. Do not stand there staring.'

There is a voice to drive the chaps demented.

I took my place at the back with the scholars—people like Joey Randy whose da took the big stallion once a week up to Penyard, behind Cyfarthfa, and collected six guineas, and living on immoral earnings as plain as your face, said Dewi. There was Owen Bach, spit and image of the Wild Welshman who tamed the mad bulls down the Vale of Neath, and Davie Half-Moon who was bats round the chimney, like his poor old mam and dad. Mick O'Shea of Connemara was there, thicker in the mouth than a Chinese, and girls, too, though none worth a mention, our Gwen being the best in sight with her seven teeth missing in front, and ghastly when smiling. For me, indeed, there was only one female there—Miss Bronwen Rees.

Sit with your chin on your hands and watch from the back of the class.

Small, she was, large at the top and small at the bottom, and with a fine dignity. Black was her hair, flowing either side of her face in waves of mystery. And her face I have seen but once before when my father took me fishing down to Giant's Grave. Calm and pure was that face in the shop window. The Madonna, Dada explained, but did not tell more, though I recall that she had a baby in her arms and her red heart outside her dress, but it was her eyes.

It was her eyes.

'Bryn Evan, kindly pay attention.'

'Yes, ma'am.'

Dewi, who kept a list of all the useful females, had her age down as seventeen, my Bronwen. This would make her twenty-two when I was sixteen, the marrying age, and I have heard of wives much older. Take Mrs. Alfo Morgan, for instance—she took her Alfo to the altar on the day he was thirty, and she was knocking sixty, though both were Church of England, and any damn thing can happen in that lot, said Gran. But very happy, these two, with good morning kisses on the doorstep when Alfo left for mule-skinning at the tannery, and good evening kisses when he came home at night. And after a good beef dinner they would kiss good night and Alfo would slip down to the Castle Inn for a moonlight with Rosie Carey, the bar-maid, and often enough come home at dawn. 'Suits me,' Mrs. Alfo Morgan used to say, 'let Rosie begin where I leave off—she gets Alfo and I get the wages.' Not such a fool as she looks, says Gran.

But this, as my father said, is a wreck of a marriage, and I had planned it more convenient for me and Miss Bronwen Rees of Abergavenny.

'You listening, Bryn Evan?'

'Yes, ma'am.'

Gwynedd and Gwent it was again this morning. Miss Rees always started the day with some pathetic yarn before getting down to the horrible business of twice two are twenty-six. For some ten days now we had been on this yarn about Gwynedd and Gwent, a pair of twins, girl and boy, and how they got lost in a forest, according to Gwen, for, to be truthful, I never heard a thing when my Bronwen was speaking. Apparently, they were taken by a witch to a gingerbread house which had a sugar chimney and in bed there was a dog dressed up as a gran. I never really got the hang of this Gwynedd and Gwent pair, because every time my Bronwen mentioned them Gwen would swing her pig-tails in the front row and grin horribly with no teeth, and this would set me bored and heaving, for anything that took my mind off Bronwen was unwelcome.

'Bryn Evan, are you ill?'

I gripped my hands in my lap. 'No, ma'am.'

'You are making some astonishing expressions—you realise this?'

'No, ma'am.'

Very educated, she was, with a voice of gold, and sometimes, although she said she was English, she was really Welsh inside, for she'd get the pastor's *hwyl* up her red dress and wave her arms about, going to the window to face the sun with

24

tears glittering in her eyes, which is perfectly understandable, for if you've got a heart as large as Miss Bronwen Rees you'd very likely be affected by beautiful children such as this Gwynedd and Gwent getting lost in a forest with dogs and witches. I used to weep with her, I remember, fist on the desk, the tears running hot on my cheeks.

'Is there something wrong with me, Bryn Evan?' She stood back, examining herself.

'No, ma'am.'

'Then why are you staring?'

'Not staring, ma'am.'

'What was I talking about?'

'Pardon, ma'am.'

'I was talking about Gwynedd and Gwent, wasn't I?'

'Yes, ma'am.'

'Right, you. If Dyfed is Pembrokeshire and Brychain is Brecknock, what parts of Wales are the old Welsh kingdoms of Gwynedd and Gwent?'

Well.

Here is a terrible bloody situation.

'Stand up when I speak to you, Bryn Evan.'

Sweating cobs, I stood, and I heard Billie Softo giggle next to Gwen and saw her thump him, for though I treated her rough, she would die for me, our Gwen.

'Very well,' said my Bronwen. 'I suspected that you were not listening at all, so now please tell me what you know about Gwent and Gwynedd.'

I began to shiver. Accusing faces were turned to mine. Distantly, I heard the thunder of Cyfarthfa Works: through the single window streamed a shaft of golden light. I thought: O, sun, O, *sun*!

'I am waiting, Bryn Evan.'

And out it came, in a stuttering rush of words; of dogs and witches and a gran; of sugar chimneys and a door of honeycomb, and Miss Rees listened, her face stricken.

I closed my eyes to the perfume of her as she drew nearer.

Eh, dear me, females smell beautiful.

Gwen smells of stew, the stains being on her pinafore: Sharon smells of spices. My gran has a plum-pudding smell,

25

and of lavender from the little blue bags she sews into the lining of her cloak. But the best smell of all comes from my mother, this being a cowslip smell, as if she had been sitting all day in their fields above Merthyr, and made chains of them and put them in her hair. And so did Miss Bronwen Rees smell good that day as she stood beside me tapping my desk with her ruler: this, as I say, is an April smell and comes with walking hand in hand with your mother.

'Oh, Bryn, look! Beautiful, they are. Cowslip time is best of all—could the whole world be as pure and lovely!' said the ghost of my mother.

'Talking I am to you, Bryn Evan, remember!' said Bronwen.

'Take my hand and we will run,' cried my mother. 'We will go from this dirty old place down to the forest of Rheola. You ever seen the Vale in cowslip time?'

'I am asking you for the last time, Bryn Evan. Bryn *ap* Mostyn, indeed! The *ap* is not acceptable to English law since the Act of Union in 1536, and you know it. Dogs and witches and grans, indeed! Sugar chimneys and doors of honeycomb, indeed! I will blutty teach you to stare at me!'

'*Cariad Anwyl!*' cried my mother. 'Oh, my precious, what a beautiful day!'

'Take that, and that, you blutty little Taff!' cried Bronwen.

Distantly, through the thumping pain of the ruler, I heard Gwen shrieking. Very surprising, it is, to be thumped by your mam in a cowslip field after all that loving.

We went home hand in hand that day, Gwen and me, made whole by the same pain; she having collected a couple that were meant for me, and stripes on her little fat behind that sent Gran raving, fists clenched, and it took Dewi and Ifor to drag her back from the door.

'Now, now, my lovely,' said my father, smoothing her, 'the children are not decapitated. I will have a word with Miss Rees this evening after Chapel, see.'

'By God, Mostyn, if she lays hands on these children again ... !'

'Mind, she didn't really mean it, Gran,' I said.

26

'Didn't really mean it! Look at your sister's bottom,' and she up-ended Gwen to show me.

'Never mind hers, look at his,' said Dewi. 'Like a Carmarthen slaughter-house. What was she hitting you with, man, pig iron?'

Gran said, 'Mostyn, you will see her tonight, for if I go, as God is my judge . . .'

'Shall I slip down, Dada?' asked Dewi, innocently.

'Let the punishment fit the crime,' said my father, 'she has not committed murder. Ointment on bottoms and enough hatred for today—I will visit Miss Bronwen Rees. Removal of the *ap*, indeed! I will give her 1536 and the English Act of Union.'

I was glad he didn't go.

Ridiculous, come to think of it—a daft old pair like Gwynedd and Gwent coming between me and Miss Bronwen Rees of Abergavenny.

4

ABOUT this time, when I was eleven, the workers were trying to form a decent Union, and were coming pretty skinny with anyone who would not help them to do this, such as belting into anyone who decided to work on when the Union said to stop. New Benefit Clubs, which were the beginnings of the movement, were springing up left and right in Merthyr about this time, and since the intention of the Union was to get a rise in wages, masters like Crawshay and others naturally took exception to the idea, and formed a Union of Masters themselves. Thereafter, anyone suggesting a shilling a week extra was naturally assisted out of the job by the boot, and anyone who suggested forming a Union of Workers was accused of a crime against humanity. Generally, the way this was stopped was by sending round a list of names called a blacklist of trouble-makers, and this, I heard say, was perfectly understandable. For higher wages, said the masters, only resulted in drunkenness and debauchery and idleness, and this was against the law of God. So much against the law of God was this that pulpit preachers, Chapel and Church of England, were slipped a couple of sovereigns to condemn the Unionists from the Big Seat, and special gates of Hell were erected for any man going in the same direction as the Tolpuddle Martyrs, for this lot, apparently, were absolute sods. This scared the workers, and many pulled the forelock in front of Cyfarthfa Castle and Dowlais Manor, hoping the masters would raise them a penny an hour, but all they succeeded in getting was a cut of five shillings a week since the price of iron had gone down a week last Sunday. Right, you, said the Union: we will make you more scared of us than you are of the masters, so they invented the Scotch Cattle. These were very special Unionists who dressed themselves up in skins and put cowhorns on their heads, and roamed the mountains after dark lowing and bellowing and visiting the homes of scabs and blacklegs and breaking their fingers and burning their furniture. I remember lying in bed with sweating dreams of my beloved Bronwen skirts up and rushing over Hirwain Common with about five hundred Bulls after her shouting improper suggestions, but mostly they confined themselves to putting the boot into simpering workers.

'It is a scandal that men should have to resort to such intimidation,' said my father.

'It is a scandal that they cannot get decent wages without having to beg or fight,' said Dewi.

'Hush now,' said Gran, 'there's a good boy.'

Dewi was always getting hot under the collar about now, talking about the greed of the employers and places like Liverpool and Bristol having been built on the slave trade by clergymen wearing out their knees on hassocks and the bishops set up in six-course dinners in their palaces while the children of the factories starved. But it was mostly the slave trade that got him agitated, though this was finished, said my father: talking about black brothers and white bastards and places like India being built on blood, and if he had his way he would nip the tabs off every collar back and front and tie bombs on the carriage of Queen Victoria, though none of this was her fault personally, apparently, for the wool was being pulled over her eyes.

Sharon said at her book of Shakespeare, ' "So I told him, my lord; and I said I heard your Grace say so: and, my lord, he speaks most vilely of you, like a foul-mouthed man he is, and he said he would cudgel you." ' She looked up. 'If it is not Queen Victoria's fault, then why tie bombs on her?'

'Because she is a symbol, stupid,' replied Dewi, scowling.

'What is a symbol?' asked Ifor, lying face down on the horse-hair sofa, salt-pickling his fists, for the railway navigators were in the district again, and anything under six inch rocks they took on the chin without so much as a blink.

Gran said, 'Praise her on the harps and cymbals, is it?' and she went on peeling her spuds.

'Oh, God,' exclaimed my father.

Dewi said earnestly, 'It is political, Gran—nothing to do with music.'

'Religion I am talking, mind,' said she.

'Then you are the only one,' said Dada.

'Oh, aye?' Up with her then, sparring at the bosh. 'But I am the only one talking decent! The house is full of fist-picklers and revolutionaries, and I will praise who I like on the harps and cymbals without asking anyone in by here.'

Dewi said, bitterly, 'And do not talk to me about religion. They shout the cause of the masters in the name of God, they bless anything they can get their hands upon for an extra half a sovereign. That Parson Williams—he hands out the rights of God's little creatures and goes rook-shooting every Sunday morning after the service, the swine.'

'Aye, but he is Church of England,' said Gran warmly, and my father groaned aloud, saying:

'We started off with the Scotch Cattle and the Unions. How the hell we have got into harps, cymbals and rook-shooting I do not know. I'm trying to read the paper—do you think we might have some peace?'

Ifor said, 'Up at Nanty, day 'fore last, a mule kicked a packer and knocked him dead. So the drovers loaded it and loaded it, until they broke its back.'

'Oh, Christ,' whispered Dewi, 'it is nothing but cruelty, cruelty....'

Bang, bang on the back, and I nearly fainted with fright. Gwen opened the door and Pietro Bianca stood there, five foot two of teeth, hair and burning eyes. Mexican by nationality, anarchist by nature was Pietro, and he was only here because of my father's free-thinking. I am having no rules and regulations in this house, he used to say: each to his own, each to his whim: free expression do mould the nobler characters. Dewi leaped up, crying:

'Come in, come in, Pietro, boy!'

'Long live Mexico!'

'Long live Santa Anna!' cried Dewi.

'Death to President Polk,' said Sharon, at her Shakespeare. And Gran said:

'Take Pietro down to the cellar, Dewi, there's a good boy, and try to keep the bangs within reasonable limits.'

'The bomb he made last Tuesday brought the bedroom ceiling down,' said Dada. 'And do not shoot up, man: there are already two holes in the kitchen table.'

'Will you sing for us again tonight, Pietro?' begged Gwen, for when Pietro got going on his mandolin it was as good as any Welsh harp: and he would sit by the grate with tears on his face, singing patriotic songs about what the bloody Americans were up to in his beloved Mexico, and how Santa Anna, his national hero, would hit hell out of the savage invader, while he, Pietro Bianca of Veracruz, would personally attend to the barbaric American President Polk.

Strange brothers I had, come to think of it. There was Dewi the poet, the revolutionary; tall, lean and calm. There was Ifor, all fifteen stones of him, no sooner the word than the blow, his eyes brooding malevolence for anything six foot in boots. And romancers and hard drinkers, both; fighters both, their shirts open in winter frost, chests sprouting black hair, and my father kept them on a leash like chained tigers. Keep these two apart until Gran or I come, he used to say. Hit them with the nearest thing handy, but keep them apart in the name of God.

But Dewi was his cross. And what the devil Pietro Bianca

was doing in Merthyr at a time like this was beyond my father's comprehension, though there are some queer old folks in the place about now. He will lead Dewi to the gallows.

'Your fault, mind,' Gran used to say. 'Since we had the free-thinking we have had to drag them to Bethania, and the house is full of Shakespeare, pugilists and revolutionaries—I don't hold with it, Mostyn!'

For my part it amazed me how Pietro used to turn up on the nights we had the stew.

No women, I think, should be loved for mere beauty, for you can pick that up at sixpence a time. By stew they should be judged, and because of stew, married. Lovely, the smells a good cook can bring to a house, and I personally do not mind if Irish stew lingers a while, though Gran acted very strange over this—leaping from the table the moment the meal was finished, throwing open doors and windows and beating it out with swipes of a rag. Stew is all right in its place, said she—on the hob or in the stomach, but I am not having it sitting around the house for days after.

'This stew I smell all the way from here to Old Berhania,' cried Pietro.

'That means he wants some more,' rumbled Ifor.

'It is Irish stew made by a Welsh cook, and she is wonderful!' And he leaped from the table and embraced Gran, smacking her a kiss on both cheeks. 'This is the most wonderful cook from Nueces to Grand River!'

'Oh, go on with you, Pietro,' said Gran, very pretty with her. 'Another helping for Bryn, is it? Get plenty under your belt, boy—first day at work tomorrow.'

I will always remember that year of 1846, because this was the year I began work with Dada and the twins up on the Old Cyfarthfa.

Coal was in our hearts, for we came of a long line of coal, but we Evan family were never colliers: it was pack-mules and rafting in the old days, it was barging and flat-boats now, yet there was also sunshine in our bodies, for our Granfer Ben was born on Welsh wool down Carmarthen way, at Llanstephan by the sea, and was soft with the little lambs come spring, with milking and shearing with his dad, and growing a bit of wheat till the gentry cheated them of their land by the act of enclosures, and sent them packing on a donkey. Down to the Cynon Valley they came and settled there as porthmen, which is the trade of drover, and every summer they would work the Welsh fairs and gather the cattle in batches, driving them across the mountains as far as the borders of Kent.

'Big men, remember,' said my father, 'working with people like Richards the Drover, and you can see his grave today in Aberdare Old Churchyard.'

'*Whee!*' Sharon sighed, for Richards the Drover was more important in the Merthyr valley than Queen Victoria.

'And your Granfer Ben was a specialist, too,' said Dada, warming to his pipe, 'and he held court at Abercynon Basin, shoeing the cattle for the long marches to England, and tightening the leather pads on the geese.'

'Aye?' I was breathless, hypnotised by the romance of my Granfer Ben.

'Pads I have seen on chickens walking over Mexico,' said Pietro Bianca.

'Aye,' said Dada. 'But geese are cunning old things, preferring to laze away their lives to walking three hundred miles into England, and they used to knock off their pads ten miles out so your granfer had to carry them. . . .'

The wind is doing his tonic-solfa in the eaves; a night-owl is shrieking from the hills of the Beacons. Red the firelight flickering on my father's face.

'. . . a couple of geese he could manage, but when he was fifty miles out and eight up and couldn't be seen for beaks and feathers, your Granfer Ben started getting ideas.'

'Necessity being the mother of invention,' said Gran.

'Aye, so he warmed pitch on the march and drove the geese through it on the hop, and then, adding insult to injury, he chased them through a bourne of sand, and when they came out they were soled and heeled.'

'Wonderful!' we all cried.

'Marvellous!' shouted Pietro.

'Thereafter, not a lot of notice was taken of geese limping on the march to England, and any important protests were assisted along by Granfer's boot. Very famous he became between the Old Bridge and Castle Inn, Abercynon, and Swansea, it being said that you could hear his army of geese coming a mile off, their pitch boots clattering on the flinted road, playing hell to each other about drovers in general and your Granfer Ben in particular.'

'It do take a man and a half, mind,' said Gran, 'to get the upper hand of geese—are they the same in Mexico?'

'They are the same, but bigger in Mexico,' said Pietro.

'Everything is bigger in Mexico,' said Ifor. 'And then?'

My father continued, 'But when the wit is out the ale is in, and what with fighting for right of way on the mountains—which was the habit of the old drovers—and stopping at every mountain inn between here and the city of London, you greatgranfer became less than normal, and died. Alone, your Granfer Ben landed in Dowlais, in coal.'

'Down at the Starvo, and he worked deep,' whispered Gran, reflectively.

'Aye, a dirty old mine was the Starvo,' said Dada. 'You remember Richard Griffiths, who owned it?'

'I do,' answered Gran, 'since my mam scrubbed for him. Took a thousand pounds off old Sam Homfray while we were starving in Hollybush Level—a thousand pounds, mark me, on the turn of a card.'

'You should have a revolution!' cried Pietro.

'We have had a revolution,' said my father, 'and it has been crushed. We have had our riot of bread or blood, and that was also crushed—as you will be crushed in Mexico, Pietro Bianca.'

'Never!'

'It sings the same tune, Pietro—in Merthyr or Veracruz: the weak go to the wall, the strong flourish. They own too much, their power is too great for us, they are backed by the Church and guns. We had our Frost, you have your Santa Anna—a hundred years from now their names and movements will be dead.'

'Never, never! Mexico will come through the fire, Mexico will rise again!'

'Give him some more stew,' said Ifor.

They spoke more, but I did not hear them, for I was sick in my stomach in the face of Pietro's pride of race, and his rejection. I left them to their reflections, I remember, and went out the back, and the stars were like little lamps in the redness of iron-making, with Pontyclun and Penydarren mushrooming with light as the cauldrons were stirred. The soil of the garden trembled beneath my feet. Queer, I think, is talk of coal, for it reaches out fingers of rags and bones. And I thought, standing there, that below me gaped the caverns of the past, and in these lonely places lay the bones of men, women and children long dead, as one with coal: in darkness, in the rat-runs, in the metallic plonks of dripping water; in the Cyfarthfa levels in a feast of greed. The door opened behind me and the kitchen light cut the back with a yellow sword. My father said:

'The revolutions are dead for now, Bryn—remember this. One day it will come on the flood of the world; but the petty fights, the squabbles, the thousand dead are as nothing, and greater than this will not come in your time, or your son's, or his son's. Work, I say, forget the revolutions.'

'In coal, Dada?'

Square and handsome was his face in that strange, rosy light.

'Coal is in our blood, Bryn. Coal is in your heart from the day Granfer went down the Starvo, and to the fourth generation it do put the strain. Bed now, is it? Leave the coal to granfers.'

5

ALTHOUGH the Old Canal at Cyfarthfa went out of general use some years back, my family had been employed there as drainers and pulling an occasional tub-boat through it with slack coal from the tips. But the night before I was due to start work with Crawshay he transferred my father and brothers to the big Glamorgan Canal running from Merthyr to Cardiff.

'We start as hauliers, Bryn, and we end as contractor—you wait!'

Out at first light and on to the cobbles with us, Mostyn Evan and three sons, and we went down the murky street with our hobnails hitting sparks off the kerbs of Bridge Street. Boots out we went, in a barge-man silence, with mouse-trap tins under our arms and Gran's oatmeal inside us, and enough to freeze you solid as we went past Thomas Street and over the Iron Bridge by the ironworks for a last haul on a tethered tub-boat and take him down to the Dynefor Arms. This done, we collected Nell, our Cyfarthfa mule, and took her down to Fishpond and the head of the canal, for there was a big consignment of rails going down to Abercynon, and this was us—special delivery.

The wharf was thronged with ragged Irish; men and women just come in from Fishguard with droves of children, and now waiting for casual labour on the wharf loading rails, and not enough strength in twenty of them to raise a ten foot length, poor souls. Still as dark as winter curtains as we pushed a path through the hungry Irish and a voice boomed from the darkness in Welsh:

'Any Taffs by here?'

'Aye!'

Mr. Ephraim Davies we found, the agent, writing on a box. Excellent, this agent, not to compare with Man Arfon, his sub-agent, who was an unborn bastard when it came to the poor Irish.

'Mostyn Evan and three sons,' said my father.

'*Diawch!* Breeding, are you? For now, is it?'

'Three and a half,' said Dewi, pushing me up, and I stood level with belts and stomachs, seeing above me ringed the starving faces of the Irish, pinched and pale in the first streaks of dawn.

'Name?'

'Bryn Evan.'

'There's a lovely old Welsh name. Age?'

'Eleven, sir.'

'Do not call me that, young man—reserve it for the English. Address?'

35

'Fifteen Bridge Street, Merthyr.'

'Now there is a select community. Educated, I expect?'

'He is the scholar of the family, Dewi excepted,' said Dada. 'Miss Bronwen Rees, and six-inch stripes on his rear to prove it went in.'

'Nothing like it,' said Mr. Davies. 'And I could do with a bit of education from her myself, if I could manage it. Three-pence a week extra for reading, writing and arithmetic, thank God for generous employers. Hauling, is it, Mostyn?'

'We will teach him the run of it, Ephraim,' said Dada. 'This time tomorrow he will have the hang of the mule.'

'Three and threepence a week if he runs it, if not—out! By God, here is another giant of industry to stick it up the workers,' and he swept me in with thick arms, shouting, 'Welsh, any more Welsh?'

'Irish, mister!'

'In the name of the Holy Mother, man, get us in!'

'Away!' roared Ephraim, arms folded.

They pressed about him in their rags, they held their shivering babies to his eyes, they begged, pleaded. Ephraim cried:

'And would you employ the starving Welsh in Ireland, man?'

'All one nation—Celts.' This from a skinny Irishman, his head black curls, and I pitied him. 'Not bloody English, mind—*Irish*.'

'Then give me English if I am to sink to damned Irish. Who do you think you are, you people—brothers and sisters?'

'Aye, under God.'

They pulled at his sleeves; a woman knelt before him. A young girl came up, her dress ragged; about Sharon's age, and still beautiful under the hunger.

'Take her for wages. We starve, man, we starve!'

Ephraim Davies bowed his head. 'Go and beg of Crawshay, do not beg of me.'

'You damned Welsh swine!'

'And do not blame me—do not even blame Crawshay, you stupid fools. You should have thought of this before you left Ireland!' He stood on the box, crying, 'Welsh, any more

Welsh out there?' and they raised before him a forest of arms.

'Man in Heaven,' said my father, and pushed me on. 'Never have I seen so many.'

'It is the new famine, God help them,' said Dewi.

'They would take the bread from our mouths,' whispered Ifor.

'They'd need a ten pound hammer to get at yours,' said Dewi.

They eyed each other, like dogs hackled for fighting.

It was the same in most families these days: one side cursing the agents for keeping the Irish out, the other cursing Crawshay for bringing the Irish in. Like a flood they were pouring into the Top Towns with their crucifixes and holy water, their lovely little Madonnas propped up in the little square windows, and bleeding hearts were ten a penny between here and Pontypool: their glorious women of the long black hair and peaches and cream, if fed; or little scrags of humans burned out by men and hunger before they were twenty. But work, mind—grant them that—work till they drop, and for a crust, not money, and this was the trouble, for they undercut the Welsh wages. But once they got a sovereign or three in their belts they were mad sods for the ale-houses and the fighting. And since the Welsh were not backward in this respect, either, it was the fists and boots on Saturday nights, especially after the six-week-pay, with Welsh scum this and Irish bastard that and Chapel botherers here and Popish swines there, though it was the women, any nationality, who usually got the thin end of it. Blame not the starving Irish, or the poor little harlots on the doorsteps of Chinatown, said my father: blame the masters for allowing such conditions to exist—blame them for bringing in the walking ballast that will work till its stomach is lying on its back-bone; blame Guest for the cholera and Charlotte for no decent water supply; blame Hill of Plymouth for his belief in upright living while children withered and died on his porch; blame the iron-masters of Penydarren and Pontyclun, the Butes of Aberdare, the owners of Mountain Ash, Hafod, Dinas and Pontypridd—blame the whole rotten lot of them from north to south and east to west of Glamorgan and Monmouthshire who came to Wales for easy pickings and bulbous profits: and blame the Welsh masters also, said Dewi, for we are not blameless.

As we left the Irish on that first day of work I saw an Irish boy standing on a tump, watching me as we passed: thin as a Handel lute, he was, and his arms, bare to the shoulder, were blue with cold. There was only me and him in the world just then, and to cheer him I smiled and gave him a wink. For answer he drew himself up and the pride burned fierce in his eyes. His lips moved.

'Welsh bastard,' he said.

No matter, for I would rather be a bastard than hungry, and it was away with me, Dada and the twins to the wharf where the barges were waiting, their giant snouts biting into the grey, winter dawn. All around us the rails for Spain were tolling and clanging as the levers got under them: bedlam here, with men and women stripped to the waist in the frost, rushing overmen yelling orders, mules neighing under the whips and women arguing, fists up, like an Irish Parliament, everybody talking and nobody listening.

'Yours, Bryn,' shouted my father, and tossed me the mule's traces, and I had no sooner got them than she rounds with her rear and comes hooves up, trying to catch me a fourpenny one, so I slammed her one in the chops to quieten her and brought my knee up into her belly, and at this she grinned, as mules do, wagged her head and came after me like a spring lamb.

'That is better,' I said.

Jed Donkey came next, he being billeted with a hundred other donkeys, and I went round the stamping ends, looking for him, and found him instantly, which wasn't difficult since Dewi always insisted in plaiting the tail of the donkey himself with red, white and blue ribbon, which, if you stop to reflect, is the colour of the Union Jack. Getting in beside him I gave him the elbow to start with, and he gave me a look to kill since I smelled of work, and work was something this particular Jed had never been guilty of. Little wonder that this pair went broody when Dewi was around, with him nuzzling them and feeding them sugar, and them saving hind-leg belts for any-

38

thing in trews who happened to be passing, including Dada.

'Get over, you swine,' I said, and I had him out in the dawn before he knew what day it was. Harness them up, Nell and Jed Donkey, unwind the thews for barge-towing, get them up on the snout.

'Number one!' shouted Dewi above the clanging of the rails, and pointed.

'That means us,' I said, and ran them to the front barge which was deep in the stomach in finished iron: there I shackled them up, Jed leading.

'Checker out!' yelled my father, and put fingers to his mouth, whistling.

'Ay, ay!'

'Strain up, strain up!' bawled Ifor, jumping along the iron.

'If you can do any bloody better you come down here,' I said.

'No offence, man—just strain up—take the weight.'

I gave Nell my fist and the traces tightened.

'Man Arfon coming,' said Dewi.

'Room for him, too,' rumbled Ifor, thick and swarthy and stripped to the belt despite the wind. Eh, dear, here is a Hercules for you, thick in the arms and shoulders and thicker between the ears, and there wasn't a man on the wharf that morning who would have looked him over.

'Well, what have we, Mostyn Evan?'

By the light sound of his soprano voice, this one must have been standing sideways. Man Arfon, the famous. Five feet nothing in canvas leg-breeches and boots like gentry: brutal in the face also, with barn door shoulders, and there wasn't a virgin Irish safe within a mile of him, for he fed on them, said Dewi, as a hog feeds on flowers, taking them in the midst of their hunger: if this one was ever found in a ditch with a knife, the knife would be Irish, though not all the Welsh are parton saints, nor do all the pigs live in styes: given six inches' height and half a chance I would have this sod for every weeping Irish mother.

'What you got here, Mostyn?'

I would give him bloody Mostyn, if I was my father.

'Twenty-five ton for Abercynon,' answered Dada, coiling a fall. You could always tell when my father had head pains and tingling knuckles, being cold in the face when mixing with scum. Man Arfon said, 'The driver I am talking of, man, not the iron,' and he rocked back on his heels, his little eyes watching me from the folds of a shattered face.

'Leave him,' mumbled Dewi, going past me with a band-strap, and this he flung over our load and my father snatched it in the air, and knelt, anchoring, and flung it over to Ifor, and Ifor put his boots on the gunwale and heaved, his brown arms bulging while Dewi stepped over him and kicked down the trace.

'Snatching them from their cradles soon, I am thinking,' said Man Arfon.

I spat on my hands and took an inch on Nell's girth, watching the checker over my shoulder: he looked stiff in the head to me, and I began to want him. He said:

'A couple more his size and Crawshay will be scratching a beggar's arse, eh? Ho, ho!' and he boomed, stamping the dust.

He was trying me for temper, which was the way with agents and overmen, and only one in twenty were Welsh. This was the way of the ironmasters and coal-owners. They brought in the Staffordshire men first, the men of Scunthorpe, those trained in the trade of iron: from Doncaster and Worksop they brought down the English bargees of the Northern and Midland cuts. And these lorded it over us, sewing their noses to our business, wagging their tongues at the agent meetings. Bad tempers were watched; meetings of more than four Welsh were reported, and at the first whisper of a Union a man and his family could be black-listed by every master on The Top and sent packing over the mountain or into the workhouse. And the few Welsh agents and overmen were the black sheep of the fold, the worst of the lot: men like Man Arfon who was Welsh to his boots but betray his mates, his country, his religion, to curry favour with the English owner. 'My God,' my father once said, 'we come of the blood of princes, but when we are bad we are a stink to the name of Welsh; a blackness in the brain that spawns the first-rate Judas.'

Sometimes, for these few, I could weep for my country.

'Cast off, Ifor. Take her, Bryn!' called my father, and I cracked the whip over Nell's head and flicked Jed with the butt, and they put down their haunches and cranked to the load, hooves skidding.

'Has he handled mules before?' asked Man Arfon.

'Half mule he is, boyo—look at his ears.'

The overman put his thumbs in his belt, sidling along beside me as I got Jed moving. 'A cheeky little brat, I am thinking, and insolent in the eye with him.'

'What else do you expect for three shillings a week?' asked Dewi.

I think I hated them all, even my father at that moment. To this they bowed and scraped, the half-Welsh: to this men sent their little baskets of bribe potatoes. If this was Baptist, then they were Baptist, or Church of England, or anything going—kneeling in the pews with Beast, not God.

'You watch him,' said Man Arfon, as I straightened with the load.

'No,' replied my father, jumping down from the iron, 'you do the watching, Man Arfon. A couple of years from now he'll be looking for his first man, and half Welsh half English will do as good as any.'

I grinned at Dada.

Off his ale for weeks, was Man Arfon: fist on the bar and calling for rye at the very mention of the Evan family. Enemies, said Dewi later, are not worth having unless you make them properly.

But later we knew the size of the enemy in Man Arfon the Checker.

6

DOWN to the Basin with us then, with the crippled trees flaring at a leaden sky: a blue-eared morning, this one, with the hedges dripping icicles and the ice-breakers labouring up the canals and the big Camarthen drays skidding their hooves down the tow-paths, breaking it up. Aye, a wicked old winter, this one, and now well into March. The Irish were dying of cold in the cellars of China, Merthyr; father this and brother that pulling them out as stiff as boards for last rites. But, as Gran said, they'd come back to life the moment the sun came up, their laughter ringing from their hovels: pouring out of Pont Storehouse where they slept four to a bed, with Blind Tim here and Red Shaun there dancing on the cobbles to the music of the fiddles, though what they have to be joyful about beats me, said Dada. My father was always worrying about the Irish, and I wonder their God didn't do more about them, for they paid Him enough in sanctity and bribes.

' 'Morning, Mrs. Hanman!' cried Dada now, and her lock cottage slid up alongside. A giant Staffordshire puddler, this one, now aged sixty, her white hair tumbling in swathes down her back and tied with black ribbon for Thor, her seven foot man who died years since.

'A pail o'tea for you and the lads, and welcome, Mostyn Evan.' And she lifted her soapy arms from her wash-tub and I saw beyond her door the little black grate and the red flash of her fire: snow-white her cloth, her table bright with knives and forks.

'No time, lady,' cried Dada. 'Got iron for the Basin, and we are running late.' He turned to us. 'Line up,' he said.

And we came to him and lined up beside him, staring up at the lip of the wharf where Mrs. Hanman stood, hands on hips, and we said in chorus:

'Good morning, Mrs. Hanman.'

Respect will be shown, said my father, especially to widow ladies.

Last week Mrs. Hanman was down in Neath, and Dai Half-Moon got caught with the rowdies, till Mrs. Hanman came up. And she stepped him under her skirts and got stuck into the rowdies, and when she stepped off him, said little Dai, the rowdies had vanished and she was licking her knuckles.

With Mrs. Hanman in her cottage now, Dewi stepped off stern as we passed, and tried to lift her wash-tub and dolly which she emptied at a single heave, and he reckoned it was screwed to the flags.

On, through Quaker's Yard, on to Abercynon, the clearing house of iron for the world. Here the great warehouses and offices where half-starved clerks were bending over ledgers: on down the brick-cut and the fields where little children laboured on the frosted land; on to Lock One, the most important in the Basin. Jane Rheola, aged eighteen, is half out of her bedroom window in Lock Six Cottage, her hair hanging either side of her face, dressed pink in her new Swansea nightie.

'Oi, oi, Dewi Evan!' she shouted.

'Back into bed, girl, I am just coming up!' shouted Ifor.

There is disgusting.

'Enough of that!' cried my father, quite rightly.

'Dead you will be when you get back down, mind,' called Jane, going cuddly. 'There's beautiful, mind, a little bit of love.'

'Steady on that pole, Dewi!' roared my father. 'Dewi, lay off stern.'

'Ay ay!'

'Do not strain him, for God's sake,' said Jane.

Hot and bothered, me, by the time we got by: very attractive is Jane Rheola, but more so first thing in the morning, in pink, I reckon.

'You get about coiling those falls,' commanded my father. 'Dear me, I do not know what is happening to the modern generation.'

Found in Rheola woods by old Canal Tom when she was six weeks old, was Jane, and raised by him without a woman, and girls like this do naturally drop the tone of a decent community, said Gran.

On, on to the loading wharves where hundreds of horses were towing drams heaped with the coal and iron of The Top Towns, and as we drew closer to the Basin platforms the explosions of iron-making grew about us: great rainbows of light flooding over the skies above Hirwain and Aberdare. It was the firework display of the mountains; the music of the Crawshays and Guests, the Hills of Plymouth, the Foremans of Penydarren. The barge slid on.

'By God, they are collecting profit today,' said my father, but I could not count the profit: I saw only the loss. A tattered army of labouring Welsh and Irish, I saw; the empty sleeves, the trouser-legs tied with string. Queer old business, the more I think of it, this brotherhood of man. Dada cried, up on the prow:

'Right, Bryn, take us in!' and I gave the elbow to old Nell and took her alongside Charlie Smith's wharf where coal and lime-stone was coming in like a flood to the shovels of the teeming Irish. Here we tied up, with the sun overhead, and I unharnessed Jed Donkey and Nell and led them clear of the road. For the labouring Irish were coming for us in droves, swarming over the barge, unshackling the chains and letting under the rails with levers, and they were starting a foreman's song as we got clear, their chanting voices sweet and clear in the blustering wind.

'What do you think of Abercynon, *bach*?' asked Ifor.

'Makes your hair stand on end.'

'Some queer old customers work round here, mind,' said Dewi.

Above the thunder of the labour, the rattle of trams, the clang of steel, I heard the roaring banter of men from the Inn, and the shrieks of Scottish sopranos. Spanish labourers went by with their lovely women; gold rings in their ears, six inch stilettoes strapped to the calves. French sailors from the coasters of Brittany lounged in the weak sunlight, waiting for finished loads to take down to the Cardiff flats, and they eyed us, hating us.

'Away out of here if we want to keep our legs,' said Dada, for the rails were toppling off the deck for the stackyards. 'You got the nose-bags?'

'Aye,' I said, nose-bags being my business. And I followed them to a quiet place of trees and grass where other workers were resting, and put Jed and Nell out to grass. Here Dewi lit a fire to thaw us out, and we squatted around it, chewing vacant, unspeaking, as men do after labour.

At length, my father said, 'You see the Penydarren dram-road?'

A new-fangled Trevithick engine was fussing up and down it, pulling trucks.

'What of it?' asked Ifor.

'It sings a song of death for the barge,' said Dada.

'Eh, daft! They have been running those clumps for the past fifteen years and we are not dead yet. There will always be work for the barge.'

'Aye?' My father bit deep into his loaf, and chewed, eyes narrowed to the weak sun. 'Twelve years back John Guest put the *Powerful* and *Eclipse* on the Dowlais dram-road and worked a hundred thousand tons a year up to the rack and pinion. It takes three horses ten hours to pull a hundred tons up to Dowlais Top: the *Powerful* pulls a hundred tons up there in six. Haven't you noticed the horses shortening?'

'The horses is out, the steam engine is in,' muttered Dewi.

'Steam do evaporate, remember,' said Ifor with a burst of brains.

'Oh, God, listen to it,' said Dewi.

'You taking the mick from me?' asked Ifor, getting up.

'Already taken.'

My father said, 'Ifor, sit down.'

'All day long he do take the water from me!' Trembling, he stood, hands clenched while Dewi lounged, straw in mouth.

Trouble was coming between these two, and it was Dewi's fault mainly, for when a person is concrete between the ears it is not polite to mention it a couple of times a day. Dewi said, indolently, 'See sense, man. Is it good business to feed a horse to pull a ton when you can feed an engine to pull a hundred? It is not economic.'

'And what do that mean, economic?' I asked.

Dada said, 'Economic means cheaper, but Dewi uses the big words to take it out of Ifor.' He rose. 'Listen, you two—listen all three of you. Skinny times are coming, and we will have to fight. But we cannot fight to live all the time we fight each other.' He levelled a finger at Dewi. 'Brains are all right in the head, Dewi, but they are useless chewing in the mouth, you hear me?'

'Yes, Dada,' said Dewi, frozen, for though my father never laid a finger on us there was no saying he would never start. He swung to Ifor, saying:

'And you watch your temper—save it for the ring, or I will belt you black and blue.'

'Yes, Dada,' said Ifor, head bowed.

Excellent, I thought, and I nodded approval and chucked Dada a wink.

'And don't you make capital out of it, or I will take you first!'

'Yes, Dada,' I said.

Mind, I couldn't think of any man in the county likely to take my twin brothers in pairs, except, perhaps, the Black Welshman, the terror of the Vale of Neath; nor could I think what was coming between Dewi and Ifor these days, unless it was Rosie Carey, the bar-maid of the Castle Inn. Apparently, Rosie had been moonlighting Dewi pretty hard until Ifor slipped in the back door and beat him to it, and Dewi was now losing sleep on Rosie Carey, which given half a chance I was prepared to do myself, but at the moment, of course, she wasn't a patch on Miss Bronwen Rees, for whom I was prepared to die if needs be. Nor was Dewi the only one lamenting, for according to Dai Central Eating, whom I met at Sunday School last Friday, my Bronwen had been seen on the mountain with Taliesen the Poet, which was all right with me providing he confined himself to poetry. My father was talking earnestly, but I scarcely heard him, being busy just then cutting the throat of Taliesen the Poet.

Then I heard him say, 'We can see which way the wind is blowing. Ten years from now the barges in this valley will begin to fail.'

'In any valley,' said Dewi, glancing up.

'No—in this one, for the railway has not yet come to the Vale of Neath.'

46

This set us back a swallow, because a move on the Vale of Neath just now might be inconvenient, all three of us being committed to Merthyr in one way or another, this being the country of Rosie Carey and Bronwen Rees.

The workers were coming in from the wharves and tramroads to the Old Navigation Inn.

In their hundreds they came; the colliers of the distant levels, mule-drivers, loaders, haulers, cutters, engine-men and labourers: Welsh, Irish, Spanish, they came in an army, each to his camp on the grass; division defined by nationality, a border-post nobody crossed. The Welsh came to us, and these we knew. Flinging down their tools they sprawled on the tumps, eyes heavy with labour, and knocked off the tops of their flagons and drank, gasping. The Irish went to the Irish, eyeing us as they wolfed down their bread and water: the Spanish, no more than a hundred, went to the Spanish camp, watching the Welsh and Irish with equal suspicion. In Spanish they told their beads and cut hunks of mouse-trap with their long stilettoes, their dark eyes burning in their Latin faces. A woman, Dada said she was from Cordova, dropped down her hair, and this she began to comb in the sun, singing as she did so in a rich contralto, a plaintive melody in a minor key. The song of the earth was stilled; there was no sound but that woman singing, and on her voice stole the hatreds: the hatred of Irish for Welsh and Welsh for Irish, the hatred of both for the Spanish, and they for us. And I thought, sitting there listening to that woman singing among the switching eyes, that come Sunday the lot of us would be dusting knees in church or chapel before gilded altars or plain black cloth; praying to the same Jesus Whom we clothed in robes or rags, as the fancy took us.

'I agree,' said my father when I mentioned this, 'and I would not like His Opinion of us.'

And he sat in a holy quiet, as he always did at the mention of Jesus.

Later, when we were through the nose-bags, Dada rose, saying, 'And so, if the canal in this valley is dying, we must go where the canal is alive and kicking, and this, for me, is the Vale of Neath.'

'A move from Merthyr, then?' asked Ifor, askance.

'A move from here to Resolven, next valley over.'

Dewi said, 'But the Bargee Union is going strong in Resolven. You try to buy a barge on the Neath Canal and the bargees will break your head.'

'Can't get a barge on that canal,' said Ifor, 'it is against the Union rules, remember,' and my father replied:

'I know all this, it is not news. But there is more than one way of getting round the Union. Is there any law against buying a barge here and sailing it down to Cardiff, and from Cardiff through Baglan Bay and up the Neath Canal at Briton Ferry?'

'Take a barge to sea?' I gasped.

'It has never been done before,' whispered Ifor.

'It is time it was,' said Dada. He knocked out his pipe. 'Come.'

The contralto's song was severed as with a knife as we walked through the workers, following Dada: hands rigid in the air, she froze: all eyes watched as we took a track that led us through deep undergrowth.

'Where are we going?' I asked.

'Into a new future, into a new life,' said my father.

On a stricken door, at the end of a disused wharf, Dada knocked, and the door was opened by an aged, withered little man.

'Mostyn Evan, by the gods. You're having it?' he cried.

'I am having it,' replied my father. 'And I have brought my three sons to see it. Safe and sound, is she?'

'Safer than death,' said Mr. Eli Cohen. 'Hold hard a minute and I will take you down.'

Scarecrowed by age, jack-knifed by labour, Mr. Eli Cohen, barge-builder of Abercynon, stopped on the track and croaked:

'Six daughters and a wife, I have—seven females in all. You ever stopped to think, Mostyn Evan, what it is like with seven women stitching and darning and talking soprano, and no bass voice of a son to hold in your heart?'

'Three decent sons I have, all things considered,' said Dada.

We walked down the track in file, Mr. Cohen leading,

stamping with his stick. 'Aye, seven women I have, and four are married and living at home—three have children, two sets of twins and three singles. And all girls. Fourteen females, Mostyn—I am surrounded by women, talking women, weeping women who have quarrelled with their husbands, screaming women in napkins—women feeding and women on the breast, another at this moment in childbirth. Hey, you!' and he caught Ifor by the buttons of his shirt. 'Here is a man of strength and hair. Speak bass to me, son of Mostyn: whisper bass in my ear, for the love of God!'

'Dear me, man, you are in a state,' said Ifor, and I loved him for his gentleness, which Dewi, for all his cut and style, did not possess.

'Is the barge finished, Mr. Cohen?' asked Dada.

'Finished, you ask?' The old man teetered on his corns. 'With me aged eighty and all my labour gone? Landed with fourteen women and another expected? Finished, man? She is not even started. In reeds and damp, she is, and I am old,' and he shivered on the edge of the grave. Dada said, eagerly:

'Look, Eli, we will finish it. How much?'

'Ten pounds.'

'A sixty-foot iron loader for ten pounds?'

'If you finish it,' said Eli.

'Easy, man, if you tell us how,' cried Dada. 'We can fire the planks and bend them steamed to curve; we can get the iron forged private up in Cyfarthfa, for I know tame benders: we can pickle the timbers, make the bolts and nails. We can ballast her to a ten-inch draft with pig from the old bloomeries, but it is the planning and brains we are short of. Will you consider it, Eli?'

'Tools I have, mind, but too weak to lift them....'

'We will use them, Mr. Cohen,' cried Ifor.

And old Eli looked wearily around him. 'Could be done, but it will take time. Timber is here in plenty, if you pay extra. Dog-spikes and drifters, seamers and caulkers—tar and wool; all is available. All I have lacked till now is sons.'

'You have sons now, Eli Cohen!'

'Launch her in July!'

'Three months come Monday!'

'Sail her on mock canvas down the Old Glamorgan to Cardiff,' shouted Dada, 'and round to Baglan up to Aberdulais —Rheola and Glyn Neath!'

Our own barge!

Mostyn Evan and Sons at last!

Hell to pay rent to, mind, when we break the news to Gran.

7

CHAPEL next morning, being Sunday, for it is right to let your God know what is happening, and with an effort He might even decide to sweeten Gran.

'Not a word from anybody, remember,' said my father. 'This Cohen removal is a very delicate operation, and she is much more malleable after communication with the Lord.'

Oh, how I used to love those Sunday mornings, with people turning out mothballs and climbing into new stays, hooking black bombazine on bed-rails, with clean shirt-fronts being ironed and how do I look now, turning in circles. Eh, I adore it when the family is under one roof. In the kitchen, combing for a quiff in the cracked shaving mirror, I said, 'Dear me, Gran, I am looking forward to Bethania this morning!'

'Oh, aye? What is going on, then?' Her hand suspended on her cameo brooch of Queen Victoria, and she went to the stairs, crying, 'Mostyn, what is happening that I do not know about?'

'Did you call, my precious?' Six-foot-two of him lumbering down the stairs.

Grand my dada looked in Sunday black, the serge groaning over his wide shoulders, his waist slim, his cut-throat up around his side-boards: black, black his hair, parted in the middle, and when he walked in town the Merthyr pugilists seemed otherwise engaged, but he was scared to death of Gran, his only woman. Sad, it is, to see a man like this left without a wife, and Gran once said:

'You three bruisers get used to the idea sharp—a man like your father has need of a wife—now, don't start huffing and heaving—there is more to a woman than you have in mind. There is cooking and mending, and boots by the fire, and when it comes to good-night kisses wives are preferable to grans and mothers. And it cuts both ways, remember, for I have had my fill of men and you lot in particular. Close your mouth when you're eating, Bryn.'

'Ach, leave the chap alone,' replied Dewi. 'He is happy enough with you, and we are not having another woman cluttering up the place.'

'I am not having another mam,' said Ifor, fist on the table, and he bowed his head, his eyes bright: took it heavy over mam, did Ifor.

I was with Ifor on this. Personally, I think it is indecent to have a new wife billing and cooing in bright colours while the old one lies sobbing in black under the daffodils up in Vaynor. And I reckon the wind must have been blowing in a certain direction, for Gran could always read us like a book. She said now:

'Mostyn, this boy do not look forward to Bethania without a good reason. Something is afoot, so out with it.'

Dada replied, fingers waffling on the seams of his trews, 'It is his first girl, Mother—sweet on a girl, isn't it, Bryn lad?'

'Aye, that is it,' I answered.

'God help us,' said Gran. 'Eleven years old and he is sparking. Who is she, how old is she, what is her name and where does she come from?'

'Miss Bronwen Rees of Abergavenny,' I said.

'Well!' Gran beamed, and I was heady with her perfume as she pulled me hard against her. 'There is beautiful, the lady school-teacher, and coming to Bethania this morning to hear Mr. Emlyn Hollyoak, I hear. Church usually, unfortunately, but we can't have everything.'

'No, Gran.'

She patted and fussed me, straightening my collar and smarming down my hair. 'There is smart he is! Never be indifferent to your appearance, boy. And clean underwear is as important as a clean suit, and a man is tidy if he is clean on the

51

skin, the collar and the boots, isn't it?'

'Aye, Gran,' replied Judas.

'Clean underwear especially, see, since you never know when you are going to have an accident.'

This accident business had been going on ever since I could remember, and by rights every man jack of us should have been down six feet. With this she held me tightly against her, rocking and humming, which could be twice as dangerous as a run-away tram after the first two minutes of being buried in Gran. I was half-way up the stairs and gasping when my father collared me, drawing me slowly down on to his bunched fist, whispering:

'Listen, you. Nobody has trained you as a diplomat, so stop hinting. One word about the Cohen barge to Gran and you will have me to account to—understand?'

'Yes, Dada,' I said, and was nearly upended as Gwen came dashing down the stairs and flung herself into his arms. And he whisked her aloft, whooping and kissing her in circles, which I think is daft. Bloody *daft*, I call that, for I cannot stand slobbering at the best of times—showing his fist to me one moment and kissing her the next. I agree, of course, that Gwen was becoming a bit more presentable, losing some of her baby fat and with a few of her front teeth back in, but if you wanted beauty you had to go to Sharon. Smooth and haughty, this big sister Sharon, now sixteen; the image of my mother with her Welsh darkness and peaches and Irish cream. The very sight of her was sending the Town lads demented, with Robert Crocker and Albert Johns and Willie Dare sitting on the wall like tom-cats, the last-named giving me the shivers. Lots of girls were getting into trouble about this time, being hauled into the aisles in the chapels, and my father always got edgy if Sharon was five minutes late coming back from the Band of Faith; going to the window and isn't it getting dark, Gran, and do you think I ought to slip out to meet her, Gran? But the climate and the darkness have nothing to do with it, Gran always used to say, for they will do in the frost what they will do in the sun, so do not fret, Mostyn, my son.

'Speak to her, Mam, speak to her! It is difficult having no wife, and she is such a child.'

'Oh, aye?' Up with her darning. 'Do not bother yourself, boy. I am quite satisfied that in sixteen years she has collected more information on the subject than me. Stop worrying. We have brought her up decent, and this will stand by her under provocation. All right, Bryn, that is all you are getting, do not mooch about out there.'

Most embarrassing when people pass remarks like that just because you happen to be passing.

'That is the one you should be worrying about,' said Gran. 'With looks like that he will be your cross in five years' time, if I am not mistaken.'

Off to Chapel on Sundays was a treat, and we always made an impression on the neighbours. About this time the churches and chapels were full in Merthyr, for they filled or emptied according to the rate of the cholera, which had picked off quite a few in Town recently.

Amazing to me how popular God becomes when the death-rate rises.

The trouble lay in the water supply, said my father, for paupers were going down in four-foot graves, and some of the coffins were floating. The birth-pangs of the '49 cholera were beginning now, although we did not know it then, and the religious jumpers were at it in the chapels and fields, though thank God Mr. Emlyn Hollyoak of Bethania did not go in for such exhibitions, said my father.

In the kitchen with us now, under inspection, tallest on the right, Gwen on the left, with Dada and Gran on a tour of inspection of ears and boots.

'Am I right, Dada?' Ifor, beetle-browed and wide, turning in a circle.

'As right as you will ever be, my son,' and dusted him. 'Just a bit of scurf on the collar, and do not snort in the pews, man, for you are not mountain-fighting.'

Me next, and get your hair cut by next Sunday, for we are not growing poets, and I hated this, for it meant sitting out the back under a basin and Ifor cheeping with scissors while I prayed for ears. Next Dewi, easy and confident, and let's get this lot over and quick, for I am meeting Pietro Bianca who is

53

arranging two tickets for Mexico to fight for freedom, for this damned country is finished now it is toadying to the English aristocracy. Bombs were going off in the cellar these days, the idea being to develop a decent one from the shotblast powder that would put paid to an American General called Taylor, who was playing hell in a place called Buena Vista. No, Mother, I am not interfering, my father used to say: Dewi has his beliefs, and it is Dewi's neck, not mine.

'You realise he's bringing the pictures down in the second bedroom?'

'Aye, well, it is a small price to pay for complete free-thinking.'

'This free-thinking will be the death of us,' said Gran, tying bonnet-streamers. 'All ready, is it?'

And off we went in bombazine, serge, poke-bonnets and streamers, and doors came ajar and window curtains were parted for a look at the family of Mostyn Evan.

Of course, half the trouble with Bridge Street was that we were really a cut above the neighbours, though, as I have said before, there are no snobs among the working-class: really, I suppose, it was trades superior and trades inferior, and with about two-pounds-six total falling into Gran's weekly apron, we could have moved to something better. Until now, of course, my father had been saving for his own barge. Mind, had there been any justice in the world it would have hooked old Crawshay out of Cyfarthfa Castle and put him in Bridge Street for a fortnight with his back to the Taff. I suppose, in a century or so, the tame historians, said Dewi, will write about the snug little cottages of the workers and how the good employers always did the best for them under trying circumstances, but the main difficulty was that they were dealing with animals and not decent people.

'Oh, aye?' said Dada.

Aye, said Dewi, but the trouble with history is that only the ruling classes can write—like the University fops they have sent into Wales to write the Blue Books, the parsons and magistrates, the landed Members of Parliament and their lackeys, the Man Arfon traitor Welsh.

Hot, was Dewi! but I agree that Bridge Street was in a

particularly bad state that morning, after the Saturday night.

'Hush, there's a good boy,' said Gran. 'The neighbours are watching us.'

With Gran, Sharon and Gwen leading, we went, picking our way through the garbage, for it came anything from night-soil to dead cats in the Merthyr streets about now: mud streets, of course, six inches deep, with cart-tracks; narrow openings through the rows of terraced houses, and you had to keep an eye cocked in case something came out of a window. With our house it was not so bad, since it backed on to the Taff River, and all our soil and refuse was thrown into that—the same river which others tapped for drinking farther down. The houses on the Glebe Land side backed on to coal tumps, so their soil and suchlike went into the middle of the road, which was better than some, for they had gutters that ran with blood from the Shambles slaughter-house. Drains we had none, water likewise, and every day Sharon used to walk two miles with a pail up the mountain, wait for an hour in a queue and then walk back home with a pail half full by the time she got there. Sometimes, in drought, the people used to wait at the water-spouts all night, with fighting and brutalising when they thinned to a trickle, and more than once Sharon came home with an eye filled up, which sent my father and brothers raging among the spouts for the woman who had pasted her. The main trouble with the water was that the Works took priority, and the children suffered most, mortality of those under two years old being about forty per cent. Down near Coedcae Court there was a very tasty spout that ran under a burial yard, and the Irish drank from that.

'We will put a stop to it,' said Dada, 'it is only a question of time.'

'Then take your time, do not mind me,' replied Gran, 'for I have been living in this filth either here or in Dowlais ever since I can remember, and I cannot bunk to Canford Manor every time the cholera comes, like Lady Charlotte Guest.'

'She is coming round,' said Ifor, delighted. 'The Vale of Neath is over the horizon, she is coming round—boots up for Resolven.'

*   *   *

Into the chapel pew now, into a smell of well-hung clothes and tiger nuts, and the creak of stays and braces: up off your knees next minute, stricken with conscience for the week of dissipation; nervous coughs and smiles as Mrs. Ten Benyon came in with her brood ranging from Owain who topped six feet and Cynfor who was two-foot-six and whose name meant Sea Chieftain, and you couldn't see Cynfor for pew. Mr. and Mrs. Alfo Morgan were there, with Rosie sitting between them, pretty well back, being in the publican and sinner business; labourers in the rear, tradesmen up front, and if we'd had an ironmaster he would have been sitting on the rail. Up on our feet now, and I heard the congregation gasp, for a Zion minister took the Big Seat, not our usual Mr. Emlyn Hollyoak, and this new chap gave an explanation as to how his butty had been taken with the gout, or something, and that he would be standing in for a few Sundays. Deep my father sighed behind me, for this new Zion preacher's name had been linked with the Revival Jumpers up on Adulam Fields, and Dada was strong for proper nonconformity. First hymn now, to the words of Billy Twice, and there is lovely it is with Mrs. Afron Shavings on the harmonium. Bass I do like best, mind, and will be one, for I am inclined to be suspicious of throaty tenors, and it can prove injurious if you get too fervent in the higher registers, says Dada.

Now there is a commotion at the back, for Dai Half-Moon is on his ear letting somebody in, and there is a clattering of walking-sticks and falling hymnals just as we were about to land on Canaan's side. And then my heart stopped beating, and I stared over Gran's shoulder, for Miss Bronwen Rees was coming in as large as life and as pretty as a picture, all done in black, with a summer hat about four feet diameter on her head tied over the top with a sort of net outrigger that knotted under her chin. And now she is stuck between Dai and the pew, with excuse-me-pleases and trying to hold her hat on, and Little Dai all bows and shivers since he has never been in such close proximity to anything as gorgeous as Miss Bronwen Rees, says Dewi, and he is not as daft as he looks.

Sharon put her elbow into my ribs. 'Stop wagging. Dada is behind you.'

If Old Nick had been behind me it would have made no difference, now that I was under the same roof as my Bronwen, and my eyes began to smart with joy as I knew a marvellous communion of the spirit. Another peep. Now she is safe in the pew, Dai staring at her, jaw dropped, and finding her place in the hymnal. And suddenly seeing me she smiled brilliantly, lowering her dark lashes on to her cheeks as if in acquiescence to some wonderful secret.

Dear me. I began to sweat.

My father, 'Do you mind turning round, Bryn, for you are being watched.'

'The Zion preacher has his eye on you,' hissed Sharon. 'Turn round!' and when I did so the new pastor was fixing me with a terrible eye, his massive brow furrowed with condemnation, and I began to sweat more because you could not trust these boyos once they were in the Big Seat, and they thought nothing of hauling out bad behaviour for public examination. So I smiled purely at him and took into the hymn again, and the last verse of Williams beat about me in glory.

Boots scraping, coughing, books slapping, sit down again, await events.

They came sooner than most expected.

After a few notices about Sunday School and the Penny Readings and I hope every young person will come, the new Zion preacher stood up in the Big Pew, his white beard trembling with indignation, and he brought his fist down on to the mahogany with a crash that hit them off the seats in the Ebenezer Baptist.

'Are there drinkers among you?' he roared.

Well, there is a stupid question to ask, with half the male population good for twenty pints at a sitting. Toes curling, we sat.

'Are there drunkards here?' and I risked a peep behind at Dewi and Ifor to see how they were sticking it.

'For, if the sons of Baal are abroad, let them listen . . .!'

Very powerful in the vocal chords, this one, even for Zion; the boom of him battered off the faded walls: silence: the tragedy of Merthyr moaned suddenly in a little wind from the hills. The preacher shouted:

'For the drinkers will be the losers, mind! The Big Man will henceforth farm the land himself, and fair play to him, it is his property. He will turn the briars into vineyards of wine, the pure wine of everlasting life, and Satan will go to the wall. Alone will he travel in his vanity and corruption, drinking ale at the beerhouses—no more convivial company for Baal, for he must drink alone! Do I hear a confession?' The preacher glared round at us.

There was no sound but Mrs. Shenkins sobbing at the back, in the seat where her Willie used to sit.

The pastor threw his skinny hands to Heaven, crying, 'I look about me and find dust, but there is a jewel in the dust of the chapel. Is there not one man present ready to deny Baal and all his works? Must you go unsober in the days of feasting? Must you run helter-skelter at the name of the Lord?'

I was with him on this, of course, for the beer-houses were a disgrace to the whole community, with men staggering home laying into their wives. And all the time the Zion was hitting at the drinkers I was most concerned, though any moment he might start becoming personal about coveting oxen and asses, and I was a bit involved in this respect with my beautiful Bron. I took a deep breath when he shouted:

'But beer and gin do not stand alone as areas of iniquity. Does not Baal in all his glory stroll the Coedcae Spout at night, among the pails and pitchers and pots? Is there not one man, woman or child here this morning guilty of a debased thought?' He paused in the pin-drop silence. 'For if there is not one so guilty, then let him stand and claim now, and I will throw him high that he might hover like a crow in the vaults of Heaven! I cry again—let innocence stand! It is not enough to claim that innocence exists—let it stand!' And his great head with its white, flowing mane turned to me.

'You, lad—you!'

I slid my trews on the pew and got my head well down into my collar.

'You, boy!' A pause, then. 'Stand, my son, stand!'

Rigid, eyes clenched but peeping, I lay under the glare of his eyes.

'You he is talking to, mind,' hissed Sharon, digging me.

Six inch coach bolts had me screwed to that mahogany.

My father rustled in the dust-mote silence, his hand gripped my shoulder. 'Stand, Bryn—do as he says. I am here, do not be afraid.'

Shivering, I rose, and the preacher cried:

'How old are you, my son?'

Words steam-dry in the dust-bowl of the throat; the chest convulses, the tonsils sag. 'Eleven, sir.'

Opening his arms, he beamed. 'Eleven, eleven! Oh, that I might for ever feast mine eyes on such innocence!' And I heard Dewi groan aloud. 'Eleven years old. A little child shall lead them! Oh, make us all as pure as he, the golden wheat of Life! Would that this little boy's life stay unshadowed by the evils in our midst: that religion could dethrone impiety, the drunkard be sobered, the lame made to dance!'

The people were murmuring about me, a few weeping openly, others beating their breasts and sniffing, most staring up at me in open adoration of innocence. I stood a few inches higher in the magnificence of the man of Zion, his melodious voice breaking about me like waves over a rock: it seemed to snatch me up, transporting me to realms higher than the Old Bethania. And as more and more worshippers began to weep aloud the pastor cried, his arms thrown upwards:

'The day will come, and mark this, when innocence will prevail: when the miserable creatures now buried in their caverns of lust shall rise and be cleansed with the white robe of sianthood, and the cairns of Satan shall be emptied at a stroke! Hallelujar!'

'*Hallelujar!*' I shrieked, leaping on to the pew, fist trembling.

Dead silence.

Not a sound. The vaults echoed.

Clutching myself, I stared around, seeing the shocked, white face of Sharon, Gwen's mouth gaping and Gran's eyes so big that they threatened to drop from her cheeks. Suddenly, the pastor shrieked:

'Hallelujar, the boy is right. Hallelujar!'

As if ignited, the congregation jumped. Women fainted

away in the pews, burly men openly wept, children were screaming, and through the wailing and sighs the Zion cried, 'Behold! A mighty, pentecostal wind shall fill the house of the world. All tears shall be wiped from your eyes!'

'Hallelujar!' I yelled.

'Who shall be the first to confess before the congregation, who will be upstanding?'

I was just about to inform him about me and Miss Bronwen Rees when Dai Half-Moon jumped up at the back, croaking in tears, 'My sins are beyond forgiveness, pastor, they are beyond forgiveness!'

'Do not talk twaddle, man! Your sins, placed beside the Plan for Redemption, is like hitching a porridge-pot to the stern of a man o' war. Listen! The Great Revival is coming, good people, it is coming! The cock-fighting pitch shall be stilled; banished the foul game of pitch and toss. And if there are still devils among you I will prise them out of you with these two hands—every hoof, every horn! See now, the Lord, in my image, is aiming at you!' And he took aim at us as a soldier aims a musket, one eye closed. This did it. Pews were overturned, boots went up: people were crying for mercy, others pleading on their knees and the pastor's voice boomed on like the toll of Doom:

'The Revival shall come like the flash of a swallow's wing heralding the arrival of summer. Leap for joy! We will set the summer cornfields alight with our ardour like Samson's foxes!'

Somebody was blowing on his fingers like a hunting-horn, women were pulling down their hair to cover their faces, others starting the Revival Jump.

'*Hallelujar!*' It was a repeated cry now, taken up in chorus.

Gwen was shrieking with fright, Sharon up and dancing along the pews. Gran was up on a chair waving her hat with ostrich feathers, shouting something about when she was seventeen up in Dowlais, with Dewi trying to get her from behind, and as Dada come for me I fought him off, waving my arms for balance.

'Let that child stand!' roared the Zion pastor. 'Let him not be allayed! Is he not the implement of a giant purpose? Did he not fire us all with the first hallelujar?' and in a second of awed silence following this, Gran cried from the other side of the room:

'The ark has returned from Philistia, the ark has returned from Philistia!'

Going pretty solid was Gran, her hat off and cheering in tears, and swiping with ostrich feathers anybody trying to collar her.

'Leap for joy, good people!' yelled the pastor. 'Leap for joy!' and the place began to thunder as people got going. Down at the back Dai Half-Moon was prancing along the aisles with his missus swiping at him, but then, she was always inclined to the Established Church, and Miss Bronwen Rees was up on the Sideman's Pew leaping and landing flat-footed with her skirts above her knees and her summer hat over her eyes, the outrigger flying. And the Zion pastor roved among us like a great, white patriarch, his arms waving, as Moses must have looked when he was breaking the tablets.

I was half-way down the chapel, vaulting pews in pairs to get at Miss Bronwen Rees, when my father brought me down. In the shelter of a pew, hard in his arms, I heard him whisper, 'Quiet now, Bryn. Hush quiet, I have got you.'

And the harder I fought to be free the harder he held me, till I could scarcely breathe. 'Dewi, Ifor,' he shouted then, and the face of Ifor appeared above us.

'The place is with madness,' cried Dada. 'Go and get Gran!'

'Sharon and Gwen at it too, mind,' said Ifor.

'I do not want a report—go and get them, and sharp!'

Cold as ice in the chapel porch, with corpses lying round and people fanning and rubbing backs of hands and sprinkling water. Miss Bronwen Rees was brought in and laid beside me: through a hedge backwards was my Bron, with her hat bashed in and shrieking confessions that were a bit warmer than I had been led to believe, and I pitied her the indignity, blue in the face and sobbing. Gran came with the next half-dozen, in a state of collapse over Dewi's shoulder in a fireman's lift, with Ifor running beside them patting her hand, and the moment she was laid on the flags she raised her head, and shrieked:

'A match has been applied to the isolated tufts. The conflagration is ascending. Leap for joy, leap for joy!' and the corpses in the porch got up and started it all over again, so we rushed the door and got her out in the street where she crowed like a hen and went out like a light. Sharon and Gwen came out next, weeping and fighting, but Dada soon fixed them. Dewi said, squatting in the road, holding Gran:

'Will you tell me what is wrong with the human race?'

'No inquests from you, please,' replied Dada, fanning.

'Dead, is she?' whispered Ifor, white-faced, staring down.

'I doubt it,' answered my father, 'they rarely die at Revivals.' He turned to me shivering beside him. 'You all right now?'

'Yes, Dada.'

'He ought to be,' said Dewi, 'it was him who bloody started it, remember.'

'Stop that bad language,' said Gran, opening her eyes, 'for I will not stand for it. Will somebody please tell me what I am doing down here?'

'It is the Revival,' said Dada. 'Remember, you were attacked the same on Dowlais Top in '33?'

'Bring me Bryn,' said she, and I stood before her.

'Raise me, child.' She slapped Dewi's hands away. 'Raise me, Bryn, lad. Ach, I'd never have believed that I would live to see the joy of it—a child of Ben's flesh and blood leading a new Revival.' She put out her big hands to me and I hauled her to her feet. 'Aye, long may this stand amid the nest of disbelievers. Home now, for dinner, and Bryn shall take my hand. I have enjoyed every minute.'

With Sharon still unstable and our Gwen bawling aloud, we took the roads back to Bridge Street, all spare hands supporting the invalids, and Gran would not allow me from her sight. My father said inaudibly, 'And a little child shall lead them. Wait till I get you home, Bryn Evan, and I will warm your trews.'

'Aye!' said Ifor, vicious.

My father added, 'And this is the very last time Bethania receives me without Mr. Emlyn Hollyoak in the Pew. I have had sufficient of that big Nantyglo preacher to last me a life-time, and his Revival in particular.'

'Hallelujar,' said Dewi, giving me a look to kill.

8

THREE months Eli reckoned it would take to complete the half-finished barge in the reeds at Abercynon, but it was more like three years before we laid the last coat of tar; the time-table coming adrift largely because we lived in Merthyr and Eli lived seven miles south. Man Arfon, checker, was the main cause of the delay, since he devised the roster system for the runs to Abercynon, and when he knew we were keen to be down there, he charged my father a pound a run.

'No more runs to the Basin this week, Mostyn, lad,' he would say.

'But you are sending iron to Cynon twice a week!'

'Aye, man, but the economics have changed a trifle, don't you see? There is a lovely English word now—Economics.'

My father said, 'I am paying you a pound a run now, Arfon, you are not getting more. Does it matter to you what barge takes the load?'

'It does now,' said the checker, 'since you are prepared to pay for the privilege.'

'Give him another ten shillings and a thump in the ear,' said Dewi.

'The temptation might be great,' said Man Arfon, 'but it would land you on the black-list, and then you would not see the sky over Abercynon. Be reasonable, man—do I favour you free? Think of the risk I take with Ephraim Davies. Besides, it is against Company regulations to carry private goods on Company water.'

To be fair, the checker had a point there. He added, 'A bedstead with brass balls is a very prominent object, remember.'

What we were doing, of course, was gradually slipping the household goods down to Abercynon into Eli's sheds. Dada said, 'It is against regulations to accept bribes, yet you are doing it, and a bedstead with brass balls is an excellent example of Cyfarthfa iron, for it was fashioned there.'

'But I am drawing the line at Welsh dressers, mind,' said Man Arfon, 'and unless I am mistaken there is one coming now. Another ten shillings, if you please, Mostyn Evan.'

As long as I live I will remember that summer dawn, on the day I was fourteen, when we shipped Gran's Welsh dresser down to Abercynon. In moonlight, like smugglers, we carried it on a wheel-barrow along Bridge Street with fearful looks at windows, and when we got to the head of the wharf where the chief agent, Ephraim Davies, was lurking, we lifted it on to Ifor's back to save the clatter of the barrow. Very strange it was to see that dresser sliding down the wharf with Ifor's boots walking under it, and Gran, Dewi and me trying to look unconcerned. Dada came from the shadows of Number Two Shed followed by Man Arfon, a barrel in knee-breeches and bandy for letting through pigs. 'Well, well,' said Arfon. 'There is a very strange object, a Welsh dresser with boots. Travelling, is it?'

Gran said, 'It is the oldest dresser in Cyfarthfa, for Owain Glyndawr himself hung his cups on it, and it is going down to Abercynon or I am staying on in Merthyr.'

'Ay, ay. I was only wondering—do not take offence. May I know who happens to be under it, for it looks all of a couple of tons from by here.'

'Aye, solid mahogany, it is,' said Gran, patting it, 'and a good man carrying it, isn't it, Ifor, boy. You all right?'

'I will be that much better with this load off my mind,' said Ifor, jack-knifed underneath it.

'Is that the lot, then?' asked Man Arfon, nervous.

'It is not,' answered Gran. 'There is the tin bath, kitchen tables and chairs, the horse-hair sofa, and the commode in case of sickness from the second bedroom. My son is paying you for patience, Man Arfon. What you got there, Sharon, my love?'

'Chicken house, Gran.'

'God help me,' cried Man Arfon. 'Not chickens also?'

'Mattresses, chest of drawers, wash-tub and fender coming in the hearse, and half a ton of coal.'

'Coal to Abercynon?' asked Arfon, shocked.

'Not leaving it,' said Gran. 'The people coming in are Church of England.'

Man Arfon said, 'A hearse unloading on Company water! Sudden death I will have if Mr. Ephraim Davies catches me transporting this lot.'

'Worse than death you will have if it do not arrive intact,' said Gran. 'Do not strain yourself, Bryn, what you carrying?'

'The mangle, Gran.'

'Oh, aye. Put it on the dresser by here, son, for you can easily pull a rupture.' She peered under the dresser. 'You all right, Ifor?'

'Right as rain, Gran, and I know you will get going as soon as you are able.'

Clop clop in the dawn darkness, and up came Hobo Church-yard with the coal and there was a lot of pushing and barging, with Man Arfon becoming difficult about stowing things in the hold, and back we all came to the dresser and Ifor.

'Right, my beauty, all aboard,' said Gran. 'Bryn, Sharon, Gwen—lend a pound on this dresser and we will give Ifor a breather—lift on the corners—*up*!' and we heaved to take the weight off Ifor and there was a roar like a bull from under it and Ifor was arse up and ears down and blue in the face and what the bloody hell is happening.

'Giving you a pound, we are,' said Gran. 'Lift again, and easy does it—*up*!' and there was a ripping like sail canvas and Ifor bellowing and stamping hobnails.

'Anything wrong, son?' asked Gran, hands on knees now, looking under.

'It is the shelf hooks, I suspect,' said Ifor. 'Into my bottom proper they are, Gran, and begging your pardon for the language.'

'Dear me,' said Gran, 'the shelf hooks are in Ifor. It might be lighter if we took off this mangle. Dewi, Mostyn!'

'What is wrong?' asked my father, coming up.

'It is the shelf hooks,' shouted Ifor. 'They are three inches up and two with cups on,' and Dada went under for a look: very pale he was when he came out.

'Ifor is solid on the hooks,' said he, 'and it can be important to a man, so take the weight gently.'

'Is there blood with him?' asked Man Arfon, peering interested.

'Not at the moment,' said my father, 'but the gutters will run with it the moment he is free from under the thing. Steady a minute, everybody rest. I will consider this situation,' and he took out his pipe, thoughtful, while we waited breathless.

'Too late,' said Dewi. 'Look what is arriving.'

'Dear God,' said Man Arfon.

Mr. Ephraim Davies, it was, striding down the wharf, and what the hell is happening on Number Two at this time of the morning.

'Mostyn Evan and family moving,' said Man Arfon, bravely, 'and this Welsh dresser stuck its hooks up one of the sons.'

'Dear me,' said Mr. Davies, compassionate, 'there is a situation,' and he stooped, squinting under. 'To the left a bit, man. Is it getting heavy with you under by there?'

Sparks came from Ifor's hobnails, and the language that flew up sent Gran sheet-white, and shocked.

'Easy, easy with the language, you under there,' commanded Mr. Davies. 'Ashamed you should be—your poor old gran is up by here, remember.'

'God help me,' said Ifor, and my father knelt, saying:

'It is not an easy situation, son, but Mr. Ephraim Davies has arrived now, and he is technical. Meanwhile, keep the language within reasonable bounds or Gran might take exception.'

'Already taken,' said Gran. 'When he comes out by there it will be six-inch meat hooks, not Welsh dressers.'

With the rest of the family taking the weight, my father went off for a confab with Man Arfon and Mr. Davies, and when they returned, he said, 'A decision has been made. The women and children will have to leave, the trews are about to be removed from Ifor.'

And they went under and there was a lot of ripping and

66

sawing, with Ifor bawling, and eventually my father crawled out with pieces of belt and trews and Ifor went like a hare coursing in the opposite direction while Mr. Davies tore strips off Man Arfon for carrying private goods on public water.

Lots of people left Merthyr about this time; like Rosie Carey who boozed the ironmasters on the day Dic Penderyn was hanged—she left and bought the Old Plough above Glyn Neath, and rumour had it that Mrs. Alfo Morgan dug deep for this, to make sure of her Alfo. Mr. and Mrs. Dai Half-Moon emigrated, too, on the boot, and were seen staggering along the road to Aberdare with bundles and their idiot son, being pelted with clods by every urchin under Pont Storehouse: Dai Central Eating, my mam's favourite at Bethania Sunday School, he left Merthyr also, being sparked by an Eli Cohen woman, and becoming keener. Mr. and Mrs. Afron Shavings, the carpenters, left, too, for Mrs. Afron started getting visions, seeing a double coffin travelling at high speed over Cyfarthfa Castle in the company of angels led by Mr. Tom Thomas, conductor of the band, blowing on a silver trumpet. Others went to the four winds when the Great Cholera came, and are not recorded—some even to England, so you can tell the panic. But one only really remembers the people with close ties to the family, like Mrs. Ten Benyon and her brood, and Mr. and Mrs. Isan Chapel next door but eight, and Man Arfon on the end of the boot of Mr. Ephraim Davies, which was poetic justice, said Dada. Last, and not least, Miss Bronwen Rees took up as mistress at a private school near Aberdulais, by the waterfall, and I had just got my teeth into a celebration quart when news came that Taliesen the Poet had been seen wandering in the same vicinity, which set me back a swallow. Robert Crocker, Albert Johns and Willie Dare also came to the Vale of Neath, their lives being practically empty, so they said, now that Sharon had gone. Mrs. Shenkins, the mother of Willie-who-died had lately been sitting out at her back in a bath of six inches of water, in desperation: but she also came to the Vale since Willie used to fish down there in the Nedd. Many, many others left when the cholera came to The Top. Away from this accursed place, said my dada. Take a chance and starve, but away, and leave the filthy place to its monumental greed that will stand for the Crawshays, the Guests and the Butes and their like to the end of Time.

Away, said Gran, to Abercynon. Now that Mr. Emlyn Hollyoak is back in the Big Seat and that wonderful preacher has returned to Zion, it will never be the same in the Old Bethania.

Abercynon!

Down to the Basin with us, and we were off that dirty old Merthyr barge sharper than monkeys and trundling down to Eli's wharf with the furniture with Dewi under the dresser this time, Ifor being with bandages, and Nell and Jed loaded to the forelocks, and at the back was Gran between the wheelbarrow shafts. Ifor was humping the tin bath, me with the mangle and Dada and the girls coming after with the chest of drawers and linen, Gran making sure that this was well presented since it came from Camarthen and was best quality. And there was Mr. Eli Cohen waiting outside his cottage door with his fifteen women shrieking and chattering hind legs off donkeys, a couple of the matrons getting the vapours when Dewi came from under the dresser, and please come in, Mrs. Evan, for the tea is ready and the kettle will be crying directly.

Invitations and introductions all round then, with Sharon and Gwen dropping their new English curtseys, and Ifor being dragged out for presentation—all fingers and fumbles at the sight of so many women, though I think it was more blood-pressure than shyness for those Welsh-Jew girls were beauties with their brown, haughty faces and glorious red hair.

And one, Rebecca, aged seventeen, came from the back, one hand on her hip and her lips bright red in her smile, and I saw in a flash that Ifor, my brother, was done over fifteen rounds. So we left him to his fate, and me, Dada and Dewi went down to the wharf, and there was that Cohen barge all shining black and stacked with the furniture for the voyage round to Baglan. Three years we had worked for this; you get out of the soil what you put into it, said Dada.

'Got a good prow on her,' cried Eli. 'She is an inch above the water-line with the household effects. The mast is spruce, the sail is best Mary Walters down in Neath Arches. Float her in an hour, and with luck you catch the high tide at Cardiff before the bore runs out.'

'God bless you, Eli,' said my father.

'And God bless you, too, Mostyn, for I am back to fourteen now that Rebecca and Ifor have met up again.'

'Ach, no!'

'Like a sis, he is,' I said. 'Eh, look at it.'

Very girlish was Ifor, turning up his boots under the apple tree and Rebecca Cohen coming the Delilah on him, and holding hands like a fairy instead of a thick-eared pugilist.

'Come on!' roared Dewi, disgusted.

Astonishing how Dewi treated women: disdainful, his dark eyes smouldering fire, his lips uncaring, and yet they died for him in their ravishing glances.

Second cup of tea for Gran, and can I slip out the back, Mrs. Cohen, and she was ready, and old Eli lined his women up on the dancing lawn in front of the cottage and snapped his fingers, and down they all went in their folds and crinolines, heads bowed, elbows wide, skirts out, and I could have shouted at the beauty of it.

'Sail aboard!' shouted Eli, and we all trooped down to the wharf, with Ifor and Rebecca lagging behind arm in arm and staring into each other's faces.

'Beautiful women you got here, Mr. Cohen,' said Gran. 'And best kept clear of this rabble of fists that I am landed with.'

'We will get together, ma'am,' chortled Eli. 'With your lot and my lot we could build a Welsh Jerusalem down the Vale of Neath, you think?'

'Many a true word said in jest, mind,' said Gran. 'See if we can manage it, for I would like to see all my boys wedded and bedded to the right women before I go under,' and she looked at my father, her eyes bright with unshed tears.

'Away to go, we are,' said Dada. 'We will not early forget the Cohens of Abercynon, and there will always be a welcome in Resolven, remember, especially at Michaelmas Fair!' and he helped Gran aboard the Cohen barge.

'Ifor, we are off directly!' cried Gran, and he came running with Rebecca flushed and watery behind him: mind, this had been going on for a month or two to my certain knowledge, though supposed to be a secret.

I got Nell and Jed Donkey shifting, and we glided through the Cohen Lock, waving and shouting to the Cohen tribe clustered on the bank, and down they all went again in their curtsey. Beautiful, they looked, clustered about Eli.

'May your Jew-God possess you, Eli Cohen!'

'His hands above your house, Mostyn Evan, I will miss your sons!'

'Dear me! *Dammo*, what lovely people,' sobbed Gran, wet and dabbing.

'If you get a tribute from a good woman again, you have her bear a son for me, Mostyn Evan?' called Eli, and this put us all pretty dull, me especially, for the thought of my father with another woman always brought me sick inside. These things are all right being joked about, but a very different kettle of fish when they happen, I say.

On, gliding along the canal, harness jingling, and Jed and Nell with eager hoof-beats, sensing that they were leaving dirty old Merthyr for good. Straight into the Old Glamorgan canal we went from the Cohen wharf, into a line of wage-slave bargees, and we were big in the chest: Mostyn Evan and Sons it was now, for we had collected out last pay-day from Crawshay and from now on it was private enterprise. And we had just run into the Abercynon Basin when Abe Sluice, the swimming pig, came up ahead and jumped on his stern, shouting:

'Where you off to, then, Evan?'

'Resolven, on the Neath Canal.'

'How the hell can you do that, without going over land?'

Dada cried, 'Down to Cardiff, into the Channel and along to Port Talbot!'

'In that thing?' Abe hooted laughter. 'Wet and dead you will be, you idiot, if you go to sea in that contraption.'

'It has been done before,' said Dada.

'Oh, aye? If the sea don't get you the Neath union will. You heard they're breaking the heads of the new bargees signing on for the Neath Canal Company?'

'Depends what you've got for a head, Abe Sluice,' bawled Ifor.

'For God's sake,' said Gran, 'do not bandy words with the unwashed, for you can always stoop to pick up rubbish. What is this about breaking heads?'

'Man's business,' said Dada, 'leave it.'

'Is it, now? If anybody is breaking my head I want to know about it. Very secretive you have been about this move, Mostyn; tell me more about Resolven, for I am just considering it. Three up and four down, isn't it?'

'And a two-acre patch, a paddock for horses, a wharf, a stable for Nell. Like a country seat, it is.'

'I can well believe it for fifty-two pounds ten.'

'Just needs a bit of repair here and there, of course,' said my father uneasily, 'but I reckoned anything would be better than Fifteen Bridge Street.'

'Well, down with my head,' announced Gran, 'for I am coming numb in the nut. Call me when we arrive at your father's paradise in Resolven.'

The sun burned down, the country shimmered and glowed with incandescent fire. The cut rippled and sang as we carved along in waving bindweed and petals, the still-water seeded with gold lace from overhanging ferns. And alongside us the poor old Black Taff, who once had watered the Romans, leaped her black arms down her oily banks. This river, as my father said, was the source of the cholera, and for months now the skeleton in rags and tatters had been wading in her depths, stalking the hovels of the Top Towns for practice, picking off a child here, a whole family there. And at night he sat on the banks of the sewer, his skull clasped in fleshless fingers, watching as the poor Irish drank from the river and the Welsh from the putrid spouts. And a month back he sent the Guests away to Canford Manor, sharpened his scythe and came swinging into Chinatown, cutting the workers down in hundreds.

It is not so much the death that counts, said my father, it is the indignity, and the evaporating agony: to die of the cholera is to die a filthy death.

And now it was all behind us. Beautiful indeed, this side of

71

the Basin, for, though the land was still ripped and torn, the sulphurous stink of the iron-making had gone, the glowing heaps of slag vanished as in a cool dream.

'What time you reckon we'll hit the sea, Dada?' I asked over Jed's ears.

He pulled out Granfer Ben's gold watch and chain. 'According to Eli we'll be bogged in the Narrows and slowed in the Tunnel at Melly. Given a two-hour sleep we should get to Cardiff at midnight, and fetch the morning Bore.'

Excitement grew within me.

At Melingriffith I would lie on my back in darkness and push with my boots along the dripping ceiling, and in oil and black water we would run, with the ghost bugguts crouching in foul weirs, claws open for the unwary hand, or leg. Eh, *diawl*! Tunnels do frit me. But also, the sea was calling me. For beyond Tiger Bay was a thirty-mile run round the coast to Baglan and Neath, working out on the swill of the Severn Bore: I sniffed the golden air, and it was salt.

I heard Dewi say, fingering the sail canvas, 'Where did Eli buy this?'

'Mary Walters, Neath chandlers, so he said,' replied Dada.

'Then the quality must be good. Who cut it?'

'Eli Cohen.'

Dewi nodded. 'And old Eli ran the clippers up the China run, didn't he? I thought so, this is a junk sail.'

'The sail of a Swiss man o' war,' said my father, 'as long as it gets me through Baglan Bay.'

Dewi flung the canvas down. 'Five shillings that we never see the sky over Baglan, and another five that the life-boat puts out from Swansea—that will cost a pretty penny.'

'Taken,' said Dada.

'Just struck me,' said Dewi, fingering his chin now. 'You ever been to sea before?'

'I am about to go,' said Dada. 'You hold Gran steady when the Seven Bore comes and leave the sails to me.'

We entered Cardiff sea-pound that led into the Bristol Channel at nine o'clock next morning. Sail up now, and we fetched Jed Donkey and Nell Mule aboard for the sea-trip.

With the wind set fair we slid gently through the moored colliers and flat-boats taking on coal from the Top Town barges, and the port about us blustered with life: coaches and horses clattering into cobbled courtyards, flunkeys bowing right and left to fine city gentlemen; ladies in hooped crinolines walked with gentry disdain before their little golden blackamoors. And among the teeming crowds of the waterfront marched troops of soldiers, their red coats flashing brass; muskets shouldered, eyes wary for the rebel Welsh, for our ancient Prince did not die in vain. He did not die in vain, said my father, and we are having him replaced by no English substitutes. Buxom serving maids with swelling tops and bustles were ladling from steaming tureens, and I watered at the mouth at the sight of those fat, city merchants forking up beef and swilling it down with quart ale pewters.

'They do themselves pretty well in the city, strikes me,' muttered Ifor.

But the mooching poor went by in droves, hands outreached to us, begging for bread. Urchins, as naked as bones, ran in circles of savage joy around a butcher's bull being led to the baiting-ring and the iron-jawed dogs. Doleful in the stocks, heaped high with refuse, a drunkard sang a dribbling song, bare toes wriggling the time. In a forest of masts, the square-rigged barques of Spain heaved at their moorings. Broken-nosed and grinning, French matelots lounged on the rails of the Brittany coasters, impounded for harbour dues, said my father, and they spat at Ifor's cheeky wave and talk of frogs.

'Where you bound for, Welshman?' This from a bearded face over a rail, the accent posh English. Dada swung his hook, grappled the ship's side, and slowed us, shouting up.

'We make for Baglan Bay, and the Neath Canal.'

'Bad weather rising in the Channel, you realise this?'

'We wait for good weather round this head and we wait all our lives, Captain.'

'You'll catch the Severn Bore, you know this?'

'That is the idea. Is the wind following?'

'Following brisk, and so will the Bore. What stern freeboard have ye?'

'Two feet.'

'Right, but keep her stern-on to the Bore or it will cost you your life.'

'Right, you,' said my father.

'Thank God for your stupidity, Welshman, though I've seen it done before. God go with you, Taff!' and the face disappeared.

'Don't sound healthy, that,' said Gran, glum.

'You batten down,' said Dada, 'and leave the sailing to sailors.'

Harlots and harpies padding along the waterfront beside us now; drunkards already rolling out of the inns, with the riff-raff quarrelling on the doorsteps and meaty clumpers flying in the smacks of fist on flesh, and the language steaming in Gran's direction was hot enough to boil Baal. In the noonday sun the last wharves slid up; the aprons facing the Bristol Channel were stacked high with the loot of the Welsh Top Towns. For nearly a million tons a year was being dug out of the mountains, a golden hoard of wealth being shipped to a hundred ports in the world: never had I realised the staggering loot that was being cut out of my country by the speculators, leaving nothing behind but hunger, poverty, disease and a ravaged land.

A million tons of loot a year from the valleys of Wales, and this was only the beginning of the tide.

I thought of my generations of farming Welsh, who had paid the price of sitting on a fortune. In the great wounds of the mountains, the sealed, fiery caverns, the places of dark, rushing water, lay the refuse of my people. In grotesque attitudes they lay, where roof fall, tram or explosion had pinned them. In the jammed ventilation doors of the galleries, lipped by flood-water or incinerated by fire, sat the husbands, wives and children, trapped in the same instant, the same scream. Upturned pit-ponies and donkeys lie in company, their flesh preserved, embalmed by the last pressure of the crush in unknown salts and stinks. Hoof and hand entwined, they lie, the refuse of a foreign profit that was shovelled out with the furnace slag, by a foreign hand, of a thousand furnaces and bloomeries from Hirwain to Blaenafon and Cyfarthfa to Swansea. Let the patriot Welsh remember Cardiff docks, the

74

pus of the ulceration which men call profit, gained at the cost of pure Welsh and Irish blood.

'You all right, Bryn?' called my father.

I nodded.

Strange, I thought, that I should remember my people at a time like this, as if they had been borne along before my eyes on the flood of black diamonds that were pouring into the holds; and their death-knell, it seemed, was the tolling of the rails being loaded for Argentina and Peru, France and Spain.

Industry, progress—yes: but not at the price as high as this.

I saw a tattered generation of dead that day. Six abreast, they came across the sky: the wizened colliers, the tattooed miners with their head-bumps and scars; the furnacemen scalded by the iron flash, the cancerous breasts of the women of the tin-plate picklers and the jack-knifed children of the lower levels, who, with the accord of an English Church, had been used in the two foot mine levels, where only children could crawl for coal, setting their bones for ever in crippledom. Across a landscape of engines and trams, coal and pig-iron, tin-plate and copper, they marched on a cloud, this stricken army of my Welsh dead.

'Wait for me,' said a voice.

We were through the sea-pound lock now, and Dewi and Ifor were back on board. My father's face was expressionless in the vicious light of the sun. The barge swung as the sea hit her along the shanks, the white-topped rollers hissed and sprayed from the Severn lying east.

'You'd best get the legs out from under that donkey, Mostyn?' shouted Gran.

'There'll be no panic, if you let him stand. He knows what's happening.'

'Got one foot in my bath of washing now, mind.'

'Ach, don't bother me, you should see to your washing!'

'And I'm getting as wet as a herring down here, remember!'

Dada rose at the tiller. 'Dewi, Sharon—cover your Gran—don't stand there mooning—see to her!' He grinned up at the marching host. Glorious they looked in their thousand, marching across that summer sky. 'Wait for me,' he said.

I stared at him from the prow, and the sea leaped, hissing wet on my face.

Behind my father I saw the sea-lock dying into the land, and behind that I could see the day-shift iron beaming on the clouds above Dowlais as the bungs were tapped: I heard the faint thunder of it, bellowing and reverberating over the sea. All this I saw through the image of my father's face, through the humped shadows of his eyes, through his transparent cheeks and hair. And he winked at me and looked again at the sky, for the sun was glowing in a new majesty, breaking over the earth a single shaft of golden light, and in that beam the army marched. I shivered, gripping myself, watching my father as he cupped his hands to the flare of his pipe, smiling at the sky.

I heard his voice, not in echo, but loud and clear above the hammer of the wind and the tramping hobnails of the marching dead.

'Wait for me,' he said.

And I knew then that the vision I had seen would one day be real to me, and on that day my father would be safe and dead, leaving me to suffer it.

9

OUTSIDE the pound the wind sweetened into pleasant whispers, content now we were in her parlour, and the sky opened wider and poured the summer morning over us: a zephyr fanned from the east of the Severn, and the ribbed canvas of the sail rose and fell like the breast of a sleeping woman. Laden on the wind came the tea-smells of the Asian clippers, the spices of India, cinnamon of the South Seas and ground coffee from the bubbling fire-pots of the Brittany coasters. In full flight were noses that morning off Cardiff sea-pound. Dear me, there is a strange thing is a nose, stuck upside down on the face to keep out the rain, and with holes · yet beautiful in some degree, according to the occupant—smooth and graceful, like Sharon's, for instance, or broad-beak and busted like Ifor's, spelling manhood. But it is the soul behind the nose that speaks—nostrils flaring in the lover, put sideways for kissing, and very windy in passion. Or twiddling to the scent of fried bacon, itchy when smeared with butter, but best of all when in repose, like now—drinking great draughts of autumn woodland and salt flung high from the caverns of the drowned.

Danger, it tells of, also. I saw my father raise his great head and sniff at the wind, which is the sniff of the savage to the rustle of undergrowth.

But, of, there were some glorious whiffs off Penarth that day. Very fancy is Penarth, but she do turn out some very strange smells: pot-herbs and onions from the Italian cargo-bummers, garlic from the bunged-up French, curry from the Indians, turbanned and jewelled. Persian tobacco drifted under my nose from the hubble-bubble hookahs of the grimy bunks, and there is only one way to smoke, said my father, and that is through a tin bath for purity. Had God given me a choice between a tongue and a nose, I would have chosen the latter. For the tongue can betray for the taste of money, as Judas for silver; can speak evil, can be seduced into corruption, or scornful, inarticulate with fury or as smooth as buttered honey with insincerity. But the snitch is noble, silent in service, its only crime being to turn itself up occasionally. And through the glorious plunder of the nose that morning knifed the Severn tang as the plug came out of the Bore, and there was spray in the wind as we swam easily around Penarth Head towards the white-foaming Flatholm and Lavernock.

'We got there yet?' Gran had loosened her buttoned boots and stays and was sitting with her feet up, her hat over her eyes, bulging black.

'Got there, woman? We are not even started,' replied Dada.

And nor were we, for there was a great wastefulness on the sea, with the sail flapping anger, and every time the barge rose at the prow the Welsh dresser went along on its rollers and hit Jed Donkey a butt in the rear, and rather this dresser than me, for he was hind-hoof-happy under less provocation. Gwen and

Sharon were going green round the gills as we ran goose-winged and free on the Bore in a world of buck and roll, and the white horses of the Head neighing after us as the basin emptied between Clevedon and Newport.

'Stand by with the paddles to steady her,' said Dada, for we were starting to go like a feather in a puddling-pit in hisses and roars.

'Five knots, you reckon?' asked Ifor.

'If we keep at this rate we will shoot past Neath,' said Dada.

Everything appeared normal at this stage, with Gran very perky and actually singing sea-songs about being down among the prawns and winkles with cockles for dinner and sea-weed for a bed, though inclined to be wet, wet, wet, with Dewi and Ifor, the idiots, bawling the chorus. Personally, I think this is tempting Providence, and I reckon Davy Jones lifted the lid of his locker and took note of the landlubbers, for next moment the wind came down in howls and the sea leaped up in fury.

'Paddles out, lads,' roared Dada. 'Hold her steady!' And Dewi and Ifor swung out the big oars.

'Bryn—drift anchor away!' came next, and I flung it out as Eli had told us, but personally I was becoming frit to death. For white-maned seahorses were after us now and people were hanging over the side, and suddenly, to my horror, I saw that my gran was head down and boots up underneath the horse-hair sofa.

'Bryn, see to your gran!' yelled Dada, cranked over the tiller, and I jumped into the hold, a little shocked, also, for one rarely thinks of grans with lace-frilled drawers and real knees, they being mainly floor-length people. And every time I heaved to have her out the bloody sofa rolled up and hit her back under again, and the stuff she was turning up must have taken the stain and varnish off every Big Seat from here to Port Talbot.

'Dewi, Ifor,' she shrieked, 'get me from here!'

But they were on the oars, so I took a grip on Gran's heels, eyes clenched for modesty, braced my toes against the Welsh dresser, and heaved, and her high-buttoned boots came off and I was arse over ear in the scuppers, still holding boots, and I reckon they heard my gran up by Tusker Rock, and just then Nell Mule wandered up and sat on the end of the sofa while Jed Donkey started hitting hell out of the Welsh dresser.

'Bryn, for God's sake, what are you doing to Gran?' yelled Dada.

'Stuck under the sofa with Nell on the end,' I shouted, 'and Jed Donkey by here belting up the dresser.'

'He is doing what?' cried Gran, peeping out, shocked and pale.

My father came down then, flinging chickens aside and heaving up the henhouse, and I couldn't see either of them for feathers, but he got Gran under the armpits and lifted her out and sat her on the kitchen table: very unhappy she looked with her hat down over her ears, and the moment she got her boots back on she swung one into Jed Donkey's rear.

'Not fair,' I cried. 'The dresser started it, mind.'

'Look, woman!' said my father. 'Will you stop this palaver about dressers and donkeys? D'you realise, if the sea comes any higher we're likely to swim for it?'

'And I hold you responsible, remember!' cried Gran. 'Not my idea, coming on this mad-brained voyage down the middle of the ocean.'

'What is that?' I asked, finger up, listening, for there was a strange hissing noise above the roar of the sea and chattering of chickens.

'That do sound ominous, Mostyn,' said Gran. 'Sprung a leak, have we?'

'Stop that Jed Donkey!' bawled Ifor from aft, and we swung round. And there, as large as life, with one hoof up and the other in the bath, was Jed Donkey piddling over Gran's weekly wash, and this all damp and rolled for ironing.

'Now, now, no recriminations,' cried Dada, soothing her. 'Donkeys are more important that ironing, and we will see to him later.'

'Ay ay,' said Gran, evil. 'See to him I will. This barge will be half a ton lighter if that Jed Donkey crosses my path.'

'Do not be ungenerous,' said my father. 'He is a house-trained ass, but he had to go somewhere. Bale!' and he went double-bass, so we baled, for when this happened we knew which side our bread was buttered.

Well! If the Danes had been off Aberavon in long-boats that evening, they would have bolted back to Skagerrak at the sight of us blazing along in Swansea Bay. Rolling, pitching, shipping it, trying to beat the turn of the tide, we ran into the mouth of the Neath River, poled and towed past Giant's Grave and up to Neath Abbey, which was smoking and flaring her ironworks like a place demented, and out came the puddlers and rollers and scarecrow Irish, all waving and cheering us, for it is not every day of the week that a twenty-two-ton coal loader runs up to Red Jacket with a sail in tatters, its crew at the oars, a mule and donkey aboard and fowls in the rigging, to say nothing of three women hanging out starboard and baling with chinas.

'Make a good impression, remember,' cried Dada, rushing about and tidying up, 'these Red Jacket canal folks come very smart.' *Ach*, wonderful my father looked that summer evening as we took the sea-lock into the crosscut that joins the river and canal: stripped to the waist on the prow he stood, bantering with the lock-keeper, his muscles bulging like an ancient Phoenician who had been this way before, and Ifor and Dewi naked to the belts, faces straining skywards as they heaved on the oars. On, on in a clang of drop-hammers as dusk came down, with Lord Vernon's Briton Ferry behind us mushrooming fire and hundreds of furnacemen working like dancing dervishes against the exploding fire-balls of redness and the clouds flashing and glowing to the streams of scarlet and yellow. Live ash rained down into the cut beside us; worse than Merthyr, I thought, but soon came the moon over a lovely land.

'Right,' said Gran, 'spruce up. Shirts back on, bonnets tied, tidy now, like your father says,' and she hauled up her kitchen table and tin bath and started pulling canal buckets to flood out her washing.

'Can't you wait an hour or so, woman?' demanded Dada. 'It'll still be light at the Old Navigation.'

'Things need sweetening because poor old Jed miscalculated,' said she, and this heartened me because five miles back he was due for the knacker-yard, and now he was one of God's little creatures and we are all caught short at one time or another.

The colliers were thronging down the path for Cadoxton pit as we slid past the town all twinkling fairy lights in the gathering gloom, and the stars came out, stepping above the alders arched against the sky, and I saw, reflecting on the clouds from Swansea to Pontardawe, the bomb explosions of the iron and copperworks and heard the shriek of engines and the whine of mills.

'Worse then stinking old Merthyr, I am thinking,' said Ifor.

'What we got for a change from dirty old Dowlais, then?' asked Gran.

'You will see,' said my father.

The cut grew quieter, the banks garlanded with summer flowers: coloured birds began to dart and sway over the water as we got deeper into the fair country, and the people were more countryfied, the men very stiff in good suits and dubbined boots, the women prim in poke-bonnets and whispering behind their hands shyly at the sight of strangers, and every other minute Gran was pulling Sharon and Gwen up on the stern, and the three of them going down in deep curtseys to families strolling along the tow-path. Now we reached the aqueduct at Aberdulais mill, the junction of the Tennant and Neath, and a woman came out of Lock Cottage with her daughter to work the paddles. Welsh dark and beautiful, this pair, and with a fine dignity, their black hair flowing free as they ran the wheel. The paddle jammed, which was an act of God, said Sharon, and my father jumped ashore and freed it, and I saw a soberness in him for this woman, with bows and please allow me to do it and think nothing of it.

'Dear me,' whispered Dewi, rubbing his face.

'You leave him be!' commanded Gran, suds to the elbows and flinging water.

Through the lock now, into a golden land where coo-pidges were whimpering and willows weeping, and the bright cut winding through a country of honey and milk and great swathes of green over the glorious mountains, and Ifor cried as the Aberdulais lock receded, '*Dammo di!* You see her, Dewi? I would rather be chased round a mulberry bush by that than rushed by a couple of dozen, eh, man?' and my father swung instantly to him, saying softly:

'Mind your mouth, or wash it. You keep those remarks for the beer-houses, for one day you'll know the difference between a lady and a slut.'

And Ifor, to my astonishment, grinned at this, and leaped down to the path, elbowing me out of it, walking saucy, his boots punching out.

'Did you hear me?' shouted my father, growing horns.

'Yes, sir,' said Ifor, instantly, back in his place.

'The woman heard you—back and apologise.' On the towpath with him now, flinging Ifor back. I saw Gran make a face at Sharon, and lend a secret wink.

Very strange is fate, I think, that a man can search the earth and never find a mate, yet sharpens his boots on a path over a valley, and there she is waiting.

I swung the tiller now for a second look at the daughter of the beautiful lock keeper, and Gran whistled a tune at the sky as she hung out her smalls.

'Manna from heaven, isn't it, boy. You at it, too?'

Don't miss a thing, this one.

But when we started to pass the barges running down to Neath, murder took a hand, with the local bargees looking down their noses and their women looking the other way, and eyes were glowering in dark, Silurian faces: blood and race do not count a lot, said Dewi, when the bread is being eased out of the mouth, and we were strangers. But the tin-plate workers from the Works above Aberdulais on the Nedd gave a welcome, strangers or not; straight from the Dandy-fires, their cheeks patched red with the heat, they clustered in their white smocks, the melters, picklers, tinners and branders, and waved and shouted, and Gran lined up with Sharon and Gwen and went down in curtseys while we got up and bowed, for there is nothing the Welsh like better than good manners.

'My, there is an industry!' said my father. 'If they can make tin we can carry it, and not likely to dry up, either—they have been feeding tinned beef to the Army since the time of Waterloo.'

A canal overman in breeches called from the bank, 'Mostyn Evan, is it?'

'Aye!' replied Dada.

'Come in from Neath on special ticket?'

'That's us!'

'Welcome, Evan. Report to the Company early, remember, to get clearance.'

'First thing tomorrow, sir,' said my father. And he turned, not interested, staring back in the direction of Aberdulais. Got it terrible bad, my dada.

On, on, with Ifor panting up red in the face and sweating, and my father put a hand on his shoulder as he jumped aboard. On along the cut now, free of the river lock—on past Gollen and Clyne and Melin, on to Resolven.

10

THE Old Navigation!

Here is a tumbledown; a ragged, rickety three-storey canal inn, used by the early bargees and drovers, with a rusted, creaking sign twenty feet up to prove it. But no drovers drank here now, for their bodies were dust with the souls of people like Granfer Ben, though their obscene shouts still echoed along the tracks above Sarn Helen, the old ones say: no bargees rested here on the way to Neath Abbey, for many were drowned at sea and down twenty fathoms off Scarweather and Tusker, or lay faint in the old canal grave-yards. But the Old Navigation still stood as their tombstone, ancient with her memories of coloured crinolines and knee-breeches in the days of Dadford and Jonathan Gee, though Tom Sheasby built the upper lengths, and was arrested before he finished it, while working over at Swansea. It is necessary, said my father, to know who gave this heritage.

'I don't now who built it, Mostyn,' said Gran, hands on hips, doing a tour, 'but the chap who charged you fifty-two pounds ten ought to be arrested also, for you have been fiddled.'

'What the devil did you expect, then? Buckingham Palace?' asked Dada.

'Outwitted, Mostyn—that is the word,' Gran persisted, and good reason for such statements, for there was scarcely a window whole in the place, sheep very comfortable in the tap-room and not a slate in sight on the north aspect. On we went on the tour of inspection, Gran in front, everybody following, including Nell and Jed Donkey, they naturally being interested, and out the other side faces were longer than kites. Gran finally said, 'Well, I will hand you the odd two pounds ten for it, boy, and you can keep the fifty instead of the heritage.'

No soul in some people, mind. Dada said:

'Stables at the back for the donkey and mule, remember.'

'I do,' replied Gran. 'And with their permission I will move in there and they can come in by here, for this place is not fit for pigs, let alone decent Chapel people,' and to my astonishment she began to cry.

Panic all round at this, with Gwen and Sharon also bucketing, and everybody but my dada patting and smoothing them, and for heaven's sake dry up, said Ifor, or you will start me, too.

'Mop up,' said Dada, stern. 'Are you Welsh? Do you expect a new life to be a bed of roses?' In contempt, he sniffed. 'Dry as bones you would all be on the coffin ships before you reached Boston. Can you imagine Granfer Ben dissolving in the eighteen inch bunk on the ship that hauled him to Salt Lake City?'

'Ach, yes,' answered Gran, drying up. 'It do put a different complexion on things when explained like that.'

'It do,' said my father. 'Meanwhile, get shifting, for there are enough women here to eat the place. Sharon, Gwen—away for the buckets, pails and mops and get one room presentable —and heave out those sheep. Dewi and Ifor will haul in the furniture—all sleep together tonight. I will bed the animals.'

Strange, my father: one moment a dutiful son, with yes, Mam, no, Mam: next moment a husband.

'*Cariad anwyl*, my Mostyn!' whispered Gran, adoring him.

'Aye,' replied Dada, 'and your job's the cooking—get moving, for I am hungry.'

The only way to treat them, mind: females work better after taking a belting.

'That might even come later,' said my father.

But trouble was upon us within a couple of hours of arrival. The tap-room had been scrubbed out, Dewi and Ifor were getting the barge tarpaulin over the roof of the north aspect; two rabbits I had clouted for supper were on the boil; dusk was having a word to a hunter's moon when I went with Dada over the bridge and into Resolven village for groceries.

'And do not be all night about it,' called Gran, in her element. 'The buns are in with spuds, the table laid, and I want this over before candles.'

'Back in half an hour latest. Come, Bryn.'

There is a pretty little village, this Resolven, half asleep in the dusk and with smoke from the miners' fires standing as straight as brooms against the clear, blue night, and the stars pale, but big enough to pick from the sky with fingers. We had just got to the start of the village street when Alehouse Jones Pugilist hove in sight four sheets in the wind, being a sailor, and put his thumbs in the slips of his trews, barring right of way.

'Into the gutter,' he said.

Let me be clear on a point. The road was about fifty feet wide at Resolven Square, but his request meant changing direction. We stood, the three of us, just looking, and Alehouse said, 'Strangers, is it?'

'Mostyn Evan and son, just arrived in Resolven, sir,' said Dada, sweet, 'and been sent for groceries, so kindly let us pass.'

The colliers started coming off shift, jumping off the drams that were clattering into the village, even from afar as the big pits of Cadoxton and Brynoch: out of the inn came Evans Brewer: Eynon Shinbone left his shop with knives and sharpeners dangling on his blue and white apron; urchins by the score were eyeing me. And my father did an astonishing thing then; he knelt on the road, saying softly, so only I could hear, 'This is a man who fights for sport. Never fight for sport, Bryn, only for honour. By now, your brother Ifor would be mixing it—and to what end? Do you give or take a broken nose for fun? And pity this poor man, for he is heavy in the head. First we will try him with reason, eh?' and he rose, saying to the bruiser:

'I am not a fighting man. Yet must I sell my honour to save myself a hiding? Let us pass, and I will buy you a quart in the public.'

The blood rushed hot to my face, and I closed my eyes; the gall was bitter in my mouth. Terrible when, at his first trial of strength, you realise that your father is a coward. To lose my shame I took myself with my brothers down to the Old Iron-works outside Merthyr last spring, and you Welsh swines *out*, before we shift you! Ifor, Dewi and me, and the three of us flattened against a tram with furnacemen coming at us with ladles: swerving to boots, shouts of gusty laughter, and I heard Dewi's voice in a dream, 'Run for it, Bryn lad, run!' and we went like devils after saints with half the Staffordshire men after us.

Now, I opened my eyes and looked up at my father.

'Coward,' said a woman, and the smile left his face.

Dada said, 'Of course, when you are called this you do not step in the gutter for anybody, including God Almighty,' and he stripped off his coat, putting it into my hands. 'Home to Gran, son, and tell her I might be a few minutes late with the groceries.'

The mountain fighter was swinging back for room, spitting on his hands, the crowd was buzzing with excitement, and joy.

'Dada . . .'

'Go,' said my father, and stooped, thrusting me through a forest of legs and belts, and I ran, but when I reached the river I ran up the bank and stared back. The canal is nearly empty now, for the railway strangled it of life; the lovely locks are rusted with years of forgetfulness, the runs which I shall always love are narrowed with silt, as if Nature had done what she can to heal the knife-wound in her breast. Yet sometimes, even now, as I stand in this place at dusk, I see my father again as I saw him then a lifetime ago: handsome in his white shirt, he stood, his head black curls, waving me off, and he was smiling.

I ran like a hare coursing. Along the tow-path I went, skidding over the wharf, up to the Old Navigation and hammered through the door, to slide to a stop on the flags, staring, gasping for breath. Everybody was up on Gran's white cloth with their knives and forks set, waiting for supper, and Gran was at the top with a pair of boiled rabbits lying like naked babies on the big white and blue dish before her.

'And what time do you call this?' she asked.

I cried in agony, 'A seventeen stone mountain-fighter has got Dada in the crowd down in Resolven, and bets are being laid and blood is running in the gutters!'

Nothing happened. Ifor grinned, Dewi looked bored, Sharon tossed her head and Gwen went on playing with the cloth.

'Alehouse Jones Pugilist?' asked Ifor.

'Aye!'

Gran said, 'Up at the table sharp, Bryn. It is bad enough one being late and I will talk to him later. How can we eat boiled rabbit without salt and bread?'

I stared at her, and she added, closing her eyes and putting her hands over the rabbits, 'For what we are about to receive make us truly thankful, and may God have mercy on this Alehouse Jones Pugilist.'

Aye, the Neath canal is a barren river of Time now, the Old Navigation where I made love to Rhiannon is just a pile of old stones: no longer it stands rubbing shoulders with beautiful Resolven, stark black against the stars with the wind doing his tonic-solfa in the eaves which Ifor mended; no longer the screech owls of Rheola let fly on the ridge that Dewi mended. For a man came with a telescope and tripod and set it up in the valley and peeped on cross-hairs and brought down his hand, and a banderole went in, then a centre-line peg. And next came the navigators of Limerick and Lancashire with railway lines and sleepers, and they took the main line through the garden and a branch through the tap-room and out of the kitchen where Gran laid her table. Then, first in singles and later in pairs, the big Corsair saddletanks of Brunel raced through it at twenty miles an hour. Most of our dreams went when the Old Navigation came down, but you can't tear the soul out of a place where people have lived: demolish it, ransack it, but the wealth is still there on the breast of the land, said Gran; the people are still there in mist; the lovers like Rhiannon and me still go up the back stairs hand in hand.

Ghosts now, most of us who once lived in the Old Navigation.

Listen.

The land is sick of it, and so am I. We are all sick to death of being second best, of quality being booted out by quantity, of honour by greed, of Wales being milked dry by the few in the face of the many, and we are sick, too, of the tap-room patriots on high benches who wheedle for English favour, and we have been in bed with these, said my father, since the iniquitous Act of Union. If the canal must be strangled in the stupid name of Progress, said he, then strangle it in the name of Wales, who owns it: if the land must be laid waste by ironworks, coal or new-fangled railway, then ravage it in the name of the Welsh, not the English, for the English have been plunderers from Glasgow to India and back via China, and we, the cousins of their door-step, got it early because we were nearest. Aye, to English board-rooms go the profits, he used to say—and carted there by the traitors of Wales, remember, for you do not find the English wheeling barrows. If an army of peasants had to die, if a host of children had to be starved and an ocean of tears flood the valleys, then let this happen in the name of Wales, by the Welsh, for the Welsh, not for some foreign gentry class who have never seen the skies over places like Merthyr, Dowlais and Swansea, and do not intend to.

'There is only one answer to it, mind,' Dewi remarked.

'Aye?' replied Dada. 'Well, violence is what they have preached to us and handed to us from under the skirts of their Church and Parliament. But nothing is solved through violence. You can shoot, you can bomb, but you will land back where you came from, because they are experts in the trade when the occasion arises. They will spread their words on honey, preach tolerance, invoke the gentleness of their particular Christ; but, by God, Dewi, if you threaten their profit, they will teach you the art of violence—remember the Chartists, the Luddites—have you heard of Botany Bay, their slave trades? There is no madder dog than an English country gentleman.'

Personally, I am not much concerned with the politics, save that I would hit everything English back to England if I had my way, for I remember the agony of Cyfarthfa. I am much more concerned with my Vale of Neath.

The canal, which I loved, is dying. But in her quiet places the sedgewarbler still sings, also the mavis and night-jar: still the corncrakes fly, still the herons stand on one leg in the old Nedd. But, when I was very young, the Vale was alive and singing. In the days when my father put out Alehouse Jones in eight seconds flat, the people were alive. Tough, aye, but *real*—not the milksops that Wales turns out today. Down Resolven cut the barges used to run, with Dolly this and Dolly that laying into the towropes, hooves skidding, flanks steaming, with the old summer moon lying on his back heavy with his meal of June. Smoke drifts up, in dreams now, from the hooped canopies of the bargees; hares and hedgehogs simmer, the last in gipsy clay; rabbits bubble in the big, black pots of the cabins.

Gone, all gone.

Gran has gone long since; indeed, most are gone, including my dark, sweet Rhiannon, but I see their faces clearly, as if it were yesterday: I hear again the run of the Nedd, smell again the sweet, sour earth-smell of the cut: aye, all the song of the earth is with me, and through the mist of the years I smell the perfume of Rhiannon.

I keep telling of Rhiannon, and do not mean to, for she did not come to me in those early days when the only decent road in the Vale was the canal winding through the alders, long before the Great Western Corsairs came roaring through the Vale, turning the milk sour in the pails, driving the pigs demented, aborting the cows.

Yet, such is the miracle of memory, that it only seems like yesterday that my father brought us in from the Bristol Channel and into the Neath Canal, to the lock where I first set eyes on Rhiannon, and the crumbling wharf of the Old Navigation at Resolven.

II

FOR the next week, too, we were still at it, up sharp at dawn, the women in sack aprons like labouring Irish and swilling floors, and isn't it damned filthy and absolutely disgusting, and a passing bargee informed us that it was last occupied by a Mrs. Duffy of Cork, and I can quite believe it, said Gran, and if I could get my hands on Mrs. Duffy she would land in County Wicklow. No good trying to explain that this was about eight years back.

'You all right up there?' called Dada, for Dewi and Ifor were up in the gables mending the roof, and I was hauling up slates and tiles on a rope and pulley. Dada was bricklaying along the wharf and Gwen cleaning out the stables. Soon, with the glass back in the windows, the wind of the cut was sweetening the rooms, and we had even got the floor boards mended in the second bedroom, for Gwen, within an hour of arrival, had landed back in the kitchen in a shower of plaster and petticoats. Now she said, her eyes going big at table:

'Nine barges came down the cut today, Dada, and fifteen went up, and while doing Jed's stall, I did wave to them, but only three waved back.'

I saw my brother flick a glance at Dada, and Ifor said, 'Tub Union runs it strong round these parts, I am thinking. First he sends Alehouse Jones to give us a greeting, then he will not wave to a baby.'

'He can keep his union,' answered Dada. 'We have another here—the family, and it will take some breaking.'

'A handy size, mind,' said Dewi. 'They say he has a hundred and seventy members. We have seven.'

Sharon said, 'This morning I did speak to Betsy Small-Coal. Sick and scared they are, said Betsy, because they are poor, and we are strangers.'

'Not strangers,' I interjected. 'Welsh.'

'It do not count for much these days,' said Gran.

Considering that I was unimportant in the family, being in the middle, I never understood why my father selected me for discussion of points of policy.

'Dada is shouting for you, Bryn!' shrieked Sharon, and she added, whirling out of the kitchen, '"My desolation does begin to make a better life. 'Tis paltry to be Caesar; not being Fortune, he's but Fortune's knave!" Bryn, where the devil you got to?'

'Coming now just, Juliet,' I shouted, for breakfast, dinner and tea we were into this Romeo chap. Through feathering leaves, her face patterned with sunlight, I watched her, book in hand, her face smooth and proud. Scrambling from the canal I rubbed for a glow, and she drifted on tiptoe towards me, hands floating, crying, '"How cam'st thou hither, tell me, and wherefore? The orchard walls are high and hard to climb..."'

'If you will go from here, I will leg my trews on,' and I left her to her dreams and Shakespeare, and found my father leaning against the empty stable, smoking at the sun.

'Listen to her,' I said. 'Stark raving, she is—no rhyme or shape to her.'

'She is entitled to her dreams, Bryn.'

'Never make a living spouting that stuff.'

He shrugged. 'It is in the blood, and come out in Sharon. The sink awaits her, the child-bed, the endless children. Grant her Juliet, do not take her hard.'

I followed him down the tow-path, our boots polishing in the dew-laden grass, and the cut was loaded with light diamonds, the bull-rushes erect and proud, and coots skidding on their tails in panic. Reaching the Cohen barge, my father jumped aboard, vaulted into the hold, and sat, his eyes half closed to the beauty of the morning.

'I have a bit of a problem, Bryn, and need it sorted out before I pop it to the rest of the family. Sit.' He patted the gunwale, and I sat, nervous.

I was hating this, for I knew what was coming. Besides, this was Gran's business, for she always sorted the problems. After a bit, Dada said, 'Is it convenient to begin, then?'

'Aye.'

'Your nose is blown, your boots are square to the deck, the

91

coal is from under your back-bone?' His eyes switched under his dark brows.

'Yes, Dada,' I answered, rigid, for this appeared important. Then:

'You can remember your mother, lad?'

'Aye, of course.'

'How long has she been gone?'

I replied, 'Five years back come December.'

'A long time to be without a mother. Don't you think you could do with another?'

'Another mam?'

'We don't need one?' He was making it easy, judging my expression.

'Of course not, Dada—we've got Gran.'

A dog-fox barked from the woods of Rheola, and the vixen replied, her voice strong on a wind of perfume, for this was scything time, which is a smell of crushed apples in hayseeds, and bruised grass. We watched, unspeaking, as a barge from Glyn Neath slid past us: the bargees nodded briefly, and fine they looked with their brown, bulging arms sweating in sunlight, their flannel shirts open to the waist, and red neck-ties for taking cooling water.

'Do not look so ferocious, man,' said Dada. 'It has been done before.'

'A second wife?'

'Another wife.'

'Same thing.'

'It is not. Supposing I bring one in?'

I said, turning away. 'Gran would throw her out.'

'Gran would not throw her out, for she suggested it. Good grief, I should never have started this—too young, you are.'

'I am not!'

He jerked his pipe at a couple of Glamorgan canaries pecking in the field. 'You see those two old crows? This is the way of it—in pairs. Beef bulls and door-mice, rabbits and rodents —a man is happier, son, with a woman of his own.'

I said, getting up. 'You've got three—Gran, Sharon and Gwen.'

'How old are you?'

'Knocking fifteen.'

'You sound more like twelve. Backwards in some directions, isn't it? It was silly of me to mention it, and I'm sorry.'

I said, bitterly, 'Now you make me small because I do not agree with you.'

'That is better. Now you sound like a man.'

'It would be terrible to have another woman about,' I said desperately. 'Sort of indecent, it would be, with you and her married, and in the same bed you had with mam.'

'Is marriage only the bed, then?'

The blood was pounding in my face. I whispered, 'You make Gran lay her place at table, and now you talk of bringing in another, to take her place!'

'Whoah, man, do not take it hard!' said he, and brought his fist to my chin, pushing me sideways. 'It was only a suggestion, to get the feel of the family.'

'Who is she?'

He played with his pipe, uncertain, then smiled up. 'The little lock-keeper down at Aberdulais.'

'You seeing her?'

'Only from a distance. She's got a pretty daughter, you noticed?'

I nodded, smiling with him. Relief was claiming me; the horror was passing. The sweat ran in a little trickle on my forehead, and I wiped it into my hair. Dreadful, mind, the more you think of it. My father said:

'I heard that Miss Bronwen Rees has been seen in the vicinity.'

'Aye,' I replied, joyful. 'Gone in as school-mistress down at Aber—near the lock.'

'You still keen on that Bronwen Rees, boy?'

There are times in life when clothes go sideways, when the collar of your shirt is lying on your shoulder and the buckle of your belt is lying on your hip.

'Keen as mustard, but the age is wrong, see?'

'Have you seen her lately?'

'Not since leaving Merthyr.'

'You miss her?'

'What has that to do with getting a new mam?' I asked.

'Nothing. Just that I thought it worth a mention.'

I was warm inside for him then, eyes closed at the thought of Bronwen: excellent, it is, when people are considerate about the things you think important. Strangely sad was my father's face.

'You all right, Dada?'

'Aye,' said he, and, sighing, got up. 'I will raise the matter again when you are five years older. Back home with us now or we will both be pixilated.'

All this, I suppose, was the outcome of the new free-thinking that my father was always talking about these days. There was Sharon becoming an actress and down with the Penny Gaffs every Friday night, there was Dewi making bombs and planning a revolution in the cellar with folks like Ianto Fuses, and Ifor setting up a punch-bag in the stables, getting into form for the Black Welshman, the giant navvy who lived round these parts. And all this on top of Gwen looking up hollow trees for fairy Espionosas, and now Dada going mooney about the Aberdulais lock-keeper.

No good can come of this free-thinking, I say: since it started, me and my gran were the only folks normal.

Later that day there was a fine wind rushing down the valley, with the trees waving green along the cut, and there was a strange excitement in the air: bright and foaming the old Nedd, throwing up her arms to summer.

Special, that June day, also, for my father went on foot up to Pont Walby and came back to the Old Navigation waving a piece of paper.

'Mother!' Over the cobbles he skidded, and into her arms, and she held him away as mothers do with sons, and wagged her head, beaming.

'Oh, Mostyn, I am so glad!'

'Coal hauling—special consignment from the Company at standard rates—three trips a week from Glyn Neath to Giant's Grave!'

'What is happening?' cried Dewi, rushing in from the stables.

'A contract, a contract!' shouted Sharon, dancing.

'Three trips a week, it is a fortune!' I said.

'It is a fortune all the time you can keep the rates. Two shillings a ton free on board is fair payment; it gives a thirty per cent profit to the Company, and is about what they clear with their direct employed.'

'Then the Union has no cause for complaint.'

'You don't know Tub Union,' replied Dewi. 'It depends how he takes it.'

'On the chin, if needs be,' said Ifor. 'Does Tub Union and his mates own the Neath Canal?'

My father said, 'A lot depends on what happens when we go up to Pont Walby in the morning.'

'You will get up all right,' I said. 'The trouble will begin when we start coming down.'

'Oh, ah,' said Dewi, 'hark at that! The babies are from their long clothes at last, eh?'

'Growing up fast,' said Dada. 'We had a perfect example of it earlier this morning, didn't we, Bryn?'

It brought me ill at ease. Terrible, it is, to be at odds with your father.

Gran said, fussing and patting him, 'No trouble now, Mostyn. No difficulty with this old Union thing now, promise?'

Next morning everybody was up at first light, with Gran sawing at nose-bags and running the small-beer, and Sharon dancing around and quoting very happily, she having just got a job as live-out kitchen-maid over with the Vaughans of Rheola. I was grooming Nell and Jed Donkey, Ifor and Dewi sweeping up the barge and putting pipe-clay on the Turk's Head on the tiller: beautiful, that Turk's head, my father's joy, with its white, flowing tail and intricate patterns of laced whip-cord. Everybody was out to make a good impression and make friends all round, though it seemed that Tub Union would be the main enemy.

Not one of us gave a thought to the Black Welshman, for he was a railway navigator.

'You heard that the railway company is working on the Pencydrain viaduct, Dada?' asked Dewi as we went aboard.

'It will end like the Merthyr tunnel,' said Dada. 'I heard that has come to grief.' He took the fall from my hands and coiled it neatly on the barge prow, and beyond him the cut was all misted, with shafts of sunlight striking the run in patches of hay-seed gold. 'Eight shafts dug and Mr. Ritson, the engineer, at his wit's end, for the thing is losing money.'

'Shows the intention, nevertheless,' said Ifor, bracing off with his feet. 'You don't build a viaduct, mind, unless you intend to build a railway.'

'It will come to nothing,' said my father. 'Stephenson himself has said that a railway through this valley will never be built—the gradients are tremendous.'

'Brunel don't agree with him,' sang Ifor, teeth gritted as he thrust with his pole against the wharf. In bindweed, we slid on to the breast of the cut.

'Aye, Brunel says it can be done, Dada.'

My father spread his hands. 'All right, all right—in ten years' time. By then we will have bought up the Company and we will sell out to the Great Western for a hundred thousand pounds! Easy, easy!'

'Now I know who is Dai Dafto,' said Ifor. 'Take her, Bryn, lad—give the butt to that lazy Nell Mule. Here we come, Tub Union.'

Glyn Neath!

Going up for our first barge of coal, Dada cried, 'Take her, lad!'

For a moment he paused in labour, smiling at me, and then he winked, and I winked back. The wound was healed. Trembling with joy, eager, I turned to Nell, bawling, 'Up, up, away! Give it her, girl!' and the old mule flung her weight; the trace became a bar, spraying water on the thong: damp smells arose in the skid of hooves. 'Give it her, Nell. Lay on!'

'Fend off stern!' I heard my father shout. 'Well done, Bryn, lad!'

I cracked the whip over Jed Donkey's head, for he was walking still in his nose-bag, never reckoning to pull a pound till ten o'clock in the morning.

Eh, wonderful it is on a cut first thing in the morning, in slapping water and mist and shafted sunlight, with the air fresh and clean blowing down the land, and behind you your father and two big brothers, going up to Pont Walby. The women were out on the doorstep waving, of course, but naturally, we did not spare them a glance. But very proud, me, with my shirt open to the belt, hair parted in the middle, yorks under my knees and a red choker knotted on my shoulder: stepping so light in greased hobnails I hardly touched the mud.

12

NEVER have I seen the like of Mr. Jeremiah Alton, the English Pont Walby agent, with a broad-brim felt hat two sizes up on him, a black funeral coat with buttoned alpaca knee-breeches and a plum-coloured waistcoat suffering from a bad attack of brewer's goitre. Cost him a fortune to get it that size, said Dewi.

' 'Morning, Mr. Alton,' said my father, jumping ashore at Glyn Neath wharf.

'You are late, Mr. Evan,' and he stared up at my father, beef nose wrinkling under his spectacles, chin vegetating, most luxurious, and the hum of him at that time of morning would have flattened the small-beer in the manse. Dada said:

'With respect, Mr. Alton, it is not in the Company contract what time I report—just that I carry three times a week from here to Giant's Grave.'

'Your tune will change when the railway arrives, my man. You will have to get up early in the morning to beat that.'

'When it arrives. Meanwhile, I am not your man, sir. I am partner to a contract. Where do I load?'

Note-book out now, very official, licking a stub of pencil. 'Contracts in this valley are not very important, Mr. Evan. Men, too, are ten a penny, which you and your kind will learn. It is the barge, the donkey and the mule the Company fiinds important.' Removing his spectacles, Mr. Jeremiah Alton

97

peered at us standing with shovels. 'Welsh fighters you got there, by the look of them.'

'Butter will not melt in their mouths.'

'I am delighted to hear it. The railway navigators are astride the road at Pen-y-Dre.' He smiled thinly. 'Led by the Black Welshman.'

'Bridge building?' asked Dada.

'Railway building, or have you not heard? And the Company does not want trouble.'

'None from us, Mr. Alton. That I can promise you.'

'Then keep that promise, or you may land back in Merthyr where you came from, for I do not like your style.'

'Nor I yours,' said my father. 'Tell me the bay and we will lift from under your feet.'

'That would be wise—also Man Arfon's, for I am leaving this very day, and he will be running the wharf tomorrow.'

I saw Dewi turn away with a groan. Strange is life. When you want to make a new start Baal comes out from under the stones with instructions for you to crawl on your belly. And now Man Arfon, sacked from Merthyr, was a top dog in Pont Walby. Mr. Jeremiah Alton turned, shouting, 'Irish, Irish!'

A ragged, burly overman ran up and I could smell his panic from here.

'Bay Five. Load priority—get this barge out of it.'

'Aye, sir!' He pulled his hair. 'Certainly, Mr. Alton, sir!'

'And report to Mr. Arfon tomorrow that it was late starting contract.'

'Yes, sir!' The overman swung, his fist high. 'Right, into it. Move, move!'

I saw shovelling labourers rise and stare; men, women, children. Dropping their shovels in a panic, they ran, pushing empty trams into a branch line, then rushed back, flung their tools high on coal tubs and seized the buffers of heaped trams, dragging them towards us.

'Stand clear!'

'Come on, come on!' shouted the agent.

'I said move, you lazy swines!' yelled the overman. In rags, sweating, their eyes and mouths white in their masks of coal, the Irish labourers flung themselves to the task with a panic born of hunger. I pitied them. With levers they tripped the trams forward to the incline, running with them and leaping aside with shouts of warning as they struck the timber baulks. The coal gushed into our barge. One tram empty, drag it into the branch: another one up with a rush, trip it, leap aside.

'Trim down the spills!' shouted Dada, and we flung off our shirts and jumped into the barge hold with shovels. I saw young girls working above me, stripped like me, their hair tied back with string, hauling on the lines, grunting like animals, their iron-studded boots hitting sparks on the concrete. Whips curled and lashed in pistol-cracks over the flanks of horses: reluctant mules were getting the butt-end or the boot.

It was a scene of Hades; of sweat, brutality, hunger, pain.

I cursed this Pont Walby agent, I cursed the masters, I cursed my country.

Pausing in the shovelling, I gasped at Dewi, 'Right mess we have landed in—Man Arfon on this wharf, and he do not like Mostyn Evan and sons. I reckon we'd have done better slogging it out in Merthyr.'

Dewi spat, wiping his mouth with the back of his hand. 'You have to kill a hundred Welshmen to get a pound of brains,' he said.

Out of the Glyn Neath wharf we came and drifted past the Nedd River with our first load of coal, and the four of us pretty sober, too, for it was news to us that Brunel had actually started line-laying down at Neath.

'The Swansea Valley might have been better to make a start,' said Dewi. 'There is no talk yet of a railway going through there.'

'We will meet the railway when it comes,' said my father. 'One trouble at a time.'

'Some coming up now, by the look of it,' I said from the tow-path.

We were on the Old Levels between Morfa and Glyn Neath, the Nedd River sparkling and lovely under the midday sun, with a string of Company barges making upstream, their animals cranked to the swim and hard under the whip: on our bank the rushes were thick, and lying among them, blocking our way, were some five coalers with their crews on the river path.

'Slow us, Bryn, it's a stiff flow—slow us!'

Leading Jed Donkey through the bargees, I brought her into the reeds. The moment Dada and the boys jumped down they were ringed by men; these were the Company hired who did not own a barge and never would. Mostly colliers once, as Ifor said later; the older ones shortened by the galleries, their head-bumps and coal-tattoos telling their old trade. But some were young, and brawny handsome.

'You the new lot from the Old Navigation?' asked one, an ox of a man, and over his eyes were the scars of fighting, not coal.

'Aye,' said my father.

'That right you got a Company contract to run from Glyn Neath to the Grave?'

'I have,' said my father.

'Got a paper to prove you can run on this water?'

Dada patted his pocket. 'The contract is in here, but you have the truth of it because I have told you.'

'We are seeing that contract, Mostyn Evan, or we are running you off this canal.'

'Then come and get it,' said my father.

Hands in my trews, I wandered closer to Dada. You could have shot holes in that silence of clenched fists and squared boots; then Ifor said, 'You want to mix it, bargee, you start with me,' and Dada said:

'You realise, man, that while we fight the owners profit? What are you stopping, right of way?'

The bargee weighed my father: this man's eyes were good —bright blue in his tanned face. He said, 'Now that the railway is coming the barges will be starved. They have cut us to two shillings a ton free on board now, and when the railway runs they will cut us again.'

'There will be enough loads for all,' said Dewi. 'If they build six railways, there will always be loads for the barges.'

'Oh, aye? Do not lecture your betters, lad, or I will be bloody livid with you. Less barges we are wanting on this canal, not more.'

'Anyway,' said Dada, 'Stephenson says they will never succeed in building a railway—he says the one in eighty Hirwain gradient will beat the engines.'

'And Brunel says he will build it, and we back Brunel: that is what Tub Union thinks, and I am Tub Union.'

My father showed no surprise. 'We will stand with you against the railway, remember: we will join your union, we will obey its rules. Tell us what you stand for, man?' Tub Union's voice rose:

'Against the railway, against the entry of scabs like you. We stand for the Vale of Neath bargee, for better wages, and respect for trade. And we had troubles enough before you came. Do you realise the railway navigators have a log across the cut down at Tonna? Playing pranks, while we have bread to earn.'

'What are you doing about it?' asked my father.

'What do you expect? It is the Black Welshman. He is backed by five hundred navvies and we are only a hundred.'

'Dear me, you are in trouble,' said Dewi.

'The Black Welshman!' whispered Ifor, smacking his fist into his palm.

'Aye,' said Tub Union, 'and he is going for the men, not the boys.'

'Strikes me you want more bargees, not less,' said Dada. 'Are you aiming to remove that log?'

'Talk sense,' came the reply.

'And if we remove it, will you sign us on?'

The bargees grinned, loving it. Tub Union said, 'Mister, you touch that log and the big Negro will boot you out of this vale and save us the trouble.'

'And if we do shift it, and Black Sam, too?'

'By God,' said Tub Union, 'if you beat the Negro we will sign you on.'

'Money in advance,' said Dada, and fished out four shillings. 'Is it a deal?'

'I like clean men, too,' said Tub Union, and spat on the silver. 'Cards when next we meet if you clear the log. Good luck, man. The big black will peg you down and draw the bones from your bodies.'

'It will be an enjoyable experience,' said my father.

Back south down the canal again in a drowse of morning heat, with the fields flashing green and the river leaping silver as we swam alongside, loaded to the gunwales with Pont Walby coal. The sky was a basin of varnished blue flung with billowy bed-sheet clouds from St. Peter's wash, and the great mountains dozed on their shoulders in the valley, their heads circled with little haloes of mist. Joe Stork was standing on one leg in the shallows, fishing, not the least interested in bargees, badgers crawled to earth, otters were hunting in shrill whistles. Past Melin we went in the canal, with Gran and Gwen hand in hand at Resolven, dropping in stately curtseys, all prim and mockery, and went into shrieks of laughter when the four of us lined up on the gunwales and bowed back to Dada's command, our mole-skin caps dusting our boots.

'All right, son?' called Gran.

'Dando!'

All fun and laughter, he was; hard to believe that he was going down to visit the Black Welshman, the man who had taken Owen Bach, the son of *Owen Bach y Crugau*; famous in the Vale was Owen, the mad one, as they called him, since he found men too tame to fight and used to take on wild dogs at the Lamb and Flag Bridge and in Margam Park on Sundays, from what we had heard. The Negro took him in forty seconds flat, the bargees told us, and nothing had been seen of Owen since.

The lock at Aberdulais appeared deserted when we arrived, and only when I began to swing the paddle did the door open and the keeper come out: pale and proud, she looked, smiling with cool politeness as my father bowed. Shadows were under her eyes, her hair dull, her lips colourless.

''Morning, Mrs. Mortymer,' said Dada, shifty in the boots and nervous.

'Good morning, Mr. Evan.'

'Well, are you, ma'am?'

She dropped a hint of a curtsey. 'Well enough, sir.'

I glanced around for her daughter, but the cottage appeared to be empty.

'See you coming up, more than likely, eh?'

'More than likely, Mr. Evan.'

And that was that: very dull, my dada, as we dropped back into the canal, and he did not speak again until we reached Pen-y-Dre, though I noticed Dewi and Ifor exchanging some jerked thumbs and nods of understanding.

'How much do they pay these keepers?' asked Dewi.

'The cottage and ten shilling a week.'

'Looks half-starved to me, that woman.'

And still my father did not speak.

'Here comes a handy looking lot,' I cried from the tow-path.

This was the first time we had seen the navigators at work in the Vale, though they were ten a penny up in Glamorgan Vale, where the railway came earlier. But these navvies must have been special; never in my life have I seen men such as these. They were bringing the railway end-on up towards Tonna, and they were burning out quarries to bottom up the permanent-way, we heard later, for the ground was marshy: a single line of seven foot gauge they were building, and rather them than me, for the going was tough. Stripped, like the Irish, the navigators laboured, amid the clatter of the trams hauling up the stones and muck, the horses rushing pell-mell and neighing in shrieks, galloping, then swerving free, the horse to the right, bridle-lad to the left—slipping the hooks a second before the tram struck the tripping-baulk. Up went the tram, out came the muck, spilling down the embankment: men go in with shovels to spread and level and rammers to consolidate.

They lose a boy a week down here on average, said my father, but there are more where they come from, horses being dearer than boys: when you see a railway in this country you are not looking at genius, he added, you are looking at blood.

And these were the men who built them, the great Stockton to Darlington, Liverpool and Manchester: men of the Shropshire quarries, tinkers from Ireland, the giants of the northern counties and the coal-bumped little colliers of the Midland pits—anyone with enough guts and strength was flocking to the navvy gangs of men like Peto and Brassey, who employed them through grasping sub-contractors.

'Take her slow, Bryn,' called my father, and the navvies

straightened, resting on their tools as we slid past them, for here the railway was coming within feet of the cut. Irish, Spanish and French were here among the English; blacks and even Chinese could be found among the navvy gangs: fighters all, hard-drinkers all; thumping for ale in the canal inns and the publics of Neath and Swansea, and they were better hunters than leopards of the women, anything from sixteen to sixty, said Dewi, leaving a trail of children for the Guardians of the Poor wherever the railway took them. With sullen looks, unspeaking, they regarded us: trouble has a strange perfume, coming in sliding eyes and tense muscles.

'There is a log across the cut,' shouted Ifor.

'That is what we have come down for,' said my father.

I am not given to easy panic, but I reckon there are certain times when one whistles and looks the other way, for there were three of us and Dada that morning, and about five hundred navvies.

'Remember what happened to Ianto Fuses,' said Dewi.

'No need to tell me,' I replied.

A week last Friday, according to gossip, Ianto Fuses came down this way and collected a log. Sixteen stone was Ianto, and a bar-room revolutionary, and he moored his barge, went up the embankment, bowed low to the navvy foreman, and would he be good enough to shift this log in the next ten seconds or hell would come loose for navvies, and their foreman in particular.

Didn't know what hit him, said Ifor. Woke up in bed with a steak on his eye and had it later that day for his dinner, not knowing if he was in Pen-y-Dre or Swansea.

'Slacken that trace, Bryn,' called my father as we came up to the log, and he leaped down on the tow-path beside me.

'Shall we come, too, Dada?'

'You three stay were you are.'

As I tethered Jed and Nell, the navvies started coming down to the tow-path. Lounging on the bank, they cut wedges of tobacco, chewing it and spitting on their boots, or rolled it and smoked, their clays cocked up arrogantly in their whiskered faces.

'You after trouble, son?'

'No,' I said.

Big and brawny, these men, yet some were quite small; wizened gnomes from Cumberland, said Dada, but graft and exploitation in the pits had condensed them in ferocity. One about this size, but young, wandered up, gave Nell one in the ribs for luck and lounged on a gate-post beside me, his eyes glowing hatred.

I recognised him instantly. He was the Irish boy I had seen begging for work of Ephraim Davies, the agent, in Cyfarthfa, nigh four years back. Glowering, he pursed his lips, making a rude noise in my face.

'Well done,' I said. 'Now do it with your mouth.'

'You after trouble, Taff?'

'Set them up,' I said, pushing Nell out of it, but my father said, pulling me away:

'Bryn, for God's sake—must you choose a time like this?'

'Begging for it,' I said.

'Then take him in your time, not mine.' He wandered through the bunched navvies, his hands on their chests, pushing them aside, as a man can do without giving offence. And through the path he made I saw the log again, lying over the canal: at the bank end a Negro was standing, and he was a foot taller and wider than any man there, including my father. Feet splayed, naked to the waist, he grinned, his teeth appearing white in his face, and flung away a shovel, putting his fists on his hips: like some primitive god he stood motionless, his great, muscled body glistening like watered coal. 'You got a log, bargee!'

Hands in his pockets, my father joined him. 'Aye, did your gang put it?'

'I put it, Taff.'

Dada nodded, scratching his chin, deliberating. 'And I shift it, eh?'

'That is the idea.'

It was the age-old song of the drovers—fight for right of way. My father lighted his pipe, very interested in this log, then suddenly hit it on his boot and dropped it into his pocket, always a sign of trouble.

More navvies came down from the embankment, their eyes

bright in their faces at the prospect of a fight; these were the men of the randies when they broke out on pay nights and drank everything in sight, who lived in their shanty hutments alongside the line, made their own creeds of honour, and fought to the death at the drop of a hat. For these there was but one form of transport—rail; barges, to them, were a joke. The Negro said:

'I put it, Taff, and you shift it, or get back home where you came from.'

My father rubbed his chin. 'A new game, is it?'

'An old one—right of way: to see what the white Welsh are made of.'

Dada nodded. 'You talk cheeky with enough to back you.' He put his foot on the log. 'And if I shift this thing do I get down the cut?'

The Negro said, 'Not so easy, man. After you shift it you tangle with me.'

My father said, 'It's the log I'm worried about, black man. I can take you any day of the week.'

The expression on the faces of the navvies changed from interest to incredulity, and the Negro scowled, made a fist of his hand and thumped it into his palm.

'By Christ, Taff, you got it comin'!'

Dada grinned, and I knew what he was up to. The temper of the Black Welshman was known throughout the Vale: he was most dangerous when he was ice-cool, and my father was rattling him. Now, waving his arms out of his shirt he tossed it over to me, gave Black Sam another happy grin for luck, and waded into the canal.

'He strips well, Sam,' called a navvy. 'You best watch him.'

Silence. Even the sun froze: the water of the canal moved in ripples to Dada's legs as he positioned himself beside the log. Suddenly, he ducked, taking it on his shoulders, entwining his arms along the bark. He splayed his legs wide to drop height, the fine muscles of his back tensed and knotted, and he grunted deep in his chest. Relaxing his grip, he ducked out again, panting, then dipped his hands into the water and flung it high, smoothing the coldness over his face and chest. Ifor shouted from the barge:

'I say leave it, Dada, it is a two-man load.'

'One-man load for a dirty black nigger with a hide like me,' shouted the Negro in sudden anger, and I saw in a flash the insults, the kicks; the brutality of the whites, and the chained labourers of the American plantations under the lash of men called human.

'Black Welsh is dirty Welsh down in Tiger Bay!' he shouted.

'Not with me, Welshman,' said my father, taking another grip on the log.

'You will do, Taff, 'cause you are nearest. You shift that log, then I'll tan your arse like a baby.'

Suddenly, the log rose, and Dada was under it. Straightening from the waist, he held it, the end waving as he fought for balance, and I saw the sinews of his thick arms corded, the great biceps bulge and vein bright blue. Sweat ran in quick flushes down his back. I held my breath. Neck cramped under the load, face scarlet, eyes clenched, my father turned slowly from the waist, a foot out, feeling for a hold. Step by step, with agonising slowness, he moved towards the bank, and the Negro went back a pace, nodding approval.

'Give the old man credit!'

'He'll need more'n that—he still got to land it!' They pestered among themselves in a rising babble of oaths and encouragement, they shoved for a better view, bawling, their faces aflame, and I hated them. The boy-navvy yelled into my face, 'If he lands that log he still got Black Sam—murder him!'

I did not answer. I was dying inside for my father. Another wading foot, feeling for a firm place, and the log was tipping precariously. Always, it seemed, he had to fight to keep up square with the rent, either masters or mates. If it was not employers, it was people like Tub Union for membership, or Alehouse Jones for the fun of it—sent by the Union, a pawn in the game of hunger. Now the navvies were turning him into a dray-horse, for right of way, before setting him up for a beating by the most brutal man in the Vale. The boy beside me said:

'When he collects his, you get yours, remember, and no scarpering for home!'

I had no time for reply. A voice cried, 'Brunel!'

The navvies moved uneasily, the name of Brunel going through them like a fire, trapped by the spectacle of courage and the arrival of authority. Brunel was their idol. I saw a trap arrive on the road above me in bowed greetings.

'Hey, Sam!'

The Negro half turned from my father.

'Watch it, Black Sam—Great Western people coming!'

'Ritson, too ... !'

Three gentlemen were standing on the bank just above me: one was quite small, wearing a soiled frock coat and striped trousers and a top hat too big for him.

'Brunel,' whispered the boy navvy, 'the one in the middle.'

With an expressionless face the man on the bank watched the scene below him, and his navvies moved nervously, like schoolboys caught at a prank. This was the engineer they loved, the man of genius who was building bridges and viaducts, aqueducts and tunnels, and driving railways all over Britain. Suddenly, he cried, 'They are gaming you, bargee. Would you rather I stopped this?'

Navvies began to tear off their hats; there was no sound but the slap and suction of the canal as my father moved towards the bank, the log waving on his shoulders. Reaching it, he crouched momentarily, then ducked, shifting his grip. With fingers spread under the log, he shouted hoarsely, butted down, and threw. The log clattered wetly on to the bank.

I can see it now: my father standing in the reeds, throwing water over his sweating body, smoothing it from his face and hair, and I can hear it again—that one man clapping. It was Isambard Kingdom Brunel, clapping for my father. And the clapping was taken up by the gentlemen, and then by the navvies, and it changed to cheers that echoed and resounded down the cut. The big Negro flashed a smile at the man on the bank, crying:

'Fair play, Taff, you'm a better man than I gave credit for.'

'Thank you,' said my father, gasping. 'May we pass now, or do we tangle?'

'Any time you come down this cut, you pass, man, or you

108

call for me.' The Negro turned to Brunel. 'Just a bit of fun, sir—Welsh to Welsh during the break—no harm intended.'

'And no offence taken, I hope,' said Brunel.

'None,' said Dada, and raised his hand. 'Now be good enough to ease me out of here, for I am stinking of weeds and dead cats,' and Sam, the idiot, gripped Dada's hand and braced himself for the heave.

Too late. Dada heaved first: foot against the cut, face furious with anger, he heaved, and Big Sam flew like an angel over his head and went head over heels into the middle of the canal.

Dear me.

Now there is a hell of a commotion. Men went double, bellowing laughter: they shrieked, stamping about, mopping at their eyes. The Irish lad beside me was hooting soprano, the men with Brunel were cheering, their arms up: only Brunel was silent, weighing the situation. And the bedlam grew as my father vaulted on to the bank and stood there streaming water, and the laughter changed to shouts of warning as Big Sam floundered in fury towards him, fists clenched, his massive shoulders opening for the swing. Up on the bank now, he swung a right, and Dada's thick forearm went up, stopping it: dropping at the waist, squinting up, my father shuffled in, ducked a clubbing left, and then straightened—hitting up short. The Negro took it on the point of the chin, and teetered on the edge of the cut, arms flailing. And the hook that caught him then was glorious; a wet arm flashing in the sunlight, the fist making an arc that ended in a smack of fist on flesh. The Negro took it full. Arms dangling, he turned slowly, splashing face down into the canal.

My father turned away. 'Fetch him in before he drowns on us, Bryn.'

There was no sound over Pen-y-Dre as I stood waist-deep in the canal, holding Black Sam's head above the water; then navvies floundered in, gripping him, their actions paralysed by the speed of things and their own disbelief. Hauling the Negro ashore, they cast quick, apprehensive glances at my father as he stood on the bank before Brunel, his trews soaked and stained with mud, his hair tufted and tipped yellow with the golden dross of the canal. One of the gentlemen on the bank called. 'Well done, bargee. You will have no more truck with him, I'll warrant!'

My father said, wiping water from his eyes, 'You are right, sir. And nor will we have any truck with you and your kind.' His voice rose to a shout. 'Your navvies come to this valley as if they own the place—they cut it up for your railway, and try to drive the bargees out. But you will never drive us out because we live here—this is our home. And we were in this valley or the Top Towns before you knew of Merthyr, Dowlais, or the Vale of Neath.' He swept his arm around the staring faces about him. 'You bring in the English and the Irish. You employ the foreigners at cut prices, and they drink and whore and fight—there isn't a day's peace since they came to the place. Isn't it enough that you're carving the land to hell? Do we have to fight for right of way in our own land? Do you have to bloody starve us?'

'Mind your words, Welshman.'

'And you your railway, for I tell you this. If you want a fight you can have one. For we have been fighting in these valleys before you knew there was profit in Wales. You let us pass from Walby to Briton Ferry, or by God, it will be the worse for you. And tomorrow, if a bargee comes down here and finds a log over the cut I will go to Merthyr and bring down a thousand Welshmen, and we'll tear this railway up and toss it back to Neath where it came from.' He took a deep breath, turning to Ifor and Dewi, who were kneeling beside Black Sam. 'Is he alive?'

'Just about,' said Ifor. 'Man, you hit him.'

'Rise him,' said my father, 'for time is short. I have a barge under contract for the coasters, and we are working late. Come.'

The navvies parted as we went back to the barge, though some stood rock-still, hands bunched. The Irish boy stared at us as I shouldered him aside and hooked up Jed and Nell, and as we glided off under the animals I said to him softly, 'Now you know who you're with. You call me bastard once more and I am seeing to you right when I come by here again, logs or no logs.'

He did not reply, but before we had gone a few yards a voice rang out loud and clear, 'We can use you, bargee—you and your sons—any time, remember.'

And Dada called back from the deck, 'With respect, sir, not until you run us from the valley.'

With this, my father touched his hair, a thing I had never seen him do to any man.

'Do not look back,' he said.

In victory, in defeat—never look back, said my father.

13

AND SO we made our home in the Old Navigation, and it was good. We raised a new roof, we plastered, decorated; we hoed up and dug and grew vegetables, with Gran on her knees planting seeds along the wharf in spring and tending them through summer into glorious colours. A winter came and went, came again and flowered into another May. I remember with joy those bright nights by the fire, with my father reading from the Book and the canal outside all over ice and mist; the trees scarecrowed over a frozen land, and the old Resolven mountain shivering under a leaden moon. But it was warm and quick inside the Old Navigation, and at night I would lie in bed and listen to the ice-breakers thundering down the cut, the stamping hooves of the big Carmarthen dray-horses, the shouts and banter of living people. This noise of people is the song of the earth, says my father, for is not this business of living like a great chord of music? he asked. Granfer Ben used to ask the same questions, said Gran at her stitching. Is not living and dying akin to a great symphony, in which is born the lore and scholarship, and the marvellous wisdom of the aged? 'Mind,' said she, 'he had beautiful thoughts, except when he was on the beer, the women, or the trumpet in the Dowlais Silver Band,' and she sighed at the moon in the window. For my part, I do not agree with either of them, believing that the love of a man for a woman is the true song of the earth. And with beautiful thoughts like these I naturally hankered after my Bronwen, for come May I was in a terrible bother with the spring, the year I was sixteen.

Very tight and hot under the collar I come when I think of Miss Bronwen Rees, whom one day I will marry.

Saturday morning, one week in six this was free. Ifor was over at Abercynon sparking his Rebecca; Dewi was down in the cellar with Pietro Bianca: Meic Jones, the pot-boy up at the Vaughans, Rheola, had called for Sharon and Dada had taken Gwen up the cut for a stroll.

Not a sign, not a sound of the lock-keeper at Aberdulais lately, but this was no business of mine.

An afternoon adrift, me: polished up, pulled in, best suit on, boots shining, starched collar, washed behind the ears, very presentable.

'How do I look?'

Gran eased herself up from her flower-bed in cracks and groans.

'And where might you be going, pray?' Gay with primulas and celandine, bluebells and forget-me-nots, Gran's flower-beds blazed; the passing bargees doffing their hats to her, the women bowing, and what a beautiful sight it is, Mrs. Ceinwen Evan, and what a delight it is to see it all fresh and lovely amid the dirt of Pont Walby coal. Gran had green fingers, as people have, when they are in touch with God.

'There is nothing wrong with a bit of a stroll,' I said to her.

'Nothing at all, if you keep moving. Eh, you gorgeous, come by here,' she said, and I went to her and she held me, saying soft in my ear, 'Most bountiful. Ach, look at it!' She held me at arm's length. 'Grown from boy to a man. Down to Neath and put them on their ear, is it—here is one for a start!' and she kissed me a smacker. Finger up, then. 'But be good, remember!'

Easy when you're seventy.

'Yes, Gran.'

'No complications—you know what I mean?'

'Mamgu, *Mamgu*,' I said to her.

'As fizzy as potato wine I was, at your age.'

'I bet!'

'So fizz, *cariad*, but do not overflow. *Darro*. There's a life! Do I know her?'

I shook my head. Give her a name and she would have it all over the village.

'Well, anyway, be kind to her.'

'Yes, Gran.'

'Men are rough with women. Like Granfer Ben—didn't know his own strength. Gently, is it?'

'Goodbye,' I said. I left her on her hands and knees again, her hands deep in the rich, black soil that in time would befriend her, under Dada's flannel shirts weeping on her line.

I left her, but not in the direction of Rheola.

Aberdulais, me!

Miss Bronwen Rees, and going hot and cold at the thought of her.

I had timed her like a clock. Five weeks in six I had seen her, my Bron, when we went down to the Grave with Walby coal, all done up glorious, she was, making for Shoni's farm, probably for milk.

Six shillings I had in my pocket that day, and spent already in dreams. At three o'clock I would meet her; off to Neath with us on the first barge down, a shilling ride around Town, tea out like gentry, with Welsh cakes done on the stone, for I knew she loved these: back home in moonlight, stand on the school door-step: in the music of the water-fall, I heard myself say:

'Good night, Miss Rees.'

Pale her face in that moonlight, and her eyes like stars: lips black-red and parted, in hope of a kiss. 'Oh, Bryn Evan, my darling. Do not be like that—call me Bron.'

A shivering is in her; scared, no doubt: never had a man so close before, only females like Taliesen the Poet.

Her waist is slim to the hook of my arm, the moonlight shadows deep in her cheeks. 'Oh, Bryn,' she whispered, 'kiss me, kiss me!'

Bread and cheese now, and I ate her alive.

'Oh, gently, gently, with a woman, boy. Fizz by all means, but do not overflow. Eh, gorgeous you are, like Granfer Ben.'

'Right you, Bronwen Rees, I am grown up, see.'

'Oh, Bryn!'

'Ahoy, there, Bryn Evan!' In my dream I heard his bass voice: in my dream of Bronwen. Dai Central Eating, it was, in his little rowing boat: gormless was Dai, fishing in ten inches of water, and what my mam saw in him in the days of the Old Bethania Sunday School, I never did understand.

''Afternoon, Dai,' I said. Nearly scared my wits out, bawling like that in the intimacy of me and my Bronwen.

'You want a lift down?'

'Much obliged,' I said. 'What you doing now, then?'

'Sweeping up in the tin-works in Melin; time-keeping, making tea, all odd jobs, and keeping my ear to the ground.'

Better than the old *Trumpet of Wales* was Dai Central, when it came to the scandal, with his long nose over the gate or under the bed, one tooth snitching like a rabbit: biddings, beddings, births and black bunting was Dai Central Eating. But I was not very interested now that Bronwen was practically in the locker: sixteen, me; very determined: a sailor's farewell this was going to be—tonight or never. I was putting this particular point to her when Dai said:

'You heard that me and Tegwen Harriet are sparking very strong?'

'Tegwen Harriet?'

'Wake up, man—Cohen's number five.'

'Oh, aye,' I said, vacant.

'And if I snare Tegwen and your Ifor brings down Rebecca, this makes you and me sort of cousins by marriage, four times removed?'

'Good,' I said.

'And your big sister Sharon coming very hot with her over that Meic Jones, Rheola, and noses out of joint on Robert Crocker, Albert Jones and Willie Dare?'

'Ay ay.'

'Dewi and Rosie Carey also; there's beautiful, but very immoral, mind.'

'Very.'

'Him and Pietro Bianca still making bangs in the cellar?'

'Louder than ever.'

'Only your dada is not involved, and that will not last for ever.'

This raised my head. 'My dada?'

'The Aberdulais lock-keeper and her daughter are coming back.'

'Coming back to where?'

'Coming back to Aberdulais lock—next Friday.'

'Where have they been these last two years, then?'

'Swansea workhouse. The mother fell ill, the daughter went in with her, for debt.'

'God help them.'

The keeper was coming back. I could imagine my father's joy. Bubbling in the heart I cut across the fields short of Bryngelli, doing boot-clogs and backsteps, waving to Dai Central Eating. Vaulting gates that were not there, I made for Rheola till Dai's boat got clear, then doubled back, my hobnails two feet up in the air. Eh, I was happy for my father: after all, nothing would come of it.

Hushed in the valley of Gadlys stood Dic Shoni's farm, and beyond the farm stood Bron's school, and the little cottage she shared with her mam. Blind as a bat in sunlight was Dic Shoni, so no fear of buck-shot as I hand-sprung his gate and leaned against his barn, waiting for Bronwen to come down for the milk.

Brush yourself down, smarm back the hair, rub your toe-caps on your calves, tighten up your stock, an inch up with your trews. Heart thudding, you wait.

And on the third chime of the church bell, the cottage door came open and Bron stood there: in a snow-white crinoline and with hoops, she stood there, her floppy summer hat done over with a pink bandage. Numb, I closed my eyes to the vision of beauty, and when I opened them she had gone, as if plucked into space. High in the sky a lark nicked and sang demented; the wind of the cut fanned my face, the sun burned

115

down. Next moment I heard voices behind the barn, coming nearer.

It was the voice of Bronwen Rees.

To this day I can smell her perfume, hear that excited chattering, and her soft laugh guaranteed to make your hair curl. But fearfully now, I heard Dic Shoni's voice, too; I retreated into the depths of the barn.

Silence. Footsteps now; a man's whisper, but it was not Dic Shoni's. Trapped, I ran swiftly up the ladder to the loft, and there went flat.

Through a crack in the boards I saw them instantly below me: Taliesen the Poet, with Bron in his arms, and I closed my eyes. Pent words of love I heard then; the inarticulate sounds that spring from lovers. And amid this beauty Bron suddenly laughed, softly and treble high, as Rosie Carey might have laughed in the arms of Dewi.

I screwed up my hand, remembering the removed dignity of my mother.

Does a man ever know a woman? I wondered. Was this my mother's twin, her face of darkness, the paramour of any passing Taliesen, a slut in straw?'

I shut my eyes and pressed my hands over my ears.

Give me men.

Enough of good women to last me a lifetime.

14

No place like the Vale of Neath when it comes to gossip.

And the family of Mostyn Evan over at the Old Navigation were not left out of it, for the Welsh are very interested in neighbours.

Very respectable on the face of it, that Mostyn Evan and family, the bargees; twice to Resolven Zion every Sunday, with bows on all sides, and aren't they a picture, and all but one of them a credit to the community: upbringing, it is, girl, upbringing. Ach, yes—bangs in the cellar, true, but queerer things than bangs in cellars do happen in Resolven, be fair. Strange, though, that Mostyn Evan has no woman around, isn't it? And whiter than a shroud his moral integrity, they do say, missus. Only that Dewi do not stand close examination, nor that big Ifor doing his pugilistics. Eh, but a lovely girl that Rose of Sharon, aye, and biblical. But little Meic Jones Rheola will turn her into two, given half a chance: ah! hot as hell, that Meic Jones, same as his da, mind—got them running screaming down at Swansea ten years back, as fast as they could pull them from under him, Constantinople harems don't come into it, man. But nothing against that Sharon, save that Shakespeare—isn't healthy, too much Shakespeare, says our minister, though his activities do not stand examination, remember. And that Bryn not normal, you ask me, though Dewi is his dada's cross, mind, oh, aye!

Dewi, Dewi, *Dewi* . . .

Slander, slander, bubbling in the ale, gurgling under the aprons; invectives coming from starched white collars, whistling over the cobbles, around street corners. In the frothing bars from the Lamb and Flag up to the Plough, Glyn Neath; in pit, in kitchen, in cornfield, it was Dewi, *Dewi*!

And that little one Gwen not quite the ticket, also: sad, sad it must be for that grandmother. Talking to the teacher, I was. Given her up, see. Twice two are eight. You know what? Down the bottom of the garden she was feeding a sparrow. 'Bread for the sparrow,' she was asking for, and when her gran went with her she was feeding a viper. In touch with the Devil, I say.

But always, always it came back to Dewi.

Anarchist, agitator, and Rosie Carey, and Mrs. Alfo Morgan used to stoke the fire up at the Lamb and Flag. 'The pillows are in constant use,' she used to say, 'as Alfo rolls out one side Dewi rolls in the other. Not that I have actually witnessed it, mind, but there is always speculation. Suits me fine, girl, as long as I draw the wages. Another pint, Mr. Talfarn Davies—first one to settle the dust?'

And Gran used to say, 'That Dewi is the talk of the village, Mostyn. Not decent, I call it, sharing a woman.'

'The cheese is that much sweeter when nibbled by another mouse,' said he.

'You ought to be ashamed of yourself!'

'Better Rosie Carey than a girl like my Sharon,' said he at *The Cambrian*.

'It is all part of the free-thinking,' exclaimed Gran. 'Never in my life will I agree with the free-thinking.'

'That is the difference between you and Rosie Carey,' said Dada.

'Is it wrong to be respectable now, then?'

But Dewi apart, we were as respectable as anyone else on the canal about this time, for the bargees of Wales must not be confused with those of England. And while George Smith, the canal reformer, had his hands full up on the big Midland canals, and fighting spare-time to bring ten thousand children out of the brickfields, he never had to come down to Wales. And if we had a bad name at times, this was brought in. Men like Baccy York, for instance, he came down from Worksop with his three wives and first ran on the Swansea cut: Laddie O'Brien, handy with a knife, he came to Giant's Grave, and Beef O'Hara, one of Tub Union's men, running from the '47 Hunger in Mayo. There was Joby Canal, who beat his children every Sunday with a switch, to stripe the God out of them, and Randy Bandy who lived with his sister and had four children by her, all dribbling idiots, working up from Melin.

'None of these compare with that Abe Sluice,' said Gran.

'A swimming pig, is that Abe Sluice,' said Ifor.

'The Company would bring them in from Tokyo for a farthing a ton less, free on board,' whispered Dewi, fist clenched.

'Where is that?' asked Gran.

'It do not matter, Mam,' said my father.

'If it do not matter then why mention it?'

'It was mentioned as a figure of speech, Gran,' explained Dewi.

'That is a queer old place for anyone to come from,' said she. 'And I think that Abe Sluice came from there. But hospitable, give them credit. I was hauled aboard for a cup of tea, and I do not forget it.'

Down from Chester was Abe Sluice, drinking and fighting, and the pair of them living more by poaching and theft than carrying Company goods. This was the scum that was coming in from England—but hospitable, of course—oh, yes, said Dada—give you the top brick: pushing dead cats out of the way when filling the kettle from the cut.

'Mind, that tea tasted queer,' said Gran, reflectively.

'And I can tell you why,' said Dewi.

'Hush,' said Dada instantly, 'enough!'

Many of the foreigners had built cabins on the Company barges, and lived aboard, but most of the Welsh lived in cottages. And any day of the week you could see the English barges tied up in the passing-places along the cut, doing their debugging, and you will not believe it when they say that I have never seen a flea. Aye, sitting in long lines on the bank, these English, de-nitting their hair and bathing the yearly bath in the canal, naked as bones. And moored alongside was the barge with the cabin door and window sealed up with paper, and brimstone burning inside—ten thousand hoppers in the bunks screaming their heads off and billows of smoke rolling over Resolven.

I am not against people keeping themselves clean, said my father, but I am against the English coming down here to do it: the bugs were caught north of the border and ought to be laid out up there, not here.

In Merthyr, Dowlais, Pontypool—any place named, it was just the same: decent Welsh homsesteads before the coming of the industries, now seats of Baal in all his glory. Down one side of the street the Welsh were with bibles under their arms, going to Chapel in black serge and crinolines, very devout with their measured tread: down the other side of the street the foreign workers would be fighting and jeering and doing it in the gutter.

Dewi said, 'The product of the English system of class, the great unwashed. They would have us be like them but we will never be like them, because we are Welsh.'

Queer old characters, mind, these English bargees, and not so much their fault, said Dada, as the fault of the English canal system: up in England the canals were hundreds of miles long, and the bargees, unlike the Welsh, lived aboard. And they were brutalised by cramped quarters and never belonging to a community. Most of the Welsh were a cut above them— like Tom Daniels' family: down to Neath he would go with a load of coal, all done up in mole-skin trousers and bowed greetings on every side to neighbours. But the English used to act like savages. The women wore cauliflower ears and broken noses and could swear like their men-folk to blister Baal. And every pay night when the agent forked out their wages in Bethel Street in Ferry, they would roll up to the Cuddlecome Inn and sink quart pewters and hell would come loose with their fighting; women biting and scratching and tearing off skirts in a ring of cheering men from the railway. An indelicate place, this Cuddlecome Inn, apparently, and therefore I was anxious to visit it. For there was talk that they had tap-maids dancing in the saw-dust with enough fore and aft to stop the heart of a mummy, and ladies flocking up from Neath and Swansea, with Cushy, the landlady, blowing on a bugle at six o'clock in the morning and back to your own beds, ladies and gentlemen, I'm having no hanky-panky business, mine is a respectable establishment.

'There is no such place,' said Dada, finger levelled at me, 'and kindly remember it.' Bang, bang, bang on the back now.

And Dewi raised his head from Fred Engels, and winked. For my part, I thought it colourful to have Baal in all his glory rampant above the door. Very fascinating, this Cuddlecome Inn.

'Come in, come in, Pietro!' shouted my father from his corner, and I saw Gwen look up from her drawing with anxious eyes.

'Aye, come in, boy!' cried Dewi, getting up.

Pietro Bianca bowing to Sharon now, hat sweeping the floor. He kissed Gran's hand. 'Just a few friends I have brought to visit, Dewi Evan, is it all right?'

'Friends are always welcome,' said Gran, 'bring them in, Pietro.'

Well.

Six came in, burly, bare-footed, ragged: like cut-throats of the Spanish Main, their great dark eyes shining from the caverns of their hungry faces.

'Down in the cellar, boys,' cried Dewi. 'Bread and cheese sent down later, is it, Gran?'

'As much as they can eat,' said my father, reading *The Cambrian*.

Gran whispered to Sharon, 'Upstairs and take down the pictures in the bedroom, there's a good girl.' She swung to my father as the last of the guests disappeared. 'You are encouraging this, remember. Thieves and vagabonds. I never thought I would live to see it. Oh, Mostyn!'

'Patriots,' said my father. 'Cut them bread and cheese.' Rising, he went to the cellar door. 'Dewi!'

'Yes, Dada?'

'Reduce it to Marx and Engels if you can; keep the bangs within reasonable limits and the bullets horizontal.'

For myself I was not much one for the politics, with bombs under the Whigs and Tories and President Polk if ever he visits Grand River: being up and coming in the female stakes I naturally found more to interest myself nearer home, especially since Bronwen Rees had fallen from grace. And although Ifor reckoned that Cushy Cuddlecome's place never existed, I had noticed a few going along the tow-path down near the Tennant worth a hammering, with neat swings of their hips, which some people find delightful, and black tumbling hair and red lips. Not that I find such people over-attractive, but by the come-hithers and blown kisses they hand out while I am on the fending-poles, it would appear that they have a need. And for this reason alone, I would be prepared to sacrifice myself on the altar of womanhood once a week, as Dewi said. This, I think, is the most beautiful thing I have ever heard Dewi say, and shows that, Karl Marx and Rosie Carey apart, there is, deep inside him, a wonderful nature.

'I shall not tell you again, Bryn—forget this,' said Dada.

'You keep clear of that Cushy Cuddlecome, or you account to me,' said Gran, looking evil. 'What happened to that beautiful school-teacher?'

'Folded up.'

Ifor rumbled, shadow-boxing in the corner, 'She is walking out with Taliesen the Poet.'

'Oh, my poor, poor lad!' cried Sharon. Dressed like a fruit-seller, was Sharon, with posies in her hands, and a woven rush basket, 'How now, that you are crossed in love? Is she fair, or dark? And what fine creature wooed her from your heart?'

'Oh, go to hell,' I said.

'Bryn!' said my father, removing his pipe.

Crash, crash! from the cellar, and he leaped up and caught the Granfer Ben clock as it dropped for the hearth. Down came the pictures in the second bedroom. Plaster trickled down from the ceiling.

'Oh, my God!' whispered Gran, holding her heart.

'They are building a new social order,' said Dada, putting back the clock. 'You get on with your knitting.'

'I have drawn a pig upside down,' announced Gwen.

'Oh, coz, coz, coz,' cried Sharon, dancing around, her hands beseeching, 'my pretty little coz!'

Ifor, naked to the waist, sweating, was thumping the boxer's bag in the back, snorting and grunting with each blow. 'I will give him Black Welshman,' he said in his teeth.

Gran frowned at her knitting. 'You know, Mostyn,' she said, 'sometimes I tend to think this house is a little bit less than normal.'

'Reflect that they come from you originally.'

'I was beginning to wonder how I could be held responsible,' said Gran.

Night.

The Old Navigation sleeps.

A hunter's moon is flashing along the canal; otters are whistling from the Nedd, badgers rolling in grunts at their earths. Dai Half-Moon and his idiot son are coming through the lock at Aberdulais; the sky is afire with the glare of the tin and copper works over Seven Sisters, the clouds apple-cheeked from the ovens of Ystalafera. I was weary to death and black with a day of coaling, coming up from the Grave behind Dai Half-Moon, and the silly sod gets stuck on the river gate with the tide going out, and began barging about in the dark like a hundred-ton frigate. Up on the prow went Dada, fending off, and shouted, 'Dai, get your old heap shifting so decent men can make a bed—what ails you?'

'Trouble with this gate, Mostyn, son—stuck jammed, it is.'

'Where is Jones, the Keeper?'

'Gone, man, haven't you heard?'

Tom Jones who took over the Aber lock when the beautiful keeper and her daughter left two years ago. Dada turned to me. 'You heard that Tom Jones has finished?'

'Finished this morning when the woman came back, and her daughter,' I said, looking away.

'You might have had the grace to mention it.'

'Forgot,' I replied. 'Dai Central told me last Monday—this is the first time since we've been down.'

'Where did they get to?'

'Debt,' I said. 'Swansea workhouse.' And Dai Half-Moon shouted:

'Hold up, Mostyn, while I lever the paddle. And stop butting me in the arse.'

'Mind that language,' cried Dada.

'Comes to something when we have to work the locks ourselves,' called Dai.

It was a two-barge take, this lock, and when Dada jumped ashore and helped Dai free the paddles I slid our barge in beside Dai's, and the idiot son on the knee of his mother slobbered over the gunwale beside me, and I shivered.

'The cottage is empty,' cried my father from the bank, but I scarcely heard him: black the water swirling in as we rose, the wind breathed, fanning the moonlight. On nights such as this, when idiots stare and lock-keepers vanish, the aerial creatures fly, like the Flying Viper of Nedd Fechan, which Gwen fed with bread, and the Green Lady of Craig-y-Llyn bearing her necklace of wild berries—in mid-winter Ifor saw her, and not a berry in sight on the hedges.

My father jumped back on to the barge.

'There is a smell of sweetness in the cottage, and it is clean,' said he. 'It is not a pig-sty like when Jones had it—clean as a pin, but she is gone again.'

'Can't be,' called Dai Half-Moon. 'The Sluices reckon they

saw her here with her girl midday, after you and me come down.'

'Gone again,' said my father, and sighed as a man sighs when nails go through his hands. At me, he said, 'You could at least have told me.'

The stars were as little moons as we swung past Dai Half-Moon into the open country, and the trees above us dripped silver in that madness, for it was a night of witches and besoms and canal bugguts.

There was a great emptiness in my dada for the lock-keeper, for she had torn his blood.

Stock still my father sat on the prow, disdainful of the distant brawling from the canal inns along the cut, for this was pay night when they were at their best, with drinking and whoring with the paid women they brought up from Swansea and Neath : not much time for navvies since he had hit out the Black Welshman : even less now they had brought the railway line up within sight of the Old Navigation, the centre line pegs missing the east corner by ten feet. Marvellous, it was going to be when the big saddle-tanks came snorting up the valley, trying to get a sleep after a night-shift.

Dewi said now, 'A little noisy on the cut tonight, Dada,' trying him out.

'Aye, damned disgraceful, it is.'

For there had been talk that the beautiful lock-keeper, Mrs. Mortymer and her daughter, had been up half the night since returning, never daring to step outside the cottage now that the navvies had brought the railway up above Tonna.

'I reckon they drove her out,' said Dada, fist in his hand.

'Like they will drive us out of the Old Navigation,' said Dewi.

'Oh, aye?' This rose my father, stiff on the prow, chest bulging enormous.

The navigators were a curse to the community, said he, and he was right.

Every beer-house was filled to overflowing, no woman safe on the streets, with Dai this and that knocking on the little navvy cabins that stood beside the railway, doors coming open and the Welsh going in with fists and the navvies coming out with boots off, wiping split noses and holding broken nuts. Just the same down in Neath since they arrived—knocking the helmets off the policemen and hitting out English red-coats, though naturally, the Welsh had no objection to this in the main. Aye, a funny old time was the 'fifties, the more I think of it, with the Welsh dusting knees in the chapels thanking God for coal and ironmasters who were making their lives a misery, and refusing to join the Chartists, which were the only hope they had got, said Dewi. Once all was lovely here, said Dada, but now Baal was about in gorgeous raiment: the maids were up in the attics mooning about the boys, the boys were riding cock-a-hoop and very loose in the mouth; rivers of ale were flowing over the inn counters and the Devil down in the cellar trying on the girl's stays. Sad, it is, said he, when a country loses its proper disposition, and I tell you all this—I will set fire to the house before I accept a drop in standards and show you the heat of hell—and you, Dewi, are the one copying this navvy trash.

'Yes, Dada,' said Dewi.

'You and that Rosie Carey, it has got to stop!'

'Rosie Carey, Dada?'

'You know exactly what I mean. You, too, Bryn . . .' and he levelled a finger at me. 'Your old gran is right, I am beginning to believe. And you, Ifor . . . !'

'Me, Dada?' cried Ifor from the tow-path.

'It is long past time you married Rebecca Cohen or I stand shamed before old Eli—can you hear me?'

'They can hear you back down in Briton bloody Ferry,' said Ifor, grinning wide, and this made my dada grin, too, he having a voice like a fairground barker, then some, especially when he got on the subject of virtue.

Wonderful to see my father smiling again, with all the sadness of the woman keeper left behind him.

In moonlight, bright and clear, we slid along, tired to death: above us the black trees nodded together in wind whisper, trying to recall the last lovely summer: coo-pidges, early from the nest with their voices not yet broken, cooed treble from Rheola.

Running footsteps in the night.

Gusty breathing now and stifled tears.

I saw Ifor stiffen at Nell's halter, peering into the moonlight.

Into a clearing shafted by the moon she ran, faltered, and fell into my brother's arms.

Half a mile up we found her mother, the lock-keeper of Aberdulais, lying across the tow-path.

Near starved, the pair of them: Swansea workhouse had left its mark.

'Quick,' said my father.

15

THERE was a marvellous investment in the enjoyment of grief when we brought the Mortymer woman home that summer night, with Gran beating her breast and isn't it an absolute scandal and Gwen gushing tears as we carried the invalid through the door feet first.

'Found her on the path.'

'The lock-keeper of Aberdulais.'

'Nearly starved to death.'

'What a damned country,' whispered Dewi.

'Quick, put her here,' commanded Gran, taking charge, 'and for heaven's sake move yourselves; can't you see the woman's nearly done?'

Pale and proud, this daughter Rhiannon, aged a bit younger than me: now kneeling beside the horse-hair sofa and gripping her mother's hand, her own eyes fevered jewels, her black hair tangled with sweat.

'What happened?' whispered Gran, on her knees with a bowl and flannel, wiping the hot brow, and for God's sake don't stand there staring, you men, but put water on the boil and heat up the stock-pot for soup.

No wonder we stared, including Dada, now he had this

woman close at last: as she lay there amid all the commotion of hand-slapping she was the image of our dead mother; the red lips bright with the fever of hunger, the same classic features of the Silurian Welsh; deep the shadows in her cheeks, her skin smooth and stark white in the marble rigidity of unconsciousness. Her daughter, Rhiannon, said softly, 'For two hours only we were back at the lock cottage, and no food, and she insisted on going to Nanty.'

'Nanty?' asked Dada.

'Nantyglo, up in the Eastern Valley. My relatives live up there—my mother's people, really, for I do not know them.'

This is strange for a start, and I saw the trouble this pair had brought with them standing in a corner, his gnome face with its imp ears peeping out of his rags, his boney hands rubbing with anticipation. Sharon said, for no apparent reason:

'She is the image of my mother,' and Dewi scraped his boots on the flags, turned away, and added, 'It is as if she has loosened the shroud and walked in from her grave at Vaynor.'

From the door I watched the girl Rhiannon: and I think I knew, although resenting her, that one day she would be mine. Gran said, sharp, 'Well, stop mooning, all of you. Mostyn—upstairs and clear out Sharon and Gwen and put them in with Bryn...'

'Oh, Gran...!' cried Sharon.

'And you change the blankets for the visitors—you and Gwen will go in the Dowlais single and think yourselves lucky. Is that stock-pot on the hob yet?'

'Raising the fire now, Gran,' said Ifor, hands black and on his knees.

'Good. What is your name, child?'

'Rhiannon Mortymer.'

I tried it on my tongue, and it was honey-sweet, as she was beautiful: as stepped from the pages of the glorious *Mabinogion*, which my father used to read to us, in Welsh, on winter nights. Gran said, 'There is a beautiful name. Hush and dry up now, is it? Your mam is coming round.'

'Mama,' whispered Rhiannon, kissing her hand.

127

And Mrs. Mortymer opened her eyes, transforming her face.

Dear me. I have come across some beauties in my time, for I don't keep my eyes in my boots when women pass. I have seen the Camarthen girls done up in their flouncies on May-pole days, and the Gower women straight and tall, ravishing in chapel black from bunned hair to toe, wealthy in the breast and with the carriage of queens, for their blood comes from ancient princes.

But the beauty of this Mortymer woman, taken close, was of her own.

The black lashes lifted, the great eyes switched in panic, seeing Dada, Dewi and me, staring down. Gran said:

'Do not worry, Mrs. Mortymer; women are here.'

'You hungry?' asked Ifor, rumbling up from the grate, beaming black. 'Got a good shoulder of mutton needing a home . . .'

'Out,' said Gran.

'Stock-pot getting hot,' said Dada.

'I told you fix the beds—out. All men out!' and she flapped at us with the flannel. 'Loafing around you frighten a woman to death. Away!'

We shuffled into the back, thumbs indolent in our belts, looking back.

I said, black moodily, 'The spit of my mam. She has no right to look like that.'

'Aye,' mumbled Ifor, knuckling his eye. 'Just seen her close, I have. I reckon it's our mam come back.'

'Bryn,' called Gran. 'Fetch coal for the hob.'

I wandered on, unhearing. All men out, is it? Then out for me, too. I saw a red hooping in the sky as the bungs were tapped; heard the clip-clop of hooves on the road to Vaynor.

'Be reasonable,' said Dewi. 'The poor bitch can't help her looks.'

Women's business, is it?

Then they can bloody sort it out.

Now they kneel beside the sofa, souping her up, and please do not take it too fast, Mrs. Mortymer, and you are all right,

128

Mrs. Mortymer, now you have landed here with us. And now we were up at table for supper, and next it was breakfast, and when we came back from Pont Walby two days later the pair of them were still in the house: first they had the woman by the fire, then she sat opposite me with her daughter, which was a crush one side since Gwen and Sharon were squashed there, too.

For nobody, you understand, sat at the end of the table opposite my father.

That place, with the empty chair, had a knife and fork laid, for my mother.

Six years she had been gone now, but her place was always laid.

And seven days later the Mortymer woman and her daughter were still in the house, and my father in his element, the fool.

At this kind of table, when there is no family joy on it, you can lose yourself in food.

Beef and mutton I like, but trout do send me demented, for in him I taste the sun of the wild places where only trout can roam. Indeed, could I have my time again I would like to be a trout, lying dozy in rushes watching ants whiskering on reed-tips and beetles in the bubbles of light-flood, sipping and shimmering in green depths or paddling in beams of sunlight.

'Sit up properly, Bryn,' said Gran.

'Yes, Gran.'

'What is wrong with you tonight?' asked my father.

I could have told him what was wrong: the Mortymer woman was there and I was here beside my mother.

Also, there was a strange sickness rising in my throat and smooth fingers clutching my stomach.

'More rice-pudding, Rhiannon?'

'Yes, please, Mrs. Evan.'

Not doing so bad this one, either—two helpings she has had already, her dark eyes watching me across the white cloth, a ghost of a smile on her red mouth. But I could not blame her going daft on Gran's rice-pudding, when cut into wads gone cold, like now, all Chinese white but brown and gooey on top;

and if anything in this world was guaranteed to bring a top set clattering down at table it was Gran's rice-pudding.

'What? None for you, Bryn?'

'No, thank you, Gran.'

'You ill, or something?' asked Sharon.

'Excuse me,' I said.

'And where are you off to?' This from my father.

I pushed back my chair on the flags. 'Just out, Dada.'

'You realise that we have not finished the meal?'

Mrs. Mortymer said, 'Oh, it is all right, Mostyn.'

'Let him go, precious,' said Gran.

Dada levelled a finger at me. 'Right, but watch where you go and the company you keep. Dai Central is down with the cholera.'

'No!' whispered Gran, her hand to her throat.

My father nodded. 'They have got him up in Glyn Neath—sixteen cases.' He added, 'And don't be late—an early start tomorrow.'

I thought: away to hell out of this; leave them to their smiles that hid the hatreds; leave them to Dewi's open hostility, to Ifor's grumbling eyes as he saw in this Mortymer woman the ghost of my mam, and Sharon's simpering, putting on her best actress accent to make an impression. Damned hypocrites: all but Dada were wishing the pair of them back at Aberdulais, for all their beauty. I was at the door when Dada called, 'Say good night to Mrs. Mortymer, Bryn.'

The handle was in my hand. On impulse, I swung the door open, went through it and slammed it shut behind me. And turned almost instantly as the door was pulled open again by my father. I saw, behind his fury, the white table, the disapproving stares of Sharon and Gran and the saucer dark eyes of Rhiannon.

'Say good night to Mrs. Mortymer!' said my father, furious.

I stood there, just staring at her, and she whispered, 'Mostyn, it does not matter.' Oh, dear me—Mostyn twice now, is it: down to bloody Christian names, and we haven't been here a week.

'Bryn,' whispered my father, 'I will not ask you again.'

I shut my eyes. 'Good night, Mrs. Mortymer.'

'And Rhiannon.'

'Good night.'

'Good night, Bryn,' they murmured, eyes lowered.

Dusk and blackbirds were falling over the land as I ran.

I found my mother waiting for me by the barge, a misty foil to the decoy that was trying to take her place in my father's heart. I sat in the barge until the moon came up, and the Old Navigation was in darkness.

In a world that is dying of hunger, I hold no brief for the odd missed meal, and that is all that is wrong with this Mortymer woman. She was supposed to stay a couple of days, but every time she and Rhiannon hooked out their bundles my father pulled them back. They saw us into May, and with June came summer clad in her gay green rags, and looking into the sparkling Nedd she painted up her face, calling the sun to warm up her bed of rushes.

Come July, they were still in the house, and every time they got up to go my father opened his shoulders and screwed them in tighter.

'Now, listen, you,' said Gran, 'I will have no more of it. Who the devil do you think you are—head of the house?'

I did not reply. Up to my elbows in my trews, head lowered, I stood out the back while Gran laced me. She cried, 'When you own a house you will say who sleeps under its roof, and not before—you hear me?'

'Yes, Gran.'

'Don't just stand there saying nothing!'

I said, 'Not only me, remember—Dewi, Ifor and Sharon— they got no time for them, either.'

'The moment he chapels her I am going from here,' said Dewi.

'Me, too,' muttered Ifor.

'Count me in.'

Gran now, face scarlet, foot tapping. 'Then go, all three of you, but I tell you this—nobody will come between them, because he deserves her. Try as you like—put the house upside down. Go to Mexico or America, go to hell, but leave my son alone.' Sinking into Dada's armchair she began to cry in gasps and wheezes, rocking herself, stays creaking: the three of us looking at boots mainly, but we did not go to her, though usually there was panic if Gran cried.

'Gran . . .'

She swung to the wall. 'You leave me alone!'

A bitch is that Mortymer woman: Dewi called her this, and I call her it—a damned bitch for coming in between us.

Bang, bang on the back. 'Can I come in?' cried Pietro.

'Oh, God, no!' said Gran, very damp. 'Not Pietro at a time like this . . . !'

'Come in, Pietro!' sang Dewi. 'Come in. There is a better revolution going on in here than ever you'll get in Mexico.'

Supper over, and I was whittling a new gaff in a corner. Dewi was mending harness, for Pietro had gone, Ifor was out gathering two sovereigns of a gentry purse up on Resolven mountain; taken on Dai Swipo of Skewen, two stone larger: even heavier in the head was Ifor, these days, bruising with mountain-fighters inches up and thicker in the beam, but a tidy little hoard was going in his chamber under the bed. Dada said over the top of his newspaper:

'You remember that Pont Walby agent I tangled with?'

'Mr. Alton, the English?'

'Aye. He died on Friday. Being buried today.'

'No loss to the Welsh,' said Dewi, 'for he hated us.'

'He was followed by a worse one—Man Arfon, and he is Welsh. You heard he is booked for a plum job with the Great Western?'

'Plum jobs for those who grovel to the owners,' I said.

I was glad Man Arfon was moving from Pont Walby. From the moment we had met we had hated each other, and I knew he was only biding his time to get even with me.

'According to Dai Half-Moon he is going as an inspector,' said Mari Mortymer from her chair opposite Dada.

'Inspector?' Dewi laughed. 'More likely as a checker, for this is his trade. Man Arfon doesn't know a rail from the arse end of a mule.'

My father glanced up. 'Easy, Dewi.'

'Well, she's talking daft!'

'I am only saying what little Dai told me,' said Mari Mortymer, softly.

'And I was there when he said it,' observed Rhiannon coldly.

Got a bit about her, this Rhiannon, and I was becoming interested.

'You believe all Dai says and you end up as skinny as him,' I said lightly.

'But a dear little man, nevertheless, and sad about his son, isn't it?'

Sharon said at her King Henry the Fourth, 'Dai Half-Moon is a little scrounger, Mrs. Mortymer. There is not an ounce of the Christian in him.'

'I am still sorry for him, and for his son.'

Dewi said, 'Little Dai gets by on sympathy and theft. He would cut his mam's throat for the price of a pint.'

'You have to get up in the morning to get the hang of Dai Half-Moon.'

'I did not know,' replied Mrs. Mortymer. 'He seemed a good little man.'

'He is a better little man than most give him credit for,' said Dada.

Terrible is the silence of a house at odds with itself: see the agitated fingers, the nervous thrusting of the needle, the switching eyes; and the room changes colour, I have noticed: from the warm pink of kindness and understanding comes a faint flush of green, and coldness, and there is a shivering and a desire to hurt. And in that silence Mari Mortymer rose, put down her sewing, gripped Rhiannon's hand in passing and began to lay the table.

'Thank you, girl,' whispered Gran.

In the cracked mirror over the bosh I watched her lay that table, polishing each knife and fork on her white apron, smoothing the cloth at my father's place. And when she laid my mother's place, she paused, face lowered, and I think she might have been with tears. Softly, she said:

'Are you up at Pont Walby first shift tomorrow, Mostyn?'

'Aye.' He puffed at his pipe in the corner, the match flaring. 'Pig iron for a change, so we will come back clean.'

'Rhiannon and I will be coming with you.'

He glanced up. 'What takes you to Pont Walby?'

'It is part way to Nantyglo. Leaving tomorrow, Mostyn.'

Dewi glanced up and flickered a wink at me, and in that moment I hated him.

'What's this? Who is leaving tomorrow?' asked Gran, putting down the stew.

'We cannot stay for ever,' said Rhiannon, getting up. 'A family is entitled to be a family, and not living with strangers,' and her mother added:

'It ... it is better this way, Mostyn. Anyway, I was on my way to Nanty when you brought us in, and thank God for you all. But my mother and father-in-law are expecting us, and it is time we left here.'

'But you will be coming back, Mari?'

She shook her head. 'Not coming back, Mostyn.'

Gran turned slowly to Dewi and me. 'Now perhaps you are satisfied!'

'No, it is not their fault, Gran,' said Rhiannon. 'This is a house of ghosts. At first I thought it was only Granfer Ben...'

Mrs. Mortymer gestured with empty hands at my mother's place at the table. 'It is not only Granfer Ben—it is a house where the mother has not really died. Tonight we will pack the bundles. As I said, Mostyn—it is better this way.'

I do not know why I said, 'You come from Nantyglo?'

'No, from Carmarthen—Llanstephan—the same village as your old granfer.'

'It is queer, mind,' murmured Dewi, 'that you have been here weeks and we don't know anything about you.'

'That is because you have not asked,' replied Rhiannon, her eyes on fire.

Butter wouldn't melt in this one's mouth, but I bet she was fighting Welsh when she was roused. Dewi nodded. 'That is fair. Your husband's people up in Nanty, you say?'

Mrs. Mortymer shrugged. 'They were in Blaenafon iron—I married my Iestyn in Blaenafon. Later, the Mortymers moved to Carmarthenshire, back to the farms. My husband was killed in the Chartist riots in Newport, when trying to escape capture.'

'Tell them about your son,' said Dada, his head bowed by the lamp.

'I had a son, and his name was Jonathan. He was ten years old. He was killed two years back, working with the navigators. I let him work in their cabins, for money was short—sweeping up, making tea, with oiling bolts and nuts spare time. But one day they were short of a tripper, and they put him on the embankments, and the tram spilled and trapped him, and he died.'

'Thank God you have Rhiannon,' whispered Gran, and I saw Dewi shifting his behind uncomfortably on the stool: hot as hell, me: damned swine, me.

'Rhiannon is adopted. When I first came to Lock Cottage, Jonathan found her wandering, and brought her home.' Mrs. Mortymer smiled at Gran. 'Things have not been good for me, but I thank God every day for my Rhiannon.'

Dewi rose and went to the window. 'You are right when you say that our mother has not really died, but she will die in time.'

Sharon now, up on her feet and blazing, 'That is a dreadful thing to say!'

'But it is true. It is us children who have kept her alive, not Gran, not Dada!'

'Oh, please, do not quarrel,' cried Rhiannon, and Dewi repeated, thumping his fist into his palm, 'And I am next in line to Ifor when it comes to this responsibility—it is he who demands her place be laid at table, and I have backed him.'

'At a time like this the family should be alone,' said Rhiannon, and got up.

'Please do not go, Mrs. Mortymer.' Dewi turned from the window, smiling. 'I apologise for my behaviour to you. I did not know your man died fighting with the Chartists.'

'You want to get your values straight,' said my father, and the sound of him shocked us. 'She is accepted now, is she, now you know her husband died for the spirit of revolution.' He lumbered up. 'You are right, Mari, it would be best for you to go. One day, when I have got rid of this lot, I will come to you.'

'Mostyn, for God's sake,' whispered Gran.

Not staying in this morgue for supper. Away out of this, me.

If good women are so disturbing, we will find out what the wicked ones are made of.

16

NOBODY can really tell you about Cushy Cuddlecome's place: you have to drink Saturday night quarts in there to get the hang of it, and Friday night is no fool either, and this was the Friday of the six-week pay.

I ran fast down the cut, and there was a strange sickness rising in me at first, so I rested when I got to the Melin lock and watched the navvies at culvert work on night shift, with their whooahs and whip-cracks as their big horses towed the pipes: some were mares, but many were wonderful animals—entire horses from the blood yards of London: great white creatures with bodies steaming in moonlight. Panting, I shivered, remembering the *Y Ceffyl Dwr* the Water-horse who lived in the foam-cascades of the Mellte, whose hooves did not touch the pastures and whose mane floated in the clouds. Bogies and ghosties do bloody scare me, mind. Blood-curdling shrieks from the cellars under Neath Abbey, vampires who get through windows and cotton on to corpses even in the death-chamber, to say nothing of the church bells tolling in the sunken city at the bottom of Llyn Crymlyn. The poison-fish of Garn, the Frog of Hepste, which is the spirit of a hanging, do frit me stupid. Frit, frit to death I come when I see the winged serpents of Erwood and the Flying Dragon of Pont-Neath-Vaughan. It is all right somebody reading what I am writing now in a hundred years or so and calling me a Dai Dafto, for they do not live in my time. I tell you, I have seen them. Ghosties and canal bugguts, which the Midlanders brought into the Vale—these I often see, and when a clawed hand reaches up from weirs and such-like, you have got to watch it. I have personally witnessed the rock and water fairies milking cows, and into the milk they mix a herb potion, and go on a randy like the navvies on this stuff, dancing naked and singing in December frost: skidding on ice and playing touch-me-last, their lips stained black through eating windberries: windberries in December, mind—enough to frighten chapel folk to death. Lots of things happen in this Vale to congeal the blood: things like dancing corpse-candles, cocks crowing at midnight, pigeons perched on coal-tips, and buggy bo's and hobgoblins by the hundred, and these, remember, are not to be confused with the *tylwyth teg*, the fair and terrible ones, for these can be sods. I have known a pair of *tylwyth teg* chase Jacki Scog and Wil Screech home through the bogs after a thick night down in Neath, hanging on to their coat-tails and putting in the boot, and Jacki and Wil arriving in the Square, Resolven, emotionally done up and physically exhausted, and it took another three quarts to get some sense into them. Then take old Modryb Ann of Mellincourt; although she is not in my time, my father takes her story for gospel, since Dobi Revival, the preacher, told him, and he got it from Dai Swansea, who was second cousin to the mate on the ship that carried old Modryb Ann's nephew.

Dreadful, horrible is the story of old Modryb Ann, as told by her nephew.

Mind, all her life old Ann acted queer, with nightly visitations from a scarecrow in fetters who knocked on her lattice window round about midnight. And although the neighbours saw old Ann let him in, they were not particularly concerned since there were quite a few of the locals up to the same trick, and they were not wearing fetters.

But it was different, indeed, when Ann's nephew came home from the sea.

Bangs on the door and clanking at midnight, so naturally, he got up, and there, as large as life, was a grey mare standing on the cobbles and a skeleton standing by the door. 'Come in,' said Ann, opening it, and her nephew peeped through a crack in the floor, and watched the skeleton enter the kitchen. 'I am come for you,' said the skeleton, putting on a cloak. 'Sit a bit, boy,' Ann replied, 'I am not quite ready,' and she went into

137

her bedroom and came back wearing a shawl. 'This is the third time of asking, remember,' said the skeleton, 'tonight I am come to claim my bride,' and even as Ann's nephew watched, his heart turning to stone, the skeleton took old Ann's hand and gripped her waist, and they danced together on the cobbles of the kitchen. 'Right, you,' said the skeleton, 'we are off directly,' and he ran old Ann through the cottage door and on to the horse and they were away, the pair of them, and not a living soul in this valley have seen old Ann since.

The only corpse in this valley that doesn't possess a grave.

I can personally guarantee that this story is true, since I got it from my dada, and he got it from Dobi Revival, who, as his name implies, tends to the religious.

Some queer old things have happened down the Vale of Neath.

But nothing as queer as Cushy Cuddlecome's.

Away from the navvies now, with their threats to the Old Navigation: away over the aqueduct at Aberdulais I went like hell's hammers, and along the Tennant canal for Skewen, and I heard through the flowering moonlight the high shrieks of tickled women and the bass roars of men, and suddenly, round a bend on the tow-path, the Cuddlecome Inn came frowning up and blazing with light from its big, bay windows.

There was a shivering in me and a wet sweating, caused, perhaps, by the running, as I crept up to a cracked pane of glass and peered within.

Here is a dreadful sight for decent people.

Gran would have thrown a fit with legs up at the view.

The tap-room was jammed with elbowing, snarling men with pewters in their fists: ragged navvies on a randy from Brunel's railway, gipsy Irish, Frenchmen, Spaniards with gold earrings, and labouring Welsh. And they were roaring a chorus at the ceiling, boots stamping the time to the music of a melodeon played by an Irish tinker in a corner. And amid this convivial company, most with their back teeth awash, danced a tap-girl in crepe and scarlet, tight in the waist and most pleasant at the top, with her black hair swinging in plaits and tied with red ribbon.

I was beginning to realise I had a fever on me, and I reckon it went up ten points.

'Got a heart of gold on her, Welshman,' said a voice beside me, and I turned to it, shivering. Dim in the yellow light stood the Irish boy navvy I had first seen up at Cyfarthfa, and later when Dada flattened the Black Welshman.

'Ay, ay,' I said, nodding.

'Though it's not the heart that matters so much,' he added, 'but the beautiful things that go round it.'

'Do not be disgusting,' I said, shocked, and got my boot on a brick for a better view.

'Ach, no offence,' said the Irish. 'But since I'm arrived to meet her after the drinking, I'm flattening every chap round here with an eye on me rightful property.'

I weighed him. He had grown a bit. But even with a fever on there's a spare Welsh hook for an Irish chin, especially round the Skewen area.

'Are you married to her?' I asked, taking him off.

'I am not.'

'Then hop it.'

'Listen here,' said he, tapping me. 'She's not me wife, per- haps, but that woman's me food and drink and me pride and comfort, and if you continue to crack that window with your eye I'll paste you one that'll land you back in Cyfarthfa.'

'Fair enough. Shall we drink first?'

'It's a bountiful idea. Will a quart suffice ye? What's your name?'

I told him. He said, 'And mine's Tai Morlais, which is Welsh in the sound, though I'm as Irish as the fiddlers of County Mayo.'

I jerked my thumb at the tap-room. 'And she's as Welsh as a leek. Can't you keep your dirty hands off other people's nationality?'

'I would if I dare,' said Tai. 'But there's few educated Irish women round these parts, an' the ale tastes the same when the women are as soft as in Mayo, and so is Sian Edwards. Will you leave her free for me?'

I saw the girl instantly, profiled in dark beauty against the swinging lamps, her lips red and open, showing the straight white lines of her teeth in her sudden, tinkling laughter.

'Sure, I'll do my best,' I said, taking him off again, 'but I can't guarantee it . . . for you've got no authority, hobnobbing with decent people.'

'I'll have one on your chin at the first intimation,' said Tai.

'If you can reach it,' said I.

We shouldered our way into the bar. I was too excited to notice Dai Half-Moon cranked over a pint in the corner.

Into a swirling fug of tobacco and ale we went, elbowing a path through buckled stomachs and hairy arms, deafened by their bawdy, stamping chorus, which was all about a sweet Swansea girl who had fallen for a buck navvy from Working-ton, and how she shamed her dad and finished in the work-house with her guilt, and some bargees and navvies were in tears at the thought of her, since ale, when taken in quarts, has more ways than one out of a man. And Cushy Cuddlecome, the best pillow in the Vale, was standing on the counter, her size twelves stamping the time an inch from my nose, her sack dress billowing around my ears. Mop-lace cap awry and hanging down, fat face puckered up, she was bellowing the navvy chorus, one bare arm beating the time, her fist holding a quart of Cuddlecome Special, while below her a pair of wizened Irish navvies, an inch taller than leprechauns, danced an Irish jig, arming each other around in whoops of joy, their kicking hobnails raising the saw-dust to the screeching of an Irish fiddle.

'And around again we go me lovely boyos!' bawled Cushy, and stooped, heaving a big Lancashire bargee up on the counter beside her, and the pair of them prancing up and down now, lifting their knees in whoops, overturning tankards, flat-tening fingers and raising curses, with roars of laughter billow-ing about us as she up with her sack dress and showed her red garters.

'Good heavens,' I said, for it is disgraceful what a decent community can sink to when invaded by the likes of these: no prude, me—do not start that—in fact, pretty broad-minded, all things considered, but a middle-aged lady's legs do deserve to go under tents, especially venison haunches like Cushy Cuddlecome's.

Beside me Tai was hammering the counter for service, and getting nowhere, but as the tap-girl in scarlet and crepe swept by with her tray loaded I lifted a pair of pewter pints, and I had just got my teeth into mine when the sack dress came down and I was under Cushy Cuddlecome in a tangle of bare hams and petticoats.

'Away out of this,' I said, fighting free, and we got to a corner.

'Skin off your nose.'

'Spots on your belly.'

We drank like seven-foot colliers. Dear me. There is nothing in this world like the cold douche of a strong home-brew when it takes its dive to its death: explodes the lamp-light red in your clenched eyes. Open the gullet, and tip, for practised alers never swallow: drown, and come up gasping.

'Two things Cushy is good at,' cried Tai, 'and one is brewing ale.'

Aye, I thought, and if my dada was here just now he'd be raising six-inch lumps. Thoughts of my dada quietened me: very ashamed I felt with that pint inside me.

'You hungry, man?' shouted Tai.

'Starved.'

'Got money?'

'Six shillings,' I cried.

'Enough to drown us. Six shillings is ten Cuddlecome Specials apiece and a pair of Swansea tarts.'

'What is a Cuddlecome Special?' I asked, knowing that Swansea tarts were pastries with jam in, like by gran made back home. Eh, gorgeous, those tarts, Swansea or otherwise, made special for Sunday tea, crisp and brown but puddingy at the bottom where the jam had soaked in, and biting hot to the tongue.

'Hey, Bryn!' yelled Tai, and I pushed through the drinkers to a little table where Sian Edwards was working with a carving knife, slicing slices off a leg of lamb and hitting it between hunk doorsteps of black bread.

'Strangers, is it? There's handsome!'

141

Marvellous, mind, when beauties call you that.

'Ay, ay!'

'Never seen you before,' said she, 'but I've had an eye on your brothers!'

'You know him?' asked Tai, askance.

'I do now,' said Sian, and the look she gave me then sent me cold at the knees.

'My friend Bryn Evan,' announced Tai, and bowed before her, his mole-skin hat collecting the sawdust, and while he was down there with his neck in my hand this Sian Edwards went all cuddly in the shoulders and sweetened her lips at me, and I was just removing the table to get at her when Tai came up again and steered me into a corner. There we bit deep into the lamb doorsteps.

'Any good?'

'Aye,' I replied, 'but cheese and onion I prefer, mind.' Cheese and a Spanish onion is a meal and a half, I reckon, especially in summer to keep the flies away, said Dada, for my gran made cheese with a bite in it, never allowing it on the table until it could open the larder door and climb up there by itself, and we ate it, Dada, Ifor and me, like starving pariahs.

'You dry, Bryn, lad?' asked Tai, considerate.

'Dry as a powdered bone.'

'Jebers, this can't be,' said he, and swivelled on his stool to a bench where two brawny navvies were watching a cock being dressed for the ring, and he lifted one of their quarts and put back his empty, then shared the quart with me. And we had just parted our knees and getting into it when a fight started on the bench, for it is a mortal sin in Cushy's, apparently, to sink another's pewter : and while this was on Tai filched the other quart and we drank deep and gasping.

'Free beer is alive, eh?'

'Alive and kicking,' I said.

'This is nothing, man. Dead and buried you will be before you are finished. Where you going to be when your house comes down?'

'What do you mean?' I was seeing three of him.

'When Black Sam pulls down the Old Navigation?'

'Black Sam, how many wild horses, and what regiment of Guards?' I asked.

Tai held a bargee yorker aside and spat neatly in the spittoon and it belled like the toll of Doom. 'The railway pegs go right through the Old Navigation, says Black Sam. Out of the back door and through the front, according to the pegs, for I helped lay them.'

'The pegs miss us by twenty feet,' I shouted, getting up.

'Now, now,' commanded Tai, 'do not get your bowels twisted. Just giving you the tip, that's all. Your dada flattens Black Sam and Black Sam flattens the Old Navigation: an eye for an eye.'

'My dada will kill him,' I whispered.

'And while he is at it, a couple of thousand Brunel navigators. Drink up, boy, for you look miserable to death.'

I began to sweat. Sitting there swilling it down, waiting for the Swansea tarts, I began to sweat cobs, for the frippery women had started to come in from Neath and Swansea, and there were things going on in odd corners to make your hair stand on end, with dancing going on in the bedrooms and stop-it-Joes and please-don't-Derricks going on left and right: hollers and groans, and tables overturning in shrieks, glass crashing in tinkles and drunks teetering about on wooden legs, and hell was coming loose in a corner with the cock-fight.

Suddenly I saw my father's face: through a haze of sweat, hops and blasphemy, I saw him: Gran came next, spinning at her wheel, then Sharon, strutting about in a shawl as Desdemona.

Very strangely, also, I saw the face of Rhiannon.

'Excuse me, please, I am going from here,' I said, getting up.

'Back door only,' said Tai. 'Your hammering is waiting out the front.'

I put a sixpence on the table.

'Two more pints and don't forget the change.'

'At once, sir,' said Tai.

On my way out the back I saw the old men of the Vale clustered around the chimney-breast, their work-riven hands expressive before their toothless champings, for old men speak with their hands: and I saw in their sallow, ancient faces the peace of the cider-fields and gleanings, before the industry came in full measure, when the world was young. Leaving them to their chattering I parted a curtain and found myself in a rough flagged kitchen: here a bright fire was blazing: turning on a spit was a naked sheep; steam was billowing up, flames spearing blue and gold to his hissing fat, a martyr of Mankind.

Being about six pints aboard and now hot enough to boil a kettle on, I bowed to him because at the time it seemed polite. 'Good evening,' I said.

The spit turned his blistered face to mine, and I saw in his glazed eyes the agony of his slow roasting, and he looked to me that moment as alive as a market-day sale: hand him back his horns and hooves and he'd have been through Cushy Cuddle-come and up the mountain.

Sian Edwards appeared just then with a carving knife and a plate to remove his left leg. 'Wrong house, boyo,' said she. 'First door on the left and second turning right.'

Even in that swimming room she was beautiful: no freckled school-girl, this, with carrots for hair and a tiger-nut in her cheek: this was eighteen, I reckoned, her arms round and white, her fingernails unbitten.

'Did Tai tell you I was his girl?'

'Aye, Sian,' I said.

'Well, I am not, for I am Welsh—Gower Welsh, mind, which is real, and it is Welsh to Welsh I have in mind. Is that handsome brother of yours still putting it over Alfo Morgan up at the Lamb and Flag?'

'So they say.'

She came nearer. 'Beautiful family, mind, especially that Dewi, though your Ifor was not behind the door when they handed out bodies. See now, here is a key. If any member of your family do fancy an hour or two with Sian, they are welcome, though I naturally prefer the males.'

Kindness do come from unexpected sources, and she drew from her bodice a key big enough for Swansea jail, and it was hot in my hand as I gripped it in my pocket. She added, over her shoulder, 'First floor, first left, first door. There is gorgeous is a midnight visitation,' and she leaned over, eyes shut, and kissed my lips. 'And be careful lest you land in with Cushy.'

First floor, first left, first door, and don't land in with Cushy.

If Dewi or Ifor saw the ceiling over Sian's attic it would be a bloody miracle.

Coming in from the back I heard a low whining from the other side of the fire: through the half-open curtain I saw the tap-room drinkers at it in a fury and fights were starting: the fighting cocks were locked in a steel embrace of beaks and spurs and blood; money chinked in saw-dust.

Again the faint whine, and I went round a board to the other side of the chimney-breast.

On the trundling-wheel that turned the spit a little dog was working: behind the tattered tarpaulin that was supposed to protect her from the heat, she treadled blindly, eyes closed to the spiking glare.

'Ay, ay, *fach*,' I said to her, and she paused to stare, then trundled like something demented, afraid of a stick.

You keep your god of men and leave me mine.

'*Dammo*, girl, wait a bit,' I said, stroking her and she turned her frizzled little face to mine. Picking up my ale I tipped the pewter to her mouth and she drank madly, not knowing ale from water, eyes rolling in fear.

'You drink,' I said. 'Anyone stopping you I will flatten.'

No sound I heard then but her gusty breathing: in a scrape of scorched pads, tongue lolling, she started off again. Her back was burned pie-bald where the coals had jumped; near blind, she was, where the fat had spattered.

I wept, but I think it was the ale.

Then, as if called, a woman parted the curtains leading to the tap-room: a woman with the body of a yard broom and a face like a hatchet and what the hell is going on here and get out sharp, or you will get this instead of the bitch, and she raised a stick.

'Only giving it a drink,' I said, in sudden fury.

'And might ye realise the sheep's in flames next door?' Bog Irish, this one. Out, *out*! Feeding the thing beer, indeed! You'll have it as tipsy as a coot!' She stood before me in her rags and madness, her skeleton arms waving; this single-fare ticket that was the tragedy of Ireland: the ballast that could walk from the famines and unload itself at Fishguard.

I shouted, 'The thing's nearly dead, woman. If you don't water it occasionally you'll be turning the spit yourself.'

'Well, the bloody cheek of it! Did ye hear that? Beering up the tread-mill is against the regulations, and I'm hauling you up before Cushy Cuddlecome!'

Ducking under the rod, I slipped the dog's collar and hooked her off the wheel into my arms. 'Now, then,' I said, and went for the door, but she swished the stick, and I took it on the shoulder, staggering back. She shrieked:

'Take that! You put that dog back on the treads, Welsh-man, or as God's me judge, I'll flog the livin' daylights out of the pair of ye.' Turning, she screamed, 'Beef O'Hara, Mick O'Shea! Will you come and handle this Welsh hooligan?' and she swung another, but I ducked it.

A voice from the bar shouted, 'What's happening to the spit? Sure, the sheep's on fire and goin' to a bloody cinder!'

Crouching, I darted for the door, but the stick came down and I took it on the face. 'One move, ye limb of Satan,' whispered the woman. 'Just one more move and I'm splittin' ye skull for you!'

Back went the tap-room curtains, then a mob spilled into the room, Cushy Cuddlecome leading; shapeless, her face flushed to its rolling fat, her dress untied at the waist. 'What's up?' she demanded, gasping.

'It's this mad Welsh. He's after stealing the wee animal entirely, an' it's me for stoppin' him.

Cushy put up her fist. 'Put that tyke down, son, for I'm warning ye. Put it down or me and mine'll hand you a shellack-ing that'll last ye down to the fourth generation. . . .'

'What ails ye, Bryn?' shouted Tai. 'Have ye gone de-mented?'

'Aye,' I said, and stopped, gripping a firing-iron. 'And if anyone wants this dog, they come for it.'

'I'm coming,' said Beef O'Hara, and hooked up a chair, snapping off the legs, tossing one to Mick O'Shea. 'Take him either side, boyo, by God we'll give him thieving Welshman.'

The back door went back on its hinges as I lifted the firing-iron, and it butted Cushy in the rear, sending her floundering into the others: Dewi came first, ducked a chair-leg from Beef O'Hara and laid the prettiest left hook I have ever seen on Mick O'Shea as he rushed. Pietro Bianca kicked Beef's shins and Ifor clubbed him down from above: my father came in through the tap-room, leaving a trail of dead and dying and hauling women aside. Holding Cushy at arm's length he shouted, 'What are you doing in this filthy place?'

He shouted again, but I did not hear him, but I saw him shimmering in a world of sweat and pain: I remember dropping the firing-iron, I remember the little dog howling; then nothing.

Later, I heard Dewi say, 'Soaked with sweat, he is, his shirt is sopping.'

I opened my eyes to an avenue of stars and rushing trees, and felt the strength of Ifor about me, the grip of his thick arms as he took another lift on me, and he rumbled deep in his bull chest:

'What was he doing in Cushy's place, anyway?'

'That's what Dai Half-Moon wanted to know,' said Dada.

'Thank God for Dai Half-Moon for once,' said Dewi.

In my fever I made a mental note to crack the skull of Dai Half-Moon.

'Dada . . .' I said.

'Hush, Bryn, Ifor has got you.'

Silence now: an otter whistled from Rheola. So clear I heard him, and saw his whiskered snout: urgent whispers on the tow-path as they hauled me around and I smelled the tobacco smell on my father's hair, its curls rough on my face, and heard through his loins the thumping of his boots as he carried me.

'Is he just plain drunk?'

'Don't be a fool, Ifor. Dewi, put your coat over him, he is shivering to have his bones out.'

147

'Is it a fever?' asked Dewi, covering me in my father's arms.

'Here, give a hand,' whispered Dada. 'Hurry, for God's sake. The boy has the cholera.'

The cholera. The *cholera*!

You dodge the thing in Merthyr and pick it up at Cushy Cuddlecome's.

17

THERE are many ways of dying with the cholera, the old people say, and this varies with the religion of the patient. Church of England folk, for instance, take it pretty hard according to the Welsh Nonconformists, being boiled to a puddle, a foretaste of things to come. Roman Catholics, considered by the Established Church to be equally misguided, rarely pull through, while disbelievers, who worship pagans like Cushy Cuddlecome, die worst of all; in froth, shrieks and speechless agony, also, these die, their spines arching to the satanic heat as a stick withers in fire, the soles of their feet touching their heads in the final paroxysms of dying.

One thing was certain. Whatever the religion, if you caught the cholera off Dai Central Eating, or anybody else in the 'fifties, you were almost surely booked for cloud eternity. However, a few did get through for one reason or another. There are some, said my father, though qualified for Heaven in some respects, were unqualified in others—such as midnights spent in tap-rooms in the company of doubtful young ladies, and others so contaminated with navvy brew that a self-respecting cholera germ couldn't get a proper hold.

And since you come into both these categories, said he, I am not surprised to see you alive on the fifteenth day, which was an important day with the Old Cholera.

I opened my eyes to bright sunlight, I remember, with the fever broken, and saw beside me the face of Mari Mortymer: sheet-white that face, the cheeks proud and humped with weariness, the eyes black in shadow, as if the cholera had entered the stable in his rags and bowed with his scythe before her.

'I am here, Bryn,' she said, and I turned towards her, seeing the agitation growing on her face. And then her eyes opened wide and she rose in the straw, ran to the stable door and flung it wide, shrieking, 'Mostyn, Mostyn!'

If she had set the barn alight she could not have caused more commotion.

Out came Dada with lather on his face, cut-throat razor waving, then Gran, already bucketing and supported by Rhiannon and Sharon. Ifor was blundering around shouting with joy, and even Dewi wandered into the yard, grinning, his thumbs in his belt. Like a family of old retainers they came to pay me court, standing strangely silent at a respectful distance, for there must have been cholera germs as big as banana spiders flying off me still. Mari cried:

'It is broken, the fever is broken. Oh, Mostyn!'

From his eyes, skidding over the yard cobbles between them, came his love for her.

'Where is Gwen?' I asked.

'Up at Glyn Neath, she will be back soon.'

Ifor shouted, 'Back down at Cushy's first opportunity, eh, man?'

'You can pick up some queer old things in Cushy's, eh?' said Dewi.

'Do not attend them,' said Mari. 'Very impertinent, they are—you have never been within a mile of that dreadful place, have you?'

A man's woman, this one. 'No,' I said.

Gran now, mainly unintelligible, blowing and streaming one moment and smiling the next, and thank God he is going to be all right now, my prayers having been answered, the special notice given out in Resolven chapel being mainly responsible. 'And down to skin and bone, he is, poor boy.'

'Mostly in the buttocks,' said Dewi. 'For a boy of his age it shows mostly in the buttocks.'

'Aye, when the buttocks sink on a man it is a sign of general dilapidation,' said Gran.

'We will have to build you up, Bryn.' My father was unusually quiet, and I put this down to his displeasure. Mari said quickly:

'Good beef broth is what he needs, eh, Gran: if you put it on a skid-tray, Rhiannon will bring it.'

'Up on your feet this time tomorrow, remember,' said Dewi, 'do not make a meal of it.'

Rhiannon came nearer and my father drew her back. 'Thank God you are better, Bryn,' she said.

And with this Sharon wept softly, her hands over her face.

It took a strange path, this cloud of relief and love hanging over the house.

I lay back with all the sounds of the stable about me, the rustling of mice, bird-quarrels, the comforting chinking of Nell's chain, the stamp of Jed's feet: all the song and smell of life flooded into me; the golden scent of straw, the acrid tang of urine, while through the open door came the reedy earth-smells of the cut. I listened for sounds of the house, but none came: as dead, that house, its laughter coffined in its relief, perhaps.

'Friend of yours, Bryn.' Mari now, kneeling beside me, holding in her arms the little Cuddlecome bitch, and it strained and whined to be near me, and pretty good somebody had done her, with her body fatter and her coat brushed clean.

'Why are you in here with me?' I asked.

She rose with a shrug. 'Somebody had to nurse you. Gran was abed when your father brought you in. Doctor Brodie came from Glyn Neath and put the pair of us in the stable to keep it clear of the family.'

The wonderful Doctor Brodie who later gave his life to cholera, for the people of Glyn Neath.

'How long have you been here with me?'

She was rolling up her sleeves and tying back her hair, being with business.

'This is the fifteenth day. Hush now, and rest. A strip-wash for you first, and then Gran's broth. Fighting fit you will be with that inside you.'

'Hey, Mari!' called Dewi from the yard, and he and Ifor carried a brimming bath and lowered it on to the skid-tray and threw her the rope, and she braced herself, heaving, and skidded it into the stable.

'Everything off, remember,' called Dewi. 'You cannot do him justice all done up in night-shirts.'

'Eh, go on with you,' said she, very pretty with her.

'Every mortal stitch, remember—off!' bawled Ifor.

Yet when they turned away their faces they were not with smiles, I noticed.

I turned my eyes from her as she bent to me.

She said she was a mam, but she looked more like eighteen. Indecent, it is, to lie helpless before a woman, one so young. And there is obscenity in the body after cholera: the sunken ribs, the sagging parchment of a belly that once was ribbed with muscle, the white, scrawny loins of the aged. I clenched my hands, and she said:

'Do not make it hard, Bryn. Indecent, they are. Personally, I do not put much store on this business of privates.'

'Not proper,' I said. 'Only you and me in by here.'

'Would you have me call your dada and give him the cholera?'

She had my night-shirt in her hand and I stared at it. She said, 'Good God, man. I put it on, surely I can take it off,' and I grinned at this.

'What about you getting it, then?'

'Old boots, me, she said, sluicing water over my body. 'And I have had it once. If the scythe don't chop you in half first time, it only skins your ribs next. Front done, over you go. Much better looking that way round.'

I saw behind her the tip of Resolven mountain with her head in the clouds, and the sun raging golden down the cut where the rooks were holding the annual Parliament in quick flourishes of the wind.

'Do not go, Mari Mortymer,' I said, and though her hands paused she made no sign that she had heard me. Later, she wrapped me in a towel and I lay back as she went to the door and combed and tidied her hair. She said:

'Welcomes are like door-mats, Bryn. They wear out under the feet.'

*   *   *

Dusk came, with bats, and I listened to the banter of the cut as the bargees went down to Briton Ferry: distantly, I heard the hammering of the railway navvies. Mari was sitting on a stool by the stable door, the dog was sleeping under my hand: lazily rose the Vale moon, in dripping silver. I said:

'How near is the line?'

'Gone past us—up half a mile to Rheola locks.' Beautiful her face against the rising moon. 'They missed the house by thirty feet.'

'I haven't heard the Corsairs going through.'

'There is argument about a branch line, your father says. He has been down to Neath seeing Mr. Seth Cowbum, the solicitor.'

She smiled at me in the half light, adding, 'There is a gorgeous name, Mr. Seth Cowbum!'

'Rather him than me,' I said.

'There is an agent called Man Arfon, and he wants the house down for the branch line.'

'Man Arfon!' I slowly sat up.

'Rest yourself, he will never be a match for your dada. Some dada, you have got, you realise this?'

'Yes.'

'Do not be a grief to him, Bryn. Girls like Sian Edwards are not his style.' Getting up, she wandered to my jacket hanging on a nail and fished out Sian's key, and this she held in front of me, smiling, impish. 'There is bad luck,' she said. 'Must have missed it by inches.'

Hot and cold now. A terror, this one. She said, still smiling, 'Were I a man I would give Sian a run for it, but sixteen years old is only a boy.' She emptied her hands at me. 'Drink, if you like—fight, chew, smoke if you like, but do not seek out the secrets of girls—not yet. Give it a rest for a year or so, there's a good boy.'

I did not reply, and she winked. 'Hot to melt she will be for you by the time you are twenty.'

With this she stood on the stool and put the key on the wall-plate in the eaves, saying, 'She hands out more attic keys than the flesh-pots of Gomorrah, that Sian. And even if you got past Cushy you'd find them queueing at the door.' She tucked the key out of sight. 'Sian Edwards is yours on the night you can reach it.'

Some woman, this one. I gave her a grin.

'All the time in the world, Bryn,' she said at the moon, 'all the time in the world. And now, up on your feet as soon as you like, for I'm sick to death of being cooped up in this stable while you lie there like a lazy old lump.'

'Do not go, Mari,' I said.

'Stay around here with you hooligans? Not on your life.'

'Do not go, Mari,' I said.

They said I slept for three days after that, and when I awoke I asked for my sister Gwen, but she was still up at Glen Neath, said Mari.

But it was her eyes.

Eyes, like the tongue, can betray, but they cannot lie.

'Gone, is she?' I asked.

'Yes, Bryn.'

'The cholera?'

'Aye.'

I bowed my head, 'How ... how long?'

'Last week we took her up to Vaynor, to be with your mam.'

I wept.

'Do not make it harder, Bryn; most of the tears have been cried.' She held my face in her hands. 'For the sake of Dada, and Gran ... ?'

'Aye.' I did not say more.

In the 'fifties, in Wales, we shut the door and turned the key.

Later that night my father came into the stable and wrapped me in a blanket, and carried me into the kitchen. And while they were preparing to sit at table there was a great palaver about is he too cold or too hot, and setting me straight, and Sharon fetched a pair of bricks out of the oven and wrapped them in flannel. I sat there lording it over them, stinking of goose fat.

It was the first time since my illness that Mari had been in the kitchen. I watched her smooth, proud face; saw the flushed beauty of Rhiannon, her eyes rising at me over the white, starched cloth. I saw my father's questioning glance at Mari, and saw her secret nod.

I saw, too, that Gran's lips were trembling. Sharon was sitting stiffly, her eyes red, sick of weeping: my brothers were in a holy silence.

After Gran had served the supper my father rose at the head of the table, and said, 'Grace indeed tonight, O Lord. Bless those who have been taken from us in Thy holy Name; my wife, and Gwen, my daughter; keep them in Thy heart. Our thanks to Thee for bringing my son back into this kitchen, cleansed, free of the cholera. The people of this house give thanks for the blessing of Thy holy Name, O Lord Jesus.'

Nobody moved for a bit after this, but when Mari broke her bread, my brother Dewi broke his also, his dark eyes smiling at her: there was no sound but the ticking of the clock.

I watched them.

One by one, they broke bread with Mari Mortymer, the last being my father. Then suddenly Ifor lumbered to his feet like a bear with honey. Mari and Rhiannon opened wide eyes at him as he took Mari's hand, and drew her to her feet.

In silence, my brother Ifor led her to the chair that belonged to my mother, and set her there facing my father at the head of the table.

Head bowed, she sat, unmoving, her fingers twisting in her lap. And even when Ifor took his place again, she did not lift her face.

My father picked up his knife and fork and went at his supper.

'Eat, woman, eat,' he said.

18

AND SO, in summer, my father took the woman Mari Mortymer to Resolven Zion and brought her out as wife. July, I
think, is a bad month for a marriage, since there hangs in this
month the threatened death of summer. *Calan Haf*, which is
what the old ones call it, is the month for me, the very birth of
the summer year. On the first day in May I will take my
woman to the pastor, for I will not parade a fruitful lady
before the gold of a dying year.

But *Calan Haf* or *Calan Gaeaf*, May or November, it was
good to have a mother back in the house again.

Never have I seen such a palaver as there was in the preparations for the bidding; everybody up at cock-shout, Ifor in
the bosh, and me, Dewi and Dada under the pump shaving
extra close and shouting for slippery eel for cuts, and for days
now the women had been prancing around in crinoline bunting, with yards of this and that over their arms and holding it
up to the light, speaking with pins in their mouths and scissors
and needles in their fingers.

'How do I look?' asked Ifor, going in a circle in the yard.

Very tarted up was Ifor, in his long white gown, coloured
ribbons pinned to his shoulder and more flying free on the end
of his long, white staff, the official uniform of the marriage-
bidder.

'What you doing tonight?' I asked, peering inside his gown.

'Gran!' he shouted. 'Bryn is sissying me again.'

Out she came with fists and threats, and you'd better get off
if you have nothing better to do, and then Dewi appeared
dressed the same, clomping over the cobbles in hobnails.

'God, no!' I said. 'Ribbons in the hair, too, is it?'

Mind, it was not fair to take the water, for this bidding
business was a pretty affair, and much better than this stupid
new-fangled post for a penny idea.

'Right, you,' said Gran. 'Quiet, everyone. We will have this
done properly, or not at all. Recite slow, clear and do it in

chorus,' and Ifor and Dewi, after a bit of boot-tapping and nicking, cried:

'Pleased I am to relate, we being bidders of a wedding between Mostyn Evan of the Old Navigation and Mistress Mari Mortymer, both residing in the hamlet of Resolven...' They faltered, staring at each other.

'Oh, for God's sake!' said my father, distressed.

'Forgot it, Da.'

He shook his head. 'Whoever suggested this pair of nitwits for the bidding...' and Mari's voice rang out:

'Come on, come on! "Back home after the wedding..." Come on!'

I was creased with laughter, stamping about.

'Do not be a pig, Bryn!' whispered Rhiannon, eyes afire.

Fingers locked on their stomachs, eyes turned up, shoulders swaying like a pair of school-girls, they continued, 'Back home after the wedding there will be clean chairs to sit upon, a leg of mutton and home-fed pork to eat, boiled by the bride personally...'

'Boiled by me personally,' said Gran.

'Boiled by Gran personally, also for each guest a quart of Cuddlecome brew...'

'Lamb and Flag brew, if you please,' interjected Dada. 'I have had enough talk of that Cuddlecome place to last me six weddings.'

'...Lamb and Flag brew, with small-beer for the ladies and children. Please to come, then...'

'Oh, Ifor,' wailed Mari. 'Be happy for me. Glum as coffin lids you are, do not look like that!'

'Bloody daft we look, mind,' said Ifor, brushing ribbons.

'Stop that!' cried Gran. 'Dafter you will end if you do not go into it proper. Right, finish it, and remember that nothing Welsh is daft.'

'Please to come, then,' they sang, 'and bring a hen, a turkey or a chicken—even a piece of bread, which the house can afford.'

'*Anything* the house can afford,' groaned Dada, lathering up. 'Some queer old characters we will have arriving sending that cuckoo pair as bidders.' He levelled his shaving-brush at them. 'And remember one thing—do not accept money.'

'Aye, Dada,' said Dewi, and my father turned away, saying, 'I do not agree with this, Mother. You realise they will be boots up in every establishment from here to Swansea, and we won't see them till Easter.'

'One whiff—one sniff at their breath and they will have me to account to, you understand?'

'Yes, Gran.'

'And try to look happy!' begged Mari.

I stood on the horse-mount as they went off, sending mating whistles after them.

'Enough of that, you—into the house,' cried my father.

'Eh, bless St. David! That was a glorious summer day in old Resolven, and the things Ifor and Dewi brought in filled the house. There was a pair of canal ducks from Dai Half-Moon, while Mrs. Ten Benyon who was living down by Neath Abbey sent a soup bowl. Mr. and Mrs. Isan Chapel sent a painting of a child found drowned, and Eli Cohen sent a pig on the hoof, led by Willie Dare, who went all coy and simpering at the sight of Sharon. Cushy Cuddlecome had a keg of ale rolled up by Abe Sluice and sent her regrets for absence, for there were three potential customers at the Old Navigation, and Cushy always had an eye to business. Mrs. Willie Shenkins baked eight pounds of bread, and brought it personally, with congratulations to Mari, breaking down on the doorstep. There was a cracked wash-basin from Dai Central Eating, who, thank God for our Doctor Brodie, was over the cholera, and I swear the swine unloaded it on to me. Mr. and Mrs. Alfo Morgan sent kind respects and Rosie Carey a pillowcase with Valentine hearts entwined with roses, very romantic was Miss Carey: Mrs. Hanman on the Old Glamorgan came with five meat hooks and half a leg of mutton, which Gran cried over, saying she couldn't afford it. There were dozens of well-wishers, and Ifor and Dewi were loaded with gifts from folk you would never expect, like Mr. and Mrs. Abe Sluice, and even Betsy Small-Coal sent a sampler she had stitched herself with 'Together' embroidered in silk on satin, and where she got the money from for that I shall never know, said Gran.

Mind, it is when you go up in the frock coat and down in the wooden suit—this is when real friends remember you, said my father.

'Aye,' said Gran, 'that is the answer. Up and down without a stain on the soul.'

Naturally, though, we took note of the people who hadn't sent anything, for though there is good in everybody and some of the poor souls can't afford it, according to Gran, there were also a few mean bastards who could and didn't, said Ifor.

I will always remember my little marriage because it was to Rhiannon: but nobody in Resolven hamlet will ever forget the summer day in July when my dada married beautiful Mari Mortymer.

Very stiff and starched; nervous laughs and coughs, and dust on the velvet collar and a piece of cotton on the crinoline: the men of the family stood like statues in the yard: the women held their hearts with palpitations, and Gran got a fit of the vapours just before we left, and had to be fanned round.

All right to laugh, mind, but a very exacting business is a marriage.

But, oh! These two Mortymer women, Mari and Rhiannon, do take the breath.

'Slip the big one over the county border,' whispered Dewi, 'and I would wed her myself.'

'Bryn!' called my father, and I ran to him. 'You are youngest son, so your new mother will ride with you. Take the big mare Mr. Ephraim Davies was good enough to lend us,' and my heart was thumping with pride as I led lovely Mari up the mount-steps, and helped her on side-saddle, then swung my leg over the mare's back, gripping Mari with my forearms.

'Right,' said Dada, tightening the girth, 'make yourself scarce—but no risks, remember—no big fences. Injure her, and I will see to you.'

'Yes, Dada.'

'See you in Chapel, Mari!'

'God willing, Mostyn.'

Like a Greek god I felt sitting there on that big mare's back, with Mari in my arms. The wind moved over her face, and it was perfumed to my nostrils.

Do not be mistaken: I was a boy no longer. Six-foot-one in socks, a bit stringy round the flanks perhaps, but coming thick in the shoulders and thews, and a blurr of hair coming on the chest. And the yard was filled with people, every barge coming down the cut was mooring up and their crews piling ashore, standing six deep around the gate with their flannel shirts and mole-skin caps, the men touching their hair as I took Mari past with a stately tread, for this was a mare for special occasions, the women dropping down in curtseys, the little children bowing. Too much for Gran: nearly soaked, was Gran, and we had not even started. Down went Rhiannon and Sharon, fingers clasped; firm friends, these two. And as we reached the gate I looked up at the small attic window of the Old Navigation, and saw in the eye of my mind the small, white face of my beloved Gwen.

Still: dry up; enough sadness for a wonderful day.

'Eleven o'clock at Zion—don't you dare be late!' cried my father, and there was a thunder of banter and clapping in the yard.

'If you catch us first!' I cried, and gave the heels to the big grey mare, and we were away, hooves thumping along the tow-path until we came to the Nedd bridge, and here I tamed her, and we took it slow, walking in shafted sunlight and bridle jingles into the forest tracks of Rheola.

Just me and Mari in the whole world, then, walking in hoof and heart-beats in the ancient forest of Rheola.

Shon Seler Shonko, the Poacher of Rheola, was untying his snares: wild in the eye was Shon, fresh back from Van Land for taking salmon from the Towey over in Carmarthenshire, and he staggered back in his rags, the coney hard against his chest.

Good hunting, is it, Mr. Shonko?' cried Mari.

Broken mouthed, he grinned at her, and I saw on his skinny arms the lash of the blood-soaked triangles, for a clergyman-magistrate had him for a ten pound hen, and ten years Shon

Seler Shonko did, less the voyage out and back.

'Good luck, missus! Oh, ah! Good luck, I say, lady!'

He walked alongside us, hand on the bridle.

'Got to go now, Shon,' I said.

In his riven back I saw the misery of my generation.

'You take the coney, missus? Take the coney and eat it for the wedding breakfast, eh?'

'Hop it, Shon,' I said.

'No, wait,' said Mari. 'You want me to have it, Mr. Shonko?'

'Ah, missus, by Christ I do. You have it for the luck of it, comin' from a rag-tailed old sod like me—will ye take it, in good nature?'

'And pleased to, Mr. Shonko,' said she, hooking up the rabbit.

'And right good fortune to ye, missus—a good and gentle man wi' you!'

'God bless you,' she said, and pressed his filthy hand.

And she spurred the mare with her heels, shouting, 'Goodbye, Mr. Shonko. Put some speed in it, Bryn, lad—are we hanging around all day?'

'When he come a-hunting ye, I'll send him opposite way!' roared Shon Seler Shonko. 'Isn't proper that a man should transgress such an apple of a woman!'

We thundered over the moss of Rheola, swaying through the massed trees, ducking under branches, shouting with excitement, as if she was my bride being pursued, and not my father's, with Shon Shonko's rabbit in my pocket and the big mare lively beneath us.

'Stop!' commanded Mari, and turned in the saddle as I reined the mare. 'An apple of a woman, is it?' She blew out her cheeks and made herself big. 'Transgressed, is it? But it do depend, Shon Shonko, on the manner of the man doin' the transgressing!' and she shrieked with laughter.

In a stamping of hooves and quickening hearts we went past Crugau, turning south before the House of Vaughan, and there was a love in me for the woman soon to be my mother.

Heisht in Chapel now, waiting for the bride, sitting in

beams of sunlight watching the dust-motes dance. Listening to Mrs. Tref Hopkins on the harmonium with Mrs. Arfon Shavings turning her pages: coins and keys rattling, trews square on the mahogany, boots square on the floor. Dubbined toe-caps and socks with no toes in, shirt-fronts with no arms and tails, boots with no feet in come up from the pit, sleeves with no arms in pinned at the shoulder. Da Point-Five is propped in the pew, trews with no legs in, singing *All Things Bright and Beautiful* in a glorious bass. Up for the hymn now, alpaca bulging on the shoulders of the colliers, Butcher Shinbone is standing in a pool of blood. Billie Softo is standing in his rags, dreaming of bread and butter: collywobbles from Mr. Evans Brewer, dreaming of ale. Give him a glance, shift your boots on the boards, for the collies become booms and the wobbles become thunder, and he goes blue and bucolic, does Evans Brewer, and explodes in sherry scarlets and foaming fizz and frothing golden ale in a sheet of white gin and cider amber, expiring on the pew in a gentle zizz. Sure as Fate it will happen one day, says Dada.

Lovely Tom Davies is there as sidesman, and the medical profession very well-represented, with Mrs. Teague the Herbalist who did our Gwen's whitlow and cured Dai In and Out's yellow jaundice by enchantment, and he wasn't in and out of the Vaughan for a month; also good at the lobe-cutting for children with rickets, top half ears only being evident in Resolven.

'Oh, look!' ejaculated Gran, behind me. 'Here comes that beautiful Zion Revivalist!'

'You know him?' asked Rhiannon.

'She should do,' I said, 'he practically transported her a few years back up in Merthyr Bethania.'

And down the aisle came the preacher like some gigantic patriarch, white mane of hair flowing, spade beard over his waistcoat, and behind him came a young man, tall and handsome. Rhiannon whispered excitedly, 'The preacher's name is Tomos Traherne, and the young man is my cousin sort of.'

At this the young man turned and smiled at her, his fierce, dark eyes softening in his face, and I made a mental note to keep an eye on him.

'*Duw*,' said Sharon, 'he can be my cousin sort-of any time he likes.'

'Hush, you lot,' whispered Gran, 'here comes the bride.'

Large and handsome my father looked in his frock coat and trews hired special from Hobo Churchyard, and Mari was young and enchanting on his arm: as regal as a queen she was, her face lifted in a smile as she walked to the Seat, and we got into the I do's and sicknesses and cherishings, which brought out Gran's bedsheet handkerchief which she kept special for weddings. Then Moses Thomas gave out the bessing hymn and Mrs. Tref Hopkins opened her shoulders and we were into the *All Hail the Power*, which was Mari's selection since she used to sing it back home in Camarthenshire. A good old corker, this one, and I reckon the Lord Jesus enjoys it as much as I do, and the Resolven congregation let it fly that lovely morning of my father's wedding. Bass and tenor, soprano and contralto, in full harmony, and the rafters shivered to the blast of sound when something moved in the pocket of my coat.

Sweating, me, and I put a curse on the soul of Shon Shonko.

'You all right, Bryn?' asked Rhiannon prettily.

'Right as rain,' I said.

Back to life had come that Shonko coney and now kicking me in the ribs like a six foot collier.

Trying to sing now, as if nothing was happening, and stuffing the bloody thing back into my pocket every time it popped out.

'*Diawch!*' rumbled Ifor behind me. 'Hey, Bryn, lad,' and he tapped me.

'What?' I said, turning.

'Do not look now, man, but there is a coney sitting up in your pocket.'

'A what?' asked Sharon.

'A coney—sitting in his pocket,' said Ifor.

'Do not talk daft,' replied Sharon.

'Hey, Gran . . .' muttered Ifor, while I cursed him, stuffing the coney back.

And just then it was up and out and running along the hymn shelf hitting up people's hymnals, raising shrieks of delight

162

from the children and walking-sticks clattering as bruisers like Dai In and Out tried to hit him cold. And then, to my horror, I saw the Revival preacher fixing me with an eagle eye.

'He'll have you, mind,' said Sharon, 'bringin' coneys into Chapel.'

Now the coney was sitting petrified between Dada's boots, now snitching round the hem of Mari's dress, giving me palpitations, for the very last thing ladies love is things like mice and conies going up and under. Now he was prancing along the harmonium, and you could see he was wondering how the hell he had landed in here from the forest of Rheola, and every kid in the place was up on the pews pointing and shrieking before being dragged down and stifled. And then I went sweating cold, for one moment he was sniffing at Mrs. Tref Hopkins' boots as they went up and down on the bellows, and next moment he was under.

'Gone up Mrs. Tref Hopkins,' rumbled Ifor in my ear.

'Do what, love?' asked Gran, taking a breath for the last verse.

'Bryn's coney, Gran. Just seen it, I have. Gone up Mrs. Tref Hopkins, see.'

'Aye, indeed, son. We will have a good strong cup the moment we are back. Sing up, there's a good lad.'

I watched Mrs. Tref Hopkins in terror, for she was already off the note and in trouble with the bellows, and never in my life have I seen such an expression on the face of a lady, which is perfectly understandable because harmoniumists have a right to perform safe in the knowledge that Rheola conies will not start walking up their legs, especially in Chapel. Now the last line coming up and she hit the keys in glorious crescendo, getting the *hwyl* right up her apron, and next moment she was boots up and music down, with the coney rushing out and people kneeling and fanning her and is she all right now and for God's sake fetch Mrs. Teague the Herbalist, since Mrs. Tref Hopkins do not appear to be herself this morning.

'Excuse me, please,' I said, 'I am going from here,' for that Revivalist preacher was on his way down the aisle towards me, his staff striking the flags like a Swansea gaoler.

Bright sunlight hit me in the porch, and there, to my

astonishment, stood Shon Shonko the Poacher as large as life, grinning like a barbary ape and with a string of conies hanging from his belt.

'Just come wi' a few more, I 'ave,' said he. 'That lovely bride, she took my hand—me, old Shon Shonko, an' I reckon she's entitled to a few more rabbits for the wedding breakfast, oh, ah!'

Very fast I went down to the river, to save me the sin of murder.

'Why!' yelled Shonko, indignant. 'No call for that, young fella—that's no sort o' language, and you just received the blessin' of Chapel!'

I did not stop until I reached the Old Navigation.

19

THE year my father brought Mari Mortymer as wife to the Old Navigation was like a bright eye in a face of joy. A new man was he, re-born, even larger, it appeared to me; singing in the tub before the fire while she swabbed him after the Pont Walby coaling, digging in the garden, with cheery waves even to the passing men of the new railway. It is amazing to me the effect a good wife can have upon a man, and I am sick and tired of stories about shrews and harridans with six-inch tongues lashing their men into one gin-shop after another, and I am not surprised they get belted occasionally.

'Aye, well, that is it, see,' said Gran. 'It do depend largely upon what direction they are sent from. A Baal hand-maiden can be picked up in saw-dust, but you got to sweep the dust of the chapel to find the jewel that is one like Mari,' and with this she got into the moral virtues and contrary vices, adding, ' "A prudent wife is from the Lord, and whoso findeth a wife findeth a good thing, and obtaineth favour of the Lord." '

Which was a pretty sweeping statement, it was proved later.

My father had found a beautiful wife, but with her came a beautiful basket of trouble.

I suppose, looking back, you can't expect to hit out a man like the Black Welshman and get away with it, or make enemies of people like Man Arfon who was now large in the new railway, to say nothing of the uneasy peace between Dada and Tub Union for working a private contract.

Summer faded into autumn, and spring came again over the blazing land, bringing kissing-time, and this had a deep effect on the family.

'Where are you away to, then?' asked Gran.

'Taking this up to Rebecca,' said Ifor, holding his new tin ear up to the shaving glass. Glorious was that cauliflower Ifor had collected in his return with Dai Swipo, tight-screwed into a ball and shining like a sea-lantern, and I would personally slam one of mine in a door if I thought I could mutilate it as good as Ifor's.

'Time that girl was married, Ifor,' observed Mari at her stitching.

'Ah, when times get better, girl.'

'Times will not get better, only worse,' said Sharon. 'They dropped us another threepence a ton, you hear that?'

I had heard it, and it had set my father deep in his chair, furrowed; the new railway that was belting past the Old Navigation was getting bigger and the bargees thinner. Brunel, the genius, had done what Stephenson said could not be done—linked the wealth of the towns of Aberdare and Neath, and collecting the vast tonnage of Merthyr Road, Hirwain, Glyn Neath, Resolven and Aberdulais had poured it into the maws of the sea.

The opening of the line last September was a highlight, with the Crawshay band loaded on to a truck pulled by a saddle-tank, blasting martial music from Hirwain to Neath, and nearly hitting the big black clock off the mantel with Gran out in the garden shaking her fist at the trombones and tubas, for brass bands sent her raving, especially serpentines and things like that. And I remember, when she was up in Merthyr, she used to suck lemons in front of the Brass Band Cyfarthfa, which usually put paid to them, for nothing will fill up a serpentine quicker than somebody sucking a lemon while the bandsman is blue in the face and up in the top registers.

'Welsh harps it is for me,' she used to say, 'and damage I will cause blasting brass bands, especially Cyfarthfa, for it is money the workers are wanting from Crawshay, not music.'

But back to the kissing-time of the spring of '52.

Great developments were afoot between Sharon and Richard Bennet, Rhiannon's cousin sort-of. Big and handsome, this chap, with a Welsh fire-brand of a mother and an English agitator for a father, both now dead. And though he lived with his gran and Tomos Traherne in Nantyglo, he appeared to spend most of his life down here at the Old Navigation.

Very polished and educated was this Richard Bennet, with bows on the doorstep and showing his arm to Sharon, but also too bright in the eye for Rhiannon to suit me, and I didn't reckon it healthy.

A dreadful state I was in that spring over my lovely Rhiannon.

Hot and bothered, I was, when she was closer than a yard, and I nearly threw a faint every time he cast a glance in her direction.

'Good evening, Mrs. Evan.' Low he bows to Mari; then in with a stride and a white smile on his tanned face; now his hand goes out to me and Dada, and he had a grip like an elephant in gloves.

This was the Wednesday that Sharon got the vapours.

I have never seen this happen before: I have seen her hot and swearing over a chap, but never actually faint, and she was out cold for fifteen minutes.

And Rhiannon was nearly as bad. 'Oh, Richard!' cried she. 'I haven't seen you for days.'

Isn't healthy, I say: apparently he didn't work for a living. He had fine clothes, plenty of money, and didn't work.

'Don't be ridiculous,' said Rhiannon, from the bosh.

'Mind your own business,' said Dewi.

When nobody was around I looked in the mirror: see the coal-black face, the red-ringed eyes, the white mouth. Smelling of mule, too, after a day down the pit. And in comes this Bennet chap all braveries and fancies, with a buttonhole in his coat big enough to bury him, ducking his head under the door.

'Good evening, Bryn!'

'Come in, Dick, lad!' cried my father.

Later, out the back, Dada said, 'Listen, you. When a man offers his hand to you, you take it, whether you like him or not—understand?'

I leaned against the mangle, empty and unequal.

'You owe it to Sharon, you owe it to Rhiannon—I'll not tell you again.'

But it was good at home on the nights that Richard Bennet did not come to visit. Oh, I do love it when the family is all under one roof and the doors are shut tight to keep the mice out, with the stars of the cut so big that they threaten to drop out of the sky. Like tonight.

'Hold still,' commanded Gran, with Ifor's head in her lap, and her doing his excellent cauliflower ear: expert with these was my gran, having learned the art of a hot and cold compress from pay nights up in Dowlais where the average a month was one per head of the population. Rhiannon was on the hot compresses and Sharon on the cold, doing her Shakespeare acting in between. Mari was smiling at her sewing, Dada deep in his chair, legs thrust out: Dewi, book up to the lamp, was into *The Triumph of the Working Classes over the Capitalist System,* and I have a sneaking idea who it was lent him that one.

And Sharon, with Shakespeare in one arm and Richard Bennet in the other, is in form in the middle of the kitchen. '"Oh, coz, coz, coz, my pretty little coz, that thou didst know how many fathoms deep I am in love! But it cannot be sounded: my affection hath an unknown bottom, like the bay of Portugal."'

Some queer old things this Shakespeare chap do come out with at times.

Dada said, removing his pipe and folding *The Cambrian,* 'Sara Siddons, now deceased, retired prematurely because of the competition.'

'Easy with that hot one,' complained Ifor. 'Setting the thing alight, you are, Gran.'

'Hot you will have to have it, son—no good lukewarm.'

'Raising lumps on it.'

'It would have been less complicated had you ducked,' said Dada.

And Sharon, dancing to Ifor with a rose in her hand is showing enough of the deep divide in her sack dress to kill a curate. ' "Ah, you poor, sweet little rogue, you! Alas, poor ape, how thou sweatest. Come, let me wipe thy face..." ' and she bent to Ifor, smoothing his cheek, whispering, ' "Come on, you whoreson chops—ah, rogue, i'faith, I love thee...." '

'She do the acting well, don't she, Gran,' observed Ifor, beaming.

'She do it a bit too near the knuckle for my liking,' said Gran. 'Pin up a yard or two in front, there's a good girl.'

'Oh, Gran!' Flushed and stamping is Sharon, her artistry denied.

'The free-thinking do not allow you to parade half naked—pin up!'

'Ach, let her be, Mother,' said Dada. 'It is only in the family.'

'It is disrespectful to her brothers—pin up.' Gran slapped another cold poultice on Ifor's ear. 'And you keep still. Who's she supposed to be, anyway?'

'Who are you supposed to be, Sharon my rose?' asked Dada at his newspaper.

'Doll Tearsheet in Henry the Fourth Part Two.'

'Where did Part One get to, then?' asked Gran.

'Ignore that,' said my father.

'Who is this Doll Tearsheet? She don't sound savoury to me,' said Gran.

'A cheap whore with a heart of gold,' said Sharon.

'Excuse me,' cried Mari, leaping up. 'A cup of tea for everyone, is it?'

'A what?' whispered Gran, shocked and white.

'Oh, Gran, it is only in the play!' protested Sharon.

'It might be, but I am not having such language in the house.' She levelled a finger at Dada. 'This is your fault, mind, you have encouraged her!'

'My dear girl—do you realise this is Shakespeare?'

'Aye, and I don't like the sound of him, either. The house is going to the devil since he came into it.' She put her fist on Ifor's ear. 'Enough's as good as a feast. Let us have a little more of that coz coz thing and the bay of Portugal, and a little less of these cheap whores with hearts of gold, you hear me?'

'Yes, Gran,' said Sharon.

'And pin up!'

For my part this Shakespeare chap do sound all right to me since I prefer to look a thing in the face than hide it under banana leaves for dirty people to find. And the people this man makes do please me, the great kings and courtiers, and also the little Doll Tearsheets, for I have seen some fine ladies under parasols I would not put in the company of this Doll, who was sweet in kindness, according to Sharon, and I would heave cobbles at the hypocrites who dress like gentry and act like harpies.

'You can find dirt anywhere, if you insist on looking for it,' said my father once. 'This poet Shakespeare makes us each a lute and on this lute we can play his words to a song of our own. Each singer sings differently. You take the Song of Solomon, for instance. You can find in it glory and goodness and love: but another will tear aside its tapestry of gold and spy beneath the nakedness and lust.'

Often, to hear my father speak, you would think he came of the bards. One thing was sure: at Granfer Ben's knee he had learned of beauty, and been educated in English and Welsh, and although he was of the barges, he was no ordinary bargee. Also, but I do not wish to be unkind, I think my poor old gran was a lot to blame for Granfer Ben going to Salt Lake City: nothing, not a thing in common, said my father.

'The saint will interpret life as the saint sees it, the monk behind the sanctity of his walls: the vile will find vileness in purity; in love of the body they will see the sexual behaviour of the animal. The unctuous will always play hypocrisy, which is the cardinal sin of men: do no look elsewhere than Jesus if you want the sight of a man, and remember that he found beauty and goodness in the harlot as he smoothed his foot in the sand.'

And now, he put out his hand to Sharon, saying, 'In the Penny Gaffs of the Swansea Michaelmas Fair I have seen your Granfer Ben play the great Falstaff.'

'You know of Falstaff?' cried Sharon, kneeling at his feet, eyes wide.

'Aye, and Pistol and Bardolph, Hotspur and Mistress Quickly of the Boar's Head Tavern. Aye, girl, you are not the only one to know of the great Shakespeare—I grieve I do not know more,' and then, to our joy, he rose from his chair while Mari watched him, smiling; he cried bassly, ' "Thou art as valorous as Hector of Troy, worth five of Agamemnon, and ten times better than the Nine Worthies. Ah, villain!" ' and with his arms out he paraded the room, shouting:

' "A rascally slave! I will toss the rogue in a blanket!" cries Falstaff.'

' "Do, if thou darest for thy heart," ' shrieked Sharon, delighted, ' "an thou dost, I'll canvas thee between a pair of sheets." '

'At this point music is played, and I am a page,' said Dada, strolling and humming loud, his hand strumming a make-believe lyre.

'And I do not like the sound of that, either,' said Gran.

'What, the music?'

'The canvas and sheets bit. Now stop it, Mostyn—I wish no more of it.'

'Oh, Gran!' cried Sharon, beside her now, arms out and loving her.

'Never you mind,' said Gran. 'No more of it—and mind Ifor's ear.'

And there are some who are monsters of virtue, yet we adore them.

Everything stopped at that moment while a Corsair went through on the line with ten ballast trucks behind it for station building up at Hirwain: in smoke and steam it bellowed past the window, and the Old Navigation shook to the depth of her foundations, as if navvies were hammering dog-spikes into the soles of her feet.

'No more cheap whores with hearts of gold, is it?' said Gran at length.

'I promise.'

'Or that Doll Tearsheet?'

'No more Doll Tearsheet. Just the old coz coz business from now on.'

And so, with Sharon laying snares for Richard Bennet and me courting Rhiannon and getting nowhere fast, with the railway getting bigger and the canal smaller, we went through the golden summer of the Vale with love impending but getting no nearer, and with anxious pockets.

But with one undying consolation.

Michaelmas Fair!

I am getting that girl under cover in a wheatfield or die doing it.

20

GREAT were the preparations for Neath Michaelmas Fair, with people up at dawn prancing and preening in mirrors, the men yanking at trews, shaving close and polishing boots; the women rushing around half-naked, their arms crossed on their petticoat chests, taking out crackers and curling, tightening stays and pulling on stockings, and for God's sake wash under the arms for a change, you men, said Gran, for you never seem to think of such places. Even Cinders, my little bitch, got a bath, and Dewi was out in the stables most of last night tying up Nell's mane with straw and rosettes and plaiting Jed Donkey's tail with red, white and blue ribbons. Beautiful looked our barge, too, all decorated with bunting and autumn flowers, the great Turk's Head on the tiller freshly pipe-clayed by my father for the barge competition, with the long, white tail of the first stallion he had owned blowing straight and proudly in the wind of the cut.

'Bryn,' shouted Gran, 'don't stand there idling—get the things outside on the wharf!'

'Can I help?' cried Rhiannon.

'You catch this end,' I said, shifting a box, but Ifor came up then, stripped to his black trews, and lifted it clear for the prow of the barge, to sit upon: taking on the famous Alehouse Jones in the booth, said Dewi, and God help him.

'Got the small-beer and eats?' called Gran.

'By here.'

'All ready, is it?' asked Sharon, swirling in with petticoats and bright pink crinoline, her hair flying free on her shoulders, and Dada came next with Mari on his arm, Gran all bunned up in black and cameo with a tin of her cold rice-pudding under her arm, and away to go we were, with Ifor first aboard; daft as a brush he looked, sitting there naked to the waist and his fists on his knees, but this was the custom.

'Right, cast off!' called Dada, and I coiled the mooring-rope and tightened the trace and took my seat beside Rhiannon. Dewi was at Nell's head and down the cut we went in golden morning sunlight. There is lovely it is to be travelling to the Neath Michaelmas Fair, and the clouds all wispy in the October sky and your best girl beside you. Always will I remember her scented sweetness that day, her hair black curls under her poke-bonnet and down to her waist in white ribbons, and beautiful pink her crinoline, sparked with white roses. See her face patterned with shadow and sunlight, Iberian in darkness, the lips curved red, her eyes bright and strangely light. Proud as a cocker I was that day, with her hand in mine, Mari and Dada behind us and Gran and Sharon bringing up the rear, and my elephant brother half naked on the prow, biceps bulging, ready for the best in Wales.

'They are turning out for the Fair this year, right enough!' cried Mari, and so they were, for the villagers were walking in thick swathes down the valley, pouring from the cottages of Melin, Clyne and Gerwen in a medley of colour, the children scampering in Sunday best, the women in bright crinolines and bonnet-streamers, laughing shrilly under their poke-bonnets. From the lock cottages came the keepers, being flicked by their wives for hair and scurf, sons and daughters being lectured on special behaviour, and striped bottoms it would be for hob-nobbing with the navvies, male or female. The cut was alive with barges as far as I could see, many of them loaded with brass and silver bands, and already blue in the face with them, the conductors standing in the prows beating the time. Choirs from the Neath and Swansea valleys were there, too, and at Aberdulais the crowds thronged in over Seven Sisters. From the tin-plate works came the melters and boxers, the sorters and branders; the men wearing the white smocks of their trade of tin, their blood mixed with the Celts of Cornwall: the fire-maintainers were clutched in groups, each man with a cheek scalded crimson from the flare of the hearth: flat-chested came the women picklers, their breasts given to the poisonous prick of the sorting knife. The blind came, too, for eyes are given in return for tin and copper: the maimed came on crutches, and a few Dais cut-in-half were carried by the wrestlers and fighters. Owen Bach I saw, in a majesty of strength, fists on hips, straight from the bull-taming in front of the Lamb and Flag, Glyn Neath. Thundering down the railway came the snorting Corsair engines of Brunel the genius, bringing down the wealth of The Top, the puddlers, rollers, rodders, furnacemen and their families, all done posh and waving greeting to the bargees, and I saw Bili Jones and Wil Shout, the drovers, standing close with Hobo Churchyard between them and he hadn't a leg under him which brought Dada up and shouting delighted, 'Good man, Hobo!'

'Oh, sit down, son,' cried Gran, 'a minister might be watching. Dear me, this family do stoop to pick up nothing.'

'Bryn, look!' cried Rhiannon, and her grip of my knee took me light in the head so I almost fainted. 'Oh, just look at that beautiful Rosie Carey!'

A very fine sight was Rosie Carey, high in the breast and short in the ankle, done up in white for purity under a big, floppy hat, bowing this way and that to the gentlemen, and smiling, her teeth flashing white against the crimson curve of her lips: gorgeous woman, and I could have eaten her with haricot beans and gravy, and I saw her mouth open in delighted surprise as Dewi came up behind her and pinched her under the bustle.

'There is a huzzy, mind,' said Gran, evil.

'Oh, no, she is lovely!' cried Mari, who was the loveliest there.

'It do go deeper than the superficial, though,' said Gran. 'Some queer things are happening at the Lamb and Flag, I hear,' and so there was, for rumour had it that Alfo had his hand in the till while Mrs. Alfo was upstairs in their big fourposter hitting up the pigs: down in the tap-room was Alfo, night-shirt billowing as he counted out the takings, 'One for you, my Rosie, one for me, none for Mrs. Alfo, and one for Coventry.'

'No smoke without fire,' said Gran now. 'Folks reckon he's got a cottage up in the Midlands all set for Rosie Carey, and I do not think it decent.'

On, on through the patterned gold of the canal, past the junction with the Red Jacket cut and down we went past the big dry dock alongside the river where the big two hundred tonners were on the high tide, all gaily decorated with streamers and bunting, and along the banks the boys and girls were gathering to give us a cheer, and among them was Sian Edwards and Jane Rheola, and Sian winked.

'Ay, ay, Bryn Evan!' cried Sian, and went all cuddly, slapping at her hands.

'Ay, ay,' I replied, sweating bricks.

'Got another, has he?' said Jane, praying. 'Should be a law against it.'

'And I bet she don't know what day it is, eh, Bryn Evan?'

There is a pair of bitches for you.

Red as a turkey wattle was Rhiannon, her fingers twisting in her lap.

'If you so much as blink, he'll have you, girl!'

Rhiannon said, lifting her eyes to mine, 'You ... you know those two?'

'Never seen them in my life.'

'Is that a fact?' said Sian, with ears like mice. 'Sinking Cuddlecome Specials with that Tai Morlais and I had to fight him off. Dear me, woman, you do not know what is coming to you!'

'Be warned!' cried Jane, her finger up as they went off. 'Last time he landed on Cushy, but you may not be so lucky!'

In a black silence we sat then, and thank heaven nobody else had heard them because of the celebrations, and I devised special tortures for Sian Edwards and Jane Rheola if ever I caught them running.

'What did she mean, that last one?' whispered Rhiannon.

'Nothing. Just trying to cause trouble,' I said.

For this was a relapse I had been trying hard to forget, and it was Rhiannon's fault, anyway, making a fuss of that chap Bennet. A couple of months back I had taken Sian's key off the stable wall-plate and popped down to the Cuddlecome Inn, but I got the directions wrong and I was first floor, first right and first door, which landed me in with Cushy, and I was out following bottles and boots from Cushy screaming blue murder and the Irish Shrew and Sian, and now doing my best to live it down.

'Don't tell me you go down to the Cuddlecome Inn!' breathed Rhiannon.

'Good lord, what next!' I replied, disgusted. 'You ought to be ashamed of yourself, saying such a thing!'

'Oh, look!' she suddenly cried. 'Here comes Richard.'

If he had worked it he couldn't have come at a better time. Barbed hooks were in me as I saw him shaking hands with Dewi on the river path, and he waved, making secret signs to Sharon who whooped with joy, knowing of a tryst.

I sat in funeral cloth, my heart clutched in green fingers. Rhiannon said, as he vaulted the bank and walked away, waving, 'Ach, he's a good one that. You know his dad was English?'

'I am not surprised.'

She sighed. 'Many things he taught me when I was young and mam took me up to his gran's in Nanty. You know that hawthorn buds taste bread and cheese?'

'Of course,' I said, unaware of it.'

'That you can make pop-guns out of elder branches?'

'Everybody knows that,' I said testily, never having heard of it.

She laughed softly, and I hated her, and she said, 'He used to catch dumbledores in Canterbury bells, but I cried and he let them go.'

'Daft old things they do up in England.'

She began to shake silently with frail laughter, and the ire rose in me, clenching my hands, and I saw this Bennet coney staggering back with me after him, hooking his head off: later, he was laid out in the marble rigidity of death, and Rhiannon was beside him in widow's weeds, weeping while I sat in the Petty Sessions with a gaoler either side in a malign silence, unrepentent.

Now I said, archly and uncaring, 'I suppose you will spend your time at the fair with him and Sharon?'

'I will give some thought to it,' said she with a twig of a smile, and I sat there mortified in a rising heat of blood, while she, arrogant and larkish under her poke-bonnet, did not spare me a glance to see the effect.

'Horrible, you are,' I said. 'You do not take after your lovely mam.'

'Nor do you after your da,' said she, tartly. 'I am not as thick as I look, mind. You would never get him sinking quarts down at Cushy Cuddlecome's and hobnobbing with the scarlet ladies!' and she tossed her head.

'I have never been out with a scarlet lady!'

'Easy in front there,' said Dada, his chops on my shoulder. 'No need to boast of it to all and sundry.'

'Bryn is being a pig!' cried Rhiannon.

'So I gather,' said Dada, 'but do your best to confine the battle to within family limits, for they can hear you over in Swansea.'

The streamers, the music, the laughter beat over us in a rising tide of joy and sound, and I slipped an eye at Rhiannon. She was sitting in a splendid, savage beauty, indignant to my glance.

'It do not need the penny post, remember, for things to get around,' she said at nothing.

'You are an inch-minded bloody little bigot,' I said, with ice.

At this, for no apparent reason, she began to bucket, her fist thumping in her lap, and her nose went stuffy and her eyes red and wet, and I was glad.

'Oh, Bryn!' whispered Mari, distressed.

'Will somebody inform me what is happening up there in front?' cried Gran.

176

'It is Bryn being a little pig to Rhiannon, and making her cry,' said Sharon.

'But this is terrible!' cried Mari, holding us together. 'You must not quarrel on Michaelmas—and look, it is such a beautiful day!'

'I hate him!' breathed Rhiannon.

Everybody coming up now, stroking her and saying how I ought to be ashamed of myself, with daggers and sighs from Dada and an arched, understanding eye from my new mother. And between us, me and Rhiannon, sat a big English lout whispering to her words of consolation and sneering his lips at me.

I sat in a numb trance, listening to his untidy, English voice, and I swore that anything English that crossed my path that Michaelmas Fair I would hit back over to London via Cardiff.

'I hate you, I hate you!' cried Rhiannon, all bunged up and soaking.

'Oh, Rhiannon!' whispered Mari, shocked.

'I do. I hate you!'

'That makes two of us,' I said.

Bloody good start to the Fair you come to think of it.

Down the cut we went, with the crowds between us and the Gnoll getting bigger every minute, with great engines thundering down the railway with flats of bawling navvies, most of them bawling improper suggestions, and I saw my father cutting his knuckles on his serge. Then a few on the opposite path started winging bottles and such-like at Ifor who was still sitting stripped on the prow, and to his credit he didn't raise an eye when cabbages and carrots started bouncing off his nut, for dignity is a hell of a thing, mind, and has to be preserved, especially since this carrying of the champions had been going on since the canal opened in 1796.

'But the sooner we get ashore the better,' said Dada, sitting starboard of Gran and fending off rotten apples and bananas, but nothing shifted Rhiannon for every time I tried a conversation she was nose up to drown in a rainstorm. Also, navvies with six-pound swedes started getting at Ifor, and as the range shortened one parted his hair like a cannon-ball and the next hit him arse over ear off the box, and this naturally raised my father's ire, since he up and shook his fist and called them a shower of bastards, and this set Mari very dull, but Gran didn't hear because she was collecting swedes. Baccy York was chewing tobacco on the bank and his three wives already pretty tipsy; also Tub Union with his bargee bodyguard, all paid up members of the Lodge, and they all came down to meet us as we tied up, their little fat women all starched and stayed in best bombazine and hats with ostrich feathers: very truculent looked Mr. Tub Union.

'A word with you, Evan,' and he removed his clay and bowed deep to Mari, and she went down in a curtsey before him.

'Not business, I hope.'

'It is business every day in the business of living. You realise that we have been dropped on the rates of haul and will drop still lower now the rail is here.'

My father sighed. 'Look, *bach*, the sun is shining and it is Michaelmas Fair—must we talk rates of haul?'

'Talk today or starve tomorrow—take your pick.'

'The old collieries will stand by us,' said Dewi.

'The old collieries will load with us until they get railway sidings, then they will leave the Company, and we will leave the Vale.'

'I say it again, Tub Union,' said Dada, quietly, 'there is work for all.'

'There is work for the Company bargee, Mostyn Evan, but work no longer for the private contractor.

'So where do we go from here, then?' asked Ifor, lumbering up.

'We go nowhere,' replied Tub Union. 'We were here before you came—you go back to Merthyr.'

'And if I refuse?' asked Dada, polite.

'Then we bloody shift you.' He bowed to Mari. 'Begging your pardon for the language, ma'am.'

'Excellent,' said my father, 'and begging my wife's pardon for the language, you are welcome to bloody try. I am running a private barge on this canal with permission from the owners, and here it stays.' He shouldered the bargee aside.

'You will regret this,' said Tub Union.

'I have been regretting things all my life,' said my father. 'Most of all, I regret joining a Union that brings a threat to a paid-up member. Now call aside your dogs and let my women pass or I will whistle up mine and clear you from this bank.'

The crowd surged about us, the children with stick windmills and tinkerbells running in scampering joy across the Big Field of Gnoll House. Great dray horses from Cyfarthfa Yard came six abreast across the meadow, a white-smocked ostler at each bridle: rattling their brass medallions they came, their hides flashing in the sunlight, their hooves stained with ox-blood, the feathers dusted with flour. And the judges fussed about them, while in the circle they had formed beautiful Arab ponies high-stepped like country dancers.

In a square of ropes the poor were being hired for the kitchens and fields of the gentry, and I pitied their wan faces; standing in their rags as the agents and farmers barged among them, feeling their muscles and crying, 'Art thou hired, lad?' and pinching the fetlocks of the mares and pressing their stomachs to see if they were in child, shouting, 'Should thou work for me, girl, thou'll work tidy,' and many had already been hired, standing like cattle with straw in their mouths. Redcoats who had marched across Sarn Helen from Brecon Garrison lounged on their muskets, eyes switching at the Silurian swine: big men of the northern counties of England who had drunk their ale between Fort Nidum and Senny, and by the grave of Dervag, the son of Justus, had slept in a night of studded shields and strange, Roman oaths. They watched us. For lately there had been rail-greasing on the Hirwain gradient, and the giant engines were sliding backwards, so the Great Western was taking no chances.

Rhiannon I saw in a gap of the crowd, but she only put her nose up.

Lost, I wandered, looking for Tai Morlais among the cheap-jacks, the poultry and bread stalls where dumpling house-wives were duffing up butterpats with good luck signs. Fortune-tellers were there in tinker robes and bangle earrings, Welsh weavers in a swish of shuttles. In a storm of gaiety and colour,

179

in a clash of tambourines and shrieking of fiddles, I bumped into Mrs. Shenkins, the mother of Willie-who-died.

''Morning, Mrs. Shenkins.' I knocked up my hat to her.

''Morning, Evan *bach*. Seen my Willie, have you?' She turned her wet face to mine, grizzled by the rain, snow and sun of sitting in the open these past seven years, praying for the chill that would send her to her Willie.

'Not this morning, Mrs. Shenkins,' I said.

'How am I looking, boy?'

She was tanned like teak with the weather, as square and strong as a horse. I said, 'Pretty delicate, you ask me, Mrs. Shenkins.'

'You reckon I'll last another month or two?'

'Doubtful, missus. Any day now they will slam the lid and drop you to your Willie.'

'God in heaven,' said she, 'them's bountiful words. Can't live without something to look forward to, can we?'

Sobbing, she left me. Later they told me she lived to the age of ninety-four.

Dai Central Eating I hit into next, staring up at the Booth of Dentistry, tapping his big horse tooth and trying to rake up the courage.

'Painless extractions it says, mind,' said he.

'Painless or not, it is the least you can do for Tegwen Harriet,' I replied.

'Though it don't look too healthy,' he added, and neither did it, with a half-naked savage prancing around the stage with a headdress of chicken-feathers and a pair of bruisers hitting on a big bass drum, and another blowing on a serpentine.

'No good thinking about it,' I said, assisting him up, for one good turn deserves another, and this one put me on my back six weeks with the cholera.

Painless extraction it was, sure enough, since you couldn't hear Dai hollering because of the drum, and when I uncovered my eyes I was in time to see the curtains closing and Dai going through them with his boots studs up, and nobody saw him for days.

Rosie Carey I saw next, kneeling on the grass in all her frills and fancies, with her arms around Billie Softo while he got into a meat-pie big enough to stop an elephant.

Beautiful Rosie Carey looked kneeling there with her eyes closed and Softo skinny in his hunger and rags, hard against her. And I seemed to hear, about the bedlam of the crowd, the beating of her heart.

'He didn't steal the thing,' cried Rosie. 'I paid for it. You leave him be, you big, heartless bastard.'

Forlorn, I went, dying for Rhiannon but too proud to hunt for her: wandering past the sweet stalls, the tiger-nuts, gobstoppers and Spanish juice; heart-shaped hundreds and thousands, cashous, bull's eyes, lotus-beans and mottoes, kali pink and yellow, humbugs, jelly-babies and stick-jaw. On the great beer-stained trestles stood the belted barrels of ale, and big brown drays with flowing manes and whipping tails stamped and snorted in their nosebags while their bury drivers, stripped and sweating, rolled up the casks. And in the middle of it all Cushy Cuddlecome was hitting out the stoppers and shrieking with delight as the foam ambered and hissed.

'Out wi' ye bungs and fizz, ye gorgeous whampo!' she cried, all done up in pleated crinoline and very blousy, and I swear she was six pints in the wind although the sun was not overhead. 'Throng up, throng up, me beautiful men, for the tide's never out at Cushy Cuddlecome's, can ye hear me, son?'

Mr. Emlyn Hollyoak she was addressing, and very stern the preacher looked among the crowd, sallow under his big grey topper.

'Sure to God, there's nothin' wrong wi' a drink, your gracious,' cried Cushy. 'An' there's fine value given in me inn, for what we miss at the taps we make up for in the beds!' and she howled at the sky, fist up, her great breasts shaking. 'When it comes to us Sodom and Gomorrah can put the shutters up.'

Not good enough, of course, and people took note of it, like Mr. Waldo Scully, the Inspector of Nuisances from Neath, though it is true his business was mainly burial and drains, but he instantly came up, very official, licking his pencil. 'Miss

181

Cuddlecome, this is Michaelmas Fair, not a den of iniquity, and it is my duty to warn you ...'

'Ach, bless ye beautiful soul, yer honour,' cried Cushy, going down in a curtsey, 'I'd not offend a hair of yer head, and I'm only after slaking the thirst of the community, for they're a long time dead. Will ye have one on me to liven ye?'

Roars of laughter from the crowd at this, of course, and I pushed my way out ears down in my collar. For I knew that come starlight Cushy would be knee-deep in ale and navvies and fists up, looking for a fight, and I would rather tangle with the Black Welshman than Cushy when she was man-hating instead of man-loving.

Pietro Bianca I saw next, to my astonishment, prowling on the edge of the crowd with a placard on his chest saying 'Help Free Mexico' and his cap in his hand, and I went to him instantly, for I hadn't seen him in months.

'Pietro!'

'Bryn Evan!' His face glowed, and he cried, 'Long live Mexico!'

'God help Santa Anna,' I said. 'Where you been these months?'

'The bombs I have, the money I have not. Explosions I put under the scabs and blacklegs. You spare a penny for Mexico?'

I got one into his cap. 'Aren't you with Dewi these days?'

He glanced about him. 'Dewi is with the new revolution in Nantyglo. Under Richard Bennet the Chartists will rise again. Bombs I put under strikebreakers now, but bigger ones I will put under President Polk—me, Ianto Fuses and Dewi Evan, we fight for freedom.'

'Ay, ay,' I said, and left him. From Veracruz to Grand River they could keep their Mexico: Dewi was right, there was enough trouble to feed on at home. Through the dancing, the joy of the Fair I saw, on the road to Neath, a ragged column of burned-our poor, the sallow refuse of the tin-plate works, with their few possessions clutched against them, trudging to the workhouse.

Betsy Small-Coal I saw next: shapeless was she in her sack

182

dress tied at the waist with rope, and very worried about her man Joby Canal.

'Seen my Joby, have you, son?'

'No, Betsy,' I answered. Bald as a gnome was her Joby, and with ants in his trews. Nine months a year he was on the navvy tramping-ticket, working up to Darlington with news of the railway building, a walking navvy newspaper. A few weeks in Swansea jail, a fortnight at home with Betsy and the kids, then off again, leaving her full with another, and him no more than four-foot-ten in his boots.

'Always at Michaelmas my Joby comes home,' said Betsy.

At night she tramped with the coal she picked off the tumps, living in a hole under Neath Abbey by the ironworks: once she had six children, now she had two, but do not worry, woman, said Joby, there are plenty more where they came from.

'A good little man is my Joby, mind,' she said, watching me.

Pickpocket, loafer, a little scrag of a waster without a single redeeming feature.

'First-rate chap, Betsy,' I said.

The crowd bustled about us in warmth and smells of hot cloth.

'Aye,' said she. 'Every night I thank God for my Joby. For although he has faults, he do not trifle with the fancy women, nor does he leather the childer these days.'

He had covered more beds on the Stockton-Darlington than a blanket factory: the only reason why he had stopped belting the children was because he was worn out belting Betsy.

Wistful, she smiled about her, and her face was beautiful. 'My, there's a lovely Fair—good to see people happy, isn't it?'

The only hope of Heaven for men, I think, is that they are made in the bodies of women.

'You talk about my Joby, you give him a good name, see, Bryn Evan.'

I bowed deep to her.

Tai Morlais was walking arm in arm with Sian Edwards

and Jane Rheola, in whoops and giggles and toffee-apples. 'Just off to see Alehouse Jones duff up your Ifor—you coming?' he shouted, and I shook my head.

'Took enough duffing up himself, today, haven't you, *cariad*?' called Sian.

'Poor soul, she has rejected his advances,' said Jane Rheola.

On the wrestling green I saw an English lout, and if it wasn't the one Rhiannon had been talking about, he was good enough for me. Like Atlas he stood naked to the trews in a ring of gasping people, doing a muscle control: the sun was flashing on his rippling shoulders.

'Five shilling to any man who can throw the Cumberland Strangler!' bawled a barker, strutting about, and I saw the bargees and colliers pressing the ring tighter, wiping their mouths with the backs of their hands while their women threatened with parasols and wagging fingers, and just you dare—just you *dare* make an exhibition of yourself and I am home from this fair fast.

'Five shilling, missus,' grumbled a navvy. 'Not to be sneezed at, woman.'

'Then try it—just you try it.'

It was a job for single men. Hands in trews I wandered up, weighing the wrestler, and sensing an opponent in his law of the jungle, he turned, his green eyes switching over me with the speed of a serpent.

'Where is Cumberland?' I asked a bargee.

'North of England, ye dafto,' said somebody, so I vaulted the post and landed in the ring.

'I am on,' I said.

Up came the barker instantly. 'You wrestled before, son?'

'Aye, when it comes to five shillings.'

The crowd grumbled in its throat like bulls scenting blood. The barker roared, 'Throng up, throng up! A local boy is about to tackle the Cumberland Strangler. Give heavy, good people, give heavy—pay the lad for courage!' and he passed round his top hat.

I threw off my coat and waved out of my shirt; unlacing boots, I watched the wrestler. He walked in circles now, like a caged tiger, flexing his big shoulders, his great fair head sitting square on his bull neck, his forearms cording and bulging as he opened his hands, and I knew by his marvellous set of tin ears that he came from the professional rings of the gentry. About thirteen stones I reckoned him, a couple more than me, but I gave him more than three inches in height and had ten years on him, at least. Suddenly, still kneeling, I stared through legs at Dewi's face.

'What the hell are you doing in there?' His eyes were horrified.

'Five shillings,' I said.

'You stupid idiot! D'you realise he's a professional?' said he on all fours. 'Bryn, he'll cripple you—this is wrestling, this isn't fists.'

'Then vanish before he does the pair of us.'

'I'm coming in,' he gasped, scrambling up.

I heard him land in the ring behind me, but I did not turn to him, and I could hear a lot of barging and pushing and do you realise he isn't even eighteen and you hop it before the Strangler starts on you, and next moment there was a scream from the women and cheers from the men and Dewi was spreadeagled on the grass and the Strangler dusting his hands. Back came Dewi through the legs of the crowd. 'Did you see that? I tell you, he's a killer!'

'Hop it.'

Dewi scrambled up. 'I'm going for Dada!' and he up and dived for open country.

'Right!' shouted the barker. 'The Cumberland Strangler will now assist the local lad out of this ring in two separate pieces.' He paused. 'Make a ring, gentlemen—right, boys, into it!'

I turned to face the wrestler. The noises of the fair died in my ears.

We circled, hands out, stooping, looking for a hold. Strange the eyes of a professional wrestler: as green as June grass, this one's, the brows jutting and humped with bright hair, the cheekbones criss-crossed with thin, white scars. Hypnotic, these eyes, expressionless and cruel. Licking his thick lips, he moved a hand at me and I smacked it down, still circling. Suddenly

185

relaxing, he straightened, but I saw the trap and did not go, and he spat sideways, and winked, grinning.

'Take it slow, lad,' he whispered. 'Got eight kids need feedin'.'

'I got ten,' I said.

'You drop an' you get brass just the same, Taff.'

I saw in his face the face of Richard Bennet.

'And you call yourself a wrestler?'

'Right, you want it, you get it,' he breathed, and feinted, stepping in with the speed of sparks, snatched my wrist, twisted at the waist and flung me backwards, and as I hit the ground he landed elbow down and I didn't know if I was in Neath or Nantyglo. Gasping for breath, I rolled away as he came after me like a cat, snatching and clawing on all fours, but I flung him off and scrambled up, and no sooner was I upright than he did the same bloody thing again and I was legs waving and down while he pounced and held me momentarily before I twisted from his grip, floundering across the ring.

'Six to one on the Cumberland!'

'Take fives? Fives I am taking against the Welsh!'

Bets now, money chinked, pencils being licked, men roaring and women saying it was a damned scandal because he's only a boy.

'On't ear or backside, Taff?' said the wrestler, coming like a baboon. 'Take pick,' and we closed, chest to chest, instantly locked in a finger grip: now arms entwined, now bodies straining in a sweating, gasping hold. But I was with the advantage and I heard the wrestler grunt deep in his chest: hooking my leg round his, I heaved, and we collapsed, him underneath: rolling over, I got him above me and he dropped straight into the scissors. Face turned away, gripping the grass, I pressed him, and he went sideways, staring up, groaning with the pain of it.

'Fours!'

'I'll take fours on the Taff!'

'By gum, ee's a randy kid. Do 'im, lad, do 'im!'

I bowed my head and squeezed and the Cumberland gasped aloud, arms waving. With ebbing strength I shifted the scissors to get him higher, and dug my fingers into the earth turning all my strength into the paralysing hold about his waist. He was crying aloud now in a sustained roar from the crowd, beating at the grass, and I rolled again, jack-knifing him, switching my cramped ankles.

'Oh, Bryn, please do not hurt him,' I seemed to hear Rhiannon say.

'Oh, Bryn,' cried Rhiannon, 'when you get to know him he is very sweet.'

'Oh, you Taff swine!' shouted the wrestler. 'Oh, you sod.'

Somebody in the crowd shouted. 'Evens I offer—sixpence to sixpence, bet returned.'

'How do it feel, Cumberland, takin' it instead of givin' it?'

'Aye, but he isn't done yet!'

'In the name of God!' gasped the wrestler, and I stared at him, slackening the grip of my legs.

He inched towards me, his face agonised. 'Aw, there's an evil thing in me belly, lad, and by gum, it's fair killin' me—for heaven's sake lay off!'

Instantly, I slacked him more, and he bucked high, kicking himself free and leaping upon me, his hands around my throat. Locked, we rolled, and as I threw him away he scrambled up and had me in an arm-lock, lifting from behind, and I fell face down. Somehow, I rolled upright, and he hit me with a fore-arm smash that I don't think they would have allowed up in Cumberland. Blood swam over my eyes as I clenched them to the glare of the sun, and he hit me again, bringing me to my knees. In sweating, brutal heaves he was clouting me with everything but the bucket now. Up and down like a wet sack I went with that bastard belting me. Shoulder-throws and flying mares I had, the last being very inconvenient, I discovered; also somersaults. And as I blindly pawed the air to see where the hell he had got to I collected shoulders and elbows, stomach punches and knees, and the backs of his heels every time I went down. And then, as if to add insult to injury, he began helping me along with his boot every time I was on all fours, which, when you stop to consider it, is a very humiliating thing to happen in your own home town: round and round I went with the Cumberland Strangler booting me and every boot he put in made me more angry, so I finally staggered up

187

and faced him, and when he rushed I tabbed him with a glorious left hook that sent him staggering into the barker, and the pair of them went floundering into the crowd to roars of approval from the onlookers, and the instant he was up the barker fetched me one with his bugle, and I took it and went out like a light, to awake next moment cradled in Rhiannon's arms.

'Oh, Bryn, my precious,' said she, and Dada said it was the most lovely sight he had ever seen; me lying there in Rhiannon's arms with her tears dropping on my face, the crowd sniffing and wiping and a few buck navvies actually breaking down, which is perfectly understandable when you get a battered hulk like me being cradled in the arms of a beauty like Rhiannon; it is enough to break the heart of a Swansea slaughterer.

Away we went eventually, Rhiannon supporting me, with the crowd parting and smoothing us, and when I passed the Cumberland Strangler I slipped him a wink, he having achieved in three minutes what would normally have taken me three weeks.

21

LOOKING back, I suppose the family fortunes began to change in that autumn when I was eighteen. The wages of colliers and ironworkers in the valleys were being cut by the masters, and although the Company truck-shops were outlawed by Parliament twenty-one years ago in '32, most towns of the Top, for instance, were still running them, and charging a quarter more for goods that could be bought on the open market. Anti-Truck societies sprang up, and were fought and closed down by the owners, who reckoned they had a right to make profit out of their workers' food when the prices on world markets went down. And although, to his credit, Crawshay never owned such a shop in Merthyr, other owners were not so particular, and defied the Government, opening shops in Abernant and Aberdare, Nantyglo and Maesteg and a score of other places. People became poorer, things became tighter, and the bargees of the Vale of Neath were some of the first to feel the draught, for the railway was collecting what trade was going faster every month. Slowly, our runs to Briton Ferry began to be cut, and Man Arfon, the new railway superintendent at Pont Walby, was in his element.

'Well, Evan,' he used to say, 'that is the pity of it—supply and demand. Who wants barges when the railway carries quicker and cheaper?'

'The railway will never run us out of business, Man Arfon. Time will show that they will always need the barge.'

'That I cannot envisage, Evan. Foresight, that is what you lack, see.' He tipped a flask to his lips. 'Like little Bryn by here—hoping to get married soon, is it?'

'Get back into the hole you came out of,' said Dewi, tying ropes.

'Got a list of names, I 'ave, down my hole, Dewi Evan. A randy old drunk, am I? Too mean to give away my hypocrisy, am I? Enemies are not worth having unless you make them properly, is it? By God, Dewi Evan, you have made one here.'

Dada said, 'We thought we'd seen the last of you, Judas. What are you doing here at Walby?'

'You got me kicked out of Merthyr, and I landed on my feet,' said Arfon. 'Overman, you might call me now—or superintendent of liaison over the canal and railway. There's a beautiful English word that—*liaison*. Judas, is it? Toadying up the English, is it—a stink to the name of Wales, Mostyn Evan?'

'I am come for coal, man,' said Dada. 'Tell me the bay.'

'There's a dear little woman is that Rhiannon, Bryn Evan.'

The sweat of fury was running down my back.

'Tell us your master, we are here to carry coal,' said my father.

Man Arfon straightened. 'Now that Jeremiah Alton is dead, I am master here.'

'Don't fool with us,' said Dewi. 'Who do we go to for coal?'

189

'Back to Resolven where you came from. One run a week from now—take it or leave it.' We stared at him.

It was the beginning of the end of us. The railway was collecting one firm after another with their little concrete platforms. The Canal Company shares began to drop. With haulage competition greater every day, with the railway loading free-on-board at half the rate of the barges, the bottom started falling out of the market.

In a world of private enterprise, where the Devil takes the hindmost and cuts the throat of his grandmother for a penny a ton less, the first victim of the system is free enterprise. One night Tub Union with eighty men knocked on the door of the Old Navigation. Tub Union jerked his thumb.

'Out,' said he. 'I have told you before, I will not tell you again. Out.'

'I go when the Company discharges me as a private contractor, not before,' said my father. 'I am hauling for the same cost as the union men, I charge nothing for wear and tear.'

'Out,' said Tub Union.

Man Arfon, big enough to kill us, and now Tub Union doing it final.

Things always come in threes, said Gran, and Gran was right.

'A letter for you, Dada,' said Sharon, bringing it in.

It was morning, I remember, a bright summer day. Dewi was over in Nantyglo with Richard Bennet, Sharon was dressed ready for a Penny Gaff down in Neath, Ifor was cleaning harness out the back and trying to spin out the oats for Nell and Jed Donkey.

'What is it, Mostyn?' asked Gran at the bosh.

'An order to remove,' said Dada, turning away.

'To remove what?' asked Gran.

He went to the window, staring out. 'To remove ourselves from the Old Navigation—they are bringing through a branch line, and we are on the curve.'

'But surely, the land is ours,' said Mari, coming in, her face pale.

'The land is not ours, it belonged to the Canal Company.

Now the Company's sold out to the railway, and they are our landlords for the ground rent.'

'I always said it was not worth fifty-two pounds ten,' said Gran, flicking off soap suds.

'What are you going to do, Dada?' I asked.

'I am off to Town to see Mr. Cowbum.'

'With a name like that he'll be able to work miracles,' said Gran. 'Ach, well, I always thought I'd end in the Poorhouse.' *Rock of Ages* she sang then.

'I will come with you,' said Mari, swinging her hat off a peg.

'And me,' said Sharon. 'I was just going to Neath.'

Which left Gran and Ifor and Rhiannon and I at home; the fact is important.

'Oh, God,' whispered Gran, broken, after they had gone. 'I don't know what will be the end of it.' And then she straightened and made a fist of her hand. 'The first railway navigator coming in by here to soil the place I will hit from that yard to Cyfarthfa.'

'That is much more like it,' I said.

But I think I knew, when that letter came, that it was the end of us. First Man Arfon, the traitor Welsh, then Tub Union, leader of a Lodge that turned on its members, now Mr. Seth Cowbum and into the hands of solicitors.

'Trust in the Lord,' said Gran, after Dada, Mari and Sharon had gone.

Aye? But I think he had his hands full up in places like Merthyr and Dowlais, and must have been doing up laces when the Black Welshman came up to the back door. For some time I had been expecting this visit, for you do not hit out navvy pugilists and expect to get away with it. Alone with Rhiannon in the kitchen she was making big eyes at me when I heard him at the back.

'Morning,' he said.

'Good morning, what can we do for you?' asked Gran.

'Come to knock in pegs for the railways surveyors,' replied Black Sam.

'Is that a fact?' said Gran, going Irish. 'Shall I crack your skull with this now, or will you wait till me son comes home?' and she picked up the Irish shillelagh Granfer Ben used to pay the rent with up in Dowlais.

'Put that down, woman,' said Sam, 'or you will have a piece of my mind.'

'Indeed? Well, I'm always gettin' pieces of mind from people least able to afford it. Say your bit and go.'

'Surveyor!' yelled Black Sam. 'You'd best handle this, man, for I've met with a shillelagh solicitor. Shall I toss her aside?'

'You can try,' muttered Ifor, hands on hips, coming in from the stables, and his eyes were dancing bright under his lowering brows. I got beside Gran, shouldering Ifor back, and saw in the yard at least a hundred navvies armed with picks and shovels and mandrills for blasting.

'What the hell's happening here?' I demanded.

Up came the surveyor, fussy in frock coat and top hat with notebook and pencil and maps, five-foot-two in boots, and a nose as purple as the vineyards of Babylon. 'Come now, my good woman,' said he, 'it is all signed and legal and according to my papers the owner has been informed.'

'The pegs go through the back door and out the front,' said Black Sam, loving it, 'so the house comes down.'

I said, 'My father was notified about four hours ago—is this what you call signed and legal? He is down in Neath consulting a solicitor.'

'And nobody's coming in here till he gets back,' rumbled Ifor.

The surveyor tapped his papers. 'But it is all official, a legal undertaking.'

'That is the word,' replied Gran. 'I am off to fetch the shotgun. Anyone left in that yard in the next five minutes will be undertaken six feet down and without a service. Nobody touches this house till my boy comes back.'

Man Arfon now, hands in his trews, wandering up front.

'Trouble, is it?'

'I might have known you were in it,' I said. 'This branch could serve the Kerry Flat and still miss us by a hundred feet, and you know it.'

'Essential that it goes through your rooms, Bryn Evan. There is a very beautiful word now—*essential*. Will you tell me how you can stop it?'

'We cannot,' I answered. 'But I tell you this, Man Arfon. And let there be witnesses. You are superintendent, you are liaison between the railway and the canal workers. I appeal to you in the name of the workers. If you touch this house we will take you to law—you only, you, Man Arfon.'

It triggered him. He moved uneasily in his boots. The surveyor said:

'But this is ridiculous. The railway company is the sole owner...'

'And he is the Company representative, so we will go after him—Man Arfon,' I said. 'And if we win, Man Arfon, my father will break you.'

The agent pulled out his watch. 'I will give you three hours. At two o'clock this afternoon the drays will move in.'

I looked at the sky. The sun was an incinerating glow in an ocean of red petticoats, shafting over the green country in royal splendour, nearly overhead.

'My father will be back by then,' I said.

With muttered curses and threats, the navvy gangs moved out of the yard.

'And that has got rid of that lot,' said Gran. 'Good for you, boy!'

'Took him rigid,' muttered Ifor, fist in his palm.

'What do we do now?' whispered Rhiannon, her eyes big.

'Barricade the house,' I replied, 'until Dada gets back with the interim injunction.'

'Never heard of that one,' said Gran. 'It do not sound decent to me.'

'And if Dada is not back in time we fight for right of way, old style, to gain an hour or two.'

'The Black Welshman is mine,' said Ifor, pushing up, his chest swelling.

'I'm glad you suggested it,' I said.

We bolted the doors back and front and nailed the windows, I fetched the shot-gun down from the attic; Ifor split a barrel and handed out staves, and we brought Nell and Jed Donkey into the kitchen with nose-bags and Cinders, my little bitch, ran around whining and smelling delighted in the air of pent excitement, and in the molten heat of the afternoon, giving us an extra hour of grace, the navvy gangs came again; flinging down their tools as far away as Melin, they came to the scent of blood, for word had gone around that the Evan family would fight. They spilled into the yard from the cut, staring at the windows, their bodies stained with the yellow mud of the earthworks and streaked with sweat. I saw on the road beyond them two teams, the demolition gangs, the ten-inch timber baulk with chains, drawn by three giant dray-horses: with this tool they could slice the Old Navigation clear of her foundations.

Man Arfon, however, did not return. Opening the landing window I looked down on the big Negro and the gang surveyor on the cobbles below.

'It needs an hour still, before my father returns,' I called. 'But we will call it legal to fight for right of way.'

'It is legal enough, I will have no brawling,' cried the surveyor, instantly agitated. He knelt with a chalk. 'First peg here, Black Sam. Knock me a peg.'

'The first man who does so gets this,' I said, bringing up the gun. 'But if you have anything to fight with, we will send a man down.'

I saw Black Sam lick his lips. Like an animal that hungers, he stared up at Ifor and me.

'I need an hour,' I said, 'and I've got the champion of the Vale.'

'Not while Ah'm standing,' said Black Sam, grinning.

The surveyor pestered about him, fuming, threatening; the navvies pressed about him, urging him on in banter and threats.

And my brother will hand him the same he got off my da,' I said, to fume him. The Negro grinned wider and unbuttoned his coat, flinging it away. Magnificent he looked in height and strength, then, the sun flashing on his great body. Beside me Ifor was trembling with excitement. Below us the navvies were packing in droves into the yard, bawling, shoving, yelling up at us.

'Make a ring, Black Sam!'

'I give threes on Sam!'

'Taken.'

A Welsh voice shouted from their ranks, 'You'd best get it over quick, Sam, before his dada gets back.'

'Is he coming down or do I come and fetch him?' asked the Negro.

'Give me a knee, Bryn?' asked Ifor.

'Aye.'

Gran cried then, 'Oh, God, the black savage will kill him!'

'More than likely,' I whispered back, 'but it should take half an hour, and by that time Dada will be back.'

In the kitchen I filled a bucket with water and followed Ifor out into the yard: seeing the bucket, knowing that soon the bright spring water would run red, the mob rumbled in its maw, thirsting. And as we came mid-ring the surveyor rushed up to Ifor, squabbling in protest in a falsetto whine, and Ifor stooped and seized him and threw him high into the fists of the crowd.

'Right, you, Black Sam,' said Ifor a moment later, and he lifted from my knee and wandered towards the Black Welshman, grinning, his black-maned head thrust out, inviting a blow. Thick, heavy and tall though he was, my brother looked a pigmy as he circled the Negro giant.

'Good afternoon,' said Sam.

There was no sound in the world just then but the padding feet of the fighters.

Ifor was in first; a snap left, and the Negro slipped it, grinning back. Cagily, they circled, left fists out, right hands cocked. Suddenly hunching his thick shoulders, Ifor shuffled in, flatfooted, shooting up a stream of lefts to Sam's face, ducked a right counter and hooked a vicious right to the body and swung the same fist to the chin: the blow was square and on the point, and I think I knew the outcome, for Black Sam hardly blinked. But then, with the speed of light, Ifor stepped back and hooked a glorious overarm right flush to the head, and as

Sam fell forward, he swung heavily to the midriff. The Negro gasped, and went on a knee, then, amazingly, buckled up and sat on his haunches, grinning stupidly.

'What's thou doin' on t'arse, Black Sam?' cried a navvy.

'Well done, Taff!'

The crowd mumbled and mawed, swaying for the sight of blood.

'Up and do 'im, Sam!'

A North Country roared, 'Stay on backside, Black Welshman: half a bar I got on the White Welsh!'

Ifor sat on my knee as Sam got up and swayed back to his second.

'You watch him, man,' I whispered.

'He do hit easy, mind,' said Ifor.

'And so do you. Keep him off, for God's sake, till Dada comes.'

'To hell with Dada,' said Ifor. 'This baby is mine.'

A man shouted then, 'Three to one against the Welsh lad!'

'Taken.'

'Milk-sops, these bargees. He'll be on his back next round, as God's me judge. Will anyone give me sixes against him?'

'I will,' cried Gran from the back door. 'Milk-sops, is it?' cried she, going Irish. 'If the granfer were here except the grandson your black baby would be half-way over Swansea. Sixes I'm taking, man,' and she came out into the ring with Granfer's mole-skin cap on her palm.

Banter and roars at this, with the navvies loving it.

'Gran, back in the house!' I shouted.

'Indeed, I will not. Sure, there's enough of your granfer in him to eat this big fool!' and she gripped Ifor's shoulder, yelling, 'If ye tangle with the blood of Ben Evan, then you pay for it. I'm taking six to one against me grandson, and I have the money here to prove it,' and the sovereigns leaped in her hand.

'Time!' roared somebody.

'To the devil with the time, I'm taking the bets,' cried Gran, and went round the ring of kneeling navvies with the money flowing into her mole-skin cap.

'Gran!' shouted Ifor. 'Out of it!' and he rose, gripping her bustle, but she slapped him away and fetched him one on the side of the head that nearly buckled him. 'Six to one I'm offering, are ye taking?'

'You're on, missus!' bawled a ginger navvy, dancing her in a circle, and they came from the crowd, pushed Black Sam aside and linked hands, dancing her in a ring, fists up in the air, their clogs raising the dust and whooping like a tribe of Cherokee Indians, while Gran, her skirt lifted, swept in and out of the howling navvies with her cap spilling copper and silver.

'Dear God, it's terrible,' said Ifor, close to tears. 'She's spoiling my life's ambition.'

'Rhiannon!' I shouted. 'Come and fetch Gran out of it!' and Rhiannon came scuttling into the yard and started pushing and heaving, and just then Ifor left my knee, went into the crowd, fended Gran off with one hand and hit Black Sam with the other, and he was head over heels among hobnails, and when he got up he was breathing murder, switching his stance as he rushed. Ifor waited, then let fly with a glorious right-hander, which is the way to beat the right-hand-forward. Sam took it square, tottered and fell. Ifor turned and came back to my knee. He had not been absent ten seconds.

'And what d'you think of that?' cried Gran. 'Is it still sixes, ye sons of heathens?'

Hats were going up, money was spilling, odds were being shrieked as Rhiannon managed to tow Gran back into the house, and I reckon they could hear the row up in Bethel Street, Glyn Neath. For the yard was now filled like mackerel in a barrel, every corner of it jam-packed with ragged men and boys, the refuse of the mountains spewing from their holes in the embankments and culverts. From the cooking-pots of the navvy shanties came the whores and mistresses, the crones and beauties of the cut and railway. Ifor whispered, 'There's some ripe ones arriving now, Bryn. Any sign of Dada?'

'Come on, lads!' yelled Gran from the back door. 'Cover your mouth with your money. Six to one I'm taking on me grandson. It's the best chance of easy money since me husband duffed up Dick the Drover outside the Plough in Clyne,' and she dangled the frying-pan and hit it with a hammer. 'Out and finish it, Ifor, boy!'

'Time!' I shouted, and lifted Ifor under the ribs, and Black Sam met him with a looping right swing that took Ifor's legs from under him, and the moment he was up fetched him another that would have pole-axed an ox.

Bedlam now, as I ran out, hauled Ifor to his feet and started slapping his chops to bring him round, and Gran and Rhiannon ran out and helped to get him on my knee and every time they did he rolled sideways like a drunk, and there was Black Sam sparring up before us shouting insults above the roar of the navvies while Ifor was rocking around on my knee not knowing if he was in Resolven or Swansea.

'Did he hit me?' asked Ifor, dazed.

'He did,' said Gran, 'and he'll do it again unless you get up and square off to him.'

'You ought to be ashamed of yourself,' I shouted at her.

'Where is he?' asked Ifor.

'Big as a barn door, he is,' cried Gran. 'Oh, me son, won't you lift off and see to him in the name of Granfer Ben? For you're fighting for right of way. It's the drover's fighting, you see, and legal. Just up and hit him, lad.'

'The big black one in the middle, is it?' asked Ifor.

'Time!' she yelled, and hit the frying-pan, but instead of getting up my brother Ifor just flopped about, going in circles on my knee with his eyes crossed and the Black Welshman towering above us shouting insults on the family and the navvies bellowing for Maniac Square, shouting for their bets. And just when the commotion was gathering height Gran suddenly stooped, lifted the waterbucket and swung it at Black Sam's head and he lay back into the crowd with his arms wide and his feet up, and as if this wasn't enough she flung Rhiannon aside and dived among the crowd, swinging the bucket and not losing a drop, and everywhere she went she left a trail of dead and dying behind her. Very undignified it was, to see Gran laying into people with a full bucket, putting them out right and left with Rhiannon on her bustle being towed along behind her. And there was Ifor, the Champion of the Vale, still on my knee and flopping about from the four-

198

penny Black Sam had caught him. Very ashamed I felt, and I closed my eyes, and when I opened them again Gran was still at it and gathering speed and my father was coming through the crowd by the stable door in a very fancy trap with a pony and a fine gentleman, and will somebody please explain what the hell is going on as he vaulted over the side.

I got Ifor on to his feet and left him swaying and ran over to my father, crying, 'It is Black Sam and Man Arfon came with surveyor's pegs, so Ifor fought for right of way until Gran started into them with a bucket.'

'I can see that,' said my father, 'and it appears she is still at it,' and so she was since she was right in the middle of them now and swinging like mad and navvies were ducking and howling and the slow ones going down like pit-props, and the language steaming up was driving Gran into a frenzy. And just before my father got to her they were raising Black Sam on to his feet, so she lay back and swung him another and he was down again with six on top of him.

'Mother, for God's sake!' cried my father, shocked, for though he basically had nothing against anyone hitting out navvies this does not make much of an impression on a Swansea solicitor of the grade of Mr. Seth Cowbum, who was standing in the middle of the yard now, watching the slaughter with sad eyes through his pince-nez glasses.

A God-fearing type was this Mr. Seth Cowbum, and very severe he looked as he examined my Gran, in his high starched collar, his goatie beard munching, and the place was filled with shrieks and screams as the navvies started spilling out of the stable yard with Gran after them screaming like a caged lunatic.

'Mother!' bawled my father in his fair-ground voice, and she stopped dead, did Gran. With her hair down to her waist and her eyes on fire, she dropped the bucket and stood guilty before him. Pitying her, I ran to her and gripped her hand and we stood together before his wrath.

'A most disgraceful exhibition, I must say,' breathed my father, his face stern.

'Not her fault, mind,' I said. 'Fighting for right of way, I told you.'

'Quiet, you!' said Dada. 'I do business with a Swansea solicitor and bring him here to avoid violence, and I find it already on the go. To say the least, I am most ashamed.'

'Injunctions do not keep the house up,' I cried. 'If Gran had not slammed in they would have had the roof off.'

Very sorry for herself my Gran looked, standing there with her fingers hooked before her and her eyes cast down, but up came the Swansea solicitor with his hand up and very benign, standing there like a string-bean, smiling.

'Mostyn Evan,' said he, sonorous, 'there are times when court injunctions are issued over the ashes of burning property, and they are useless when they arrive late. Force, sometimes, must be met with force, and proves more effective than legal scraps of paper. Would it avail us if the house was down?'

'No, sir,' said Dada, looking simple.

'Would you,' said Mr. Cowbum, all collar and whiskers, 'would you have looked with pride on a cowardly woman who had sat within, and wept?'

'I suppose not, sir,' said my father, standing sideways in his boots. 'Very sorry, I am.'

'Excellent.' Mr. Seth Cowbum, the solicitor very eminent in Swansea, bowed low before my gran and swept off his topper. 'Good woman, may more like you bring forth your kind and build the Empire, and in passing save the time of the legal profession, which invariably arrives too late. With your kind permission, ma'am, I will escort you back to the house.'

'Oh, sir!' cried Gran, undone, and she backed off and went down in her best gentry curtsey, and just then Rhiannon came back from the house and went down, too. Beautiful it looked, you know, with that revered gentleman all side-whiskers and frock coat doing his professional bow and my gran at his feet, her head bowed, her skirt a black stain on the cobbles, and the navvies that were left in the yard were dumb with enchantment, doffing their mole-skins and lowering their faces, for good manners do get the best of us, even those who do come from pigsties.

'Your son apologises, ma'am,' said Mr. Seth Cowbum. 'And I will take the problem from your capable hands, and if the Great Western Railway encroaches on your property henceforth, it will be the last illegal thing it does.'

Straight he stood then, in grace, his arm hooked, and my gran got up and took it and away they went, the pair of them, stepping like a brace of Arab stallions, nodding and bowing to all and sundry, through the stable yard and round to the front entrance.

'Sod me,' said my father. 'I am two sovereigns lighter on a legal injunction and she gets it free with her boots and a yard bucket.' Deep he sighed. 'She has been doing this kind of thing for years, and she always do finish with the upper hand.'

22

AUTUMN blustered into winter, and the branch line came through, missing us, like the main line, by about twenty feet. Icicled, frosted, piled with snow, the Old Navigation sat in the throat of the railway and the giant Corsairs of Brunel rattled through, belching their steam and smoke into the kitchen on their way to Aberdare, flinging soot and sulphur into the bed-rooms along the branch to Rheola. Standing square to the on-slaught, the old inn groaned and rasped her timbers as thou-sands of tons of coal, iron and limestone thundered past her foundations. Cracks appeared in her walls, hair lines that widened into crevices from ceiling to floor: the roof began to sag, and we shored it; the windows jammed and we took them out, eased and replaced them; the doors would not close. And at night we lay wide awake in our beds and listened to the wheel-spins and snorts from as far up the gradient as Pont Walby and Pencydrain. Below us the loading bays of the Clydach tram-road roared and thumped on the night shifts, the black diamonds of Resolven, our own colliery, rushing in a sea into the jaws of the trucks while our barge was tied up empty on our wharf. One trip after another was cancelled, one contract after another was stopped. By the time spring was blowing her warm winds over Sarn Helen the barge rates dropped lower still, the hauls became fewer, the canal shares cheaper still. It was two a month now, and lucky to get it from a sneering Man Arfon.

But I do not remember the year of '53 because of the skinny times, but because it surely must have been the most romantic in the history of the hamlet since 800 years and the times of the Normans. Dai Central Eating started it by leading Tegwen Harriet down to Aberdulais Baptist, the new chapel, which sent old Eli cackling with delight, but he cackled a different tune some eight months later when Tegwen rose like a ship under sail and landed him twin girls. Then Ifor stood before Tomos Traherne, the big Revival in Zion, Re-solven, with Rebecca Cohen on his arm, and not before time, said my father, for Rebecca came so hot that particular June that you could boil an egg on her, said Gran, and with Ifor not knowing what day of the week it was, the attic was cleared and the bundling bed laid out. On wet Sundays, when Rebecca visited, it was upstairs sharp with the pair of them on twin pillows and Ifor with his boots on and Rebecca done up to the ears in mail bags and sail canvas, which I firmly believe is the most beautiful Celtic custom, though with Ifor's hair standing on end when they came down for supper it do not do a great deal for the blood pressure. 'I cannot get that pair up past Lyons Row quick enough,' my dada used to say, and the following year he achieved this and nine months to the very day Rebecca's hair went redder still and she came even lovelier in the face with her and gracious with curves, especially in the front, and Eli went down to Neath for special Benediction, and when she propped up a girl he went to the very edge of his grave. Gran reckoned she had the answer to this, of course.

'Mind,' said she at tea-time, 'I have known herring exactly the same—only one roe in five million is male—right in the middle of the soft ones. This Cohen family is doomed to the breast and the womb and old Eli had better make the best of it.'

'It is an attractive theory,' said Dada, getting up from table and putting his feet up with the *Cambrian*.

'Of course,' said Gran, 'it could well be that those Cohen

girls are not doing it properly. There are the rights and wrongs of going about these things.'

Mari said swiftly, 'Another cup, Gran? Yours is stone cold.'

'Eh, no,' said Ifor, munching, 'you come wrong about that— my 'Becca knows everything about those matters.'

'Aye, but there are certain antics you got to perform, and you know it, Mostyn.'

'Excuse me,' said Sharon, spluttering in her tea, and going out.

My father said, sighing and putting down his paper, 'Do you think we might change the subject, Mother? We have had Ifor's assurance that Rebecca is well informed on these things, and from what I have seen I am also quite satisfied.'

'It is the bustling and corseting that is mainly the answer, mind,' said Gran.

'The what, darling?' whispered Mari, her face bright with love.

'High in the front for a girl, broad in the beam for a boy, see: bustling and proper corseting is the way to make the selection.'

Other romantic things happened. Mrs. Ten went up to eleven on Man Arfon, though I never did understand what that was supposed to mean. Jane Rheola and Meic Jones, the pot-boy once sweet on Sharon, should have kept going in Rheola Forest, but didn't, which was a happy thing, I think, for a lively little girl was Jane and it was only a public duty to turn herself into two, in or out of wedlock. Taliesen the Poet married Miss Bronwen Rees and had a son they called Algernon, for there is nothing like keeping the Welsh flavour when you are in love with Wales, like her, said Dewi; he still extremely keen on night visitations to the Lamb and Flag, Glyn Neath, and he do not arrive up there for washing his socks, said Sharon, who was still going strong on the travelling players and the Neath Penny Gaffs.

Also, we had a funeral at the Old Navigation that spring, though nobody died, but more of this later. Nevertheless, it do go to show what a queer old place the Vale was about this period.

Finally, my butty, Tai Morlais, married Sian Edwards in his navvy shanty in Lower Dulais, where Mr. Brunel was forming a base for the building of a new railway in the Swansea valley, and Tai and Sian jumped over a chair, which was about the closest the navigators got to a wedding service. On that great day, after receiving the invitation, I climbed into my best suit and my tallest collar; spruced up, broomed down and polished, and intended to hobnail it over Seven Sisters, but Fate intervened.

'You mind what you're up to,' said Gran. 'Evil folk, these navigators, remember.'

'Oh, no Gran, please,' interjected Mari, shocked. 'You are speaking of his friend!'

'Not evil, when you know them,' I said.

Mari said, at her stitching, 'You going alone, boy?'

'Aye, Mari.'

'Good excuse, is it, with Richard coming this evening?'

'As good as any,' I said, rubbing boots. 'A pretty good pair, with Mr. Seth Cowbum coming, too.'

'You leave Mr. Cowbum out of it,' said Gran, pointing with a comb.

In fact, some very strange things happened that spring, with Dewi out most nights with the new Chartist movement up in Nantyglo, and Gran acting queer.

'Rhiannon might like to come with you, Bryn,' whispered Mari.

'She's got Richard Bennet,' I said, gruff.

Drive you daft, see, what with one and another of them. Aye, very pulled in and perfumed was my gran these days, curling with hot irons before the shaving mirror, patting and preening, and how do I look, and would I pass in a crowd: not that I care either way if he comes, or not, for Mr. Seth Cowbum must lead his own life—anyway, he'd drop me at the nearest lamp, for he has yet to see me in fierce sunlight or on an off-day, for every woman over seventy has an off-day. And my father, lighting his pipe in the corner by the grate, would wink and eye Gran sideways as he folded up the *Cambrian*.

'Rhia would come if you asked her, Bryn.'

'Aye,' and I kissed her face; the only mother I had ever had, this one, and, in passing, the most beautiful woman in Wales.

I was just getting old Nell into the saddle in the yard when Rhiannon flew up to me all black curls, peaches and cream and crinoline; flushed and breathless with her: 'Oh, Bryn, take me with you!'

'But you haven't been invited, woman!'

'But Tai and Sian would not mind. Oh, take me!'

'What about Richard Bennet—isn't he arriving here?'

'That is why I want to be with you. Oh, Bryn!'

Nearly in tears.

You know, bloody daft are women, and I do not understand them. For months now I had this Bennet chap stuffed and cooked for breakfast, dinner and tea.

'Pretty rough, these navvies, remember—curse to make your hair curl.'

'Oh, my precious, I would not mind!'

'Right. Hurry up, then.'

And she was away shrieking, to come back a full hour later all done up gorgeous with her hair piled in ringlets and a pink crinoline and a big, white, floppy hat lying on her shoulders, and red and blue bonnet streamers flying.

'There is a good boy now, waiting for Rhiannon,' said she, wagging a finger, and stood waiting until I caught her at the waist and put her side-saddle on Nell, who rolled an evil eye at us, for there is no romance in the life of mules, as is widely known.

Honeyed and dark, this new Rhiannon, with the wonderful mystery of her womanhood swelling at her breast, and great was her dignity, chin up, smiling down. And I was just clip-clopping out of the stable gate with her held before me when Gran came dashing out of the house, yelling:

'Bring her back this minute, you hear me? Navvy weddings are not fit for virgin women. Bring her back, I say!'

So I gave Nell the heels and we were off down the cut at a gallop, shrieking, with my father's bass laughter and Mari's contralto echoing behind us.

There is beautiful it is to be clip-clopping along on a mule with the sap rising in tree and manhood, and the one you love obedient in your arms, and all the green of a new year falling about you, the April banks swarming with buttercups, celandines, and the woods behind hazed with bluebells and bee-hum and shafts of gold emblazoned in the glades. Sweet and warm was the wind, perfumed on my face by the breath of Rhiannon. Carelessly, I said:

'Why this sudden need to be with me? Usually, when Richard is down from Nanty I do not get a sniff.'

'I am afraid of Richard,' said she, her eyes cast down. 'Besides, I have always wanted to see a navvy wedding.'

'End up in bed with the groom, unless you're careful,' I said, and tightened the rein, determined that she would not trifle with me, for she was often bunned up and skinny with me, while she was the water on my throat. I swung old Nell along the drovers' track below Sarn Helen and across the Dulais Valley, and the sun was all hot and merry with him at the thought of summer and larks were diving and trilling in a sky of varnished blue. The great country of March-Hywel, stained with its blood of warriors, swung up before us in a blaze of morning, with great haloes of cloud-smoke flowing over our heads. Here, fifteen hundred feet above the shimmering Bristol Channel, Neath and Swansea were patterned in fire and smoke below us, with Skewen and Morriston blazing like hells demented in mushrooms of flame and sulphurous billows. Taking Nell short on the bridle, I lifted Rhiannon down into my arms, and held her, and such was the strength in me that I could have tossed her high in gay laughter and not snatched at a breath.

'Like a bull elephant you are,' said she, commanding. 'Put me down, Bryn Evan!'

Nineteen and fourteen stone and six-foot-two, I was, and looking for trouble. With one hand I could have held her still, but could not, because I loved her.

'Eh, dear me,' I whispered, and reached for her after laying her down, but she twisted away with the speed of a serpent and was on her feet in a gust of laughter, skirts up and flying down the mountain in a rhythm of ankle-drawers trimmed with lace, the huzzy. Hobnails pounding, I went after her and caught her below the hill of Caru, collapsing her in a tangle of petticoats and curls, and we lay together, Rhia and me, snatching at breath, and I kissed her amid gasps and protests.

'Hei up!' she cried. 'You are eating me alive.' She showed her arm. 'And look, the bruises!' Flushed and panting she was, and not all come with the running. 'Bread pudding, am I? Biting out lumps, you are.'

'I am sorry.'

'I am not,' said she. 'Let us have more of it, for you are not exactly greased lightning, Bryn,' and she closed her eyes and pouted her lips for kisses, but I turned from her.

I turned from her because often, when Richard came to visit, she was frugal with me, and tarty, like gooseberry pie without the sugar in, and when he was around I heard but the whisper of her, and never her song. It is always astonishing to me how beautifully God put the body together, yet took such little care when he stitched up the soul.

Her eyes were troubled when she said. 'As restless as an old cow's tail, you are, man. Is it angry with me, boy?'

'Bloody daft you would call me, were I to explain it.'

At this she reached out mothering hands, and held my head, swaying me and humming, which is the mother in the lover when I wanted her as a girl. I pulled myself away, and got up.

Wandering away, pushing old Nell aside, I went to the top of Caru and stared down over a golden land, seeing the cut lancing silver through the hills and the Nedd all flashing white and gleaming through the rocks of Clyne and Tonna. Lying on an elbow, I thought of the Roman legions which had rested here, the kisses taken and given by fierce Silure and Italian; the Spanish lovers of the lost decades in tears of birth and dying: here, in the place of sun and wind that I call Wales. Oh, beautiful Wales, I thought, on whose breast we are lying, you and me, Rhiannon, whose blood is noble and has coursed through ancient princes. 'Do you understand, Rhia?'

'It is all a bit complicated for me,' said she, coming up and lying beside me. 'Tell me, Bryn, tell me what you are thinking!' and she caught my hand and pressed it against her breast, and the softness of her stilled me. Still lying, I said:

'You will not laugh if I tell you of a story my mother told me, when I was ten years old? You want to hear how God made the earth?'

'Aye,' said she, in warmth and secrets.

I said, holding her, and looking down on Wales, 'In six days God made the earth, and on the seventh day he rested, as is told in Genesis. You listening?'

'Ears shivering,' said she, eyes closed.

'And he went from his workshop to his couch, and slept. But the wind moved over the land, stirring open his door. And God looked into his workshop again and saw that his task was not yet finished since he had a small barrel of clay and a large barrel of vision and enterprise left over. "I will make another nation," said he, getting up, "and because I am at the end of the alphabet, I will call them *Welsh*." You still with me?' I asked her.

'I can hear the beating of your heart,' said Rhiannon, like a cat in cream.

I continued, 'So he made the Welsh, and because he had put little clay, he made them small in stature, to get more of them. And he put them down on a plain and watched them mate and bring forth, and this they did readily, said my mother, because their blood was of the hot Iberian. And then, five hundred years later, which to God was a moment of Time, he looked again, and they had come to thousands.'

I got up, looking over the land, and said, 'But although they were fierce in love and war they were uncultured, and God knew then his only mistake, and said, 'Of course! How can a people of small stature, filled with vision and enterprise, see into distant places when they live on a plain? So I will make their country with mountains. Snowdonia, and Dinas and the Black Mountains and the Beacons!' You hear me, Rhia?'

But she was sleeping, not given to poetry, and I went from her to a quiet place of bushes and stood there filled with a great excitement, looking down on my mother, my girl. For a man can mate with a country, make no mistake. There, on that April day up on March-Hywel, I heard the cry of the bards. In sword-clash, I heard the song of a lost age of princes, the cries of the feudal lords, and saw the skin of the beast Lee and heard his talk of felons: the hammering of scaffolds, I heard, up from the Marcher Lordships; the squalid poetry of Tudur Aled, whom my father hated. My eyes filled with tears and I began to tremble, and I knelt on the soil that bore me and thrust my fingers deep into its earth, and listened to the song. In all my dreams of possessing Rhiannon, in all the stuttering panic of lips and heart and loins, there was a greater need in me than Rhiannon, and a greater, deeper love. This was a mother of haughty pride; a land cleansed by her rejection of the conqueror.

I got up. The wind was cold on my face, I remember, and I looked at my hands. The fingers, the hands, the wrists were stained with her soil, where I had driven them. And there was a great joy in me, a calm in me: one with my country.

Rhiannon was lying asleep where I had left her; the mule grazed nearby.

And I went to Rhia, and knelt, touching her foot, and at this she awakened instantly, starting in panic, then smiling, her hand to her throat.

'You come back to me, Bryn?' she asked, softly.

'Aye, Rhia.' I was cool with her, having no need of her now.

'You believe I love you?'

I did not reply, and she said, looking away:

'You want me to prove that I love you, Bryn Evan?'

So beautiful she looked, lying there, with the redness flying in her cheeks and her eyes dark in her face. I seemed to hear her voice as from a great distance:

'You want me bad, you take me, Bryn, for I am your girl.'

I remember only that I held her, and she said, in gasps:

'Oh, God, Bryn. Oh, God, you hold me!'

Even on the best of us, says Gran, some rust do stain the mechanism of the soul. With a little human assistance it do easily polish off, though.

'Up a dando, quick,' I said, lifting her to her feet. 'Up quick, before you are in trouble. No chapel up by here, no Methodist preacher up on Mynydd March-Hywel. Done decent, it will be, with a ring and proper service, because I love you.' My hands were soiled, I remember, and I held them to my face.

'And I love you, too, Bryn, *cariad*,' she said. 'For all the

Richards coming and going, I do love Bryn, my sweet, my precious. Up away, and dando! Last one down to Hendre is a maniac,' and she was off again down the hill with skirts up and me after her, dragging Nell Mule.

It is not really much good trying to tell of a navvy wedding, when they go on a randy: you have to be there yourself to witness it. And the randy they turned up south of Crynant on the day Tai Morlais, my butty, married Sian Edwards, is talked off in the Dulais Valley to this day.

'I'm frit,' said Rhiannon, as I wheeled Nell down the last slopes above Crynant and we approached the encampment.

'If that's all that happens to you, I'll be thankful,' I said. 'You realise randy navvies are hot enough normal, without you setting fire to them?'

'You shouldn't have let me come,' said she, pert and nose up.

There is no sense in some people, so I did not answer, but clamped her with my arms and reined Nell Mule through the hutments of the compound, and doors came open and windows blew out and craggy faces and hair appeared and look what's coming, for God's sake.

One moment peace and quiet, next a commotion, with dogs bounding up snarling and cats going like bullets, and the earth street a clamour of ragged children and shrieking crones.

On we went, with Rhia white-faced but waving and bowing with brightness, and a few of the women curtseyed, give them credit, and a group of old navvies pulled off their caps on doorsteps as we passed.

'Where you bound for, mister?' This from a hulker naked to the trews, washing in a barrel, hair tuddled up, wet flesh gleaming.

'Tai Morlais' wedding breakfast!'

'Straight through, and best you come early, for Tai won't have a bloody leg under him in an hour.' His hands paused and his eyes traced Rhiannon from toe to face and back again. Like a wet tiger he looked, standing there watching.

'Bryn, love, you won't leave me, eh?' Shivering, she was.

'Depends how you behave. By the time the wedding is over

they won't know you from Sian Edwards. Just act natural and keep close.'

Cheap-jacks and hucksters were unfolding travelling stalls outside the rough huts, and as we rode deeper into the compound the music of fiddles and squeeze-boxes greeted us. The crowds grew thicker; thick-stemmed, hairy men, all stripped to the waist, were rolling out barrels of ale or tossing them high on to their brown shoulders: boy-navvies rushed past with piled loaves and pails of butter from the crowded tommy-shop on a corner. Black-dressed and bunned-up, the navvy wives watched in lounging unconcern as we passed: a dogfight under Nell's very nose now, and a fist-fight in one of the huts, by the sound of it, with furniture over-turning and glass splintering in coarse oaths and shrieks from a woman.

'Don't look very healthy,' said Rhiannon, shivering, and gasping.

'Didn't I warn you? Anything Welsh in skirts they have for dinner, and you look tasty done up like that.'

'A pig you are, Bryn Evan. Dear me, look at this!'

Flouncy women now, six of them, done up in red and blousy, waving fists and gin bottles, and doing mock curtseys to Rhiannon as we trotted by, and up with them, shrieking hoarsely, and the language floating up on the gin sent me sheet-white and shocked, and I'd heard some in my time.

By a well in the middle of the encampment a great bonfire was burning and a whole calf was turning on a spit, with a swaying crowd of navvies and their women laying out benches for the celebrations, and a butcher, beefy and red, sharpening knives; people shouting in a score of dialects from Scotland to the Welsh border, and wizened old navvies already dancing in circles to the music of a melodeon, their arms going up like dervishes. Now a gipsy dancer in a scarlet skirt and bangle earrings, her long, black hair flying as she spun and swayed to the screech of Irish fiddles. And behind her I saw Tai Morlais, fists on his hips and staring. Gone was the boy, this was a man. Deep-throated, he called:

'Bryn Evan!'

'Ay ay!' I shouted.

Through the people he came, swinging men aside. 'Bryn Evan, Bryn Evan!'

'So you got her, eh?' I shouted in the commotion, and slipped off Nell and lifted Rhiannon down, and he gripped me with big hands: fine and handsome he looked, did Tai; all done up in mole-skin trews with red stockings and high-laced boots, and the finest velveteen coat over a scarlet waistcoat with pearl buttons, and his tammy, bright blue, with a sleeping-bobble swinging on his head.

'Where's Sian, then?' I yelled above the clamour.

'Ach, do we need her when there's crackling like this around?' Low he bowed to Rhia. 'A woman should be full in the haunch and firm in the calf, so you're the loveliest dinner I've seen since the old days of Cushy Cuddlecome.'

'She's me friend, Tai,' I said, taking off his Irish. 'She's gentry stock, and delicate in the ears, so please water the language.'

'I will, for sure, man.' He was staring at Rhiannon. 'You'll forgive the bad manners, for I'm bog Irish, lady. And it's just that I'm unsure if I'm on me arse or me elbow, for the beauty of ye is undoin' me. Ach, it's beautiful. Will ye step this way, ma'am, and I'll show ye me bunk, though the trouble is that I'm only a buck navvy, and ye'll be sharing it with another thirty, or so.'

'Can I come, too?' I asked.

'Sure, you're welcome. It's too rough for a lady, being out here and every dirty old Lancashire and what-not givin' her the eye. Come and meet Sian,' and he tossed Nell's reins to a lad and caught Rhiannon's hand and was away through the crowd with her to a hut beyond the roasting animal, and the cheers and roars that followed him deafened me. After them I went, and just in time got a glimpse of Rhia's pink crinoline as she disappeared into the hut on the end of him.

In the hut Sian was sitting on her bed, being prepared for her wedding: very off-the-shoulder was Sian, and beautiful, sitting there in her Welshness and a strange piety as the women dressed her. Bangle earrings for Sian; pale and smooth her face, but rouged in the lips where the navvy wives had painted; red was her dress, and her shoes were laced above her ankles. In simple grace she sat, unspeaking, her face in profile against the single window while the ragged wives scuttled about her.

'Sian, are you listening?' Tai bent before her, screwing his tammy. He drew Rhiannon forward, whispering, 'There's no talking in her, ye see, girl. She'll likely be a shrew after the wedding, so there's no talking in her before she jumps the chair, ye understand. It's a virgin quiet, see. An' I have her word on it, so I'm lucky.' He bent to Sian, who sat motionless, as if deaf, blind and mute. 'I'm bringing me friend and his woman, Sian. You remember Bryn Evan down at Cushy's? You recall the night he came and swiped Cinders, the wee bitch? Well, he's come over the mountain to wish us well, an' it's six sons he'll be wishin' you, woman, for although he's a Taff, he's a right good fella. Can ye hear me, Sian? It's plentiful that he's hoping for us, an' that's good friends indeed.'

No sign, not a movement she made; straight over his shoulder she looked as the women oiled her hair, which was plaited either side of her head and reached to her waist.

'I have brought a gift for you Sian,' I said and gave a sovereign to Tai.

He opened her fingers, closing them upon the sovereign. I said, leaning towards her, 'The money is split between me and Rhia. And last week I took it up to Pont-Nedd-Fechan and put it under a boulder, and when I went up for it last night the fairy offering was there, in twelve white circles of paper, but I would not take the exchange.'

'Blessed, it is,' said Rhiannon, touching her hand, 'for he did not take the exchange.'

'Dear God,' said Tai. 'There is lovely friends we do have, isn't it?'

Sian did not reply.

'No turnings and no breeches I wish you,' said Rhiannon. 'Easy births, Sian, and sons I will have for you.'

'Go now,' said one of the women, and I straightened, looking around the hut. There were about forty beds lining the rough, mud walls, some single and a few double. About twenty navvies were in there, some sitting on their beds, some in them, sleeping after shift, for they were working on the tunnel drainage, and some farther up on the Merthyr, which had been a thorn in Ritson's side from the day he constructed it. In the double beds men and women were sleeping; one bed held a family of four, and the woman was awake, with a child at her breast, sucking noisily in the strange silence, fists waving. In the middle of the room was a stove and on the fire a big black pot, and stirring it, like a witch over a brew, was a ragged, skinny old woman. Hanging out of the pot were lengths of string, each with a name tied to the end: a coney in the pot for Redbonce, explained Tai afterwards; a piece of stolen beef for Sour Billo, a quarrelsome navvy who hailed from Cork; half a hare for Dirty Tom and a squirrel for Parson, the new English boy, who prayed.

'Right the first evenin' he come in, he prayed,' said Tai, 'and Boxer came in with ten quarts aboard and let fly with his boot, and the boot hit Parson and cut his face, and the blood ran down through his fingers, but still he prayed, kneeling by the bed.'

'But he does not pray now,' said Rhiannon.

'Oh, aye, he does still,' said Tai. 'Next night he prayed the same, and Boxer threw the boot again and it knocked Parson over on his ear, and when he came round he started praying again, with one eye filled up. And on the third night he come in Boxer left his own bed and sat on Parson's, while he prayed with a special one for Boxer because he was a bastard, behaving like that. And he still sits there. Anyone throwing at Parson now gets the boot from Boxer.'

My father says there is more honour under oil-lamps than under chandeliers.

Tai said, outside the hut, 'Did you see my Sian cry, Bryn Evan?'

'Aye.'

'She cries because I'm only a navvy, and a buck Irish one, at that, and my Welsh name do make no difference.'

'Up to you, Tai, to see she do not cry in future,' I said.

But at the dancing Sian did not cry.

In a whirl of colour Sian danced in the middle of a ring of clapping, cheering navvies, with her Irish fiddlers playing for her and Tai as he armed her round in circles. Cushy Cuddle-come was there, too, with her Irish stew, standing on a dray cheering and bawling, urging the customers to drink deep, and I made sure there was something about sixteen stones between me and Cushy, for she would give out some past history as soon as look at me. The afternoon wore on into dusk, and at the first stars the celebrations stopped.

'Bring out the chair!'

The cry was taken up. 'Bring the chair, bring the chair!' The brawny creatures sho had rafted the bogs of Chat Moss linked hands, chanting:

'The chair, the chair!'

I watched them.

These were the men who drove the terrible Woodhead tunnels in Cheshire, in '45 and last year: men such as these, childish in their joy now, were those who braved the terrifying barrow-runs of the London to Birmingham; whose comrades died under earth falls and borehole explosions, or in upset buckets in the tunnel air-shafts. Who built the Paris to Rouen railway and ate with Brassey at the Feast of Maisons the year before last: these giants, now chanting falsetto and clapping at the wedding of a little Welsh serving-maid, were those who knew no law but labour; who, by their sweat, had changed the face of Britain and raised monuments greater than the Pyramids; these were the men who, within a few years, were to save the ragged, beaten British army of the war in the Crimea. I saw them anew, not as men who were taking away my birth-right of the barges, but as the new heroes of my generation.

'The chair!' The chant was taken up to a thunder, and a little gnome of a navvy rushed into the ring and placed one down.

Silence. Not a whisper. The wind blew softly from March-Hywel, fanning our faces. Rhiannon's hand was gripping mine. I see her face now, her lips parted, expectant, and I feel the tenseness of her body beside me. In the ring Tai Morlais and Sian Edwards stood motionless, as carved from stone; twin splashes of colour against the green of the mountain.

And then Tai moved. Going first, he leaped over the chair,

skidded to a halt, and turned, his arms wide. Sian curtseyed deep to him, her face lowered, and then, straightened, lifted her skirts to her waist and ran, bounding over the chair and into his arms, and they fell together on the grass in a joyful tumble of limbs as he kissed her to a bellow of cheers from the navvies. Instantly, the ring was broken. Turning, shrieking, hand in hand, they ran, Tai and Sian, and got about ten yards before the navvies caught them, carrying them shoulder high to the hut where Sian had been prepared for the wedding.

'But when is the wedding?' demanded Rhiannon, flushed in the milling crowd.

'That was the wedding,' I said.

'But they had no minister.'

So beautiful she looked standing there among the pushing, barging people, that I kissed her.

'They do not need a minister, girl, all the time they have got a chair,' I said.

'Good God,' she said, fanning, 'and where are they taking them now?'

'Give you three guesses,' I said.

23

IT was bat and curtain time as we clopped along the tow-path past New Inn towards the Old Navigation and the blaze of Rheola, and old Nell was dozy after her descent of March-Hywel and the spin and colour of Tai's wedding, now far behind us.

Sweetly, a hymn sounded then, coming to us on the clear April air, and there drifted upon us a bass unison song of men; a music that entered our dozy dream, as Nell was dozy, of a pale moon, stars and a stamp of hooves. Rhiannon, half asleep against me in the saddle, stiffened, and her eyes were large and startled in the strange light.

'What is that?'

I reined Nell to a halt, and we stood there amid the spring whispers of the cut. A night-jar sang in a frenzy of joy: on the far bank a badger, as blind as a bat, was nosing the soil for his musk, the scent of his earth.

'*Heisht!*' whispered Rhiannon. 'It is hymn-singing from Rheola House.'

Tense, we listened, and heard the words clearly:

> *Abide with me, fast falls the eventide.*
> *The darkness deepens, Lord, with me abide....*

Often, especially on Sunday nights, the Vaughans of Rheola would come up from Aberdulais aqueduct in barges with choirs, and beautiful it was to hear the full harmony of the ancient hymns, and always they sang in Welsh.

'Not Rheola House,' I said. 'It's coming from the Old Navigation.'

'Aye,' replied Rhiannon, breathing again. 'Got enough there today for a full choir—Tomos Traherne and Richard, Mam Mortymer and Mr. Cowbum come to visit Gran....'

'Counting them all that makes eight, if Sharon is home. That is a choir of men, and more like a hundred.'

Shivering was in us; there was an enmity in the night, with the hunchback trees of the cut crouching about us now, like animals for the spring. Nell, too, was trembling beneath us, and snorting, her eyes rolling white.

Opposite Crugau Farm the singing was louder. As the Old Navigation grew into shape under the Rheola moon, it came in a full throat-chorus of tenor and bass.

'For God's sake, what is it?' breathed Rhiannon.

'We will soon find out,' I replied, and gave Nell the heels and we galloped past Crugau straight and I wheeled Nell and reined her short outside the stable yard. In a blast of sound, the singing was about us now.

> *Where is death's sting? where, grave, thy victory?*
> *I triumph still, if Thou abide with me.*

Sliding off Nell, I lifted Rhiannon down, ran to the stable gate and swung it wide into the yard.

217

Packed in a tight circle in the middle of the yard were over a hundred men, and not one head turned to me at the crash of the gate. Bare-headed, they sang as men sing at funerals, dressed in their Sunday best.

'For God's sake what is happening?' I barged into their ranks, spilling and humping them before me, and they did not resist me, but sang on. Beef O'Hara I recognised first, then Mick O'Shea, the Cuddlecome drunk. Laddie O'Brien I shouted at, but he did not answer. Abe Sluice and Ditch Fielder I swung aside, furious and frightened. In the middle of the ring, standing on a rough trestle, was a pauper's coffin, and in letters stark white on the tar was painted my father's name. Mick Spit, the Midlander, I saw then, his face grieved; Bargey Boy and Dutch, Job Moses came next, their handkerchiefs held to their faces.

And Tub Union stood by the coffin in funeral black. With a Prayer Book in his hands, he turned to face me.

'Accept the Union's condolences on the death of your beloved father,' said he, deep. 'We grieve for you in this tragic loss, Bryn Evan.'

Distracted, her face stark white and sweating, Rhiannon burst through into the circle then, and gripped me, but she made no sound.

I bowed my head and the horror of it swept over me in waves, and I knew a cold and awful sickness; the bile rose in my throat, and I swallowed it down. Tub Union said, turning to the men:

'Last verse, now, and give it reverence, for this was a good man, and a brother,' and they sang, in glorious harmony:

> Hold Thou Thy Cross before my closing eyes;
> Shine through the gloom, and point me to the skies ...

Tub Union then turned to me, and said, 'Try anything, lad—one move, and we will pull you to pieces.'

Trembling, I stood there.

It was the mock burial of the scab: it was the burial, by his brothers, of a brother unwanted: the shifting of one who had refused to shift. This was the punishment for working on when the Union said stop. It was the revenge reserved for the traitor Welsh, men like Man Arfon on their way to high places in English business or government.

It was also a forecast of death for one, like my father, who was under-cutting the bargee rates by a penny a ton.

Up in Nantyglo and Blackwood, in Merthyr and Tredegar, the Scotch Cattle would scotch a man by breaking his leg when he worked on when the Union said strike. But the *Funeral of the Scab* was worse than mutilation, for it spelt the death of the soul: a Church of England service for a nonconformist man. And after the service that man was dead to the community. At Market, the wives would console his wife, and send her flowers; wreathes would arrive at the door. At school the children would play at weeping, with his children.

'God help you, Tub Union,' I said, and I turned to my father's voice, for he had heard the mule.

'Is that you, Bryn? Bring Rhiannon in, please.'

Shouldering aside men, I pulled her after me and thrust her into the kitchen; Dada slammed the door.

Hands clenched, I stared around the room.

Dewi I saw first, sitting with legs splayed, butting his fists together in his agony, his face raging and dark: Ifor was sitting in my father's chair by the grate, rigid under his command. Gran, her arms folded on the table, was quietly weeping within them, and Mr. Cowbum, the solicitor, stood with his hand on her shoulder in bewildered timidity. One by one, I saw them as Rhiannon ran into Mari's arms: Tomos Traherne I saw, magnificent in presence, hands gripping the window-sill, his white beard trembling, indignant and helpless. Richard Bennet I saw last, sombre and angry, pacing like a caged tiger, and he raised glowing eyes at me as I said:

'What the hell is happening here?'

'The little boys are playing their games—don't tell me you need it explaining,' said my father.

'You join the Union, you keep its rules,' interjected Richard.

'When I was a member of the Union I kept its rules,' replied Dada. 'When it would not take my subscription, I made my own.'

'Whose side are you on?' I said to Richard.

'Oh, for God's sake!' cried Mari, her hands over her face.

My father did not go to her, and Tub Union's voice stole into the room.

' "Man that is born of woman hath but a short time to live, and is full of misery. He cometh up, and is cut down, like a flower; he fleeth, as it were a shadow, and never continueth in one stay." '

Dada said, lighting his pipe, 'It would not be so bad, mind, if I could go down as a Methodist. Do you realise Tub Union's got a collar on back to front and I have to put up with Church of England?'

In my agony outside I had noticed this. Mari said:

'Oh, please, Mostyn, I cannot bear this!'

'You will have to, woman. They can bury me as deep as they like, remember, but I will go down six feet when my time is come, not a moment before.'

'One way or another, they are burying you, and you know it.'

My voice seemed to echo in the room, and my father said:

'Right, assume this. Now will somebody tell me what I can do about it?'

'You can shift him outside with them, for a start,' I shouted, pointing at Richard, and Dewi was instantly on his feet:

'*Diawch!* You leave him out of this or I will not be responsible!'

My father came into the middle of the kitchen. 'They will bury me alive before they bury this family. The only fighting in here will be done by me, remember it. Let Richard remember his conscience and you two remember that you are brothers, or I will take a hand.'

'I am not with the bargee Union,' said Richard, eyeing me.

'And is there a difference?' I cried. 'For long enough you have been spouting the need for Unions, of everybody being brothers and charters of decency—is this what they turn out for a penny a week?'

Mari said, wearily, 'Oh, Bryn, for God's sake stop it!'

'If they work for savages, can you blame them if they behave like savages?'

'As long as you count me out,' I said. 'I've had enough of

you and your bloody Unions to last me a life-time.'

My father said, 'Bryn, sit down and shut up, and mind your language. Listen to them for a bit: there is more and more humour in it the more you hear of it.'

Tun Union said, ' "I heard a voice from Heaven, saying unto me, Write. From henceforth blessed are the dead which die in the Lord: even so saith the Spirit; for they rest from their labours. Lord have mercy on us." '

' "Christ have mercy on us," ' said the men in bass chorus.

' "Lord have mercy on us. Our Father, which art in Heaven...." ' '

Dada grinned wide. 'Dear old Moses Shon should have heard that one. Missed his vocation, did Tub, bless him. Moses would have put him up for Lampeter Theological.' He put his arm round Mari's shoulders. 'Make a pot of tea, girl. We have got a long way to go. It is loam and shale in that yard, and they will be in here borrowing picks in the next ten minutes.'

'I say fight, Dada,' said Ifor, lumbering to his feet. 'Bryn is right.'

'And I say fight,' said Tomos Traherne, and the shock of his voice turned us all. 'They outrage the word of God: force, at times, must be met with force, as He whipped them out of the Temple.'

'Tea, Mari,' said Dada, 'for I am thirstier than a desert, being dead.' He nodded towards Tomos. 'With respect to your cloth, man, this is my house, so I will do the fighting. And let something be understood in here before we lose the sense of proportion. If I am going down in theory I am not having my face booted in before it in practice. Nor am I going out there with a mandrill to beat sense into men who are my comrades in misery. You, Mr. Cowbum, earlier talked of the virtue of Welsh beliefs, but there is no virtue in a belief unless you back it with bread. It is all right for you, sir, because you and yours are eating. But were I to take the food from your mouth you would be worse than savage in a week.' He smiled at Tomos. 'You called them mad an hour back, Pastor, and you are right, for they are mad with fear. It is a world of rip and claw, and if we live in a jungle we accept the jungle law. Today Tub

221

Union is eating me because I haul to Ferry for a penny a ton less than Union rates: tomorrow he will be eaten because he is doing the same, to feed his children. So do not anybody here talk of force or the union of ideals or the virtue of beliefs. Do not talk to me of anything save the will to change things, as Richard Bennet is trying o do, in the name of God; and do not talk to me of Jesus, Pastor, until they change.' To Mari he said, 'Now hurry the pot, woman, for I am not given to tap-room speeches and I am drier than the wife of Lot.'

After this we did not speak much, but drank the tea Mari made us and sat in lamp-light and silence, listening to the soprano chinking of the picks and the baritone grouse of the shovels; later we heard the rope-creak lowering of the coffin, and a bit to your right, for God's sake, or you will have him over: then stones and earth were thrown on wood and bass voices talked about ashes and dust.

They timed it to the stroke of midnight, and they raised the cross over the mound and left us in peace, and I left the room and went out to see what was written so that always would I remember it, this indignity and cruelty of men to men.

In the light of the moon I saw it, chalked white.

MOSTYN EVAN
SON OF BEN THE DROVER
DIED APRIL 24TH 1854
BURIED BY HIS COMRADES
IN THE UNION

When I got back into the kitchen only Dada and Gran were left, and she called to me and I went to her, standing before her like a child.

'You see it, Bryn?' she asked, mopping up.

'Aye, Gran.'

'And you will always remember it?'

I nodded.

'Right,' said she. 'Remember this too. There is a time to weep and a time to spit in their faces, and that is now. Take a shovel and dig it up. Take it far, so women do not see it, for the sight of it could dry a womb. Then return and fill the place. Fill the place in the yard, and I will look next morning.

If I see a sign of ground disturbed God help you; this is your task, for you are youngest son.' She faltered then, hand to her heart.

'And then?' I got up. 'You all right, Gran?' She nodded, smiling.

I looked at my father: strangely aged, he seemed, as if Tub Union had come in with the men and taken funeral fingers to his cheeks.

'Then what?' asked Gran, with business.

'Do we move from here?'

At this she straightened, hand on hips, but her face was pale.

'A message for Tub Union, and you will deliver that, too. Tell him that we fight for right of way. That yesterday, had he asked respectable, we might have considered it. Now not even cannons and fuses will shift us from the Old Navigation, me especially.'

'It is a mistake, Mother,' said my father, looking at nothing.

'Me and him,' said Gran, jerking her thumb. 'For we are of drover blood—me and him: us, especially. Tell Tub Union he can pull the roof down over our heads, he can dig up the foundations, he can bring through another branch line, he can burn us alive. But never, as long as I live will I leave the Old Navigation. Business as usual, it is—you and Dewi and Dada, up to Glyn Neath for the haul at dawn tomorrow.'

For all the defiance there was a sudden sickness in them, especially in Gran. Trembling, she sat there, and I cursed Tub Union.

24

GETTING into the Old Navigation that June was like trying to enter a besieged town, with the main line one side of it, the Rheola branch line on the other and its back garden specially selected by Man Arfon for a rail and sleeper stacking compound. When the navvies came and built a signal box on Gran's front patch the only entrance left to us was along the tow-path. Slowly, as convolvulus strangles a tree, the railway strangled us. Now its cracked windows stared blankly on to the embankments and rails and sleepers; Gran's flower garden was now withered under layers of soot and coal-dust. And as the railway flats and trucks thundered past us with greater loads at higher speeds, the hair-cracks of our walls widened to crevices and the crevices deepened into fissures that ran in crazy patterns from eaves to foundations. The Old Navigation was dying on her feet, and we knew it. And we were dying, too. As officially dead as if he was six feet under, my father would wait outside the Canal Company office in Bethel Street down on Briton Ferry for the occasional tossed-in haul from Glyn Neath to Giant's Grave. Defying Tub Union, he dropped his rates per ton again, and the Company snatched momentarily at the higher profit; but as the barge hauls came less and less, as colliery after colliery built access tram-roads or blasted deep into the rock for cuttings and platforms, our savings dwindled to nothing. Also, since Dewi, Ifor and me were working part time in Resolven colliery now, my father could not take a barge haul even when it was offered. Come autumn Ifor went to live with Rebecca in Abercynon, and the house was empty of his stumbling bass manners: Sharon, too, was never in the place; preferring the Penny Gaffs and travelling players, and just earning enough to keep herself. And when Dewi was not over in Nantyglo with Richard planning another anti-Truck society, he was out with Ianto Fuses and Pietro Bianca greasing the railway lines and spinning the Corsairs on the Glyn Neath to Hirwan gradient.

Which night after night that winter of the Crimean War, left in the kitchen Dada, Mari, Rhiannon, me and Gran.

And with Mr. Seth Cowbum becoming extremely bright in the eyes the following spring, it appeared to me that soon we would be more.

In a drooping, creaking, crumbling Old Navigation that bright spring day we awaited with pent excitement the coming of Mr. Cowbum.

Courting very hard was Seth, bless him. All brown topper

and kid gloves, black frock coat tight at the waist over his
corsets, mother-of-pearl buttons on a scarlet waistcoat, button-
holed and whiskered, his moustache waxed wickedly at the
ends: polished and pruned, he came trotting from Neath in
his pony and trap. And Gran was rushing about from window
to window as happy and flushed as a young maid, and he can
please himself if he comes or not for I am not bothered either
way: then up in the shaving mirror with her, smoothing the
wrinkles under her eyes, patting up her beautiful hair. Straight
as a ruler was she, and proud in carriage: this coming from the
dignity of her youth, wet or fine, down at the water-spout
behind Ynysbiben Inn, to come back with the pitcher on her
head. I can see her now as I write this, seven foot tall was she
and in bombazine black, with the setting sun red behind her
over Rheola, a Welsh woman of Samaria.

'A word to you quickly, before she gets back,' said my
father now, and we came from our chairs and lined up before
him.

In the old days up in Cyfarthfa, when we were half pints,
we used to do the same, I recall. Ifor would be on the right,
then Dewi, Sharon, me and Gwen; all dressed in our sack
night-shirts, ready for bed; lined up for the de-nitting—Gran
with the fine comb on the hair, Dada after ears, and after that
performance mouths would be prised open for great dollops of
brimstone and treacle, and it was up at first light rushing out
the back with people hollering and dancing in the kitchen. And
I can see my little Gwen now, her toes curling to the nip of the
winter flags, being done, with letters stamped across her backside, 'When empty, please return to Pontypool.'

Sweet was the sound of Gwen in my heart. My father said
now:

'A word, please, about Gran and Mr. Seth Cowbum,' and
we circled him like assassins, after the scandal. Said he, 'Beds
for the mistresses, altars for the wives, the saying goes, and
courting at any age brings fun and banter. But there will be
none of it with this pair, you understand? This is neither
courtship nor marriage, but mere friendship. Mr. Cowbum has
asked my permission for Gran to stay at his home. Amazingly,
he is a lonely man, and if she agrees to go, then it is none of

our business. So no jokes at their expense, please, for Gran is our mother, and it is from her we come. You understand?'

'Yes, Dada,' we said, in chorus.

'He will be here within the hour and bringing his daughter; who knows? If everything runs smoothly, Gran might even finish up as his housekeeper.'

'What, no wedding?' ejaculated Sharon.

'Not that I am aware of,' replied Dada. 'Chalk and cheese, this pair. But it is two women in one kitchen in by here, says Gran, and she is right. Old folks understand each other, so let them be. Tidy up and make a special effort, and anybody with a foot in the wrong place will have me to account to later. You listening, Ifor?'

'Aye, Dada.'

Gran came back just then, all very casual about the visit, and people were coughing discreetly behind their hands and talking about the weather, and the moment Gran's back was turned again we all dashed upstairs in a fever, pulling out best Sunday serge, with creases to cut your throat, and polishing up boots. Rhia and Sharon were flapping about in chemises and curlers, with stays going on and people kneeing backs and hauling on strings. And in the middle of it Rebecca arrived with Ceri, their baby girl, and most beautiful Rebecca looked standing there in the yard while old Eli and his missus drove off in the trap.

Strange the emotion of sadness I knew whenever I saw Rebecca; strange the mystery of her eyes as she lifted them to mine as I came into the yard and raised the shawl from her baby's face. Fifteen months old was Ceri now, and lusty, and 'Becca still feeding her, and you can keep your old goat's milk, Gran used to say, for there is nothing better than mother's, and Betsy Small-Coal suckled all hers up to the age of five, and Betsy knows what she's about, said Gran. Rebecca's great dark eyes moved over my face.

'Seth Cowbum and his daughter coming now just, you heard?' I said to her.

She did not answer, and Mari came up with Ifor, crying, 'Here they are, 'Becca and baby Ceri!' And she took the baby from its mother's arms and nuzzled and cooed it, whispering

226

to Ifor, 'Sit and watch, eh, lad? Do not talk unless spoken to directly, eh? There's a good boy.'

And Rebecca sat in my father's chair by the grate with Ceri on her breast, her dark eyes cast down, and I saw in her gipsy face the lost tribes of Israel, the wanderers of the Red Sea, which are the true Welsh who settled in the Vale of Neath at the time of the Romans. In a moment, for me, she was the Rebeka, one with Moses and the pillar of cloud: in her I knew the ragged wanderings of Migdol and the starving encampments of Baalzephon: she raised her eyes to mine in the mirror, and I knew with my brother's wife a strange and terrible affinity and was with her in the dust-storms and sea-waste of Pihahiroth.

Momentarily, I closed my eyes in the mirror and heard her breathing in the scur of the razor.

'Cool, lad,' said my father in passing, 'mind you do not cut yourself.'

Mr. Seth Cowbum and his daughter Miss Penelope arrived for tea at four o'clock, and there was a dreadful palaver then, with people still rushing about wiping at things with dusters and for God's sake, Ifor, try to look intelligent and no funny business from you either, Dewi, for it is a tea-party and not anti-Truck politics, and Gran running her finger around the dresser for dust. Sharon, fair and beautiful in pink, whirled into the kitchen, delighted, crying:

' "Is this the son of a friendly nation who entereth the gate? Ah, Pericles, see—he brings his regal daughter! Let honour be paid to them, sir, since soon their blood will mingle with the blood of this house." '

'Oh, for God's sake, sit down, woman,' cried my father in a panic. 'Mari!'

Always, when in terror, he called for Mari.

'Aye, Mostyn?'

'They are in the yard—where is Gran, for Heaven's sake?'

'Coming!'

'*Darro* me,' said Dada. 'All fingers and thumbs, I am. Mari, you lead the way. Rebecca, you come next with Ceri, and pin up your front, there's a good girl. Rhiannon, Sharon—best

227

curtseys, please—no half-downs. And you three ...' He eyed us.

Out into the yard now as Mr. Cowbum clattered his pony and trap to a halt, and we were low in curtseys and stiff with bows, and Penelope, Mr. Cowbum's daughter who had come to look Gran over, sank down at her feet and stayed there until Gran raised her, which I thought was beautiful.

If girls of eighteen do stir the blood, then hand me women of thirty.

Beautiful, this Penelope, her head bright curls, her brightness enhanced by Rhiannon's darkness, and her English eyes were blue and sparkling.

'How do you do, Mrs. Evan?' said she.

'How are you?' asked Gran. Precious, I think, is the tapestry of life: birth, nationality fade in the shine of good breeding; muslin and lace can match side by side on the velvet of good manners. Gran said then:

'Mostyn, my son; Mari, my daughter-in-law; Rebecca and Ceri; Sharon, Dewi, Ifor, Bryn and Gwen, who is dead. Come you in, the pair of you; thirsty as salt-cellars you must be, for it is puddling weather,' and she led the way into the house while I unharnessed the pony and put it in with Nell and Jed Donkey, and Cinders whined and leaped at me from the straw in joy.

Take a deep breath, take a hole in on the belt, into the kitchen, sit at table. Stiff at the starched cloth, you sit amid the coughs and whispers and discreet smiles of the visitors, everybody with their hands folded in their lap, and it is so quiet that stays are creaking and tums cobbling and the Granfer Ben clock on the mantelpiece in the bedroom upstairs is ticking like a death-watch beetle. Sideways in your suit, you sit, with your boots on back to front and your collar on your ear, with all the cups and saucers gleaming on their best behaviour, the spoons for afters polished and tinkling treble as people shift, the knives flashing bright from the board. This is when a table speaks, I think, dying to play its part of making the good impression for the loved one: this is when the kettle cries its best tears, the milk is cream for the first two cups, the bread smiles brown and crisp and the tea has all the scented musk of India. Mari came in with the tea-pot just then, thank God, smiling, her eyes dancing, crying, 'It is good of you to come, Miss Penelope. Long enough your father has been talking of you.' She settled herself down, with business, embracing us all. 'Been this way before, have you?'

'Often—to parties at Vaughan Rheola, and Aberpergam. Oh, it is beautiful!'

'You know the Vaughans Rheola well, I expect?'

'Once or twice I have been for harp playing, and poetry readings, and there met Mr. Thomas Stephens, the historian.'

'Well now! Anglo-Welsh, have we?'

'Hampshire English, Mrs. Evan,' said Mr. Cowbum, 'but we come as friends.'

'Interested in Welsh literature, though?' asked Dada, finding his tongue.

'Aye, but not a word you will get from me, sir,' cried Miss Penelope, and I was stricken with terror when she turned on me, and said, 'You think Rheola house is beautiful, Bryn?'

Fingers screwing, face like a turkey's wattle. 'Aye, ma'am.'

'It ought to be,' said Dewi, chewing, 'the money they spent on it.'

Sharon announced gravely, 'The grapes of Rheola are the finest in the county!'

'So I hear. And you were lucky in Resolven, for the cholera did not come below Crugau Farm?'

'We had it,' said Dada, 'but we picked it up at Skewen, and that is another story.' Mr. Cowbum said, then:

'When my wife was alive we often used to come to Rheola for the grapes. Unfortunately, she died of the cholera a year after Doctor Brodie.'

'A good man, that Doctor Brodie,' said Mari.

Silence. Words steamed dry in remembered grief. And in that silence two others came in and sat at table: my darling Gwen, and the wife of Mr. Cowbum.

'My father tells me your sons are working for Mr. Lyons now, Mr. Evan.'

'Aye. All three down Resolven colliery—but Ifor only part-time—three days a week, until Rebecca and Ceri come to live by here.'

229

'So you are no longer a private bargee?'

'With the railway here, the future is dim for the barges, Miss Penelope.'

'Already? With the increase in coaling, I would have thought you were safe for another twenty years.'

'That is where you run into loss of profit,' said Dewi suddenly, 'and when you get loss of profit, nothing is safe.'

Gran came in with the kettle then, crying, 'A good strong cup, for God's sake. Thought she would never boil. Warmed the pot have you, Mari, my love? See this old pot, you two? Had it since my dear husband was down the old Starvo—hot water we used to have them days, and pretend it was tea. Pass the bread and butter now, make yourselves at home, do not be backward.'

Like a starting-gate going up, things fly off when Gran comes in, with plates sliding about and arms crossed in offerings, and no-thank-you's and yes-please's flying up and mouths being crammed with tremendous relief, for once the chops are going the tongue cannot talk. Strange and beautiful it is, I think, this quaint shyness of God's creatures. Dewi said:

'New seams are opening up above Glyn Neath; iron is slipping, coal is taking over. They say it began with Letty Shenkins up in the Aberdare Valley. You are right, ma'am. There ought to be enough for the bargee for the next twenty years, but when the speculators start cutting each other's throats it is the common people, not the gentry, who bleed to death.'

'It is nothing to do with speculation,' said my father. 'Dewi is young, therefore he is hot. In this case the fight is among the workers, not the masters; I am a private contractor, and the Union is easing me out.'

'Then that is the fault of the Union, not the owners, surely,' said Mr. Cowbum.

'Aye, on the face of it,' answered Dewi. 'But the quickest way to kill a union of brothers is to bring in outside competition, and this the owners know, so the effect is exactly the same.'

'Right,' said Dada. 'Now remember that this is a tea-party

230

and not a political platform. Any more bread and butter, anybody?'

Cinders was lying across my boot and pushed her nose up my trews and began to lick my shin: very strange, it was, to be sitting there making polite conversation with the bitch's muzzle half-way up and licking my knee. But stranger still is life, that you can sit like this in the security of afternoon tea and yet be balanced on the tip of disaster. Rebecca's eyes were lowering and lifting at me from the other side of the table when Sharon said, for no reason:

'There was a ball at Vaughan Rheola last Friday night. Passing on the road between the lodges, I did see them, sitting on the lawns after the dancing. The moon was over the forest, the stars were beautiful, and Llewellyn Nicholas was playing on the harp.' Dreamy, she stared past me at the window.

'Trained by Miss Jane Williams, was young Nick,' remarked Dada. 'Often, up at New Inn, I have heard him play for Watkin the Weaver.'

'Beautiful looking chap, too, mind,' said Rebecca, with a burst of intelligence. 'Best looking chap this side of Briton Ferry, I reckon.'

'Aye, lovely looking,' said Sharon warmly.

'Like I told Ifor here,' said Rebecca. 'Pimply he do send me just to look at him, and he can wash his socks in my pudding basin any time he likes.'

'Indeed,' whispered Mr. Cowbum.

'Expressive, that is the word for it,' said Dada. 'Expressive.'

'Mind,' said Gran, 'a wonderful instrument is the harp. Harps I do like because they are respectable.'

'Being played by angels, that is bound to be,' observed Ifor.

'But I do not hold with balls, though.'

'Really,' said Mr. Cowbum.

With an effort, I said, 'The harp ... is the spirit of Wales. Plinlimmon and Craig Rhos, I see, when I hear the harp. And John Morgan of Rhigod Plough plays better than Nicholas, though he gets only a shilling a night.'

'Aye,' replied Gran, 'but poor old Nick is not himself these days—too much dancing—wearing himself out, like that Blodwen Davies, Ephraim's girl.'

'Does she go dancing?' asked Sharon. 'I thought her legs were bothering her.'

'They never bothered anybody else,' said Dewi.

Swiftly, Mr. Cowbum interjected, 'I was fortunate enough to hear Miss Jane of Aberpergam play to Charlotte Guest, at Abergavenny.'

'Just the same with her, though,' said Gran.

'Who, dear?' asked Mari with sweetness.

'That Blodwen Davies—all she thinks of is balls—breaking old Ephraim's heart, she is.'

'Sharon has hopes of becoming an actress,' said Dada, like something stunned.

'How very interesting,' cried Miss Penelope. 'Now, I was wondering where I had seen her before—was it in Hamlet?'

'Ought to be ashamed of herself, that Blodwen Davies,' said Gran, munching.

'As Desdemona she is a demon,' said my father, instantly. 'She played to a full house a week last Saturday in Swansea, and Mr. Macready has very high hopes of her.'

'More cake, Seth?' asked Gran, up and bustling.

'He do like that cake, Gran,' remarked Ifor. 'Two pieces he do have already, mind.'

'Well, just a very small piece, to please you, Ceinwen,' said Mr. Cowbum.

'Aye, and take the outside bit, man, and eat it slow, for it sat in the middle. Tends to raise a bit of wind, I find, when it sits in the middle. Bit for you, too, Rhiannon, my love?'

And Rhiannon took it, flashing me a promising smile: warm and together, these days, Rhiannon and me, and Richard Bennet very far over the horizon.

'Cake and fat food is the same, of course,' said Gran, blowing her tea. 'Indeed, an excess of anything can be a curse.' And my father said, quickly:

'You ... you have met Jane Williams of Aberpergam House, Seth?'

'I happened to meet her at a Llanover reception—Penelope was with me. She is both gifted and beautiful.'

'Aye, but the bane of poor old Ephraim's life, mind,' said Gran.

It is sad when the old ones begin to fade.

My father said with deliberation, 'It is Miss Jane Williams we are discussing, Mother, not Blodwen Davies.'

'Aye, well I have said it once and I say it again—balls will be her downfall, for she thinks of nothing else—losing her head to the young bucks of the county.'

'Excuse me,' said Dewi, and he was up and away and I heard his boots stamping in the yard. My father closed his eyes, fingers pinching the bridge of his nose, and Mari said with speed:

'Another cup for anybody—come on, Mr. Cowbum, you are as dry as a bone, you are. More bread and butter for Ifor, too, is it?'

'Aye,' he rumbled, for he had been eating solid from the moment he sat down and had nearly cleared a loaf. Gran got up, crying:

'Indeed not, Mari—you entertain the guests and I will see to it.'

A big saddle-tank thundered through then, with twenty tons of lime and grain for the upland farms, and the place shuddered to the thumping impact of the wheels: flakes of plaster drifted down from the ceiling as the flats whined away towards Pont Walby and the signal outside crashed the clearway. Ceri awoke, screaming and kicking, nuzzling Rebecca for feed.

'Eh, my lovely, my precious baby,' said Ifor in his boots, digging her.

'A lusty child, to be sure,' observed Seth Cowbum.

'Just needs feeding,' said Ifor, and I held my breath.

Rhiannon cried, 'Shall I take her, Rebecca, while you finish your tea?'

'With me, *cariad*?' said Mari, opening her arms and clapping to Ceri. 'Upstairs to the bedroom till mam comes, eh?'

Ifor said, darkly, 'Everybody in by here eating, except Ceri.'

Too late.

Watch them all as Rebecca, who knows no difference, unbuttons the bodice of her dress, her dark eyes lowered in the majestic action of motherhood: see Ifor's grin of relief as he helps her with her petticoat, one strap coming down: now a discussion of importance between them, in secret whispers while Seth Cowbum sat with his hair on end:

'Not that one, 'Becca.'

'Aye, it is.'

'Empty, woman—she had that one for dinner.'

'Eh, dafto! I should know—look, ten gallons, it is.'

I switched a glance at Rhiannon, and she was staring at the ceiling, hands gripped, busting inside. My father's face was a study of quiet resignation. Mari, smiling beautifully, watched as Rebecca bared her breast to her baby, and Ceri fought it, fists waving as Gran came in with the bread and butter, crying delighted, 'Why, there's lovely! Ceri having tea, too, is it? That's right, my precious—baby's being left out, was it? Forgetting all about our little Ceri?'

And Rebecca sat there in majesty, as in some ancient Pharaoh market-place, her dark eyes shining as she watched her baby suck in noisy desperation.

Later, when the moon rose over Rheola, Mr. Cowbum rose and said with dignity, 'And so, on the advice of your father, I come with my daughter to break bread with you and ask permission to carry your grandmother off to my home in Swansea. . . .'

'As housekeeper?' asked Dewi.

'We will come to that later, young man.'

'Sit down,' said Dada, as Dewi got up, protesting.

Mr. Cowbum continued, unperturbed, 'One fool at a time on the floor, sir, your turn will come later. If this is the custom of the Welsh, I ask for an uninterrupted hearing.' He strolled the room like a court-room barrister, thumbs in the armholes of his waistcoat, jabbing at us with spectacles to make a point. 'This being a house of free-thinkers, where the opinion is sought of all, not one, I come before you to ask for her company in my home on Kilvey Hill, convinced, perfectly convinced that she is wasted here . . .'

'Shame, shame!' cried Dada.

'What are you talking about—wasted?' demanded Ifor.

'I repeat it—wasted. Can such a cook, for instance, receive the credit that is her due after fifty years of service?'

'Oh, go on with you, Seth,' cried Gran, loving it.

'Father,' said Miss Penelope, 'don't make a meal of it.'

'Indeed not, I am coming to the point. I claim that familiarity breeds contempt. In this house there are many other women capable of cooking, scrubbing and cleaning—you are loaded with women, and I have none. No, do not look at Penelope, for she does not live at home. Would you believe it when I say that I cook for myself in this lonely bachelorhood, that I darn my own socks, make my own bed, sweep out my own chambers . . . ?'

Shouts of derision at this, because we knew he had three servants and two gardeners in his mansion overlooking the Tawe.

'Ill-matched,' said Dewi.

'Ill-matched, sir? In what respect? In age we are the same; in wealth also, for we can only sit on one chair at a time, farmhouse or Chippendale. She is richer than I, for she has grandchildren, and all I have is a daughter.'

'Wrong nationality,' I said.

'Because she is Welsh, and I am English? Cannot love bridge the gap of all nationality, especially a love like mine, for I will have you know, sir, that I am older than Methuselah, like her, and we are wise in the ways of nationalities.' He paused, strolling the floor, and in that silence a black bear of shape must have moved over the flags on soundless boots; Granfer Ben had left the wild herds of Sarn Helen and come to sit with Gran. And she rose, then, gathered her skirts and left the room, and I heard her feet heavy on the stairs. Undaunted, Mr. Cowbum continued:

'In culture only you might have me at a disadvantage, since on all sides I hear talk that you are the lost tribe of Israel, though with my knowledge of your history I claim this as open to doubt . . .'

'Stick to the point, sir,' cried Dewi.

'I will indeed, and I will confound you, since I claim to know more of your history than you do yourselves.' He rocked on his heels, grinning at us.

'I doubt that,' said Dada.

'It is a popular misconception, for instance, that the Ancient Britons were conquered by the Romans ...'

'It is an historical fact,' shouted Dewi.

'It is history's lie, sir, and I will prove it. You claim that the Romans left these shores, and that the Saxons arrived and drove the Ancient Britons into a land called Wales, and that the Principality was founded after the Battle of Chester in A.D. 617?'

'That is correct.'

'It is factually wrong, Mostyn Evan. See now, I am better suited and more worthy of this woman than if I were Welsh by blood. The Battle of Chester played no important part in the history of this country. Your history began in A.D. 50 with the invasion of Flintshire by a Roman general, but his name escapes me.'

'Ostorius Scapula,' I said.

'Correct, young man. And then, in A.D. 296, the emperor Diocletian divided the province of Britain into Secunda, Flavia, Maxima and Britannia Prima, the capital of which was Cirencester. And that, ladies and gentlemen, was how your history began.' He bowed. 'Now who claims that we are ill-matched?'

I said, 'It began a thousand years before that, sir,' and they turned their faces to mine. 'It began before the Romans and Saxons, even before the Celts, when the Iberians came from the east, from Pola and Treviso, Rapallo and Tarragona, in Spain.'

'Good gracious,' cried Cowbum. 'If time permitted ...'

'Time does not permit,' said Penelope.

'Take him away!' shouted Dewi.

'Give him Gran to get rid of him,' rumbled Ifor, grinning.

'Where is she, then?' asked Sharon. 'Oh, isn't he marvellous!'

My father went to the foot of the stairs, crying, 'Mother, Seth is waiting!'

No reply. The house tingled with silence. Dada said, 'I expect she's packing. I will fetch her.'

Now there was a great commotion of finding coats and hats, and we thronged out into the moonlit yard, and I remember that there was a scent of burning pine in the air from the night fires of the vagrants.

The stars were like little moons over the mountain when my father came back to the yard.

'Seth!'

We turned to him, stricken by the urgency of his voice. Dada stood in the doorway, hands clenched, his face pale, and we stared at him as he said, quite simply:

'My mother is dead, sir.'

His voice echoed strangely in the night. Mari gripped my arm, leaning against me, and my father added:

'She is sitting in Granfer Ben's chair. She is holding the mantel clock he left her. And she is dead.'

25

GRIEF is ill-remembered.

I could cant and cry down by here, but I will not. I could write the whole rigmarole from the lying-in and night-watches with candles to the incantation via floral tributes, and the end would be the same.

I had a lover, and she died.

My father had eleven pounds ten in the tea-caddie, and he spent eight pounds fifteen of it. We buried her with ham and cloves, which was the way she wanted: we had every neighbour and friend in the community to see her off—also enemies: from Dai Half-Moon and Alehouse Jones Pugilist to Betsy Small-Coal and Rosie Carey minus Alfo, by Dewi's special request. We had Seth Cowbum and Penelope and Miss Jane Williams of Aberpergam House; Eli Cohen came with his harem, also Mr. Ephraim Davies and Blodwen. Richard Bennet came down from Nanty with Mam Mortymer, and Tomos Traherne officiated at Zion, Resolven. She went on manse cloth in varnished oak with brass handles, two each side, and one fore and aft, and with Granfer Ben's black mantel clock ticking at her feet, which she once requested. She was officiated by Hobo Churchyard, and laid out by Mari.

Not even Gran would have asked for more.

And Seth Cowbum wept at the gave in shuddering grief, and had to be supported.

But my father, who had known her over forty years, he did not weep, though some others did.

But all the tears are wept now, this autumn; all the pillows are dried. Strange is grief: really self-pity, when you get down to it. Yet nothing could fill the void of our emptiness, no rallying of the spirit, no dogma of common sense could make us whole again.

Empty, we were, in the Old Navigation.

Do you know this emptiness?

By night the Rheola moon hunted in the windows; by day the August sun warmed us: yet we were as people dead: living, talking, moving, we were not alive, because she had gone from us.

We took her up to Zion, Resolven, on that hot day in June, two months back. And it seemed to me, standing there bare-headed, listening to the lovely Welsh of Tomos Traherne, that two small arms of earth reached up to embrace her as they lowered her into darkness, beside my Gwen.

And my gran was not the only one to leave home that year. Six weeks after she died Sharon dressed herself up in frills and fancies, and a coach full of Swansea Players waited on the road above Crugau Farm, and we came in a stream from the Old Navigation, loaded with a trunk and baggage, with Mari and Rhiannon very damp with lace handkerchiefs, and at the last minute Sharon got a touch of the vapours, which was the right way to go, I suppose, she being an actress, though by the standard of some of the long-haired randies she was travelling with she would more likely become a mother. Actors and actresses I do not particularly hold with, there being too much hand-kissing and bowing for my liking, and long hair on men tends to make me suspicious, while from men with perfume, like these, I would run a mile. Although, there is no general rule in this case either, apparently, since the biggest outing Dewi ever took was handed him by a lace and powder pansy with golden hair on his shoulders and smelling of ashes of roses, the first thing he smelled when he came round.

'Be a good girl,' said my father, embracing her. 'And if you fail in this, come back to me, for me and the family are your friends.'

We stood above Crugau—Dada, Mari, Dewi, Rhiannon and me, and watched the coach and four galloping along the top road towards Rheola.

And my father wept, I remember. For the death of his mother he did not weep, but he wept for the going of his beautiful Sharon, his rose.

That night, in kitchen dusk, my father said, 'Soon we will go from this place, I think.'

'Aye,' I said, at the bosh, just off shift from the Gwidab level.

'Nothing to keep us here now,' said Dewi, elbows on the table.

Stripping off my shirt, I added, 'You seen the ceiling in Sharon's room? If Rhiannon coughs twice it will be down round her ears.'

'And there is a crack in the front wall you can put a fist in,' said Mari.

Kneeling at the bath before the grate was she, stray hairs lying on her sweating face, having just swabbed Dewi down—all but his back, and now awaiting me. As I tossed my shirt away Rebecca came in with Ceri in her shawl and sat by the back window, staring down the track that led to the dram-road where Ifor would be coming. Silence was in Rebecca; the calm and quiet of her generations dead lay on her face: only her eyes spoke at times, great and liquid, like black orbs in her brown, high-cheeked face.

'Oi, missus!' I said, and jerked my thumb, and she turned her great eyes in my direction and looked at me as Jez must have looked at Jehu, and she did not go.

'You ready, boy?' asked Mari.

Black as a sweep, I was, just a sambo, with great white rings for eyes and mouth. Last week I had come under a fall, working with Ifor in a heading when a plug dropped, and Ifor yelled and pushed me clear, but a rock splinter fractured and tore my hip, and every night now Mari dressed the wound, three inches long and gaping. Night after night, it was naked in the bath with Mari, for there was no other way to do it, with her at me with a brush, scraping out the dust and poison while I chewed on a rag.

Six weeks now I had been down the Resolven drift and it seemed like six years. Dada said, glancing up from his newspaper:

'Away upstairs, 'Becca. Any fainting in here will be done by Bryn, please.'

'Too thick between the ears,' said Dewi, still chewing. 'Where there is no sense there is no feeling.'

'Come on, come on,' said Mari, waiting on her knees.

'Still got my trews on.'

'Then take them off, man.'

'Not decent. Rebecca is still here.'

Dewi said, 'Got a special. Got it cheap off the hucksters down Neath. Hinges, it do, in the middle of his back.'

'Please do not be vulgar,' said Dada.

'Oh, Bryn!' cried Mari. 'In, in—'Becca is not interested.'

Not much. I swear Rebecca was watching me in the window while I got into the bath, and it do strike me as awkward that men are expected to parade naked in front of matrons and sisters while Hell would pay rent if you asked them to show an inch of ankle. Dewi said:

'Did you go to see Mr. Lyons today, Dada?'

'Aye. Starting Monday, I am.'

'What you think of Lyons?'

My father shrugged. 'A coal-owner. You can tie them up in bundles of ten, but he is paying a shilling over the odds.'

'He gets it back in his Company shop. Did you try for pay in cash?'

'Was it worth trying?'

'A worker is entitled to the coin of the Realm!'

'Tell that to Queen Victoria.'

I said from the bath, 'You can get cash if you ask for it, but it will cost you five per cent.'

'What is that, for God's sake?' asked Ifor, coming in. 'I know the five, mind, but that per cent part do beat me.'

'Shilling in the pound,' said Dewi, drinking.

'Ay, ay, *bach*!' Bending, Ifor hit me sideways. 'Being bathed by aunty, is it?' He held my chin, making sweeting noises. 'There's beautiful, my baby.'

'Do not be bloody daft!'

Dada said, 'Lyons is not alone, mind. Every other coal and ironmaster in the country is at it—when the cost of coal on world markets goes down the price of food goes up—it is the law of supply and demand.'

'It is a bloody scandal,' said Dewi, fiercely.

'Do you think we might have a few less bloodies?' said Mari, at me with the brush.

'Oh, Christ,' I whispered.

'And a little less of that! *Duw*, what a house!'

'Rubbing holes in him you are, woman,' rumbled Ifor. 'Here, *bach*, take another bite,' and he took a knot in the rag and I bit, sweating cobs.

'Moses' tablets he has got in here,' said Mari, 'and they have got to come out. Oh, my precious, I am dying for you,' and she kissed me, and started brushing again, her fingers red. 'Convenient, mind, to have a Truck Shop in the village.'

'It would be convenient if the goods were cheaper,' said Dewi, sparring up.

'Can I come in?' cried Rhiannon, knocking the door.

'No,' I cried back.

'Aye, let her in, Mari,' said Ifor. 'What is wrong with a bit of bares?'

'Educational,' said Dewi. 'She's got to know some time, see?'

'Do not mind me,' I said, 'bring in the whole damned village.' The room began to shift around me, and I gripped the bath.

'You all right, boy?'

'No.'

'Good lad, here is another piece,' said Mari.

Dada remarked, 'If the goods were cheaper than the Tai Shop and Sam Jenkins Ton, it would not be a Truck Shop.

You pay in cash at the Tai or Ton and the cost comes out the same.'

'And Lyons collects the double profit,' said Dewi. 'The anti-Truck law was passed by Parliament fifteen years back and we've still got bloody Truck Shops—what do you make of it?'

'It is quite simple. There is one law for the English and another for the Welsh.'

'Oh, no, Dada,' said Dewi, 'that is wrong. If you want to know what they do to their own, you read the reports coming out of Lancashire.'

Distantly, I heard Mari say, 'Mostyn, I think Bryn is going out. Will you come by here and steady his head?'

Excellent was Mari when it came to this kind of thing, she having learned the art of chop and sew from her sister-in-law up in Monmouthshire, she said, and with no doctor in Resolven it was up to the women: only like doing ribs of beef, really, she used to say, but this version do make a great deal more palaver.

Now, later, there was a thinness in us, for autumn had come and gone in gold-dust and sepia and great flocks of migrating birds had wheeled over the Vale before October. Skinny is God, I think, that he do not issue autumn all the year round; sitting on a golden throne, with a charcoal burner under His waistcoat and sending blustering winds and ice and sleet down on us. Winter came, and they slept on the burning slag-heaps of Dowlais for warmth, and died of sulphur: under Neath Abbey the scare-crowed vagrants died, including the eldest of Betsy Small-Coal, which left her with the baby. The riff-raff of the navigators died in the culverts of the embankments and were pulled out feet first, stiff as ram-rods, for it was a blue-nose, coughing winter, this one, with the earth hammered into iron and the thatched roofs of the cottages all over frosty and sparkling white diamonds. Ragged and wheezy the trees of the cut and the alders began creaking rheumatic and asking each other where the hell spring had got to, with the ice-breakers thundering their steel prows down the cut, tumbling the little glaciers before them, and the great English drays straining and skidding under the lash, and one tore a hoof off outside the Old Navigation, and even the railway saddle-tanks were spinning their wheels on the Hirwain gradients and shouting for extra sand and double-headers. And the double-headers put an end to the Old Navigation, opening her wounds wider, bringing down the bedroom ceilings, kicking away the foundations of the out-house.

When the first, weak rays of spring sunlight filtered over a frozen country and the great Van Rocks of the Beacons lifted their shining heads to the distant trumpet of the sun, we were finished in the Old Navigation, and we knew it.

'We are going from here,' said my father.

'Not before time,' said Dewi. 'It is falling round our ears.'

'When are they coming for the barge?' I asked.

'Any minute now.'

'Man Arfon, more than likely?'

My father said, frowning up the cut, 'God in Heaven, he do not have that much cheek!'

'You do not know Man Arfon,' said Dewi.

Hobo Churchyard arrived late, which meant he was sober. A very good friend was Hobo, attending on the family for corpses and removals, but he could be greased lightning also, after a few good quarts. Like in the snow-drifts of the winter of '39 when he sledged the vicar down Ponty mountain: sitting on his chest, was Hobo, and whooping like a Cherokee Indian, with his top hat in one hand and a flagon of gin in the other, doing eighty over the hedges, they reckoned, and the vicar with flowers under his chin and not even screwed: the fastest trip of his life, said Dada.

Dada said, now, 'We will be better off in Big Street; play fair to Mr. Lyons, he has given us a house.'

'For which he is receiving rent,' said Dewi.

'A bit crowded, though,' added Mari, 'two up, two down.'

Tethering Nell and Jed, I went into the bare kitchen and up the stairs, instantly smelling Gran's lavender. Here, back in the kitchen, was the leaded grate with its firing irons, the snow-white counterpane of the hearth. Here, out the back, was the rusty tin bath hanging on the nail; there the cracked seat of the earthly throne, and watch yourself on that, Dada once said; the sheaf of the *Cambrian*, dated January 1856, hanging on string behind the door. Now the smells of dinner, the dismal sop of the drying-up cloth, the sud-frothing copper on wash-day Mondays. A house, to me, is a ship tossed on the endless sea of human emotions: its walls are the bulwarks, the kitchen its galley, the attic is the bridge.

'Bryn, you there?' called Rhiannon. 'Man Arfon is coming. Quick!'

'God help him,' I said.

Large as life came Man Arfon, thumbs in his trews, with the swagger of a man in triumph. And with him came a bodyguard of four—two tough railway men and two bargees—Tub Union and Beef O'Hara, who knew the time of day.

'Well, well, Mostyn Evan—off directly, I suspect?' asked Man Arfon.

'That is correct, sir,' said Dada, and I groaned within, knowing this mood.

Instantly, Mari said, 'Late already we are, Mostyn; don't keep Hobo waiting, eh?'

'When we have finished this transaction,' said Dada. 'You have come for the barge, Superintendent?'

Very plum was Man Arfon today, done up in riding breeches with a crop, a gentry waistcoat canary yellow and brown gaiters. 'Aye,' said he, 'I 'ave. Dear me, Mostyn Evan, there is a tremendous pity—bringing a fine barge like that all the way from Cyfarthfa, and now got to sell it.' He stolled up and down the wharf, kicking it.

'A tremendous pity,' repeated my father. 'You have the bill of sale?'

'Aye, by here—all three copies, and I have the money, too—sixteen pounds?'

'That is strange. I have the fourth copy, and mine says nineteen.'

'*Diawch!* There is queer. Must be a clerical error.'

'It will be,' replied Dada, 'unless I receive nineteen pounds.'

'Sad at leaving, Mostyn Evan?' He drew closer, slapping his gaiters with the riding-crop.

'Aye, man, sorry in my heart.'

'Put your every penny into it, eh? but the foresight was lacking, you must agree. Very strange, I was only thinking last night—you get me booted out of Merthyr as a sub-agent, and I land up here as a superintendent: you leave to make your fortune as a private contractor, and end up as a collier. You know what you lack, Mostyn Evan?'

'Tell me,' said Dada.

'Economic anticipation. Well, there is a lovely English sentence—economic anticipation. Don't it drip off the tongue?' He beamed. 'It do make all the difference, mind, for we are living examples. Either you got it, or not. If you have, then you finish at the top, like me. If you haven't, then you end like you, on your arse.'

'Mostyn, for God's sake,' whispered Mari, drawing near to him, but my father only grinned wide.

'The money now, sir, if you please,' he said, and held out his hand.

And Man Arfon pulled out a purse and counted nineteen sovereigns into his palm.

'Thank you,' said Dada, and turned. 'You there, Dewi?'

'Aye, Dada.'

'The money is paid and we take nothing lying down. Mari, take Phiannon and go and find Rebecca.' He tapped Man Arfon's shoulder. 'Bryn, you have always wanted this one, you have got him now. Tub Union is mine and he is going on an outing. Dewi—the railway men are yours. Anyone spare in the next ten seconds can take this fat fool O'Hara,' and he moved, pulling Man Arfon towards me as I let fly the hook. And as Arfon staggered back, shrieking, I saw my father bend at the waist, shuffling in, taking Tub Union square with fist after fist. One moment country-quiet, next it was bedlam, with Man Arfon on one knee shrieking like a stuck pig, and I dragged him upright and fetched him another and the two railway men galloping knees up and popping on the end of Dewi's boot, and in seconds he was back and into Beef O'Hara, fighting soundlessly, the image of my father with his Welsh, hooking stance. They succeeded in nothing, they took everything, simultaneously dropping cold: Tub Union moved

245

once, rising on an elbow, then fell flat again. My father stood over him, licking his knuckles.

'Where's that other bastard?' he said.

'By here.' I was holding Man Arfon up by his waistcoat and I tossed him against my father. 'You do him,' I said. 'It is like beating up Rhiannon.'

And my father seized the superintendent by his leg and shoulder and raised him high above his head and walked slowly to the canal, and stood there, poised, with Man Arfon ten feet up and screaming like a woman.

'By God, there's only a few of you,' cried Dada, 'but when the Welsh come trash they stink of the gutter. Economic anticipation, is it? Aye, well here is the damp variety. There is more than one way of ending up on your arse, Man Arfon,' and he stooped and threw him high and he fell, spreadeagled, arms flailing, into the canal.

'Excellent,' said Hobo Churchyard. 'Do I raise the corpses first, Mostyn, or do you prefer the furniture?'

'Big stuff on first, and mind you go easy with the dresser. Dewi, Bryn—fetch the bedsteads, then the table and chairs. By God, we will wash our hands of this accursed railway. Back to coal where we came from, for the love of God.'

'Sixteen Big Street, Resolven!'

The sun was high when we trundled the hearse away up past Crugau and along the road to the Biben Inn and took left over the river and into Resolven. Past the canal loading bay we went and along by New Inn, with men raising hats at the hearse and women dropping curtseys; up past the Square to Lyon's Row, and down to Number Sixteen where our women were waiting, and people were hanging out of windows and gossiping in doors and look what is arriving now, good God.

A new life: a new village with a name that stood square to the world, its chin hazed with the blue of manhood, with hair on its chest and a hook in either hand.

Resolven!

26

THE TOP TOWNS began to smoulder. They went on fire seventeen years back with the rise of the Chartists, said Dewi, and we shall rise again.

Dewi was right, I reckoned, probably for the first time in his life.

Like a giant hand laid on Wales, the valleys of the Rhondda, Merthyr, Aberdare and Rhymney clenched their fingers into a fist, inwardly seething to the inrush of the new labouring population. The great famine rushes were being repeated and the starving Irish were again being landed secretly on the coasts and begging their way to the new industry of coal. In came the south-west English, the over-spill tin-miners of Cornwall, the Staffordshire specialists, the sawn-off timber-fellers of Yorkshire and Lanarkshire: from all points of the compass they came for coal, marching in battalions down the Welsh lanes, and the coalmasters cornered them, divided them, flung up mile after mile of little terraced homes, and housed them, and then drove them underground on a seventy-hour week at one and a penny a ton, tools and candles found. The Mines Act of fourteen years back which outlawed female and child labour was flung overboard by the very men who made it, and the Truck Shops, closed by the same law, were re-opened. In the glow of the new get-rich-quick, foundering under the raw potential of flesh and blood, the owners sank coal pits on every side, deeper and bigger: new drifts were driven into the bowels of the country and the coal hewn out and trucked and barged, regardless of safety precautions, and the slag and rubbish that accompanies blood on coal, spilled towering tips and dumps over the blazing land. Ignoring social conditions, the owners shafted and dug, broke into old workings and exploited them, cut wages to increase profits and cut each other's throats in a razoring competition for rail and port and barge. And, doing so, laid acres of white headstones and new cemeteries where once was pasture. The child labour again sagged at the ventilation doors; special dwarfs were employed in the three foot seams, the eight- and ten-year-olds of a new generation, their spines set into crippledom by crawling underground, and a new generation of mothers hauled and bucketed under Glamorgan and Monmouthshire and gave birth at the face. And the obscenity is, said Dewi, that those in high office who once opposed these wrongs are now the leaders of the new merchant aristocracy. And not all merchants, either. Among them, a root of the cancer, was the old Welsh gentry, the ninety per cent traitors to the cause of the Welsh, whose ancestors had fussed and fooled with the English for favours since the iniquitous Act of Union: the gentry clergy who put on collars back to front and invoked the name of God in support of an English Church and Throne: the gentry magistrates who cried their disgust of all things Welsh, and sentenced men like Shon Shonko in a foreign language. Let their names be written on the scroll of Welsh dishonour, said Dada: let their lackey social jumpers and tame historians bolster the crime with lying pens and tongues—the Lingens, Symons and Vaughan Johnsons of the dirty books of 1847.

'Excellent,' said Dewi, 'I didn't know you had it in you.'

'I am sick to death of what they are doing to my country,' said Dada.

'Then what are you going to do about it?'

My father said, 'Better men than me have tried, and failed. Remember the Chartists?'

'Aye. And I tell you this, they got closer than you think,' replied Dewi. 'If God had not been on the side of the masters, as usual—if an officer and twenty men had not been in the Westgate, the government of Britain would have been run from the tap-room of the Coach and Horses, Blackwood. If it had not been for a man in a glazed hat...'

'What kind of hat?' I interjected.

'A glazed hat.'

Mari, sweeping up the grate, sat back and wiped stray hairs from her sweating face. '*Duw*. I've seen some hats in my time, but never a glazed one.'

'A spy, sent special down into Wales, to make the Chartists move before their time...'

'You ever seen a glazed one, Mostyn?'

'Oh, Christ!' whispered Dewi.

'And watch that language!' Finger up, she rose, the image of my gran in her wrath, and her beauty still turned every head in Resolven. 'And let me tell you this, Dewi Evan—God is on the side of goodness in the outcome, remember that.'

'It would not appear so,' said Dewi, bitterly.

'Oh, boy!' she whispered, gripping his hair. 'Do not tear yourself to pieces for people. The owners are rich and we are poor. What do you expect your dada to do?'

'Fight.'

Mari shut her ears with her hands and closed her eyes. 'For Heaven's sake give us a rest from it. I lost one man to the Chartists, would you have me lose another?' Bright and fierce were her eyes.

'If needs be,' said Dewi softly. 'What do you expect men to do—sit on their backsides and whine? Every damn Sunday you go on your knees to a Tory God in a working-class hell, and this is why you've got these social conditions.' He got up from the table and wandered the room, hackled, thumping his fist into his palm.

'Gently with Mari, lad,' said my father.

'Force must be met with force, violence with violence!'

'My God,' said Mari. 'I wonder where I have heard that before?'

Silence. Very uncomfortable, with people loosening collars and smoothing pinafores: first time Dewi and Mari got stuck across each other. I winked at Rhia over the white, starched cloth, and she lowered her eyes, great black circles in her face, and the colour flew to her cheeks: amazing, it is, how women can read thoughts.

Not much time to bother with the politics, me, save that I knew the owners were a shower of sods. Twenty-one come Sunday, me, and in need of a wife; and so full of life that I could have put my fist through the carving on the top lodge, Rheola, and not skinned a knuckle. Personally, as far as I am concerned the bloody politicians can stuff themselves under glass with aunty's feathers, and the Chartists, Lodges, Unions and Scotch Cattle can assist each other individually, with broken bottles. Chasing the women more in my line, bending the men over five foot eleven, no quarter asked and three pints made one quart, one in each hand. The only reason why I didn't slip down to see the Black Welshman now he was lodging at Pentre was because I reckoned he was past it. I topped Dewi by a stone and Dada by an inch. Not really room for you in by here, Mari used to say, sweeping up the kitchen, hold your legs up: the place for baby elephants is under brattice-cloth tents: out, *out*! said Rhiannon. I winked at her again.

A terrible effect this do have on them, mind.

Said Dada, watching me, 'Do not pester Rhia.'

'And a good example he is,' said Dewi, jerking his thumb at me. 'With the place sliding from under him all he can think of is ale and women.'

'Ay ay!'

'Thick as iron, he is—solid from the hat down.'

'Aye, man, you like to try me?'

'Any time you like!'

'Now, now!' cried Mari, finger up.

So I winked at Rhia again, and she went all cuddly and wriggling, and I could see that though she was red round the chops she was giggling inside. This is the way to get them, mind, when they start giggling.

'Will you behave yourself?' asked Dada, getting up.

Eh, dear me. Gorgeous is life.

Darro!

Mind, although I loved that Old Navigation I loved this Big Street in Resolven better, for it is good to have people living closer about you, with their smells of cooking in your kitchen and their warmth and sounds coming into your heart. And houses joined together in rows I do like especially, since they are like a gang of colliers going out on a razzle, arms linked in warmth, and here is Polly Poppit's petticoats on the line and there is Dobi Revival's new chapel shirt, and the smoke from the chimneys floats up merrily and the kids are playing hop-scotch and Devil-at-the-window. Actually, I am sorry in my heart for the owners sitting in their company parks trying to keep their loot now they've made it. For it do beat me how they expect to find human beings under all those starched shirt-front and crinolines, and when you get rid of all the palaver and rigmarole they go to bed for loving and babies just the same as us, though they would never admit it. Amber and gold is a good home-brew and excellent for the bowels, as is widely known, but all after-dinner port is good for is sparking toes on merchant bankers, says Dada, and serve them bloody right, says Dewi.

Give me a street of colliers, you can keep the mansions. Very exciting things happen down our Big Street, Resolven, and the same sweet wind that blows on Mr. Lyons, the owner, blows on us. But he do not get the dinner smell of Mrs. Pudding's steak and kidney, or see the smile on Da Point-Five's face as he shuffles along on his leather thigh-pads to bow good morning to old Sam Tommer, the overman, every day of the week.

''Morning, sir,' says Da Point-Five. 'Thank you, Mr. Tommer.'

''Mornin', Da,' says Sam, 'do not mention it.'

For when the bell-stone dropped two years back and pinned Da to the thighs, old Sam came up with an axe, and cried, 'The roof will fall in the next two minutes and it'll take half-an-hour to get you out. Do you want to live, man, or do you want to die?'

'Chop me clear, Foreman,' said Da, and Sam threw him a rag to chew on and chopped him in half, staunched him in the heading and carried him clear, and the next minute the stall went down.

'Best friend a man ever had, though he's English,' said Da. 'Took guts, see.'

Aye, wonderful things happen in Resolven. Here comes Moses Up, the sidesman, walking with Davey Down, the undertaker, in funeral black, never apart; lodging in the same bed with a bolster down the middle, respectable. Fine folk, these, and always ready to assist the community in a positive direction, said Dada.

''Morning, Moses!'

'Good morning, Bryn Evan. Off on shift, is it?'

'Ay ay! 'Morning, Davey Down!'

'Good morning to you. Very healthy you are looking, all four of you!'

'Healthy as little fleas.'

Usually pretty glum was Davey Down, which was natural, I suppose, considering his occupation, and he had never been the same since the cholera didn't get south of Crugau. Also, times were skinny for Moses Up until the new Zion went up in '63, this one being only twenty by thirty and holding a handful. And rumour had it that Mrs. Hanman, the big Staffordshire puddler, was keeping them both for six shillings a week and them only eating on alternate days, with Davey on the egg and Moses doing the bacon.

Bright the sun that spring morning, going on shift, and our boots clattered on the flags as we went up the Row, and the little gardens set neat and trim, different to dirty old Cyfarthfa. Mrs. Thrush Morgan is singing in Number Thirteen, giving the tonic-solfa a going over while she makes the beds for her two Irish lodgers Tim Dunnit and Bill Blewitt who are down the level on nights. Disappointed for the Swansea opera, was Mrs. Thrush Morgan, and now inflicting it on us, and any more of this and I am writing to the Inspector of Nuisances, said Dada, for I cannot bear sopranos who are sharp in the higher registers. Now he added:

'I hear that Siloa Congregational, Aberdare, expelled a sidesman for trying to break a strike? Hefty, the colliers are coming up there, isn't it?'

'They are not even started,' replied Dewi.

'They say half the congregation are Scotch Cattle, you heard?'

'You can never tell with the Cattle,' said Dewi. 'They get in pubs and pulpits.'

'Bombing blacklegs and breaking arms, is it?' asked Ifor.

'For working on when the Union says stop.'

'There are no Unions,' I said, 'only mountain meetings and benefits and lodges.' One all sides there was talk of Unions, but I had never met one.

'Because Unions are outlawed, that doesn't mean you haven't got them,' answered Dada. 'The South Wales Iron-masters re-formed theirs last week.'

'Flogging and burning their mates?' I said. 'If these are the Union boys you can give me the Benefits.'

'One day you will learn that the the heroes of the working classes are the Scotch Cattle,' said Dewi.

'Aye? Then let them come down by here and try it.'

On, on, up the mountain road to the level, with the dew sparkling on the short, green turf, Dada and Dewi in front now, then Ifor and me leading Nell Mule and Jed Donkey, whom we worked at the face. With my father employing little Bill Softo as mule-leader, this gave us three drams, and Lyons covered his wages in the standard three sovereigns a week we got in tokens. Ne need for Scotch Cattle in Resolven, for we were making our fortune with a four-man team, and although Lyons took your boots he didn't reckon to skin your heels in his shop, which was better than some I could mention. In two headings we worked—Dada and Dewi in one, me and Ifor in the opposite. We would take it in turns, Ifor and me, in face-cutting and pillars for one while his mate packed the roof, and every so often Bill Softo would come in with Jed or Nell and draw out the coal one side for the engine house and the slag for the tip. Doing better these days, and sleeping in the barn at Crugau with a sheep called Daisy, who was his friend, and every Friday Mari would hook him in to our house and feed him a meat meal to drop a rhino, and I had heard that odd times found him with his boots under Mrs. Hanman, and with Rosie Carey still hugging him to the ample breast, little Billie, now thirteen, wasn't doing so bad.

Up on the track to the level Dobi Revival was doing his washing, soap to the elbows in his tin bath, and he called to us as we passed, crying:

'Blessed are those who walk the path of righteousness, for they will sail to the throne of Heaven as a white dove flung into the sky by the hand of God.'

'Ay ay!'

''Morning, Dobi!' cried my father.

Very hairy, was Dobi Revival, Chinese moustache and revival beard, and his fine hair in shining waves to his shoulders: every Friday morning Dobi would be washing out his smalls on the mine level, greeting the colliers coming through, and it was harps and clouds or molten fire with Dobi, and no in-betweens.

'See now!' cried he, holding up a dripping shirt. 'Are your four souls as white as this, Mostyn Evan?'

'I doubt it,' said Dada. 'Please to let us pass, there's a good man.'

But Dobi barred the way and bared his chest of rags, crying, 'There is a guilty conscience in every sinner's breast!' and he gripped me. 'Like a tinderbox, it lies. And Heaven will strike a match and the soul will flare in torment for everlasting!'

'Oh, give over, man,' I shouted, pulling away.

'Strange, nevertheless,' said Dada, 'how Dobi can select those most in need.'

'It is a democracy of the purse and privilege,' said Dewi, pushing Dobi aside. 'It is a God uncaring, one worshipped by the insane.'

'Watch it, man, watch it!' warned Dobi, soapy fist raised high.

'You watch it,' said Dewi, 'or I'll head you into your own bloody washing.'

'Poor soul, pity him, Dewi,' said Dada.

'You are now to enter the bowels of the earth!' cried Dobi, standing in his bath. 'Filth on you, Dewi Evan, filth indeed! May Baal reach out fingers from the old workings and blister you for the blasphemy, may you sink to your bowels into the lower regions.'

And we went down the dram-road followed by threats and clods from Dobi.

But it was not all coal and politics and religious insane.

There were barge outings and country fairs and patsais and decorating the graves at Easter, and with Richard Bennet dug in up at Nanty now that Sharon had gone for the acting, there was, for me alone, Rhiannon.

Rhiannon!

The main trouble, I find, is that in the business of living together it is not the eating that matters, or the chapelling, the strolling, the talking; it is the sleeping together that do count for a lot, and no nearer that than I was some seven years back when I first marked her down for this performance. Most ladies, I find, being blessed with certain possessions, do tend to hold on to them, which I think is a pity, for things as beautiful as these ought to be shared. And there are some, like Jane Rheola and Rosie Carey and Cushy Cuddlecome, who have the right idea in this respect, and when it comes to sharing, most men can show women the way home; like splitting a plug of tobacco or an eating-tin, or a quart. And apparently, it isn't any good asking politely, as Dai Central Eating discovered when courting Tegwen Harriet. Frisky as a spring lamb was Tegwen, that day on the road to Tonna, according to Dai— going all girlish and chase-me-sailor, which naturally gave Dai confidence. But when he popped the question, she lay back, opened her shoulders and hit him boots up into the heather.

Unfortunately, the women I come across tend to the same view, with Rhiannon no exception. Very severe about herself was Rhia, and although she did once draw the curtains on that afternoon up on March-Hywel, she had changed her mind since, with a lot of slapping and shoving and how would you like somebody doing this to your sister, which is guaranteed to set any chap back a mile, for the thought of anyone even contemplating such a thing with Sharon I find absolutely disgusting.

It is unhappy being marrying age, with parents saying 'Don't you dare' and every woman in the place threatening to lay into you, to say nothing of pastors and preachers wagging their fingers and threatening hell fire, although these don't seem to miss a lot as far as I can see. And even if you did manage to collect a Jane Rheola or Rosie Carey or Cushy Cuddlecome, and came unstuck, all the God-fearing got up off their knees and put out the flags and declared it a Roman holiday.

Lately, in the absence of anything else, Polly Poppit, the new English girl, was lying on my pillow, but only in dreams. Very ample was Polly Poppit, bright fair was her hair, and very dimply when she smiled, but Dai In and Out beat me to it and laid siege to her one warm night in September. But he got the street wrong, did Dai, and also the date, apparently, when he climbed through a window one midnight and laid his head on Polly's chest. And he got the number wrong, too, for when he woke next morning he was sleeping on Mrs. Pudding. Naturally, this caused a stir, for it is coming to something if virtuous ladies like Mrs. Pudding cannot sleep with their windows open without characters like Dai In and Out climbing in and curling up on their chests.

At this point it is only fair to point out that Dai In and Out is so named because he spent most of his life in and out of the Bottle and Glass on the road to Neath. People took note of it. Not good enough. What is right for the Bottle and Glass is not necessarily the ticket for Mrs. Pudding, though I must say she's been smiling ever since.

'Why?' asked Rhiannon.

'Just thought you'd like a walk, that's all.'

'What for?'

Never had she been so beautiful as on that particular May day, all dished up in pink and white, with the sun burnishing her hair, and there was a merry flavour in her I could taste on the tip of my tongue, it being my intention to eat her alive given half a chance and the flutter of an eye.

'Where to, then?' she asked, looking pert.

I said, 'Oh, lovely it is walking up the Bont, along Sarn Helen.'

'When a boy's face shines, look behind his ears,' said she.

'Nobody's going to murder you, woman!'

'It's not murder I'm scared of.'

'You coming, then?'

'Ay ay. But put one finger on me and you will not see me for dust.'

Got the prettiest girl in the Vale; got summer in all her beauty; got eight pounds in the tea-caddie for marriage, but got to wait until December, according to Dada. 'You cannot marry on a penny less than fifteen pounds ten,' he used to say.

Fifteen pounds ten. Might just as well be fifty. Can't wait. Along the lane that led to the mountains I took Rhia's hand in mine, and there was a need in me to be one with her. In a place of white blossom we stopped in the heat of the climb,

256

and I hooked my arm about her waist and her lips were red when I drew from her, and her hat fell off, I remember, and she stood gasping in my arms and staring, having never been kissed like that before, so I kissed her again.

'Eh, I do love you, Rhia . . .'

'Loose me,' said she, pushing. 'In several pieces I am; mad apes are about on Sarn. Time for dinner, is it?'

But she did not mention this again as I stooped and lifted her in my arms, and the valley echoed her laughter as I laid her down at the foot of the wild apple tree, and the blossoms showered in the wind, and fell, pink and white about us, and fluttered in her hair.

'Bryn,' she said, like a woman.

Through a rift of her hair I saw the distant Vans spearing a sky of glittering blue, and the great Sarn Helen winding her snake of centuries through the hills of the Roman legions. And I thought that perhaps, in this place, some dark-browed ensign had lain: that the kisses I was giving to Rhiannon had been given by him, two thousand years ago, to a bondmaid Celt or following concubine: that my Welsh Rhiannon, so quiet to my touch, was one whose name was Cleo or Subara.

'Eh, Bryn, my sweet,' she said.

And in the radiance of that day I heard about us the tramp of men whose mothers hailed from Thrace and Macedonia, the white-paved streets of Rome: I saw the majesty of a passing army, and the flood-gates of our youth beat about us in a world of sun and wind and a forging of strength.

'*Diawch!*' said Rhia, sitting up and pushing away.

'What is it?'

'Dear me,' said she, 'that was a near miss. What do you think I am, man, iced cucumber?'

'I am sorry,' I said.

'I am not,' said she.

All the sounds of the earth were about us now; the sigh of the wind from Brecon, the showering petals, the larks high above us: down in the valley by Walby an ox lowed bassly and there was a smell of milk from the farms. And beside me lay Rhiannon, as if sleeping.

Bending, I kissed her, and what began in tenderness ended

in quick breathing, because I loved her, and I could not let her go. Here, I thought, but for the evil of money, we would go, Rhiannon and me: in this place of loveliness we would run, with the sky for a roof, free of the stain of coal, the scream of the trapped foot, the mangled hand. And at night, in the red glow of a cave fire, we would be as it was planned we should be, united in this gift of love, which men deride and elders call shameful: and there would be no conscience in this union, no accusing fingers, and nothing of tears.

'*Cariad* . . .' she whispered.

I heard the sound of her not on the hills of Sarn, but from across the sea, before the world was ice: I heard her amid the savageries of Gorizia. In this woman I knew delight. In a penned marriage by capture she spoke again, and her breath held the perfume of musk, which I have smelled before in the market place of Treviso: lithe was she, and quick, and her arms were swift about me as once before, when her garments were gold and her sheets saffron. There was a little woman of my blood, I remember, and she had no breasts, and she died young. How beautiful, then, this woman under the stumbling hands of my childhood. Darkness was in her face, her mouth was sweet to mine, my friend and companion.

And I knew her on Sarn Helen as I had known her before on the blood-stained marble of Corinth, before the coming of the Goidelic horde.

And now the sun blazed about us, the sheep called from the Mellte, and when I opened my eyes from the dream she was yet one with me.

'Oh, God,' she said, and her eyes were wide and startled.

I held her in strength, and she said, 'Bryn . . . you said strange things; you spoke in a Welsh I did not understand.'

'You were dreaming, Rhia.'

She said, her face turned away, 'Now we are in trouble.'

'More than likely.'

About me the land was flowing with a new brightness. Fan Lia was rearing skyward; Pen Milan of the crags was trumpeting in sunlight, and away to the east the pennants of Glas Forest were stained with red. Rhiannon said, her lips against mine:

'I do not care, for I love you. You are my man, Bryn Evan. I do not care.'

I put her face against mine, and held her fast.

27

COME autumn, the old River Nedd was alive and swirling with trout, and the salmon so thick at the weirs that they were rubbing their fins off. Folks were strolling innocently through Resolven with two-foot tails sprouting out of the backs of their collars and the women were dropping aniseed in the gutters before boiling salmon, for the bailiffs had six-inch noses when it came to smelling out the poachers, and houses were being searched for gaffs and nets. More than one went to transportation from the Vale, since God has laid it down, according to the Church of England, that salmon belongs to the gentry and is far too good for the working classes. Old Shon Seler Shonko, for instance, he got another seven years from a gentry clergyman, although Mari and my father travelled to Swansea Sessions to plead for him, for poor old Shonko was spiders between the ears without a doubt. But he went to transportation just the same, swung aboard the prison hulk in Swansea docks like a scarecrow linnet fluttering in a cage.

'Goodbye, mistress!'

'Goodbye, Mr. Shonko.'

'Going back to my old gran,' he cried to Mari. 'Don't you worry about me, missus,' which was true enough since his old gran was whipped through the streets and taken in chains to the plantations nearly a hundred years ago, for stealing a sixpenny petticoat, in the Christian town of Haverfordwest.

Sent on the Grand Tour by a clergy-magistrate who owned the water, and that was the end of Shon Shonko, and Mari wept, I remember, her apron to her face, in great sobs, for she loved old Shon, and she would not be comforted.

But happy things happened, too, that particular autumn.

Old Mrs. Scales in the Truck Shop was sent down the road by the mine company, and nobody wept over that: Ifor made another little seed-cake in his beloved 'Becca, and how he managed this I shall never know, since he slept with me and Dewi in the back bedroom. Number Sixteen was a decent little house, mind, and a palace to some of the shacks up The Top, with Mari and Dada in the room next to ours and Rhia, Rebecca and Ceri downstairs, there was only one room left for living and eating. I can see Mari now as she opened her arms to Ceri on the afternoons when Ifor was off shift:

'Come with your old gran, is it, precious? Come with me and I shall show you beautiful things, and a bag of sweets, too, from Mrs. Scales? And your mam and dada can have a little stroll up the mountain?'

And Rebecca of the flaming hair and dark face would raise her lovely eyes over the table at her husband.

And I can hear my father now, 'Mr. Lyons has done us well. The rent is low. But it is just not big enough for three families. When we get a bit more in the caddie we will shift from here, and get another bedroom, for it is not good that a family be divided.'

He need not have bothered.

Aye, in came September and set herself up on Resolven mountain with her spinning-wheel between her knees and wove great carpets of gossamer over the hedges, and the thick-eared fraternity were out every morning gathering it into match-boxes for cuts: cold and damp those misty dawns when we went to the mine, and the grass brushed back our boots and the rushes and spears gobbed soap-suds over our trews. Always, on these glorious mornings, I would take great chests of the strong mountain air, before going into the swirling dust of the mine, and I was never one for the pipe. I recall my gran used to say, 'If God had meant you to smoke he would have put a chimney on your head.' And nor do I care much for the chew and spit, believing this to be a dirty habit, but Dewi was not so particular. With Ceri in my arms I took her to the top of the Row for sweets, and Dewi spun up a sixpence, and I snatched it.

'Pick me up a plug, man,' he said, so we went into the Truck, my Ceri and me, while Dada, Ifor and Dewi dawdled up to Zion.

'Good God!' I said.

For Rosie Carey was behind the counter, not Mrs. Scales, and she was like a flower, even at that time of the morning.

'Came last night,' said she. 'Took over from Mrs. Scales. Does Dewi ever come to buy?'

'Outside now just,' I said. 'Shall I fetch him?'

'No,' said she, proud. 'Do not fetch him. Tell him that Alfo has gone to Coventry and I would not go with him. If Dewi Evan is interested, he will come in here, but tell him that I am second best.'

Lines of weariness were telling round her eyes, the matron of her thirty years having raised her knocker and come in, and Alfo Morgan, with Blodwen's till in his pocket, reckoned them that much sweeter under twenty-five.

'Mrs. Alfo turned me out,' she said then.

'Less than you deserved, Rosie.'

Deep she sighed. 'Not much good, am I?'

I shrugged. 'A plug of Raleigh for Dewi and a ha'peth of tiger-nuts for Ceri by here. One thing about it, at least we'll get the right weight.'

I saw her against the shelves, the bottles, the cheese-cuts, and saw that she was bright to tears, and with a great sadness. She threw in a nut for luck, which was more than you'd collect from Ma Scales, and I once stood with Ceri for five minutes while she sucked one to make the weight, the old sod.

'Ifor's baby, is it?' she smiled at Ceri now. I nodded, and she said:

'You come to Auntie Rosie, for a little minute?'

Ceri buckled and shifted in my arms, turning her face.

'Sorry, Rosie,' I said, taking the sweets and tobacco.

She smiled brilliantly, her head back. 'Kids are my trouble, I expect. Down by here, in this shop, I'll get hundreds.' She held herself, saying, 'One day I will have one, you see, Bryn Evan. One day.'

'More than likely. Thank you, Rosie.'

'To help me—you will tell Dewi?'

'Aye.'

'You reckon I'm worth having, boy?'

'No, ma'am.'

'At least you are honest.'

'Aye, but some don't agree with me,' I said, 'Billie Softo, for one.' The bell tonged like the toll of doom for Rosie as I went through the door, and I saw in the mind of my heart a tiny, drab room with a sacked window, and Rosie sitting there waiting to pay the rent, and her hair was white and her face aged, and past her window thronged the ghosts of her hundred lovers.

I put Ceri down and told her to run and the others were tapping their boots and where the hell have you been, outside the Tai Shops.

I did not tell Dewi as I gave him the plug: no business of mine. People have to sort it out, like me: up to them, their comings and goings, their sadness and their loves. I'd have handled it different, had I known what was coming.

Billie Softo, talk of the devil, was harnessing up Nell and Jed Donkey as we arrived up at the engine, and he was naked to the belt in a set of ankle-length pink drawers, with lace round the boots. He looked like a Turkish Delight but with nothing at the top, and seeing the spacers I froze with fright.

'Very attractive, Softo,' said my father, 'when did you collect them?' and he fingered the material, nodding approval.

'Couple o' months back, zur,' replied Billie. 'Found 'em up on Sarn.' He grinned at me with a naked mouth. 'Under a wild apple tree, they was, and blowin' as large as life.'

'Dear me,' I said, sweating, for you could never tell where Billie Softo was directioning from minute to minute. Dada said then, thoughtful:

'You know, Dewi, I could swear I have seen these spacers somewhere before.' He rubbed his chin, frowning.

'Put a sovereign on it,' replied Dewi, and Ifor said, reflectively:

'Mind, spacers do arrive in very queer places. You remember Randy Bandy, over at Cynon?'

'Like my brother,' said Dada.

'He reckoned he saw a muslin set going over Neath at two thousand feet followed by flying bandsmen on trombones and tubas, and one leg was yellow and the other purple.'

'Couldn't 'ave been this pair, zur,' cried Softo, merrily, 'for these is pink, see. Ah, a fine lady and gentlemun come up to Sarn, an' I did see 'em, and they left him special for me, Billie Softo.'

'You know this lady and gentleman, Billie?' asked my father.

'Oh, ah!' Wide he grinned at me, landing me a wink.

'But you must not tell their names, Billie—you understand?' He took from his pocket a sixpence and put it in Billie's hand. 'There now. But if you tell that lady's name, I will take it from you. You promise, man?'

'Ay ay!'

Molten lead it would be for Softo the moment I got my hands on him, and Dewi said idly, as we walked to the mine, 'You get about a bit, boy—you ever seen those pinks on a fireguard?'

'Do not talk daft,' I said, sweating cobs.

Mrs. Willie Shenkins was basketing at the door as we went into the level, sobbing as she hauled the baskets on the skip, and her coal-black face was riven with tears.

''Mornin', Mrs. Shenkins,' I said.

'My little Willie's working down Two Heading, you heard?'

'Aye,' I called.

'Mr. Lyons very pleased with him, too. Strong as a horse and twenty-one yesterday.'

'Send him happy birthdays,' cried my father, and added, 'She is a different woman, mind, since she brought him back. Good morning, Mr. Morgan!'

'Ah, Mostyn Evan!' Mr. Thrush Morgan on his haunches in the six-foot stall, and cutting happily with an Irish lad packing and dramming on him, and thank God I am away from Welsh sopranos, for he was only happy when he was in the seam. We stood against the wall as two drams went by and took the turn-out, and behind us came Billie Softo with our four drams and Jed Donkey. Alehouse Jones Pugilist lumbered by on his way

263

to his stall; always worked alone, did Alehouse, and he touched his hair to my father as he went, very respectful.

The gallery shafted here, and my father and Dewi, taking a grip on their tools and candles, turned for Number Four while Ifor and me took Six Heading, which led to the old working where Da Point-Five had caught it.

'A word with you, Bryn?' called Dada, lifting his candle-tack.

'Now?'

'No—any time—say first hour. Eight o'clock, by here?'

'Aye.' Cool the draught as Haf Benyon, aged seven, pulled the vent door, and cold on my sweating face, this sounding official. Sweet and bright was Haf's smile in the light of my candle as she sat there with her rag doll, the last of Mrs. Ten's brood, before Man Arfon's; but Owain and Cynfor, her big brothers, always worked her stall and would not let her from their sight, to their credit.

'You all right, precious?' thundered Ifor, bending to her and stroking her face, and she beamed at him, for all the mine children loved Ifor and he always carried a sweet for them; kneeling, stroking their faces upwards, like now.

Through the door and into the heading, and we crawled past Owain and Cynfor, the long and the short of it, for Cynfor had never topped five foot and he was well into the seam with his brother wedging the props.

'Come on out of it,' I said, slapping his leg, and he eased himself under the roof, gasping.

'Watch her. All bloody night she's been moaning.' He hit up with his pick haft and the coal trickled.

'Safe as a bank,' said Ifor. 'Heave over, Owain, that hole won't take two of us.' And Owain gave him some dirty old back-chat and wriggled out and Ifor wriggled in, saying, 'Tell Softo to open through—he should be here by now, what the hell is he up to?'

'Wait, you,' I said, and Ifor crawled off and sat on his haunches by the pillar, and I lighted my candle and clayed it on a board. Slipping down into the hole I smelled for gas, and it was strong. Gwidab was a good level, being damp and shallow, and although many of them got it on the chest, few died of this. But she was a bugger for damp in holes, and it had to be cleared.

'Is Haf clear of the door?' I called to Ifor.

'Aye.'

'I'll fix this. Keep Softo out.'

Ifor grunted reply, so I coiled the rope and wound it on my arm and pulled the trap over my head, then reached up and pulled the candle forward, shielding my face. The gas lit instantly, running a red flame round the face, and ended in a dull explosion above me. Rocks and stones showered on the trap.

'Right, Ifor,' I called.

He came on all fours towards me down the shaft, coughing and spluttering in the smoke, like a great, white bear coming to devour me, and he said:

'You'll bloody kill yourself one day, doing that.'

'Maybe,' I replied, 'but I'm not breathing gas.'

'That's what Da Point-Five said, and now he's got no legs.'

'Get in and cut, man, and think yourself lucky.'

'First ton for my 'Becca,' said Ifor, and spat on his hands, and swung.

Up came Billie Softo then, his face through the vent door, his candle flickering red shadows on the face. I cried, 'You shift your arse, Softo, or I'm kicking it up to Glyn.'

'You boot me, mister, and I'll tell 'em what you left up there by the Bont!' He cackled, then, holding his sides, boots waving.

'What's he laughing in doubles about?' gasped Ifor, spitting.

'You get on with your cutting.'

The last thing I do, I'm braining that damned Softo.

We drammed out after I took a run, and Ifor packed the roof and the pillars were solid, and this was good. Some colliers reckoned to shave the pillars that held the roof, but not me. You want coal you get it off the face, old Sam Tommer, the English overman, used to say; Lancashire or Wales, makes no odds. You shave the pillars and you've got trouble; any collier shaving under me goes down the road. And Sam was right. Gas-flashing he did not mind, and if he wanted speed he would thin out on the props, but the coal stayed fast in the pillars. I crawled out and cried, 'Softo, come in by here and pack for Ifor, I'm going up the heading.'

My father was waiting for me up in the gallery clear of people, sitting on a fall, long legs thrust out, smoking in the light of his candle.

'Ay ay, Dada.'

He motioned with his pipe, saying, 'Sit you down, lad, I want a little word with you.'

'Yes, sir,' I said.

Taking his time over this one, and I saw his face square and strong in the light of the candle. He was over fifty now, which was young for a collier, for there were some turned eighty—men like Cobler Johns—still working on the drams. But coal was taking its toll; his cheeks were marked, where the pit was cutting its pattern, his hair was white at the temples, and although he had not been down long, the dust was taking his chest, though the muscles of his back and shoulders bulged and knotted to his every movement.

'Time you were wed, son.'

I closed my eyes as the blood leaped into my face, and was glad of the dark.

He said, 'You reckon Rhia will have you?'

'Maybe.'

'You'd better find out, eh? If you take too long over it she'll more than likely line up another. You love her?'

I was sweating like a Spanish bull now, for I knew what was coming. 'Yes, Dada,' I replied.

'You pick and choose how you like, lad, but I want you up at Zion. May be you won't be so lucky next time. Next time you take some piece up the mountain and somebody peeps, it won't be Billie Softo. And where does that land a decent girl like Rhia?'

I raised my face to his and the drams went by in rattling thunder within inches of us, and his eyes did not falter.

'How much you got saved?'

'Ten pounds five.'

'I'll knock this up to fifteen ten, then you can wed—no, I'm

266

not having any more of these biddings, I've only just finished paying for the last one. When will you speak to her?'

'Tonight.'

'Right.' He rose. 'And now, no more of these mountain hops, Bryn, you do youself no justice. If you are going to make Rhiannon your wife you shouldn't be up the Bont sparking another.'

I did not reply, and he said, 'You don't make it easy—standing there saying nothing. You know what I'm trying to tell you?'

'Yes, Dada.'

He wiped his mouth with the back of his hand, and said, 'Save the rough stuff for the men—gently does it, lad, when you go with the women. God made them with His left hand, remember, so they are weaker than us.'

I nodded, thankful for the darkness.

'And don't try those tricks on a lady like Rhiannon, or I am having a hand in it—you understand me?'

'Yes, Dada.'

'Now away back to the stall and get those trews off Billie Softo or you will never hear the end of it.'

28

WITH the rest of the day shift we came down the mountain that dusk—Dada, Ifor and me, for Dewi had left straight for Nantyglo for a Lodge meeting, and could not spare time for tea. With tools clanking, we came down past the brook and the Tai Shops into Big Street.

Lovely, it is, to live in a street, I say, with all the excitement of the men coming home and the women sitting outside their backs and handing out all the cheek in the world. Smoke from the chimneys stood as straight as bars and the air was perfumed with the scent of burning pine, and the mist was falling with September over the Vale. Children were playing hop-scotch along the flags, the wizened granmas framed their dried-prune faces in the upstairs windows in toothless smiles of greeting, and ailing granfers crossed their boots and cocked up cheeky clays and nods.

This is when I love my people best, when the family is two hundred.

Have a peep in Number One. Here is the top dog, old Sam Tommer of Lancashire, sitting in the tin bath by the fire, like a Chinese joss, all bald head and stomach, blowing at the suds: there is his skinny missus, a shin-bone in black stockings and a face for chopping fire-wood, and not very fond of the heathen Welsh, being a cut above them, really, as wife to the overman. Mean as a razor and twice as sharp was Mavis Tommer, and every night when poor old Sam came back from the Vaughan after his glass, she would march him up and down the kitchen flags bare-footed, for some unknown reason, and this very bad for his arches, as Polly Poppit used to say. Dai In and Out was skidding along to New Inn with his seven o'clock penny; trying hard to cut it down, and all credit to him, but you could tell the time by Dai with his pint every hour from six o'clock to chuck.

'I didn't realise it was so late,' said Dada, consulting his watch, and he knocked up his hat to the Truck. 'Good evening, Miss Carey.'

'Evenin', Mostyn Evan. Seen Dewi, have you?'

'Just slipped up to a Lodge meeting, Miss Carey, but back later tonight.'

Anxious and worried looked Rosie. 'You told him, Bryn?'

I nodded the lie. Dada said, 'Nice to have you in the village, Miss Carey.'

'Welcome, I'm sure, Mostyn Evan.'

On, on down the Row, with women hanging out washing, pegs in mouths and shouting banter and others carrying steaming pails for the kitchen baths, men stepping out of trews behind neat lace curtains, starched clothes being flapped on the table for tea. In the window of Mrs. Hanman, the gigantic Staffordshire puddler, Davey Down is spooning up the stew, scrag end from Eynon Shinbone in the Tai, while Moses Up watches glum, it being his turn on the bread, and hoping for a sop. Jane Rheola is leaning against her gate, hands on hips, eyes under her fluttering lashes, lips pouting red, for Meic is on nights. Mrs. Thrush Morgan is sitting Dafydd on the White Rock again, and got him a semitone under the top G sharp, and I saw my father's agonised face, with Tim Dunnit and Bill Blewitt sitting entranced, either side of the piano. Mrs. Pudding is chopping suet on her board; cherubic and comely, Lovely Tom Davies is chopping sticks; starched up and bottled in Ancient and Modern, Mrs. Afron Shavings and Mrs. Tref Hopkins are off for hymn practice, hating each other, arm in arm; Mrs. Ten Benyon is changing her baby, safety-pin in mouth, and say what you like, says Mari, she is a wonderful mother.

On, on, boots thrusting out, abreast we go, Dada, me and Ifor, and as we reach the gate Ceri comes tumbling out and runs into Ifor's arms and he swings her high in booming laughter, kissing her face.

'Got soldiers in our house,' says Ceri.

'We got what?'

'Wait.'

Da Point-Five was reading the *Cambrian* on the flags and he turned up his ravaged face to the sun.

'Steady, Mostyn.'

'What the hell is happening in there?'

'Routine questioning—easy, man. Nobody is being executed . . .'

Ifor said, cold, 'When . . . when did they come?'

'Two of them—an hour back. They slipped in like mice, and I'm the only one who saw them. Dewi, they're after.'

'By God, I'm not taking this,' said my father, and screwed up his hands, striding away, but Da hung on to a boot.

'Cool, Mostyn, cool—it is the only way. You lay a finger on one of them and you'll be in Brecon barracks by sunset.'

'Da is right,' I said, gripping my father. 'Easy does it.'

We followed him down the back and into the kitchen.

Mari, Rhiannon and Rebecca were sitting side by side, and Ceri ran to her mother and Rebecca lifted her on to her knee, and she sat there, wide-eyed. Standing before them was a Brecon sergeant, and there was a great size to him, resplendent in his red and brass; he was young, his face square and strong and his eyes bright blue in his tanned face. Behind the door as we opened it was a soldier of the line, his musket held loosely before him. My father said:

'What the hell are you doing in here?'

'You are Mostyn Evan, the father of Dewi?'

'Have you permission to enter this house?'

The sergeant said, and I admired his coolness, 'You are the tenant. Permission has been given by Mr. Lyons, the landlord.'

'Now I am here you will need mine,' said my father. 'What you want to know you will ask outside, or do you make a trade of frightening women?'

'Oh, Mostyn, for God's sake!' whispered Mari, broken.

'Outside if you prefer it, Evan,' said the sergeant. 'We can parade the Row, if you wish, but thought you would like this done quietly.'

'We will bolster the neighbours, man. I have nothing to hide.'

They went out the back, the sergeant leading, and I felt Ifor tense his body as they passed, and I gripped him. 'You stay here with 'Becca, man.'

'Like hell,' said he, and followed us outside.

Out the back quick, and now there is a to-do, with every kid in the Row staring through the gate, fingers in their mouths, and the neighbours hanging on the fence like string-beans, and it is astonishing to me how much washing needs pegging out in these predicaments, and windows going up and doors coming open and what the hell is happening in Number Sixteen? The sergeant said:

'Your son lives in this house, Evan?'

'He does.'

'Where is he now?'

'I saw my son last an hour back on the Gwidab dram-road.'

'And why did he not return here with the rest of you?'

'My son is twenty-seven. Does he have to account to me for his every movement?'

'Do you know where he has gone.'

'I do not.'

270

'Do you?' The sergeant nodded towards Ifor and me. Dada said:

'Neither do they. I am head of this house and I speak for my son.'

The Redcoat smiled and shifted his feet. There was about him a quiet authority more usually found in their officers, and he was not without charm. He could have handled this in a much more brutal way, for he held the power of life and death over the Welsh workers. In the Top Towns, where the owners called in the military to break a strike, I have seen the Welsh flung out of their homes, their women man-handled. Time was, in Crawshay's Merthyr, when a troop had only to cut a dog in half to get obedience, or hang an innocent Dic Penderyn. But the Bread or Blood riots of '31, and the rise of the Welsh Chartists in '39 had changed the face of their authority. Yet they still demanded instant loyalty to their puppet Queen, and this, usually, was the test of Welsh fidelity. The sergeant said now, 'You are aware that your son is a member of illegal organisations?'

'If he is, then he is responsible.'

'The Chartists, for instance.'

'According to the *Cambrian*, they do not exist.

'And an anti-Truck society up in Aberdare.'

Dada grinned. 'He ought to get a medal for that. Didn't your own Parliament outlaw Truck nearly fifteen years ago?'

'It is an offence punishable by transportation to be a member of a Scotch Cattle herd.'

'God help him,' said Dada, 'he appears to have had a busy time. I wonder he managed to do a seventy-hour week. Look, man, we are tired. Say what you want of us, and go.'

'Dewi Evan.'

'Then name a charge.'

'There is no charge. He is wanted for questioning.'

'On what grounds?'

'The death of a black-leg up at Abernant.'

'That is not special, soldier. They are dying every week.'

'In the death of this one you think your son is not implicated? Perhaps you are right, but it is your duty to tell us where we can find him.'

271

'I have no duty to you,' said my father.

From the gate Da Point-Five called, 'Careful, Mostyn, in the name of God.'

The sergeant straightened, and I knew him instantly for a trainee officer: no fool, this one; he had carefully laid the trap, and we knew now what was coming. This was how they divided the patriot Welsh from the traitor Welsh. If they wanted a man for questioning, and could not get him, this was how they took the hostage. The sergeant said, taking out his note-book. 'One last question, Mostyn Evan, and be careful how you reply. You agree that you are answerable, on oath, to the Queen, to whom you owe allegiance?'

'I owe allegiance to none save my Welsh Prince,' said my father, 'and he died at her hands six hundred years ago.'

'Excellent,' said the sergeant, replacing his note-book. He nodded to the soldier by the gate. 'Take him,' he said.

'Mostyn, you fool,' said Da Point-Five.

Mari wept, and would not be comforted.

And on the third day after his going, Ifor and I waited outside Brecon Barracks, which was the place of questioning, and the gates opened and closed and my father stood there on the cobbles. His eyes were blackened, his lips were split, but there was no weariness in him.

'Is it well with Mari?' he asked.

'Aye, Dada,' I said.

'And Dewi is not home?'

I shook my head.

Ifor cried at the gates then, his fists high, 'You bastards, you bloody English bastards!'

'There is no point in rubbing it in,' said my father. 'Home now—come, Ifor—home, the three of us.'

We took the road to Sarn Helen, and we did not speak again, as far as I can remember.

29

NEXT April blossomed into May and the Vale flowered in petals of pink and white, with the big sweet chestnut up by Crugau showering its beauty of the generations and the lime trees in their seventh year flower: along the cut the bluebells swarmed, and even the primroses, normally shy of humans, blazed their yellow clusters on the banks.

And Dewi did not come.

Up in Blind Shoni's field on the road to Tonna the bees were going demented; lambs were cartwheeling in the meadows of Rheola and rams playing leap-frog. Bright as a barber's pole was that month of May, and the redcoat troops painting it up, their scarlet uniforms moving into the valley, though it was amazing how many bent nails they found on the roads. Brass bands were playing on market-days, one even arriving in Resolven square outside The Ton, come all the way down from Cyfarthfa to happify the Welsh, but it is astonishing how quickly a couple of kids sucking lemons can put paid to a set of bugles, trombones and tubas.

Off shift, my father would stand by the window, looking over the fields.

'Not seen hide nor hair of him,' whispered Rosie Carey.

'He will probably come to you first, Miss Carey. You will not keep him to yourself?'

'Not much good, perhaps, Mostyn Evan, but I would not come between father and son.'

'God bless you, woman.'

Rebecca said, putting her stomach on the table, 'Sorry in my heart for that woman, I am, mind.'

There was, between Rosie and Rebecca, an affinity.

Very flourishing was Rebecca with her second, and Ifor fumbling and fussing her, and mind the corner of the grate, love, in case you injure the brain.

'Same as everything else,' said Rebecca. 'What you don't 'ave you don't miss, but you go short of a fella and it do bring you broody.'

'It is one way of putting it,' said my father, blowing his tea.

'Gets right up my nose, it do, the way people treat her.'

'A bit up to a dream she is, though,' mumbled Ifor. 'Always mooning through the window. Quack-quack daft, I reckon.'

'The only one who is quack-quack daft is you in by here,' said Rebecca, sawing at the bread. 'Honest as an oat-grain is Rosie Carey, which is more than I can say for some I could mention.'

'No need to get nasty,' said Ifor.

'Aye? Well, there's no call for it. A sod you are, calling her daft!'

' 'Becca!' said my father.

'There you are, then,' said Mari. 'That is over. No quarrelling, you two, when you have so much to love.'

'Stuck up damned virtuous, he is,' said Rebecca. 'Before I tinged his nose he was sowing his boots all over the country. Men are all the same. One rule for them and another for people like Rosie.'

'Dear me,' said Ifor, glum, 'you do go on, don't you?'

'A lot of damned old soaking about virtue and motherhood, and off to New Inn to kill the quarts.' She added, 'And the first yard of skirt...'

Which was a bit unfair, for very temperate was Ifor these days, with nothing more than ten pints or so at a sitting, and as far as I knew he was on the tack on garters.

My father said, 'Hush it down a bit, if you please, 'Becca.'

'Don't know what's got into her these days,' grumbled Ifor.

She began to cry then, did Rebecca, in great heaving sobs, her apron to her face, and immediately Mari and Rhiannon were up and about her, whispering and comforting her, but she was in a hell of a state with her red hair down, cheeks scarlet and soaking, with Rhiannon sending Ifor looks to kill though he had scarcely said a word.

'I do not want this baby!' shrieked Rebecca.

My father rose. 'Hush, Rebecca!'

Ceri began to cry now, trying to climb on her mam, and Ifor took her on his knee and she fought him, screaming.

Damned good tea, this one, with women bawling and men shouting, and there, to my horror, was Dan Double-Yoke standing out the back with the milk from Crugau, as large as life, taking it all in. Three pairs of twins had Dan Double-Yoke.

'Oh, God!' sobbed Rebecca. 'I do not want this baby!'

'Dan Double is outside, mind,' I said.

I give the family credit. Whether it was weddings, motherhood or death, nothing could dry us up quicker than handing it to the neighbours. Rebecca mopping up now and everybody on their feet clearing the table and 'Good morning, Dan Double. Beautiful day, isn't it—different from last week—ridiculous weather for May—no shape to it. Only three eggs, is it?'

'All I can spare, Mrs. Evan—running down on hens, see. The cock got bad feet—rushing round for eight years, chasing the widows.'

'No need for the details, Dan,' called my father.

Very stitched up was Dan Double, and butter would not melt in his mouth, and his long, thin face half-soaked; but he managed to tickle up the women and Mrs. Pudding used to roll round shrieking when Dan got loose.

'Aye, Mostyn,' cried he, 'but the cock 'ave got to be dominant, see, or the girls go off the lay. How's your system, Mrs. Evan?'

'Healthy as a flower, thank you, Dan Double.'

'And beautiful!' He pinched Mari's cheek. 'All over blooming? *Ach*, oh! Give me girls knocking forty, and ample. All sizzling come summer, after a little bit of sun.' He danced Mari in a circle, his hat held high, and did a hobnail hopscotch on the flags.

'Right,' said Dada, coming out the back. 'We have had enough of you.'

'Eh, Mostyn Evan, for shame! Would you bury her alive?' He flung out his hands to Mari, eyes closed. 'The eggs are free, woman. Just give a thought to old Dan Double if this one here is taken prematurely. Wide, wide would I fling you into a universe of men. Seen Dewi, have you?'

'If I tell you that you'll be as wise as me,' said Dada.

'Lots of people looking, though.'

Night after night the redcoats wandered through the street, and very interested, apparently, in Number Sixteen.

Dan went, bowing backwards through the gate and blowing kisses to Mari.

Rebecca, I noticed, was smiling again.

Sick and tired to death of the carrying. God, I pity women: I reckon Eve must have been up to worse tricks than Genesis booked her for in the Garden of Eden, for the serpent has been at her ever since. Mari said now, holding Rebecca:

'It is a difficult time, Ifor. She will be all right soon. Try to understand.'

'Aye,' mumbled Ifor, who knew nothing of such things.

At least he kissed her when he went on dawn shift with Billie Softo.

Dada and I were working the nights, so we stayed at home.

'Thank God she kissed him,' said Mari.

Looking back, it might not have happened had Dewi been home and the shifts stayed normal. But with the heavier stall of the two, Dada linked with me, and left the inside one for Ifor, Billie Softo and Jed Donkey.

It was a mistake, for there wasn't two ounces of brains between the three of them.

Alehouse Jones, who was in the next stall, said it was a bellstone. Manuel Cotari, the Italian, said it was a face-slip that trapped them first, then took the roof. To this day Owain and Phylip Benyon reckoned that Billie was clearing the gas with a cover board and candle, like I used to do, and the stone dropped as Ifor came in with Jed Donkey.

Whatever it was, it laid sixteen tons on them, and when they roped Ifor's feet for the haul-out he would not come, said Albert Crocker, for his arms were wrapped around Billie Softo.

'She liked that,' said my father. 'Miss Carey liked that. . . .'

In the coal-blackness of my dream, I heard Rhiannon's voice from the kitchen, and its panic entered my growing consciousness; the room made shape as I slowly opened my eyes and I flung back the bed-clothes as her feet hammered on the stairs.

'Bryn!' She burst into the room. 'Accident!' she gasped.

'Where?' I was stepping into my trews.

I gripped her and we listened, and there was no bell.

My father flung open his door then and came in to me, doing up his shirt.

'Accident,' whispered Rhia, and her eyes, wide and bright, stared at me.

'Where is Mari?'

'Up the Truck. 'Becca is over The Ton.'

'Is it Fach or Gwidab?' I asked.

'Mrs. Hanman has just come down from the Tai. She reckons it is one of the Benyons. Maris Tommer says it is Cynfor.'

'God help him,' said my father.

'That's next stall to us,' I replied. 'But I didn't hear the bell.'

We were downstairs in the kitchen when Da Point-Five put his head through the gate, and shouted, 'Up the Gwidab, Mostyn—you heard?'

'Aye, now just. Did you hear the bell?'

'Not ringing it any more. Bloody thing's worn out.'

They did not ring the accident bell. It saved the panic of the whole village tearing up the mountain. Over at the Cymer colliery last July they had the same, it was said. The fire-damp went round the face, and of a hundred and fifty-six below ground a hundred and fourteen were killed outright and the rest seriously injured, and women and children were lifting the brattice-cloth and screaming, trying to kiss them back. And Cymer was only one. Men were dying in scores; every day of the week women and children went down the pits and did not come back.

So no more accident bell, said Mr. Lyons, and he was right, said Dada: let the stretcher speak, though it has no tongue.

'But old Sam Tommer don't agree, mind,' said Da Point-Five. 'He reckons the women are entitled to the bell, so they could get shawled up and down to the pit. Very musical, too. Two good legs I left under a ten ton bell-stone down the Gwidab, but I got a toll longer than the Kingdom Come.'

'Stretchers coming now,' said Rhiannon.

Mari came running then, her hair down, her eyes wild.

Dada said, holding her, 'It is young Cynfor Benyon caught it, and maybe Owain—we do not know for sure. Where is Rebecca?'

'Over at the Ynysfach Inn.'

'Best she stays there,' I said.

It was four of them: Ifor, Billie Softo, Cynfor Benyon, and old Sam Tommer. For Sam caught it half-an-hour later, they said, when he was trying to get the first lot out, and another plug dropped.

They came slow down Big Street.

Ifor came first, then Cynfor, then Billie Softo, and Sam came last because he lived at Number One: four men to each stretcher, they came, in a black procession, and there was no sound but the tramp of their boots on the ruck.

The women were standing outside their backs with their children about them, I remember. Beside Mavis Tommer they laid Sam down, and left him, and she said nothing, but stood with clenched hands staring at the sky, for this was the second man she had given to the earth. Billie Softo belonged to nobody, so they put him outside the Truck for Rosie Carey, and she came out and knelt beside him. Ifor and Cynfor they brought on, and I could hear the women sighing as they shepherded their children indoors, for it was not their turn. Mrs. Ten Benyon, with her brood clustered about her, gave her baby to Mrs. Morgan.

'Cynfor, is it?' she asked, for it could have been any of three others she had down the Gwidab.

'Aye,' said Owain.

'Dear me,' said Mrs. Ten, and knelt, lifting the stretcher-cloth.

On came Ifor, and I bowed my head and splayed my boots on the stones.

Alehouse Jones, Albert Crocker, Lovely Tom Davies and Mr. Herbert the builder brought him, and they laid him at my father's feet, and stood there, empty. Then somebody said:

'It got him on the gob-stone, Mostyn—him and Billie; quick as death.'

'Thank you,' said my father.

We stood in an aimless clutch, staring at nothing, and I saw on the slope of the mountain the trees turning up their leaves to each golden rush of the sun.

Mrs. Tommer came up then. She said, 'I got the boards in the house, Mari Evan. You give me a hand with mine, I give you a hand with your'n. Big men, see, in the turning.'

'Yes, Mrs. Tommer,' said Mari.

'Got old blankets, have ye?'

'Aye.'

'Do yours first, shall we?'

'If you please, Mrs. Tommer, thank you, Mrs. Tommer,' said my father.

'I do him,' said Rebecca, and we swung to her as she came up with Ceri.

Mrs. Tommer was kneeling, untying the brattice-cloth, and Rebecca cried, coming closer:

'You leave him, you bloody leave him, Mrs. Sam!'

I picked Ceri up and held her against me as Rebecca pushed her way to the stretcher, and knelt.

She lifted the brattice-cloth and sweat was on her face.

'He's my chap, so I got to do him.'

The wind was warm on our faces: distantly, I heard the clatter of the railway.

'Better get him in, then,' said Rebecca.

30

I HOLD no brief for the evangelical Ikes, and I reckon old Tomos Traherne up at Nantyglo was one, but luckily we only needed him for births, weddings and funerals.

God, to my mind, do have a pretty rough time round these parts, and at times He can't know which way to turn, what with one and the other of them.

'Behold thy servant, Ifor!' cried Tomos Traherne that day in Zion when we put Ifor down. 'In all his manhood and purity he lived, attendant on the Word. And now he has flung his goodness into the lap of the Vale!'

This dampened quite a few of them, but not my father, nor my sister-in-law, Rebecca.

My brother Ifor was what he was, and for this I am thankful.

And when he reaches the golden gate of the biggest seat of all, St. Peter will see him coming and uncork a bottle of the best stuff, knowing that only the strong brew would be good enough for Ifor.

In promise to Rebecca, my father took us from Number Sixteen, Big Street, Resolven, in the middle of May, and I was sad.

Sad, sad I was to leave my sweet Resolven.

The trouble with me, I think, is that I fall in love with houses. Damned near in tears, I was, when we left Big Street. No longer would I see Jane Rheola undressing at the window, but you dare not stop for a gaze, of course, or Meic would be out with a chopper, and he once chased Dan Double from The Ton to New Inn, swiping and missing him by inches: very reserved was Dan these days when Jane was in the window. No longer would I see Davey Down sopping up the fat of Moses Up's morning bacon, or hear Mrs. Thrush Morgan sharpening up the Gentle Lark and the savoury, mouth-watering smell of Mrs. Pudding's steak and kidney would no longer go strutting down the street in hobnails.

'Goodbye, Da Point-Five.'

'Ay ay, man. See you later, see.'

Bow to Mrs. Hanman, bow deep to her six-foot-two against the sun.

'Goodbye, Mrs. Hanman.'

'God go with you, Bryn Evan.'

Eynon Shinbone and Evans Brewer, bulging bulbous, stand side by side.

'*Cofion Cynnes!*'

'Aye. Goodbye, Eynon, goodbye, Evans.'

Weeping is Evans Brewer, and God knows why, for I always treated him bad.

Mrs. Afron Shavings and Mrs. Tref Hopkins now, coming with books and music, and Alehouse Jones Pugilist trundling the Zion harmonium down to the square on a hand-cart. And we stood in the middle of them all, my father and the family, and did not speak while Alehouse set it down and Mrs. Afron set the music up and people let fly.

Mr. Herbert the builder was coming with Lovely Tom Davies, and behind them along the Neath Road thronged a great crowd of people. From near and far they were coming: from the tram-roads of the levels, the colliers and miners, the deacons, the drunkards. The bargees were coming, too, rounded up by Ehpraim Davies, the old Cyfarthfa agent, and very poshed up and refined looked Ephraim, with his daughter Blodwen on his arm. And behind the people came the ponies and traps, headed by Eli Cohen and his flaming women, and Eli was up and waving his sticks. Mrs. Willie Shenkins was sobbing and mopping, but rushing round organising everything, and even Tub Union and the bargees—people like Laddie O'Brien, Abe Sluice and Beef O'Hara—were arriving.

'Good God!' ejaculated my father. 'Look what is coming!'

Resplendent in an outsize trap drawn by a brown dray came Cushy Cuddlecome with the Irish Shrew beside her and Ditch Fielder and Bargey Boy, their new fancy men, like ram-rods on the tan seats in brown hats and whiskers. Very done up was Cushy in her big summer hat, built like an hour-glass and blowing with pink and white ribbons, and behind her came the riff-raff of the Cuddlecome Brew, the Irish dancers with melodeons, the wizened Lancashire navvies and the bull-chested Irish: linking arms they came with all their bawdy banter, and even Bronwen Rees with Taliesen the Poet and their three children, and carrying for triplets was my Bron, by the circumference of her and here he is now, and isn't he gorgeous—just think I used to teach him English grammar over at Tramroadside! Aye, and this is his girl, the beautiful Rhiannon! And the fame of our going must have spread as far as the Swansea valley where Brunel was planning the big new railway, for along came old Tai Morlais and Sian on his arm in bright, gipsy colours.

'*Hie*, Bryn, lad!'

'Tai! Sian!'

In they came, fighting their way towards us amid the shoving, laughing swaying of the crowd, and he gripped Rhiannon and kissed her. In came Evans Brewer, rolling a barrel, and the ready navvies tapped it and handed out foaming pewters: in came Mrs. Pudding and Mrs. Dai Half-Moon with plates of cold rice-pudding and Welsh bake-stones, and Albert Crocker and Willie Dare set up on the pavement with a bugle and trombone, with Sam Jenkins Ton on the bass drum, and the morning was split with Welsh airs. There was Bili Ynysbont come from Tonna in case anybody fainted and Mrs. Teague the Herbalist from Cymla, and even Polly Poppit, the English girl, with her husband five foot up and seven stone odd, said Tai, and no wonder she is generous, said Sian, looking gorgeous.

'Serve out the taps, me lucky lads!' bawled Cushy. 'We'll hand them something to remember us by. Everybody welcome at the Cuddlecome, feet up and ale down,' and she stood up in her trap and beat time to the band. Mrs. Ten Benyon came, despite her loss, with Man Arfon's subscription toddling; towering and string-bean came Owain and behind him Tegwen Harriet and Dai Central Eating. Everybody came. I cannot think of one who was left out.

'Sorry to death I am about your son,' said Tub Union, gripping my father's hand. 'Bygones are bygones, Mostyn Evan?'

'Ay, indeed, man. Met my missus, have you?'

'Ach, yes—that Michaelmas Fair, remember?'

Everybody shoving over for Da Point-Five; rushing around their ankles carrying a plate in one hand and a pint in the other. Tim Dunnit and Bill Blewitt were carrying our furniture out of Number Sixteen, and I noticed a few of the village sorcerers wiping it for quality, and it would be all round the village the moment we were gone.

Mari cried, 'Remember the train is off at half-past-ten, Mostyn!'

To Mr. Ephraim Davies, my father said, 'Sir, this is the

282

wife of Sam Tommer, our overman. She is coming with us as far as Aberdare.'

Lanky and tight-fisted Mrs. Mavis Tommer stood, hanging on to tears.

'God bless you, woman,' said Ephraim Davies, bowing.

'It is a cleaner death than some,' said Mavis Tommer.

Mrs. Isan Chapel was wandering lost, looking for Isan, so I collected her and gave her to Rhiannon. Rosie Carey stood alone; I pitied her.

'No news of your Dewi, Mostyn?' asked one.

'All in good time,' said my father. 'He will turn up, like the bad penny.'

I shouted, up on a chair, 'They even told Seth Cowbum, Dada—look!'

Trotting on a little piebald mare came old Seth, sweeping off his hat to Mari, very gallant, and seeing her eyes fill with tears, I left them and all their tears and laughter, and walked up the Tai, to Zion.

''Becca,' I called. I opened the grave-yard gate.

In the Yiddish tongue she was speaking to him; it was the incantation of her race. And she knelt closer to the grave and turned her face to the sky and cried aloud, but she did not weep.

'Going now, 'Becca,' I said, drawing her up.

She said, eyes closed, 'I loved him, mind.'

'Ay, ay...'

'I ... I was a bitch to him at times, but I loved him. You believe that?'

'Yes, girl.'

'God, what a world!' She straightened in my arms. 'Just look at this stomach.'

'Rather you than me.'

'You seen my Ceri?'

'Mari had her now just,' I replied.

Empty she shrugged, looking around. 'Oh, well. Away now, is it?'

'Aye. To Aberdare.'

Heaving down on her knees in grunts and groans, she kissed the earth.

'Got to go, boy,' she said. 'Goodbye, my precious.'

I helped her up. Hand in hand we went down the hill to The Ton.

31

LIKE a mighty Pentecostal wind, the Big Revival began sweeping over the mountains that early summer, and as we travelled north to Aberdare it blustered past us down the Vale of Neath.

In a great and unfathomed accord, driven by suffering and new ideals, a harvest of souls began, gathering in small tributaries from the Big Seats of Salem to Bethania, Ebeneezer to Calfaria. Almost every denomination of the Nonconformist Church was involved; Baptist and Congregational, Unitarian and Calvinist Methodist, Wesleyans, Presbyterian and Independent, and others. And the black-clad disciples of God in the new garment trickled from the pews of Zion and Soar, Providence and Carmel: the trickle of tributaries merged into a river and the river into a flood of rhetoric bulging with Welsh *hwyl*: fists raised in barn, cottage, mountain top and valley, the new revivalists poured forth a torrent of words. Led in popularity by the great David Morgan, the wind of Heaven blew like a prairie fire over The Top. Converts flocked to the new cause. The Sunday schools were packed. Banished was the foul game of pitch and toss; prize-fighters became outcasts, drunkards were denounced from crag and pulpit, malefactors were pulled out into the aisles for torments, harlots chased through the streets with bibles and sticks. Hard-liners who had not seen a pew since baptism were now powerful on their knees most of Sunday; wool was growing on the shoulders of publicans and sinners.

Mind, until we steamed into Aberdare station that evening, I was under the impression that the coming Revival was confined to the Welsh.

'I must say I do not see how it can affect the Irish,' said my father.

'Perhaps things are different in the city,' suggested Mari.

'Can't think why we haven't heard more about it,' said Rhiannon, which, as it turned out, was the most sensible remark of the night.

Anyway, with excuse-me-pleases and mind-your-backs and whispered requests for shifting room, we managed to get all the furniture off the railway flats and set among the little crowd on the platform.

'What happens now, then?' I asked my father.

'Wait a bit and get the size of this, for I don't understand it,' said he.

So we stood on tiptoe at the edge of the crowd and listened to the fervent Revival speaker. On the platform roof he stood, a ragged, bearded bone of a man, with flowing hair and wild eyes, and he shouted:

'The dew of heaven is falling among the corn-stalks of Aberdare, sure to God! Do I see a few ears flourishing under the bonnets and hats? Lads and lassies of the great new Revival, the Lord has had a fine time tonight, indeed. For he only catches the wee fishes, d'ye see. It is the likes of us that have to salt them. Am I glowing?'

'You're the brightest light in the city, your honour,' shouted a broad Irish voice. 'You're flaring brighter than the ironworks of Aberaman and including the Gadlys, from here.'

'Could you turn up the wick a bit for us, parson,' shouted another, 'for you're still a bit dim here at the back.'

'Is that so? Then I'll turn me up an inch. Sure to God, it makes me burn the brighter, the things that are happening. D'ye know what? I was up in Higher Miskin this very day outside the Boot, and there was a Welsh friend there crying, "Milk, milk, milk!" And this very week I heard the same chap shoutin', "Cream, cream, cream!"—but that was before his conversion to the true dissenting faith. Now, don't ye think that's wonderful? To be under the influence of the chapels instead of wallowing in the poitheen like us heathen Irish?'

Cheers and clapping at this, from a crowd as ragged and

unkempt as the French Revolution, and a few looked back-teeth-floating to me.

Mari said warmly, 'What a lovely thing to say—Oh, beautiful people are the Irish.' My father said, with business:

'If I bide here all night I will not get the hang of it. Look, Bryn—you stay with the women while I knock up the Lletty Shenkins agent. . . .'

'Number six down Blind Man Groping Lane, yer honour!' somebody cried.

'Thank you,' replied Dada. 'And remember,' he said to me, 'don't let a stick of that furniture out of your sight.'

'You want to find a fool in the country, you bring him from the town,' I said.

Rhia sighed. 'Thank heavens for Mr. Lyons, recommending us to the Lletty Shenkins.'

'Don't be too keen till you get there,' I replied.

'Hey, you down there!' shouted the preacher. 'You, the fine big Welsh lad—can ye hear me, son?'

'Me?' I asked, thumbing my chest.

'Aye, indeed,' cried he. 'Ach, may God be praised, there's a wonderful specimen of manhood. Welcome to Aberdare, boyo, for Welshmen are only good Irishmen who have never learned to swim. Aye, a right welcome to you and your pretty women, including the one carrying the tub. Are ye come as neighbours?'

'Aye!' Very embarrassed I felt.

'Then you've landed among friends right enough. For the Irish and Welsh have been Celts in arms since the first landing of the Beast Cromwell at Wexford, and his right hand man, the very same year, knocked off your Prince Llewelyn up in the country of Builth. Am I correct, now?'

'Sure, you are, Patrick, me love!' shrieked a woman. 'Isn't he a wonderful fella on the history o' the exploited people!'

'Which brings me to the point, young Taff. Are ye after shifting your household goods this minute?'

'My father is coming back with a hand-cart, now just,' I cried, wishing him to the devil.

'He's doin' no such thing, me boy,' shouted the preacher, and bawled at the crowd, 'Can we stand here and watch our

286

neighbours trundlin' their goods and chattels—one man and three women, an' us not lifting a finger to help?' Roars and cheers at this, and he cried down at me, 'Where are ye bound for, son?'

'Green Fach,' I said, and could have bitten off my tongue.

'Right, me lucky lads! We'll be delaying the Revival sermon for a bit while we all give a hand with the Welsh furniture—are ye on?'

'Oh, dear,' whispered Mari, 'we ought to wait for Dada.'

I managed to collar the Welsh dresser in the rush, for one moment we were furniture and the next we were Irish, with eager hands lifting the bed and somebody else on the mangle, and out of the corner of my eyes as I jack-knifed under the dresser I saw the commode with the Revival preacher, and it was going like the hammers of hell. And as I galloped along with Mari and Rhia steadying the thing, the tin bath went up one side street and the bed up another, and by the time we were fifty yards down Station Street, all we had left was the dresser.

Well.

Ten minutes later my father wandered up with his thumbs in his trews, and with him came the Lletty Shenkins agent, a sunflower wearing spectacles sitting on a high, starched collar.

'It would appear, Mr. Evan,' said this agent, examining us, 'that they have met up with our Patrick Revival, the furniture remover.'

Mari said, clutching me, 'You cannot blame Bryn, Mostyn. He seemed such a nice man and he did sound very generous.'

'So shall I,' said Dada, and turned to me. 'If you want to find a fool in the country, you bring him from the town, is it? You big, useless gunk of a Welshman. You congenital bloody idiot.'

'Yes, Dada,' I said.

You have to see this Aberdare to believe it.

I thought I had seen some places up in Merthyr, but Bute Street and Wigan Row where the north country English lived was as bad as anything I had seen up The Top, and Hirwain and Club Row were not fit for pigs—and all owned by Lord Bute. Acres of the bright, clay soil were ponds of human filth: the cess-pits, where they existed, had overflowed and in some houses at Cobblers Row, near the vicarage, the night-soil in the ground floor rooms was inches deep.

People came out of their cottages to watch us as we passed; thin, weary creatures with dark hollows for eyes, and many of the old were shaking with ague in their tattered clothes. Filthy, emaciated children, the refuse of greed, stood in the gutters and stared at the strangers. Two men were fighting in the street outside the Royal Oak, nearly naked, snarling like dogs as they rolled in the garbage, clawing at each other and shrieking oaths.

'Oh, God,' whispered Rhia, and I gripped her hand and hurried her on. With Mari on one arm and Becca on the other, my father picked a path through the indescribable filth, and as we went we were followed by boisterous laughter, with naked children tiptoeing after us, aping our movements.

'In the name of Heaven, what have we come to?' whispered Mari as I passed her.

'It will be better down in Green Fach,' I replied.

'It do sound pretty, don't it?' observed Rebecca.

If you have seen Green Fach in the 'fifties up in Aberdare; if you have smelled Green Fach as we smelled it that summer dusk, you would have known something worse than the slums of Asia, said my father.

On, on we went, the Lletty Shenkins man leading us, and thank heaven we left the dresser in his yard, said Mari, for we would never have got it over the great mounds of garbage. And the inns and taverns were full to the windows, with elbows going up and quarts going down and men and women staggering out arm in arm and the air was split with the shriek of Irish fiddlers and the blast of melodeons and thumping tambourines. In the gutters sat beggars, men and women who were the burned-out slag of the ironworks, the refuse of profit that was shovelled away by the likes of Wayne of Gadlys and Bailey of Aberaman, and all to no end, for his works, built ten years back, was never a success. Here sat the evicted poor of the Bute rents, the crippled young and trembling aged. Here lay the young collier with the broken back, head cradled in his wife's arms; the girl-mother with her baby at her breast. Here

I passed, in tears, a ravaged generation of Welsh who were being broken on the wheel by a system of wealth and privilege that was countenanced by Church and State.

'By the Christ,' said my father, 'I heard it was bad, but I would not have come within a mile had I known it was as bad as this. One day, in return, they will hand us an English prince.'

'Dewi showed us the seven year sanitary report, but we would not believe it,' I said bitterly.

'Now we learn the hard way.'

We went on, nearing Green Fach in a glare of pulsating light, for the blast furnaces of Tye and Bryn David were tapping the bungs and salvoes of hot air rushed about us in dull cannonades, and a pillar of brilliant light shot high into the clouds with incinerating brightness, illuminating the black, forbidding country about us, the lowering hills, the crooked, squalid streets and leaning cottages. The earth beneath us trembled to the shot-firing underground. The wind was acrid with the tang of sulphur.

Rhia said, clutching my hand, 'Bryn, Bryn. . . .'

I gave her a grin. 'A little paradise, girl—wait till you see it in daylight.'

They told us that Number Five, Green Fach had only been up twenty years, but it looked more like two hundred with its stained walls and the piles of refuse at the front and back, with no garden save a pond of stinking cess-pit overflow along its unpaved street, and no light came into the rooms save red flickerings from the distant ironworks, and there was nowhere big enough to swing a cat.

'Take it or leave it,' said the agent. 'If Mr. Lyons hadn't recommended you, you wouldn't get a house at all.'

'The rent?' asked my father, mooching around the crumbling floor.

'Five shillings a week.' His strange, round eyes, bright with the inner fever of his goitre, moved over Rhiannon in quiet assessment.

There was no particular evil in him. The old French custom of *Droit du Seigneur*, of which my father had warned our women, might have died with the French Revolution in France, but it had not died in Wales. Part of the perks of Man Arfon's agency used to be the virgin Irish; this one, apparently, preferred the Welsh. It was a simple question of supply and demand; the English had the money and the Welsh had the women. Masters, sub-agents, even overmen had power over the family. In a world of skin and scrape the weakest went to the wall. Many a Welshman has starved on the drift to keep the virtue of a wife or daughter.

'Did you see the way he looked at me?' whispered Rhia, fearful.

My father said, 'No, Mr. Batey, my women prefer the pit to house-hold scrubbing. In any case, they have enough in here to keep them occupied.'

'As you wish,' said Mr. Batey.

A shadow moved over the window a moment after he had gone.

'Somebody out the back,' said Rebecca.

I flung open the door. The Revival preacher stood shivering on the threshold.

'Is this the house of Mostyn Evan and family, by any chance, yer worship?'

'You know damned well it is,' I said, and reached out, gripped him by the collar and steered him into the room.

'Where is my furniture?' thundered my father.

'Ach, sir, the situation's a wee bit complicated, if ye get me. . . .'

'It will be if that furniture is not back in the next ten minutes.'

Patrick Revival screwed his cap. 'You see, yer worship, a misunderstanding's at the bottom of it. Me friends got the accommodation mixed, and a lot of it's being delivered at various addresses in the town.'

'I can well believe that,' I shouted.

'But if you'll give me a day or two, I'll guarantee to round it up. The commode I've got here, an' the bed I can put me hands on, for I know the fella setting his aunty in it.'

'Oh, my God,' whispered Dada.

'Every stick you'll get back, sir. And what you lose I'll pay for in good money. For I'm working decent shifts down the Lletty Shenkins, Mostyn Evan, an' I wouldn't be missing a shilling a week or so.'

'How do you know my name?' asked Dada, suddenly interested.

Patrick Revival shifted his feet uncertainly. I slammed the back door shut.

'Tell us,' I said.

Strangely, I pitied him standing there in his rags. Hunger and fear was strolling in the caverns of his face and his eyes were large and fevered.

'I bumped into a fella in Royal Oak, and he was sent by your son.'

'My son, Dewi?'

'Aye, sir.'

'You know my son?'

'God in Heaven,' whispered the man. 'Everybody in Upper Miskin knows Dewi Evan, including the military. Didn't ye know he's Scotch Cattle?'

My father turned away to the window. The Irish said:

'There's not much happening round here that Dewi Evan don't know about. He's a power in the land, I can tell ye.'

'Go now, Irish,' I said, opening the door.

'An' there's a price on his head big enough to bury the entire community. What the hell d'ye think I'm doing rushing back with your furniture? It was he who sent the command.'

'Out,' I said.

After he had gone, Mari whispered, 'Oh, Mostyn!'

My father did not move from the window.

'He needs to keep away, then,' I said. 'If he comes round here he'll only land us in trouble,' and Dada turned to me, saying:

'Look at this place. Isn't he right, and aren't we wrong? I say good luck to him, for he's got more guts than the rest of us.'

We did not speak more, but stood there in the dusk of the empty room: things were changing from minute to minute. I had never heard my father speak like that before.

32

THINGS changed a great deal for us after Ifor died.

Rhia and I were supposed to be getting married in August, latest, in Zion Resolven, but that had gone by the board. Now it would be Calvinistic Methodist at Bethel, Hirwain. But it does not matter a lot which pew you select, said Mari: you could splice up at St. Joseph's, Mountain Ash, as a Roman Catholic, or stand up in Salem as a Penpound Baptist.

On our second week of working at the Lletty Shenkins, Dada said:

'Buying the old sticks of furniture has set us back a bit, boy, but we will get you and Rhia fixed up the moment we can.'

The four of us off to work at dawn that day, I remember— Dada, me, Rhia and Mari; with 'Becca left behind in Five Green Fach to do the house and cooking.

'She is near her time,' said Rhia. 'Should she be left alone?'

'Rough north country is Mrs. Robinson next door, but a good neighbour, and handy with the deliveries,' said Mari.

'No need for you to come working,' I said bitterly.

'Leave her, Bryn,' said Dada. 'It is what she wanted.'

Mari said, 'Now, what would I do sitting home in Green Fach all day, eh? 'Becca has Ceri for company, and if we are wanted she can run down to the mine. Leave it now, we have been through it all before.'

Either side of the road, men, women and children were hurrying to shift; most for the Abernant blast and forge, others for the Aberdare Iron Company, which, with the Gadlys Furnace Works, were sending every year nearly fifteen thousand tons to Cardiff. Doors were opening and slamming in the panic of the late-for-work, slops were pouring from windows, chambers being emptied in the road. Redcoats from Brecon Garrison were on the cobbles in fours, or lounging on street corners, bayonets flashing in the weak dawn light, while the people of the occupied country went to work.

'Never thought we'd drop to a Top Town pit,' I said, bitterly.

Dada laughed. 'Quite well off as a collier, though. Ten years back a roller was on an eighty-shilling week, now he's on thirty-five, and a railstraightener is cut by more than half.'

'Which is still more than we pick up.'

'That is why you have got to have me,' said Rhia. 'The third dram lifts us to thirty-seven, and we need forty to live decently.'

'Take me below and you've got a fourth dram,' said Mari.

'You stay on top,' I replied. 'Bad enough Rhia coming down.'

The trouble here was that we were paid on the dram system —the more drams per man, the higher his wages, since a cutter could cut faster than his mate filled the trucks. All over The Top about now the colliers were taking their children down the pit, for another head meant another dram. In some pits babies of two and three years of age were going into the cages on their father's shoulders and, once below, were laid to sleep or set to play while older children were put to work on the ventilation doors.

'Things will improve when the Union comes,' said my father.

'When it comes,' said Rhiannon. 'Meanwhile, I want to get married, and there is six pounds seven under the bed.'

Ifor dying had pulled us down. A very expensive thing is death.

'God, what a place,' I whispered.

For wounded soldiers from the Crimea were begging along the road to the Lletty Shenkins mine, their eyes stricken in their riven faces, their tunics pinned at the elbows, their trousers tied with string. We did not spare them a glance more than passing.

With the wages of the colliers the same that day as they were thirty years back, even a glance was costly, and the prices in the coal and ironmasters' Truck Shops were going higher every month, for industry was running down now the war was over.

'Strike action is the only way to raise wages,' I said as we went. 'Dewi said that and he was right.'

'But you cannot use strike action to get an increase,' said my father. 'You strike to resist a reduction in wages.'

In the history of the Welsh coalfields until the year 1871, long after my family ceased to exist in Aberdare, not a single strike of any importance was for a wage increase.

What we did not know as we went to work that first day in Aberdare, was that a strike of two months was about to begin against a fifteen per cent reduction. And at the end of the strike the Aberdare colliers would have to accept a further five per cent reduction to compensate the owners for the losses incurred.

See them on their knees in Chapel come Sunday; see them at communion in Church and wearing out their souls for larger profits: giving sixpenny purses for the Bible Penny Readings and silver purses for the Abergavenny eisteddfods.

Give me pigs and I will give you coalmasters.

A queer old place this Lletty Shenkins mine, and Resolven colliery was a bakestone with jam on, compared with it. Redcoat cavalry were patrolling its approaches; foot soldiers were guarding the entrance to the cage.

The cage faced me.

Drift mines and levels, where you walk into the mountain, I can stand, but ever since I can remember I have been afraid of the cage. I cannot stand the slam of the gate, the sooted cram of the sweating humanity, the sickening drop into earth: down, down to the pin-drop light a thousand feet below, in whines and shakes and rattles. Less chance of getting out, too, come flood or fire-damp. And bad on the chests, especially in Number Two stall where we were working; for every ton of coal we cut we were running out half a ton of gob.

'I am afraid of the cage,' whispered Rhia, and clutched my hand.

'Nothing to it,' I said. 'Stand on your toes and hold up your stomach.'

The colliers shoved over for her as she got into it. Leaving Mari with the croppers on the top.

I watched Rhia's face that morning, so as never to forget it. I traced every line of her, and cut it in my eye.

In plain sack-cloth she was dressed; still beautiful, though

294

her hair was bunned and tied back with string, because of the machinery. Her smock was laced about her neck high, and about her waist was a rope girdle; to her ankles her dress reached, but her arms were bare to the shoulders. Like a pale flower she stood among the Welsh colliers of the cage, though some were hefty Irish and already stripped to the belt, the smudges of coal across the shoulders and the pallor of their faces telling their trade: other women were crammed in, two being the hags of the early seams; as broad and strong as men, these, their faces blunted and brutalised by the orgy of the underground, their womanhood long vanished in the years of dramming and filling. A few little children stood at their fathers' belts, their great, wide eyes staring up at Rhiannon.

'This way,' said Dada as the cage opened at the bottom. With Rhia between us we thronged along the road to our heading with the rest of the colliers in a clanking of picks and shovels, and I watched Rhia's face as we passed the night shift stalls where the fillers were still on; men and women filling drams and packing up the roof to a chanting song of labour, their coal-stained bodies riven with sweat and flashing in the light of their candles. Ike Winchester, the road overman, was standing at the fork in the rail.

'Got another head,' said my father.

'A pretty one at that,' said Ike. Solid good English north country was old Ike, and he spoke like a Welsh, having come down to the industries years back and worked with the navvies on the Pencydrain viaduct, so he had a soft place for us. For six months he held his missus in a six foot culvert, but the second winter chilled her, and she died, so he buried her in Melincourt Chapel and left the Vale, and, like us, came north to Aberdare. My father said:

'Pretty or not, she's a dram, and I want it. Book us a third, Ike. I've got another back home in child, and she's eating for six.'

He smiled at Rhia, his fading eyes suddenly lighting up in his face, and said to me, 'A third it will be, but keep her in sight, son.'

'You watch me.'

'Your little woman, is it?'

'Aye.

'Keep her out of the dust; women are bad on the dust.'

'It's a wet seam, or she would not have come.'

He followed us down to Two Stall, hands on hips as we stripped off our shirts and crawled under the roof. 'You got gas here, by the smell of it.'

'We have got water,' said my father, spitting on his hands.

'Aye, I noticed—give her a hole, Mostyn.'

'I will do it,' I said, and knelt and swung the pick into the face, and it took, and held, and when I prised it out the water trickled. Ike pushed in his fingers and tasted it, shrugging; there was a difference between an underground spring and the still water of an old flooded working.

'Could be anything,' said my father. 'You know this heading?'

Ike said, 'Not this far. The records don't show. But if there's pressure there you would have had it before now. Pit it and I'll send down a hand-pump. Very wet on the drawers, is it?'

Rhia said, 'Shall I come back with you for the dram, Mr. Winchester?'

He did not reply, so my father stopped swinging, and looked at him.

'No, girl,' answered Ike. 'A special chap is bringing it, but it might be an hour or so.'

'Do not be long,' said Dada, 'and stand away so decent men can earn their money. Rhia, if he's starving us on a two-dram shift, better bring one up.'

'I will help you with the first one,' I said, and I took her up to the turn-out. Against the dram I held her, seeing the whiteness of her eyes in that black place, and there was a taste of dross on her lips when I kissed her.

'I love you, Rhia.'

'Ah!'

'For everlasting.'

'Eh, my sweet one,' she said against my throat.

I held her. In the distant clumping of the ponies of the higher level, in the faint whine of the cage and the iron rattle of the drams, I hold her, and her sack dress was coarse under my hands.

'That must be the deepest kiss in the county of Glamorgan.'

I said, 'The moment we can get a start we will collect another Billie Softo, then you will go from this place.'

'Ach, no!' she protested. 'It is cheaper with me, and we need money for 'Becca. Besides, I have got you down by here.'

I said, gripping her hands, 'Watch the roof. Keep your feet out from under the dram, is it?'

'One coming now—look.' She pointed down the road. A dram was coming in the flickering glow of the lamps. I turned, shouting:

'Third dram coming now, Dada.'

'Do not mind me,' he called back. 'You take your time with the woman while I dig up Glamorgan. What the hell is happening, Bryn?'

'We'll fill the third first—easy on the turnout,' I said, and we hauled the other two out of it while the third came up.

I stared in disbelief.

My brother Dewi was pushing behind it. Reaching out, he pulled Rhia hard against him, then gripped my shoulder in passing. Without a word, he pushed the dram up to the face where my father was picking out.

'Dada,' he said, and stood there in the candlelight.

Instantly knowing the voice, my father threw down his pick without even turning in the stall. 'You have been a long time about it, Dewi,' he said.

'I came when I could. They would have taken me if I had come before.'

'Which is what follows when you spend your life shattering creeds and breaking idols. Do you even know about Ifor?'

'Oh, Jesu,' said Dewi, his head bowed, 'do not talk to me about Ifor.'

'Sorry too bloody late, isn't it?' I said, coming up with Rhia.

'Oh, *hisht*, Bryn!' she said, holding me, and he jerked his thumb at her.

'Did you really have to bring her down?' he asked, bitterly.

'Got to keep the family alive till you form the Union,' I said.

My father eased himself out of the stall. 'Right, Bryn, you've had your say; now shut it.'

I looked at Dewi in the flickering candlelight: it was not more than eight months since I had seen him, yet he looked eight years older: about him was a chunky strength, something of Ifor; a man made bigger by the yellow light on his sweating body, but weariness lay in the humped shadows of his eyes.

Sitting back on the gob I gripped my hands, knowing a blind and violent anger. Rhia was hauling a third dram to feed Rebecca decent, so she could make her child, and it should have been Dewi. My father said, filling his pipe:

'They tell me you are a wanted man. Come on a bit since the old days of the free-thinking, haven't we?'

'Scotch Cattle,' I said, 'the scum of the Union. God help you if you think I'm dropping twopence a week to the likes of them.'

'Get out of Aberdare, Dada,' said Dewi, ignoring me.

I said, 'Something wrong with the comradeship of men if you have to break their legs and smash their fingers to get them in the club.'

'For God's sake get out, Dada,' whispered Dewi.

Sir John Guest of Dowlais had a herd of Scottish cattle; strong, fierce animals with black faces and curved horns. And from this the men who were enforcing the rules of the new Union took their name. They roved in herds of hundreds over the mountains, burning furniture and beating the scabs and blacklegs who worked on when the Union said strike.

Dada lighted his pipe, saying, 'One place is as good as another in this hell. Can you name a pit where I would get higher rates, with coal going down?'

'Resolven. Lyons would take you back. With old Sam Tommer dead you might even make overman.'

'Lyons employs English overmen, not Welsh. Besides, we cannot go back because of 'Becca.'

'Get out before you starve, Dada.' Dewi's voice rose. 'We are kicking out the Irish and calling the town to strike. A week from now not a ton of coal will run from Aberdare valley, for we are fighting the new wage reduction—you even heard about that?'

Dada nodded, and Dewi cried, making a fist, 'Fifteen per cent—not five, not even ten—*fifteen*!'

'The price of coal is dropping on world markets,' I said.

'You damned idiot!' he swung to me. 'Do you believe every bloody thing they tell you?'

'Now, don't start rising tempers,' said Dada.

'The owners are acting like savages!'

'And you reply by breaking the legs of your fellows. If they are savages, what does that make you?'

'If the swines go to work when the Union says strike, they take what is coming. Anyway, we do not give the orders, they come from London.'

'Then tell London to come down and starve with Aberdare,' said Dada. 'They will bring in the troops—remember Merthyr. It is a crime to strike, and you know it.'

'It is the right of every man to withhold his labour. Do they own you body and soul?'

'Damned near,' I said, 'and we realise it.'

'You're doffing your hats to them and they've got their feet in your faces. By God, these times don't breed men!'

My father frowned up. Rhia made a sweet lamenting noise beside me, her hands to her face, and Dewi cried:

'The town will stand by us. It will be a total strike, and if the Irish give out, God help them, for we'll run them from the valley.'

'Aren't the Irish people, too?' asked Rhia, softly.

'There must be a goal, woman. You must have an ideal and strive for that ideal—die for it, if needs be. This town will be in rags come winter, and still the Irish pour in, under-cutting Welsh wages. To hell with the foreigners, we fight for the Welsh. If you stop to consider individuals you become a sentimental slave.'

Dada said, 'You are too hot for reason, Dewi. Time was I thought you would make something of yourself, but I do not think so now.' He levelled his pipe. 'They will bring in troops and shoot you down as they shot you down in Newport ...'

'We will fight to the death, you will see.'

'They will transport the likes of you and Pietro and Richard Bennet—all the little men, as they transported Frost, Williams and Jones. And the big men like O'Connor, Lovett and Plaice will go free, as they went free before. The State is expert in handling revolution because it learned from France. Listen, son, listen. The owners are the State; they created it for their own convenience, they run and maintain it. And you are threatening their wealth. You can rape their daughters and get away with it, but if you touch a shilling of their money they will burn you alive.'

'*Nefoeddwen!* Then isn't it right to fight such an evil?'

'When you have something to fight it with.'

'With our bare hands, if necessary!'

'Right, then, but not with me, for I am sick of fighting. I have too many women and children, in the kitchen or in the stomach, to think of fighting.' Rising, he knocked out his pipe and pushed Dewi gently aside. 'Now away, son, for we have coal to cut and God, we need the money.'

Dewi whispered, his face white, 'So you will sit on your backside and whine about exploitation while others do your fighting for you.'

'If needs be, under present circumstances, for I have no option. Fire your belly, Dewi, but do not heat your brain—see sense.'

'If you don't give a sod for this generation, what about the next one?'

My father turned to him wearily. 'You get yourself a load of kids and then you would change your tune. Too much to lose, for us, but you have everything to gain. The next generation will have to manage while I see to this one.'

'It is your kind of selfishness that has brought us to this!'

'Away to your Workingmen's Union, son, let ordinary people work.'

'And cowardice.'

If I had not been guarding the dram he would have struck his head: Dewi dropped against me to Dada's fist, and I knelt, lowering him gently to the floor. Climbing up, he shoved me aside, staring at us. Blood ran from his mouth, trickling down his chest, and he wiped it away with the back of his hand.

'Goodbye, Dada,' he said.

I turned away: I could not bear the sight of my father's face.

Turning, Dewi left us: Rhia was bowed against the dram, in disordered weeping.

33

COME the end of that June the whole of the Aberdare valley between Hirwain and Mountain Ash was out on strike. First the Wherfa closed, then the Middle and Upper Dyffryns; the Aber Nant-y-groes and Aberaman followed, and after half-a-dozen others came the Lletty Shenkins. Short of coal for their fires, the ironworks began to blow out their furnaces, beginning with the Gadlys up to the big Aberdare. Five thousand colliers in pits big and small, in drift and level and mine, struck in the valley against the fifteen per cent reduction in their wages. The towns, villages and hamlets died that summer. Bright as a blue-bag was the sky over The Top; no smoke sullied the wash-day clouds, the gigantic cumulus that flowered over Aberdare; no longer soot and sulphur stained the summer wind; a new sweetness bloomed on the mountains, with the heather all gay in her purple dress again and the little brooks boasting clean and white from the caverns of the hills and cascading in beauty down the crags to the floor of the valley.

In July, from Aberdare to Abercynon, the children, always the first, began to die, and the little yellow coffins went trailing up the hillsides: the sick and aged began to follow, then the vagrants. They died in scores from the small-pox; of typhoid and cholera. They died in the sink-pits of Wigan Row, Hirwain Row and Club Row, and Bute Street, which is named after the landlord. Of under-nourishment and the lack of good water, they died; from the fever spouts of the Maes y dre and Darran; through drinking from the River Dare and the Cynon, and the Vicarage Well; from epidemic, endemic and contagious diseases, they died, it was officially said.

But they did not die, they were murdered, said my father.

They also died from boredom, and this I believe, for I saw them. I saw them sitting on their hunkers on street corners, staring into space; or aimlessly playing pitch and toss for pebbles, or fighting bare-knuckle with a friend to break the monotony.

They were not alone in this, of course. Up in Crawshay's Merthyr, for lack of a decent water supply that would have cost a thousand pounds, they died like flies eight years back; seventeen hundred men, women and children in four months.

In filth, in the cess-pits that their masters called comfortable little cottages, they died while masters like Bute and Crawshay were building their castles and mistresses like Lady Charlotte Guest were running for their country manors, frightened to death of the cholera.

Let further generations despise the tame historians, the crooked lackeys of the subscriber histories; those who wheedled for favour and the owner's purse to set down the lie of how my generation died.

At the hands of coal and ironmasters who couldn't afford to lay a decent water supply in a land abundant with water, or lay a decent drain in a land of slope and incline; this is how they died.

On the second week of the strike 'Becca put her fist on the table and bowed her head and clenched her eyes, and Mari rose instantly, whispering:

'Rhia—sharp upstairs with the towels and sheets. Bryn, away quick to the spout for water. Mostyn, you help—water, *water*! And boil it, remember; for God's sake do not forget to boil it.'

And Rebecca rose, shapeless in Nature's joke, and shambled wearily up the narrow stairs of Green Fach, for labour.

'Where has Mam gone?' asked Ceri, now four.

'Up to rest,' said Dada. 'You are going next door to Mrs. Robinson.'

Black-haired and olive skinned was Ceri, her eyes like great brown jewels in her high-boned, Jewish face, and dainty in the mouth. Yet there was in her the same heavy clumsiness of my dead Ifor.

It do seem like yesterday, sitting there at the table in Green Fach, listening to Mari's consoling voice upstairs, the stifled screams that floated down, the drumming of Rebecca's heels on the boards above us. Hour after hour it went on, and I can see now the bright sweat on my father's face. All that day he and I had pitchered the water the four miles return from the mountain spout, for we dared not trust the ones in Town for fear of infection, and even then it was floating wigglers and red things with ears on. At nine o'clock that night I could stick it no longer and I handed it over to 'Becca.

'Off out,' I said, hitching up.

'At this time of night?'

'Got a pain in my stomach, and it's fair crippling me.'

'I got one in my back,' said Dada. He went to the foot of the stairs, calling, 'Mari, the pair of us slipping out, you need us?'

Rhia came down the stairs, I remember, her hair tangled, her eyes bright.

'Oh, my God,' she whispered, staring at me.

'Is she coming normal?' asked Dada.

'Aye, but ... oh, it is terrible.'

'Now you know what you have got coming,' I said.

'Give us half an hour,' said Dada, 'we are both in a hell of a state.'

'I will mention it to 'Becca,' said Rhiannon.

The Irish were collecting it on the streets of Aberdare that night.

Sorry in my heart, I am, for the poor bloody Irish.

In the vagrant lodging houses, for one, they were getting it: the Welsh going in and beating them out with sticks and boots, and I pitied them cowering under the threats, hands up in terror as they stumbled down the street half-dressed.

'If anything goes wrong, the Irish get it first,' said Dada, strolling along.

'Mind, the vagrants are a disgrace,' I said.

A few years back we had five or more vagrant houses in Town, and the charge was threepence a night for a single and sixpence for a family. And with the landlords evicting the Irish right, left and centre, whole families were wandering practically destitute, and mainly the Irish. So a family would buy a sixpenny bed at the vagrant and put the family on the mattress, which sometimes laid five or six, getting them head to toe, of all sexes and sizes and most as naked as moles, to make more room; the ceilings so low in one house they couldn't sit up in bed.

'One landlord a night,' said Dada, 'smack in the middle.'

'And a coalmaster under the bed,' I said.

Blacklegs were being marched to work by the military, and a few of them Welsh, by the look of it, for they were colliers, and few Irish worked underground. I hated and pitied them; the redcoats forming them up, halting them in the road until they were joined by another or two; leaving their homes and their women and children to the scowling neighbours.

'God help them when the military leave,' said Dada.

'God help them if the Cattle get hold of them,' I said.

Red torches were flashing on the mountains, rockets were soaring into the star-lit sky: distantly, on the wind, came a faint bass lowing, like an animal in pain. The choice was not easy, said Dada; it is the torture of the Cattle or the agony of seeing your children starve.

'How much have we got left between us?' I asked.

'Twelve sovereigns all round, according to Rhiannon, counting yours.'

I nodded.

'It won't take long to dish up another twenty, the moment the strike is done, lad.'

'Aye.'

'Worth waiting for, a decent girl like Rhia.'

I nodded.

Not waiting. Not now. These days my Rhia was as much a wife to me as Mari was to my father. It had gone too long, we had been tried too far.

Not on your life. She was my woman; no more waiting.

'Try and keep decent, Bryn,' said my father.

'Ay, ay, don't worry about me, man.'

Two little pigs do live in English sties, said Rhiannon, and this little pig is in love with another. You tell me what is left to us if we do not have each other. God do understand.

Well, well. Don't see enough of Him round the Aberdare direction to know if He did or didn't.

Got my Rhia, and life was bearable. A few years from now, with the exception of life around twenty-one, I would get round to thinking about the everlasting fire, and the evangelical Ikes can make what they like of it.

They were breaking Irish windows down High Street and Irish shrieks were coming from the Boot area. For the Irish were strike-breaking when the Welsh said strike, and good Irishmen were either dead or back in County Clare direction.

'You don't have to be English to be a hooligan, mind,' said Dada. 'I know a few good Welsh ones, and there should be no nationality in street or pulpit.'

'You agree with them breaking strike, then?'

'I do not, but I understand the reasons why they do it—things come different when the children begin to starve.'

'Then you would do it if Ceri hungered?'

'I am Welsh, not Irish. If other Welsh children are at it, then Ceri starves, too; this is the law.'

'Queer old situation, if we did strike—Dewi breaking our nuts for us.'

He said, deep, 'It has happened before, it is what the owners hope for; the belly can split husband against wife and father against son. But we have twelve pounds before we sink to the level of the poor Irish.'

'The money will see us through six weeks,' I answered. 'We will be back at Lletty Shenkins long before that.'

'I hope you are right.'

Down Canon Street the Welsh mob was howling and waving cudgels. A barrel of ale was rolled over the cobbles down Commercial Street and another filched from the Bute Arms where windows were being smashed. And these they set up and foaming mugs were passed round, and in the Castle tap it was running under the doors. Down Wind Street a brass band came marching, with Redcoat cavalry prancing either side of it, and the Irish came up from Bute Street and met them in hundreds, for we saw it; a surging wave of screaming humanity, sticks and cudgels raised, and the trombones and tubas and kettles took it head on, with a six-foot Irishman putting his boot through the big bass drum, which is enough to send any decent Welshman mad and raving.

'God, what a sight!' whispered Dada as we flattened ourselves against the wall of the Black Lion. Fists were going up and cudgels coming down, with special constables going in with batons and coming out wiping cuts and holding bruises, and everybody trying to hit out the military, which is natural. Shots were clattering through the medley of shrieks and curses as the Welsh and Irish fought it out, and then a wing of the Irish mob tore off and flew down Monk Street and another made off towards the station, hitting out Welshmen with every tool God has provided since the Creation. A scene of Hades, this, with shawled Irish women racing along the gutters and little children falling among the flying boots of the colliers. One young woman stumbled amid the Irish, and lay still, her hands over her head, and immediately Dada was into the mob, flinging Irishmen aside, while I went in after him kicking at shins, for there is nothing like a good old hop to take your mind off the business in hand.

Dragging her out, we sheltered her against a wall while the mob flooded past us. I whispered into her white face, 'You all right, Irish?'

She opened fevered eyes at me, bright jewels in the pinched hunger of her cheeks, and shrieked, 'Keep away from me, ye filthy scalpeens. Dirt on ye souls for what you're doin' to me people, ye Welsh heathen!'

A voice above us cried bass:

'Are there reinforcements up at Gadlys, sergeant?' He was an officer, bright-haired and English, and he sat his horse well as it pranced the cobbles, his sabre held high.

'Only a platoon across Green Street, sir!'

'You'll need a company, for they are after the Wayne furnaces. Away to it, man!'

As the girl scrambled away my father made large eyes at me, and I shared his fears.

'Run, run!' he cried, and hammered into the mob.

We got into the back of our Number Five as the Irish mob, turned from wrecking the furnaces, came piling through the street window without opening it. And as I ducked a stick and caught an Irish jaw square in the passage I saw Rhia at the top of the stairs with something in her arms, and her face was white and terrified. Screams and shrieks were coming down the row as Welsh and English front doors went down and glass shattered, and Mrs. Robinson was hanging out of her window in her nightdress dropping coal on the invaders and yelling to go easy since her dada was born in Kerry, and Patrick Revival never lost a wink, it was said, though Mrs. Regan next door but seven lost two china dogs and a double hair mattress because her old man was Staffordshire, which was reasonable when you consider it. But it was pretty unreasonable if you were like us, as Welsh as Irfon Bridge.

Within the first minute the Irish confetti took every window fore and aft, said Rhia afterwards, and with at least twenty Irish in the kitchen and only two of us, it was naturally a little inconvenient. Side by side and hooking short, Dada and me, for you daren't swing in case you collected the dresser. And in the latter stages Mari and Rhia came down and assisted County Clare folk and Limericks through the front door with chair legs. Actually, I thought we were doing all right until an Irish navvy ducked a left hook from Dada and I stepped into it and went out like a light. And when I came to I was sitting in three feet of wreckage with my jaw sideways and Rhia kneeling beside me dabbing me with cold water and my father raging and tying up knuckles, the knots in his teeth.

'How are you?' he demanded.

'I'm lovely,' I said.

'You look it,' said he. 'How many times have I told you I'm inclined to drift on the left? If it happens again for God's sake keep on the right.'

Not an Irishman in sight now, and the town was quiet under the stars, weeping in the smashed kitchens, rocking itself with hunger. We got things more or less ship-shape and went upstairs to see 'Becca. Sitting up in bed as large as life, was she, and chewing willow bark for a headache. But she loosened her tears when I took her baby boy in my arms, and my father said from the end of the bed, 'Sometimes I think that God is sitting on the boards of the coalmasters, but at times like this He is sitting in by here, in Green Fach.'

'Becca whispered in her throat, 'Looks just like my Ifor, he do, standing there.'

'Downstairs, you,' said Mari, elbowing me. 'Give Mama's Ifor to me; squeezing the stomach from him, you are, Bryn.'

Downstairs, by the grate, I listened to Rebecca sobbing and the breathless squalling of the new Ifor Evan, and I clenched my hand for my brother. Through the smashed window of the back I watched Gomer Taff, the Gadlys collier and his three mates carrying Wil Wicker down to the New Inn on his platter, for this was Saturday night. And Saturday night, wet or fine, peace or riot, they took him, broken back included, down to the tap, and brought him back to his missus as tight as a pair of stays, and there are advantages, mind, Wil used to say, in living horizontal, for the old hen don't know if it's two pints or twenty.

'Good night, Bryn,' he cried, as I leaned on the back gate now.

I got up off the gate as he passed, and stood decent for him.

'Good night, Wil Wicker,' I said.

The Black Dare of Gadlys was going in sucks and whirls and gurgles to her underground bed of cholera: the pit-head and wheel were stark against the moon. The stars were big over Aberdare, and the wind, I remember, was weeping.

Rhia called in pent breath from the kitchen, 'You there, Bryn?'

'Aye.'

She came to me in frozen mood, her fist against her face, and stared, speechless, at me.

'What is it, woman?'

'The money is gone. Mari just found the caddie. It ... it is empty!'

Dada came then, hands clenched. 'You ... you heard? Rhia told you?'

The bile rose to my throat and I swallowed it down.

'In the name of God,' whispered Mari, coming out, 'what shall we do?'

Empty, we stood, looking at each other, empty.

All down the Row the lights were going out: faintly, the new Ifor cried on 'Becca's breast. Mari said:

'He is Ifor's boy, Mostyn, and he is not starving, like the baby Irish.'

'It will not come to that.'

'Before it does,' said Mari, 'I will go to work.'

Hands clenched, she faced him.

'You will go to work when I say,' whispered my father.

'Understand us now,' replied Mari. 'When Rebecca thins on milk for Ifor's child, Rhia and I break strike.'

'You are usurping the command of my house.'

'Call it what you will, Mostyn.'

'You leave here to work without my permission, woman, and you need not come back.'

'So be it,' said Mari, and gathered Rhiannon, and they went into the kitchen.

I touched my father.

'Leave me,' he said.

34

ON the seventh week of the colliers' strike Aberdare looked more like a town under military occupation than a Top Town coalfield. But the strikers were still defiant: burning the truck shops, bombing the houses of the black-legs and hoisting men to the top of the pit-head wheels as punishment for sneaking on to shift under Company protection. Under the threat of the fifteen per cent reduction, under the heel of the coming Union and the boot of the military, my town slowly died, leaving in its bare rooms the gnaw and pallor of hunger.

'Seven fat years, seven lean ones,' said Tomos Traherne in his beard, 'it be the law of God,' and he raised his palms upwards in our kitchen, crying, 'But the wind of Heaven is blowing over the mountains. In the death of the body through our own transgressions we are in the midst of a glorious revival of the soul. *Selah!*

'Selah,' whispered Mari, her eyes cast down.

'Selah,' I said, wishing him to the devil privately, for it was fourteen fat ones for Tomos Traherne if his stomach was a pointer.

Sad was my town, my dirty, rambling, silent, ugly little Aberdare. No longer the children kicked the pig's bladder along the flagged terraces in all their shrieks and laughter; no longer the women sang from their kitchens the high, sweet sadness of the Welsh sopranos; no longer was heard the fumbling bass and soaring tenor. In the bake of summer the town steamed. The brooks were dried in their calcined beds. Down in the Spanish and Italian houses the foreigners fingered their rosaries; the starving Irish keened and wailed in the nights. In the rake of her derelict chimneys and blown-out furnaces, in the stilled blur of her pit-head wheels, Aberdare died.

And Ifor, the son of my brother, wept at Rebecca's daily sugar and bread, for his milk was thin. So 'Becca rested. In bed most of the day to hold her strength, she stared over the sun-drenched fields, looking for Ifor. By day, while Dada and I went up the mountain to fetch water from the clean spouts, Mari and Rhia would gather the fleece off the hedges. This they spun on the wheel that belonged to my gran, making children's vests for selling in Abergavenny market, and for these a cart came once a week. Of canal reeds we wove baskets and panniers, as Mari taught us; from hazel we fashioned pegs, and Rhiannon took these gipsy style down to Skewen and Morriston, selling at the doors, and even over Sarn Helen to Brecon where they wash very white.

I remember the idleness, the boredom, the hunger of that seven-week strike against reduction. But most of all, in detail, I remember the night that the agent Mr. Batey came.

'The Spanish have broken the strike up in Merthyr, you heard?' asked Rhia.

Thin and pale she looked, her lips bloodless; yet her eyes, large and shadowed in the pallor of her face, burned with a strange, inner fever.

'It is a rumour sent out by the owners,' said my father.

Mari rose. 'It is true. Ike Winchester I saw today, and he told me.'

'Ike Winchester?'

'He is come over from Lletty Shenkins to run the Gadlys Pit when the strike is over.' Bending, she lifted Ceri against her, and there was a great silence in her for my father: scarcely a word had passed between them since the night of the Irish riots.

Tomos said, 'I heard Mr. Batey, the General Agent, has finished with Lletty, too. He is going round the Rows trying to persuade people into the Gadlys.'

'Because it is easily protected,' I said.

He nodded heavily, muttering, 'I never thought the time would come when the workers of this town would need protection from my Richard Bennet and your Dewi, and their like.'

'It is a sign of the times,' said Dada. 'I never thought the time would come when I would need protection from the greed of coal-owners.'

'Oh, God, listen to it!' whispered Mari.

'Aye, listen!' said my father. 'For you have closed your ears too long. Dewi was right and we were wrong. Force must be met with force, violence with violence.'

Sick to death of it all, I got up and went to the back door, opening it and staring out. And Tomos Traherne said, bass, ' "It is the vengeance of God on the ungodly for the wickedness of the people. . . ." '

My father got up. 'Out,' he said.

'Mostyn!' cried Mari, turning.

' "For it is the day of the Lord's vengeance," ' shouted Tomos, beard trembling, ' "and the year of recompenses for the controversy of Zion. And the streams thereof shall be turned into pitch, and the dust thereof into brimstone . . . the

311

cormorant and bittern shall possess it; the owl also, and the raven shall dwell in it . . . ! ' ' '

'Out!' shouted my father, gripping him and heaving him up, and I opened the door as Dada assisted him through it on to the cobbles, and Mari was shrieking behind him as Tomos raised his staff and held it high, crying aloud:

'This is the judgment of the Lord on those that fly in the face of authority! Here shall the great owl make her nest, and lay and hatch! Here shall the vultures also be gathered, each with his mate . . . !'

'Ay ay,' I said, throwing his hat after him and slamming the door, and Dada shouted, his hands to his head:

'I've stood that God-botherer long enough. Christ is weeping out there for the people of the town and he is sitting in by here roasting us for not going back to work. What kind of religion is that?'

'Is it religion to sit in idleness while 'Becca's child is dying for want of milk?' cried Mari.

'Oh, God, it is too big for me,' said my father, covering his face.

'But not for me!' cried Mari, bending over him. And she put her hands in her hair and pulled it about her face, and cried, 'Now I have stopped begging. It has gone on long enough, it is time the women took a hand.' She began to cry then, in gasps and wetness, and I went and held her.

'Hush, you,' I said, 'the world is crying enough. Soon it will be over, soon it will come right between you and Dada.'

'Not between us now. Oh, God, I have ploughed those hopes underground a long time ago. We are strangers.'

'Dada, for heaven's sake,' I said, turning to him.

In a sudden panic, Rhiannon said at the window, 'Heisht, Mama, *heisht*! Mr. Batey, the agent, is coming!'

'And he will go the same direction as Tomos Traherne,' cried my father.

'Oh, please, please let him speak,' begged Rhia.

No sense in this. One moment a good old-fashioned family palaver with men shouting and women crying and preachers going out head first, and next minute everybody rushing around slapping the furniture and for goodness' sake try to make the place presentable. No time for more discussion, he was in.

On the step he stood, six feet up and skinny, with his hat on his ears and his collar cutting his throat. His eyes, bulging behind his spectacles, moved slowly around the kitchen: resting on Rhia, he said:

'Good evening, Mostyn Evan.'

'Say your business and go,' said Dada, fist on the table, turned away.

'It is simple. The strike is broken.' He entered softly.

'Thank God, thank God,' whispered Mari, tightening her shawl.

Dada said, 'Now let us have the truth. If the strike were broken there would be dancing in the streets. What do you want of us?'

'It is what you want of me, Mostyn Evan.' From his pocket he brought a handful of golden sovereigns, and these he held over the table. 'What chance have you got? The owners can spill these along the streets, and here you sit without a glass of water.'

'Shift him, Bryn,' muttered my father.

'You dare!' whispered Mari, bending at the waist, her eyes on fire.

Batey said, 'You put a finger on me, Mostyn Evan, and I will run you from these mountains. I tell you, the strike is broken. In Aberaman they are going back, at Cwmdare; and the furnaces are alight at Abernant. Mr. Robinson is starting in the morning, also Gomer Taff, and the Irish will be going up in hundreds with the Spanish and Italians. Now then!'

'I will believe this when I see it,' said my father.

'You will see it soon enough,' said Mari, 'because Rhia and me are starting in the morning.'

'Well done, Mrs. Evan,' said Mr. Batey. 'You are respected in Green Fach. If you go in the Gadlys Pit will open.'

'If she goes in she leaves this house,' said Dada, getting up.

'I am with Dada,' said Rhia. 'I am with Dada because I am with Bryn. When Bryn says work, I work, and not before.'

The shock of her voice turned us all. Mari sat down slowly. She said:

'Let the baby die, then. I can do no more.'

My father said softly, 'And now get out, Batey. There is only one strike-breaker here and she can be discounted. Time was, tell Wayne, that I would have been with her, but not now. Time was I would have been first into Gadlys, for the greed of the workers is the same as the masters. But I will not break strike now, although I am not with the Union. I will not break strike, Batey, because the owners are showing worse than greed. This is a strike against a reduction, not for an increase. It is a strike against the owners who are cutting on wages to flush up their profits. And they are bringing in the foreigners to cane the backs of the Welsh: they are bringing in the starving to get their fifteen per cent. The swine can watch a two foot coffin go up Cemetery Road without the lift of a hat, for I have seen them. Now get out and look in Town for English black-legs, for you will not find them among the Welsh.'

Mr. Batey bowed slightly. 'As you wish. Good night, Mr. Evan.'

I shut the door behind him.

Mari said, 'If Gran were here tonight it would have been a different tune.'

'Aye,' replied my father, 'for she was Welsh.'

Faintly, from the room above, came the sound of Ifor crying.

Near midnight I awoke, rising up in the bed, hearing a sound.

A footstep had slurred the boards of the landing. Getting out, I opened the door. Rhiannon, fully dressed, was going silently down the stairs. I listened. The lock of the back door grated. Now, at the window, I saw her floating over the cobbles of the Row, and the moon was bright down the street where no lights burned, and the town lay silent, because of the curfew.

'Rhia!' I whispered, but she did not hear me.

I clenched my hands, knowing where she was going.

Dressing swiftly, I ran down into the deserted street and along the banks of the Dare, crossing it into High Street and along to Bute.

Now along the high pavement, flattening in the doorways, for soldiers were forming at the end by Maerdy House, and I doubled back into Cardiff Road towards Sunnybank and Blind Man Groping Lane.

Snatching at breath, I went swiftly up to the house of Batey, the agent, and there I found her.

As carved from black stone Rhiannon was standing there by the gate, and beyond her, working in his lighted window, was Mr. Batey.

A madness was in her face when she turned to me, and yet there was in her no surprise.

'Bryn,' she said.

'Aye, girl.'

I held her and she was thin in my arms, and trembling.

Suddenly she held me away, and in that light her eyes were stark white, the pupils glittering, and strange.

'You been here before, Rhia?' I whispered, and I shut my eyes to the pain of fire in me, and in the nearness and warmth of her there was comfort.

'Aye. Once before I came, but he was not here. So I waited, and he did not come. Got to have money, see, for 'Becca's baby.'

'Yes,' I said.

'You wait for me, Bryn? Mr. Batey said to come. A sovereign, it is, mind. You know Beth Regan, the Irish . . . ?'

I bowed my head against her.

'Got to have money, says 'Becca, for Ifor's son.'

I held her and would not let her go.

'Who is there?' cried a voice.

Batey was standing in his door-way, his lamp held high.

'Come,' I said. 'Come, Rhia.'

'Who is it?' called Batey.

I did not look back.

To save me the sin of murder, I did not look back.

In the kitchen I got her back into her night-dress, hushing and kissing into silence her excited chatter: sweat was on her, running in streams over her body.

After a bit, cradled in my arms, she slept, and I went up the stairs to my father's room, and knocked, and Mari came to the door, clutching her night-dress to her throat.

'My girl is ill,' I said.

My father came then, his hair awry. 'What is happening, Bryn?'

'Rhia is ill,' I replied. 'It is the fever of the starve.'

With wild eyes Mari pushed past me and ran down the stairs, and then the door of Rebecca's room came open and she stood there with Ifor in her arms.

'Dada, for God's sake,' she said.

Turning, my father put his face against the wall, saying, 'The house is split from top to bottom.'

'Death will split it more,' I answered. 'A month from now the people of this valley will be working, and ours will be dead. I am breaking strike tomorrow.'

35

AND SO, on the fiftieth day of the strike we stood in the Row of Green Fach and awaited the coming of the protection military.

Dada, Mari and I waited outside our back for the dawn shift, and we did not speak. All down the Row the word went round, and doors started coming open and windows shooting up, and dear me, Mrs. Jones, I would have to see it with my own eyes before I would believe it.

Mostyn Evan and family breaking the strike.

Their amazement changed to dumbness and their dumbness to silent fury. And breeding in the fury was their despising, and their hatred.

In a trickle from their gates, buttoning their coats, tying their aprons, they came white-faced and staring, and ringed us, and did not speak, at first.

There was old Ike Winchester from Lletty Shenkins, come down to work the Gadlys when the strike broke: Mr. and Mrs. Robinson, our north-country English neighbours, handy in the mouths but with hearts of gold: there was William Williams called Billy Twice, the old Cardie collier, now burned out by shallow seams down the Garn, and dust. Peg Skewen, the Park Pit coal-cropper, came with Noah Morgan of the Forge, Abernant. Gomer Taff from Number Ten, said:

'In the name of Heaven, Mostyn Evan, I never would have believed it.'

Standing at the back was Penrhy Jones, the minister of Siloa, Gadlys, who was our Big Seat, and staying in Number Three with his sister. Strong for his God, the Revival and for whipping them from the Temple, the men of greed, was he. With hurt eyes he regarded us, and this was the deepest wound of all.

Ike Winchester shouted, 'Mostyn, give them a week and we will all be back!'

My father did not reply. Side by side, we stared down the Row.

'And I took you for a four-square man, Evan!'

'About as straight as a scythe-handle.'

'Scab!'

'Blackleg!'

And as their tempers heated the dawn blew soft about us: sweet was the perfume of my valley after the smokeless solace of the night. Upon us they heaped dirt and insults, and when the military came marching down the Row they raised their fists and shouted in our faces. And we did not move.

About forty other scabs came, mainly Irish and Spanish, and they marched in threes with eight foot redcoats either side, muskets shouldered, bayonets fixed, and ahead of them was a sergeant. Seeing us, he halted, crying:

'You for Gadlys, Welshman?'

My father nodded.

'Line in, then!' Leaving his column, he drew his sabre, forcing a path through the neighbours, and we trooped after him to the column.

'Wait,' said my father. 'I have sick people, and I need protection.' He jerked his thumb at the house and I saw a flash glimpse of Rebecca standing with Ceri at the window.

'I can spare you one,' said the sergeant.

Penrhy Jones called, 'That is the second fool talking. He

needs no protection, his people will be safe.'

'You guarantee this, pastor?' shouted the soldier.

'Get about your business, man. Leave the Welsh to the Welsh.'

With Mari between us, we marched off at the back of the column. I looked at my father; erect he went, his eyes dead in his face. Mari's face was chalk-white and her hands clenched to the growing clamour of the mob who were piling out of their doors to greet the dawn-shift scabs.

Down Unity Street and Ty Fry the strikers were lining the road three deep, racing up from Canon and Commercial and Bute, buttoning up and belting up and smoothing straight from the bed. And in the red-tinged light of dawn they lent their bawled insults to the workers of Gadlys, forming an avenue down which we walked. Here were soldiers in scores, sabres drawn, their horses plunging among the tattered buildings of the ironworks of Wayne, their nostrils snorting mist amid the panic of the shoving crowd. On, on we went along the avenue of hatred and threats, their fists an inch from our faces as the soldiers fought to keep them back. Enveloped by their fury and insults we went, and I felt for Mari's hand and gripped it; the howling reached a new thunder as we neared the shaft of Gadlys; cold as ice that hand, and I chanced a look at her. Blood was on her face from a flung stone and her eyes were closed, the lashes ringed black on the drawn parchment of her cheeks.

On the last twenty yards to the cage the soldiers were facing the crowd; men of the Glamorgan military, their numbers swollen by the Workmen Volunteers, the traitor army loyal to the owners, and six Swansea dragoons on horse-back were anchored around the Head, their eyes switching about them nervously.

'Right into it, into it!' Musket-butts at the ready, they ringed us, with a flogging on the end of it if they lost us to the crowd.

The Spanish went first, herded like sheep, and the cage descended: then went the Irish, spitting back the insults of the ragged army of strikers thrusting about us and bawling the blackleg song. And in the moment before the drop of the cage

318

I saw, down the cinder slope of the pit, the face of my brother Dewi. And even as I stared the crowd about him swayed and broke. Richard Bennet I saw, too, dressed as a labouring Irish in a tam-o'-shanter and scarlet neck-tie, and I raised my hand, crying, 'Dewi, Dewi!'

Clearly he saw me, I knew this by his face. Putting his hands on his hips, he turned away, and spat.

The cage dropped into the pit blackness of the butcher's shop they called Gadlys.

To a pin-prick of light five hundred feet below, we dropped. And with the slam of the cage door went from there in a babble of foreign tongues to the Victorian parting, which is the division where the main gallery sweeps away to avoid running under St. John's Parish Church in the light above.

A man was issuing picks and shovels here, and I recognised him instantly despite the wavering light of the pit candles.

It was Pietro Bianca, as if stepped straight from the days of the Old Navigation, and he did not speak.

'Pietro . . . !' whispered Mari, peering, but he made no sign that he knew her.

My father gripped her arm, drawing her on with the colliers. 'Come, Mari,' said he. 'Times have changed. It is not your Pietro Bianca.'

On we went down the drift for Forge Side, the Spaniards leading in a clank of tools, and I feared for Mari, who had not been below before.

A swine was this Wayne Gadlys: she began in the drop beside St. John's and ran in a mile drift down to Fothergill, the beating heart of Abernant and the mushrooming scarlet of the furnaces of Forge Side. And the workers of Colliers' Row and Engineers' Row knew Gadlys for the bitch she was. So when the women asked the Truck for six penn'orth of accidents for a minced beef Sunday they were talking of the shambles of Fothergill; but owners don't know the difference between minced beef and chopped colliers, they said, and only the women knew what was coming up next on the stretchers of Gadlys.

And if the bell-stone and dram and hoof and engine don't

get you down Gadlys, the chances are that water would, for she was loaded to the gunwales in underwater ponds and streams and old, flooded workings.

'Watch the water,' said my father.

We went on, wading now in twelve inches, and it was evil black and oily, with Mari tying up her dress to her knees.

Now there was a great softness in my father for his wife, and I was glad.

I waded on, glancing back, and saw with joy that he was again one with her, for under the lamp of a heading he had her against the rock, and was kissing her. The overman shouted:

'First in. Mostyn Evan, the son, and the woman. Where are they?'

'Shift over,' I said. 'I am here, the others are coming,' and I threw down the tools and stripped off and there was a strange coldness in the air which, down a pit, stinks of water.

Dada said, coming up with Mari, 'Wet, isn't it?'

'Wet enough for bath night.'

Mari said, 'What was Pietro doing back up there, Mostyn?'

I winked at Dada. 'Breaking strike, like us.'

'I am not such a fool as I look,' said she.

'It has happened before,' said my father, tossing his coat and tightening. 'The lark is to stay down; you never break strike if you don't come up. The Spaniards are at it, why not the Mexicans?'

She shrugged, went back up, unshackled a dram and kneed it, spragging it along to the face for filling while me and Dada wandered round with candles belting the roof for bell-stone, though she looked solid enough by the time the overman came back: broad and teak-tough, this one, a Cardie Welsh with doormats on him fore and aft, a busted beak, and all he lacked for a cave-man was a cudgel, said Mari.

'You all right by here?'

'Another six inches and you will drown us,' said Dada. 'You got pumps?'

'We had pumps until the strike, this is seven weeks' water.'

'It will come hard on the woman—you got a spare animal?'

'The ponies are over in Park, but I got half a donkey.'

320

'Half a donkey is better than none,' I said.

'Come and fetch him,' said the foreman, and I liked his style.

In ten minutes I was back, racing with him down the gallery and yelling:

'Jed Donkey. Dada, Mari, look! Jed Donkey!'

Ragged, skinny, weary, worked out and blind as a bat. But Mari went on to her knees in the pit-water and put her arms around his neck, and cried, 'Oh, my little precious, my little Jed Donkey!'

'*Duwedd!*' cried my father. 'Last time I heard of you, you were up for the knacker-yard!'

'Sent by Gran,' said Mari, loving him, and I saw old Jed grin, as donkeys do. 'Now things are going to change.'

She was right.

But I do not think Gran had a hand in what came after that.

For three days we worked from the Gadlys, taking the drift mine to Abernant, coaling out on to Forge Side for the furnaces, for these were alight again, though only in half-blast and an eighth production which was turning Fothergill's hair grey, they said. Daily money we took home to 'Becca, and daily we faced the mob around Siloa Baptist. But Ifor strengthened and my Rhiannon rose in the bed, though not speaking. And nor did we feel so bad about the strike, for the Quakers were abroad on the streets with their Irish soup-kitchens. Often I had heard my father say that he would be mighty interested in the God of animals, and, personally, I would not dream of entering a heaven that didn't have dogs, cats, mice and Quakers, for these four are one with the greatest purity.

Conversely, I am doing my best to keep out of the hell that will be especially stoked by Welsh furnacemen for ironmasters with coal supplied by Taff colliers for coalmasters, preferably anthracite.

I sat on Rhia's bed. 'Got Jed Donkey back,' I said. 'You hear me, Rhia? Got Jed Donkey back.'

And she gave me a ghost of a smile that was once so gay.

'The fever is broken,' said Rebecca, 'be thankful for that.'

And I kissed her, I remember, and went out that day for the fourth dawn shift down the lower drift of the Gadlys.

To this day they do not know who shot-fired in Four Heading when we already had more coal in the seam than we could handle. Between the four of us we were pulling out ten tons a day, with Dada and me hewing and Mari and Jed on the drams, and we were doing this in ten inches of water.

When the ceiling came down in Four it took the shaft of the old working with it. Before the smoke was cleared we were up to our middles in flood.

'Round the top pillar!' shouted my father, and hooked his arm round Mari's waist and bent her to the weight of water coming down the shaft. 'Bryn, Bryn!'

'Coming!'

Jed was up to his haunches, and I ducked under water and knocked out the pin and the hook came free, and he shrieked and plunged for the opening of the stall with me after him, and came clear into the gallery where the flood was pounding. In the spluttering lamps this took him high, and he cartwheeled over in the blackness, his hooves cracking on the roof as the wave bore him down. Bracing myself to the flood, deafened by the earsplitting roar of water from the old working, I shouted till I was hoarse. Higher up the gallery I could see the lights of the Spaniards and above the dull roar I heard their cries of alarm as the water searched them, forcing them to climb the drift.

'Bryn!' With surging joy, I heard my father again.

'Dada!'

'Can you get round?'

With the wave splashing against the roof, the lamps were going out on the ledges above me; only one burned in wanes and splutters on the high face of Two Stall behind me. I yelled above the thunder, 'Try to get back. What the hell are you doing in there?'

'The water took us.' His voice was fainter. 'Can you hand Mari round the pillar?'

'Aye, push her round!'

Bracing my feet to the swell of the gallery flood, I clung on

to the coal. The flood was still rising up my chest yet I could
see the Spanish lights up the drift and their racing figures as
they climbed higher. Momentarily the water flowed across my
eyes and I instantly leaped, cracking my head on the roof.

'Dada, hurry! Hand Mari round!'

Nothing but the roar of the flood as the old workings let it
go. Driven by unknown pressures, the static water found life,
bounding and free as it took over the new stalls. Panic began
to hit me as it rose to my throat, but it was settling now, after
its first onslaught, and I shifted round the pillar, trying to get
into Four Stall.

'Dada!'

No reply.

With the flood dying, I stamped round the pillar, ducked
under the water and dived into blackness, groping my way
around the pillar into the flooded drift. But when I straightened for air the roof hit me down, and I knew the flood was
solid. Gasping, swallowing water, I cranked my body around
the pillar again, and straightened into six inches of air.

'Dada! Mari!'

The roof of the cave echoed, the flood washed over my face.
With death threatening, I did not recognise it: it seemed
impossible, with the gallery but feet away, that anybody would
die, least of all my father, who was indestructible; or Mari,
who was in his care. Taking a deep breath against the roof, I
ducked under the water again and crawled round the pillar
into Four Stall once more, taking the middle this time, hands
sweeping out for a hold. Something brushed my searching
hand and I plunged deeper into the blackness. Here a fresh
surge of colder water enveloped me from the old working, and
I swayed towards it, feeling the rock face, trying desperately
to keep direction. And suddenly Mari's dress streamed over
me, caressing my face, my naked chest. Gripping it, I pushed
backwards, falling to my right, and I struck the coal pillar. Up
now, into air, gasping and retching. With one hand gripping
the dress and the other pulling me round the pillar, I collected
into Two Stall, and ducked under the flood again, dragging
Mari upright against me, lifting her face into air.

'*Mari!*'

The lamp was flickering now as I shrieked her name and clutched her against me. Wading along the pillar, I pulled her to the wall. In two foot of air I laid her on the gob face down and leaned on her, and the water gushed from her in a great sickness. On her I turned, crying at the roof, 'Dada, Dada!'

In the gutting light of the last lamp, I stared about me at the coal and bit my knuckles and began to cry and call his name. Then Mari stirred under my hand, and I hauled her up against me, smoothing her hair from her face and whispering things I can no longer remember.

I do not know how long I sat there with Mari in my arms, now in pitch darkness, for the last lamp had gone out. And although the flood had not risen higher than my chest, there was a great pressure in my ears and it was difficult to breathe. I knew then that it was only the air lock that was saving us. The first penetration to free us would allow the air to escape and the water to rise to the roof. And I saw, as I lay there on the high gob, the faint glow of the gallery at the end of the stall, a six inch slit of redness reflecting in the flood.

I also knew, seeing this, that my father was dead, for the next stall, being lower on the drift, would have filled to the roof. In darkness I lowered my face against Mari's, and wept. Hearing this, she stirred in my arms.

'Whisht, *whisht*,' I said, and rocked her against me.

There was no sound then but our breathing and a faint trickling of water.

They say I must have slept, because it was over two hours later that I heard distant knocking. Louder, louder it sounded, beating me into alertness. Raising a lump, I knocked back, and sat waiting, breathless, for the reply.

It came. The colliers were at it.

They came in fire, in gas, in flood: for hero or blackleg, they always came. And I saw in my mind the panic of the houses and the measured speed of the teams: from near and far they would be coming, the firemen, stretcher-men, the miners, the strike forgotten.

The knocking became louder, developing into thumps that shook the stall. Dust began to trickle in patters down the wall

324

where they were coming through from Six Stall, I could hear it hissing into the water. And this overman knew his job, for he was taking it high above the level, by the sound of it. Coal began to fall in noisy plops, and I heard the growing hiss as the air began to escape from the trap, and felt the water rise up my chest. I listened. Faintly, I could hear them plugging the air hole, and there came the duller thuds as they picked it lower down.

'Mari,' I whispered; I could not see her face in that blackness, and she could have been dead, but for her gusty breathing.

And then I heard a voice.

'That you in by there, Evan?' From a place beyond the grave, that voice.

I yelled back, 'Bryn Evan, the son. And Mari, my mother.'

'Any Spanish?'

'None.'

'They got Spanish holed up in Number Four.'

'Nobody else in here except my father, and he is dead.'

'We are coming through, lad.'

'It is air-locked, mind!'

'Aye, we know. How much ceiling you got?'

'Two feet.'

'You need more with the woman—have you tried for a hole?' It sounded to me like Ike Winchester.

'Wait, you,' I shouted back. 'I'll try now.' Laying Mari back on the gob I shifted in the water, feeling the roof, for Dada, I remembered, was working it high, as usual. Some picked low, but he always took it high, never trusting the undercut. Beside the wall the roof sloped up. Gathering Mari against me, I elbowed along, and the air was sweeter. I cried:

'Got another six inches.'

'Get into it, and listen—can you hear me?'

'Aye.'

'Breathe easy, for we need an hour. They're building the lock-wall behind us, but it takes time.'

The dull hammering began again as they took in under the flood, and I gathered Mari in my arms, and she said suddenly, her voice clear and strong:

'Mostyn!'

I clung to her.

'Do you ... do you kiss me, Mostyn?' she said.

Bending, my face against hers, I did not dare to move, for she believed me to be her husband.

'Kiss me, Mostyn,' she whispered.

I put my lips on hers, and kissed her, and there was no sound in her when I set her free, as if the kiss had taken the life from her body. But she spoke again, in Welsh, which was her mother tongue, saying:

'Fy annwylyd, fy nghariad Cu; Cedwais fy nghalon ti aros i mi!'

Later, they dropped the wall and I tied down her skirt with my belt and lifted her into the air-lock, and the men took her.

They put her on the stretcher under the brattice-cloth when they set her down for the cage, but I would not have the stretcher because my father would have carried her, had he lived.

I held her against me in the cage going up. In sunlight I held her as I stepped on the cinders. And with her in my arms I walked down the line of white-faced people who, but a few hours before, had cursed us. And at the end of the people Rhiannon was standing, so I knelt before her and laid Mari at her feet.

'Your mam, my dada,' I said, and Rhiannon did not speak.

36

THERE was a great peace in me, standing here in the garden of the Old Navigation. And in the brilliance of that summer evening, it seemed to me that all her wounds were healed, and she was filled with a strange, urgent new life. With coal and culm the barges glided past Gran's overgrown garden; the long lines of trucks rattled and snorted up the gradient towards Glyn Neath; the house of Rheola flashed her astonishing whiteness along the road that led to Tonna.

Idly, I walked through the sagging rooms; up the stairs to Sharon's bed, and in the sweet decay of memories heard again her voice, saw again her strutting postures and fierce declamations.

Beneath the piled cinders of the kitchen grate the hearth was still with a snow whiteness. This, I remembered, was Ifor's job every Saturday, and he laid it clean with canal brick-dust. I used to brighten the knives, I remember, gliding them up and down the gritty board, and Gran would not take them unless they were shiny enough to shave in. The smell of fish on forks, said Mari, can be cured by driving the prongs into the earth.

Here is the cracked shaving mirror above the bosh; there is the punch-bag hanging from the ceiling of the back that Ifor used for the pugilistics, and I feinted and hooked it with the right as I went past, and patted it in the name of Ifor.

It was warm in the garden, the sun was brilliant, and the cut was all over golden with seed-dust and glowing in her banks with water-lilies.

Here is the Espianoza tree which held Gwen's treasure: here, in my hand, are the pearls and little glass beads she stole from Gran's needle-work box; the white rings of paper, which was the fairy money.

A barge glided by in shafts of sunlight, the bargee waved.

'Ay ay!'

'How are you?'

I got up, holding these things in my clenched hand. Standing there in all the moving beauty of the day I seemed to hear them all again: the ardent protests of Dewi, the laughter of Mari, the bass commands of my father.

Rhiannon I heard, too, her voice ringing in the room.

The kitchen was shafted with sunlight as I wandered round touching the places they had touched, listening to the music of a life now past. There was no particular sadness in me; most of the grief was now spent. I had come back here because I was complete in this place, one with the family in unity and love. It was the law of life itself that change should come about; it was the law of God that life went on.

I went down the stairs into the cellar, thinking of Dewi: of the nights when Pietro and Ianto Fuses used to come; the revolutionary pamphlets, the speeches, the free-thinking my father insisted on. And it was strange that I knew with Dewi a new affinity. In the scattered books and papers, in the rabid broadsheets of the Chartists, the wood-cuts of O'Connor and Frost he had pinned on the walls, I knew my brother standing there in the face of his past better than ever I did in the old days of his present. He, more than anything, had encompassed the death of the family in his idealistic fight to give it a new future. The very ruin of the Old Navigation seemed, to me, to relate the decay of his principles, the dust of his ambitions.

And then I saw it, pinned to the cellar door: a page he had torn from one of Sharon's books. Swinging the door into the sun, I read:

'In certain parts of the island there is a people called Welsh, so bold and ferocious, that, when unarmed, they do not fear to encounter an armed force; being ready to shed their blood in defence of their country, and to sacrifice their lives for renown.'

King Henry V of England

For a long time I stood reading this again and again.

The words, in the act of repetition, seemed to catch me up. I took the page down, screwed it up in my hand and held it against me.

The words seemed to burn against my fingers, and I became aware of a new and great excitement. I went up into the kitchen and from there into the garden. And with the paper gripped harder, I looked over the land as I looked upon it on that summer day up on March-Hywel with Rhiannon, on the day of Tai and Sian's marriage.

The excitement grew within me, stronger and stronger, and I began to tremble. In my great emptiness there came a new vitality, a strength that flowed through me. And I saw before me not a land of defeat and exploitation, but a land of triumph. I saw in the scarred landscape and the tunnelled mountains not a desecration but the glory of their wealth. And I knew, standing there, staring up to The Top, that the smoke of this year of cruelty and oppression was the bonfires of future generations, that the old order would be swept away, the old slaveries buried in the mountainous heaps of slag that one day would be green again; that the rivers now black with furnace-washings would cleanse themselves for the lives of men and women yet unborn.

It was as if I myself had become re-born, that the spirit of my country had moved in me, making me one with her in all her stubborn courage. And as she now stood purified by the flames of adversity and was strengthened and refined, so was I drawing into me the strength and determination of her greatness.

I began to walk away from the Old Navigation, drawn once more to Rhiannon. I began to run. Stupidly, obsessed with this new-found joy, I called her name.

'Rhiannon!'

I did not stop running until I reached Crugau. The train was gathering speed, a snorting Corsair pulling a new-fangled contraption of trucks and low-loaders for the industries of The Top, and I ran alongside it and scrambled aboard one, lying there gasping, staring at the astonishing blue of the sky with the clatter of the rails thumping through my shoulders as we gathered speed. And in the very power of the new inventions the joy in me grew, filling me with an exuberance I had never known before. I scrambled up, splaying my legs to the swaying flat with the wind whistling through my hair and flattening my clothes. The Corsair belched smoke, flying soot struck my face in little needles of pain, but I rejoiced in the action and movement and strength of it all. Over Pencydrain viaduct we went, rattling, bucking, with a hundred-foot drop into the valley below, and over my shoulder I saw the flowing land of the Vale of Neath in all its summer beauty. Resolven mountain I saw, and the wooded slopes of the Forest of Rheola, and in the heart of it the old Nedd was leaping down to the sea and the canal cut a staggering needle of silver through the summer gold and green down to Aberdulais. The beauty of it caught my breath, and I could have shouted with the joy of it. Now, turning, hanging on with the flat clattering and leaping under me, I saw The Top coming up in a cleft of the mountains. And the furnaces were alive again in Hirwain, the billowing scarlets and golds of their bungs cannonading across the black, burned land. The pit-wheels were revolving in blurs of light; colliers and miners were thronging through the narrow streets of TreGibbon. Smoke was billowing in black and yellow sulphurous banks across the white-washed cumulus of the Brecon Beacons, and beneath them Cader Fawr and Garn were flashing green, rearing skywards in the stricken sunlight.

On the corner of Market Street and Duke old Penrhy Jones, our Siloa minister, was ranting at the crowd: golden in the mouth and with God on his shoulder was our Penrhy, and a spade was a bloody spade, and just you look out. No Devil-shaker, this one; no false doctrines or heaping hypocrisies were his. Gasping from my mitch on the flat, I skidded along the cobbles, pausing to listen, and Penrhy cried, his fist at the sky:

'There comes to a man and a country in the greatest need a great revival of the spirit, you hear me? Then shall the caverns of darkness spew open and the light enter, and that time is now. Listen, *listen*!' He tossed back his white, flowing mane of hair and set his squat body rigid in the crowd. 'God is our salvation, and He is walking these mountains. You called upon Him in your distress and He has answered and will redeem you and pluck you to His breast as he plucked and held the people of Moses in the plague of boils and blains. Are you with me?'

And the crowd roared and swayed about him, calling his name.

'As He drowned the enemies of the people in the time of Pharaoh, so will He strike your enemies now. He comes in His great ship on the sea of His Revival. In the mouth of David Morgan, He comes. His word is in the hearts of the children, and He will feed them. The strike is over. Food will flow to your kitchens. And it is not a day of defeat, you hear me? It is a day of victory. From this time on Wales will begin to live. I see a great vision. Look, look to the west, and there shines a golden sun!'

They wept, they clasped their hands before him, they laughed with joy.

'Aye, a golden sun is shining, and it is the light of God. On what we build today will stand the new generations. Great buildings will rise, and new institutions. In this suffering we will build an empire of new learning, and great universities. And we will flow like a river to many lands, for we have gifts to bear them, being Welsh.' His voice rose to a cry, and he flung his blue-veined hands upward. 'I see an age of kings, I see a time of glory. On all sides the chapels will rise and the denominations will exalt, not in their individual glory, but in the greatness of His name!'

Stricken by his vision, I stood rooted, staring up at him. And still he spoke, holding them on the tips of his fingers, drawing them up from the dirt and squalor into the light of promise. And, standing there, jostled, shoved by the massing crowd, I seemed to see behind him a slow rent in the clouds. And from this rent a glorious light began to shine. In this light I saw the torn centuries of the past and on a great stairway walked the lost generations of a land despoiled; the blinded, the maimed by iron. The scarred colliers of the pits I saw, the women haulers, the children of the ventilating doors: all these I saw clearly, as I saw them once before outside the sea-pound of the Old Glamorgan, on the barge to Resolven; a thousand years ago, it seemed, when I was a child. And as the *hwyl* of the preacher beat about me, I turned my face to the sky. Gwen, I saw, in cloud; and then Gran, taking her hand. Ifor next, and I saw him clearly, calling to my dead mother, who was his adored. And then I saw my father, magnificent in strength, and he was laughing. For Mari was running towards him, her hand upraised, and I heard her voice above the roar of the Market Street crowd.

'Wait for me!' she called. 'Wait for me!'

And Penrhy cried, his voice vibrant, 'For the new Revival will herald the next summer like the flash of a swallow's wing. Mark me, mark me!'

Turning, I fought my way through the crowd; shouldering through their laughing, excited faces. And I saw before me the

331

straight lines of the chimneys belching flame and smoke and the whole scurry and tear of it, the clatter of the cobbled streets, the squalid, smoke-grimed buildings, the colliers going on shift in their noisy banter, for the soldiers had gone.

They were building a railway in the Swansea valley. The navvies were flooding in again, rolling down from the English north-country or marching in on the tramping-ticket; Irish, Spanish, English, Welsh, to pay a new obeisance to the great Brunel and Stephenson. In their hundreds they were coming, many with their wives and children, to fling up their wooden shanties along the line. Anything over six feet in socks they took without asking. Uncertain, I stood on the edge of the people, not knowing whether to run to Green Fach first or down to the station to sign on.

Away out of coal, me: enough of coal to last me a generation.

Penrhy cried then, 'This is the time to live, the time to die is passed. With God we will take the land forward into her new life! In the genius of our people, in the name of the new inventions!'

I ran; got a few yards and turned to Rhia's voice behind me.

'Bryn!' Gasping, she seized my hands. 'Oh, where have you been? The strike is over, it is over. Did you hear our Penrhy?'

'Aye!'

She cried, clutching me, 'Eli has just come and taken 'Becca and the children back to Abercynon. There is only me; the house is empty.'

'There is only you,' I said.

The sickness had gone from her with food, and there was a new, dark beauty in her, a new womanhood, and it could have been Mari standing there.

I said, 'I am signing on the railway for Swansea, I am getting out of coal. . . .'

'Oh, God, to get out of coal,' she whispered.

'Good money with the navvies, see, and Tai and Sian will be there. You coming?'

'And jump over a broom?' She held herself, smiling sad. '*Duw*, there is a great pain for you in me. You take me?'

'Got to do it proper,' I said. 'How much money you got?'

'One and sixpence.'

'I've got three shillings. What about Gran's dresser?'

'Worth ten shillings of anybody's money.'

'We have got to do it decent,' I said, 'for Gran's got her eye on us. Two and sixpence for the service down in Zion, Resolven, and a shilling for sidesman Moses Up?'

'That do leave one shilling,' said Rhiannon, making faces at the sun.

'Then we can afford to keep the dresser, which will put the curlers in Gran,' I said. 'If I'm signing on with the Great Western, the least they can do is carry the furnishings.'

'Tai Morlais, is it?'

'Tai and Sian. Now we will build things instead of knocking them down. You ready, woman?'

'Aye, man.'

And off we went arm in arm, for in Wales, in the 'fifties, you slammed the door on death. And as we went we heard the great Penrhy Jones shout to the crowd, 'There is no way back, my people. Henceforth, the way is forward. I see before me a great revival of the spirit, new horizons of glory, and the land shall be blessed! "Behold, the tabernacle of God is with men, and he shall dwell with them, and they shall be his people, and God himself shall be with them and be their God!"'

Aye, down Duke and across Commercial we went, arm in arm, and even down Station Street, in nudges and whispers and pointing, and jaws dropping right and left, and I heard Penrhy cry:

'On the burned out slag of this generation we will build a new Jerusalem, for the Great Revival is here. New temples shall rise for the land of our fathers!'

'Amen,' murmured the crowd, and I heard it bass, like a great wind beating about us.

Amen.

HOSTS OF REBECCA — ALEXANDER CORDELL

HOSTS OF REBECCA continues Alexander Cordell's brilliant trilogy of mid-nineteenth century Wales, which began with *RAPE OF THE FAIR COUNTRY*.

This is a brawling colourful novel of nineteenth century Wales, with all the passion, humour and Celtic sadness of RAPE OF THE FAIR COUNTRY.

It is the story of a people's struggle: slaves of the coal mines by day, under cover of dark, men unite in a secret host who burn and fight to save their families from starvation. It is the story of young Jethro Mortymer, striving to keep his family alive, and tortured by a terrible guilty love for his brother's wife.

'Running over with lust and strength . . . sin and righteousness'

The Times

'Magnificent . . . will provide hours of delight. These Mortymers are unforgettable'

New York Times

CORONET BOOKS

RAPE OF THE FAIR COUNTRY
—ALEXANDER CORDELL

RAPE OF THE FAIR COUNTRY is the first in Alexander Cordell's superb trilogy of mid-nineteenth century Wales, which continues with *HOSTS OF REBECCA.*

Set in the grim valley of the Welsh Iron country, this turbulent, unforgettable novel begins the saga of the Mortymer family. A family of hard men and beautiful women, all forced into bitter struggle with their harsh environment, as they slave and starve for the cruel English ironmasters.

But adversity could never still the free spirit of Wales, or quiet its soaring voice, and the Mortymers fight and sing and make love even as the iron foundries ravish their homeland and cripple their people.

'Ribald, bawdy, exciting, tragically violent'

New York Times

'A tremendously lusty story . . . a splendid novel'

Sunday Express

CORONET BOOKS

ALSO AVAILABLE IN CORONET BOOKS

ALEXANDER CORDELL

R. F. DELDERFIELD

MALCOLM MACDONALD

All these books are available at your local bookshop or newsagent, or can be ordered direct from the publisher. Just tick the titles you want and fill in the form below.

Prices and availability subject to change without notice.

CORONET BOOKS, P.O. Box 11, Falmouth, Cornwall

Please send cheque or postal order, and allow the following for postage and packing:

U.K. – One book 30p, 15p for the second book plus 12p for each additional book ordered, up to a maximum of £1.29.

B.F.P.O. and EIRE – 30p for the first book, 15p for the second book plus 12p per copy for the next 7 books; thereafter 6p per book.

OTHER OVERSEAS CUSTOMERS – 50p for the first book plus 15p per copy for each additional book.

Name ....

Address ....

....